The Dark Heart

By Del Smith

Del Smith

The Dark Heart

Prelude

"Growing tired?" Mordred hissed, he leaned towards his father. A smile creased his face, his tongue licking across his blackened teeth in anticipation of the moments ahead. Arthur panted out of breath his teeth bared in a grimace from his wounds.

"it's useless to continue to fight me, I have already killed most of your table and those few who remain will soon perish at the hands of my servants." Mordred waved his arms around the circle to show Arthur the dead which lay all around, but he did not need to be reminded.

"You were my son Mordred, I loved you, but no more. I know what you are, I am no longer blind to the sins you have cast over this kingdom. If this is to be my final stand, I will destroy you!" the air exploded around Arthur, his anger manifesting itself into a monster. Behind him stood his only hope, a thirty-foot-tall black dragon who's eye's gleamed ruby red.

"Is this your threat Arthur? Your pet lizard." the laugh was mad some nearby shocked at the sound stopped fighting to see Mordred lost in his delirium.

"you have no understanding of this magic; this is my true strength, and it will destroy you." Arthur shouted at Mordred.

"Arthur your time has ended and now you see the truth, I am not Mordred son of Arthur I'm….." the shouting ended; the scene began to fade to black.

The figures disappeared their argument lost to time.

Someone somewhere shouted to hear more, they wanted to know what had happened. A new landscape began to form and the person wanting to see suddenly didn't.

"No." the person cried. A cave small and dark replaced the open blood laden fields a single man hunched over a boulder a sword run through his chest a sword all too recognisable the man lay still his face white, dead. A cry never to be heard echoed into the cave as painful as any ever cried before or since but only one word could be understood through the tear-soaked voice.

"Dad."

The boy woke, thrust upright on his bed trembling as his sweat soaked sheets clung to his back. He clambered from his bed splashing water into his face from a bedside basin. His eyes were bloodshot, he felt weak and dizzy as he stumbled his way to a nearby chair. He sat with his head in his hands, his whole body shaking from the dream.

"why?" he muttered why had he been dreaming these horrible dreams, his weary eyes flicked to his bedside, a book lay open next to a picture of a man of remarkable similarity to the boy. The life of Arthur read the book; the boy cast it a dismissive look deciding it must have been responsible for the nightmare of Arthur but why did he dream of the cave? Again, he looked at the picture the man in it seemed to smile at the boy, but it was just a picture nothing could make that man smile, not anymore. Tired but apprehensive about returning to his bed the boy turned the picture face down not wanting to look into the dead eyes anymore.

Del Smith

Chapter 1

The Henge

The morning sun rose over the horizon, its light splashing through the window highlighting the face of the young man. He squinted against the brightness, shielding his eyes, he pulled himself from his chair. Snatching up his wand he pointed it to the window tinting the glass so his eyes might adjust to the brightness. Glancing over to his bed it seemed to beckon to him. A hard knot formed in his chest as though he had swallowed a tennis ball, the thought of sleep and the return to his dreams a sickening prospect. Shaking away his fear, he pulled on his dressing gown deciding to head for breakfast.

"You look like crap Jack." A well-built man was sat in the corner of the kitchen already eating his breakfast.

"Bad dreams again." Muttered Jack pouring himself a coffee. "How come you're up so early then Joe?" he asked clutching his cup to his nose breathing in the aroma hoping to wake himself.

"Just got in from my shift, Come sit down I'll make you some breakfast." Jack waved his hand in thanks seating himself at the breakfast table. He pulled over the paper Joseph had been reading whilst his brother busied himself cooking bacon and eggs.

Del Smith

The kitchen buzzed with activity, vegetables peeled, cut and washed themselves in the sink, whilst a broom swept up and disposed of any peelings to have fallen on the stone floor. Across the house Jack could hear shuffling as various items went about their business preparing it for when its occupants awoke. Outside the window he could see a brush painting the windows back to their normal white. Every morning was the same, his home, a manor house, passed down each generation of his family since as far back as could be remembered. The Manor cleaned and fixed itself, so it never looked anything other than perfect. The grass was cut, the windows sparkled and in the corner of the kitchen, wood neatly stacked itself for the smouldering fire. Jack's pet wolf, Galahad, was asleep on a rug in front of the fire. He was happily dreaming laying on his back, blissfully unaware of the noise surrounding him.

"How comes your shift was so late, I thought you were meant to have finished after midnight?" Jack asked absently.
"You know what it's like with the knights, when have I ever finished on time? Bloody paperwork kept me hours over all because of some idiot selling contraband artifacts." Joe stabbed at the bacon angrily. Jack looked at his brother properly now. They were as different as could be. Joe with his long black hair that curled down over his broad shoulders, he was average in height but as wide as he was tall and arms that a grizzly bear would have been proud of. His dark eyes and chiselled features had often placed young witches under his own unique spell.

The Dark Heart

Jack on the other hand was slender, taller than Joe by a few inches despite being the younger of the two. He wasn't as muscular as his brother, although he was hardly weak. His hair auburn like his father's that he kept short enough to sweep across his fringe. His eyes a brilliant pale blue.

"Well, I guess it happened late then as there is nothing in here." Jack said throwing the paper down. Joe placed a plate in front of him, barely had the plate touched the table before Jack started forking the bacon into his mouth. He hadn't realised how hungry he was.

"You know the papers, hardly anything bad ever gets printed. The council aren't keen on bad news." Joe shook his shoulders disgruntled.

"Thanks Joe, that was great." Jack beamed leaning back in his chair his hunger suitably satisfied.

"So, you going to tell me about your bad dreams then? They have been going on forever now, ever since …" Joe's voice trailed off, his eyes not leaving his brothers face.

"It's nothing." Jack tried to waive him away casually, he had no interest in discussing the dreams and even less in their father's death. Joe clearly wasn't convinced but seemed to decide against pursuing the subject. Joe like Jack was extremely protective of his family. They had been this way ever since their father had died. It had fallen on Joe to take up the role of protector of the family and take his father's place as a knight of the realm.

Whilst Jack appreciated his concern, he didn't want Joe to worry about him, he was no longer a child. In a few short weeks he would be going to Camelot to complete his training as both a Knight and a wizard. He couldn't count on his brother to always be there for him, he had to toughen up now.

"Honestly, I'll be ok I promise, if they get worse, I'll speak to you. Right now, I just want to forget about it." Jack smiled at his brother. They were once as close as two people could be, but when Joe became a Knight he was barely around anymore. It was unfortunate that his role had come between them. Jack had worried that his own future would drive them further apart. He resolved in that moment to ensure that didn't happen.

Joe bade Jack goodnight and trudged off to his room. Jack sat at the table twirling his wand in his hand like a baton. He was thinking of the time ahead. Going to Camelot for the first time, finishing his training, being with his friends again. Whilst he longed to see his friends and to see Camelot in person, he was secretly dreading the prospect of finishing his schooling. Once complete he would be expected to assume a role on either the council or within the knights of the realm if anything happened to either Joe or his sister Carol.

Carol was just as different to Jack as he was to Joe. Blonde haired, incredibly beautiful and smarter than the two of them combined. She also had an incredible temper which she inherited from their mother. Carol had followed in their mum's footsteps and would be joining the council. The Political elite of the country. It was the oldest political organisation left in the world. Ever since King Arthur had founded it hundreds of years before. Each generation of council member had passed down directly from a knight of the round table. It was considered a birth right, a matter of family honour to be on the council.

Jack was not sure that he wanted to be either on the council or a knight. He longed for a simple life, the idea of sitting in a chamber telling the masses how they should live their lives felt repugnant to him. Especially as it seemed to him the council had fallen far from their ancestors of legend. Even Joe, as a knight, once devoted to family honour and the all-consuming belief in the council now seemed to question their motives more and more.

As for becoming a Knight, it wasn't that he didn't want to protect people. He was after all extremely protective of those that needed it. It was more the idea something terrible would have to happen to Joe, only then would he be called to replace him. On top of that, he was hardly in the same shape as his brother. Would he be able to cope with the rigours of being a knight? Jack was more magically adept than his brother. This would more likely push his path towards the council in the long run.

He felt silly for admitting it, but he would have far preferred to become a historian, Jack was clever and had a sixth sense when it came to certain subjects, he had read every book he could lay his hands on about Camelot, Arthur and the Knights of the round table. So much history had been lost or locked away since their time and he longed to discover more. This was another reason he was so excited to see Camelot, the opportunities to discover long forgotten secrets first-hand.

Footsteps from overhead pulled Jack from his thoughts. Grabbing another cup, he poured a fresh coffee and placed it on the table. Jack's mother Emma walked in, picking the cup up without missing a beat, she gave Jack a wave whilst trying to stifle a yawn almost spilling her coffee over herself. Jack almost laughed at the sight of his mum; she was widely considered one of the country's most beautiful witches. Her sleek black hair and almond shaped blue eyes the talk of many tavern, if those people could see her now, he grinned. Her hair was a mess, looking as though she had just walked in from a hurricane. Make up that she had been too tired to remove after a late-night debating in the council chamber was now smeared across her face. She was wrapped in his father's old dressing gown, it dwarfed her small frame, she wore a single fluffy slipper, she had clearly given up on finding its pair. Jack was sure he could see the other tucked underneath Galahad.

It was 20 minutes before she said a single word, allowing the coffee to take full effect. "What time are you to meet with Michael and Kim today?" she asked.

"Three, I'm hoping to get some shopping done before though. I still need to get some bits for school." Emma nodded pulling a long list of chores from the dressing gown pocket.

"Right, well in that case I'll come with you. I need to get some bits myself, plus I'm meeting some friends for a coffee, you'd best get showered and dressed. It's been a long time since you've seen Kim and you don't want to look like you've just been dragged out of bed." Looking at the reflection in his spoon, he had to concede his mother's point.

"Jack, I thought we were going into town are you coming or not?" Emma screamed up to him.
"Yes mum. I'm just getting ready" Jack groaned. Looking in his mirror Jack saw a reflection of the man he was slowly becoming. He was seventeen years old, tall for his age at just over six foot, athletically built. He wasn't unattractive, and was often complimented on his appearance, but no matter what people said, he knew he wasn't an oil painting like his brother or sister. Both of whom had modelled during their break from education. He hadn't been offered the opportunity during his break. Joe and Carol had taken their looks from their mother and Jack had to suspect that somewhere down her ancestry there was Elven blood. Jack on the other hand took after his father, Benjamin. He never had been able to present himself with the same dignity and purpose of his siblings, much to his mother's annoyance.

Chapter 2
Salisbury

Jack waited by the stone Diasis for Emma as she gathered up her purse.

"Come on, I haven't seen Michael in weeks, or Kim in forever." He called to her. Jack was feeling nervous if they didn't leave soon he thought he might back out of going altogether. Michael and Kim were Jack's best friends, he had known them for as long as he could remember. They had been together as a group until the age of fifteen. It was when their education had paused for two years they had separated. It wasn't by choice but each child at the end of their school year once turning 15 had to cease education. It was to allow for students to increase in power before undertaking the more dangerous forms of magic, now two years later they were about to enter their final years of education.

Jack and Michael had remained close, still seeing each other as often as they could, they spoke almost every day using orbs, Jack's relationship with Kim had suffered though, it was in the last year, Kim had decided to travel in her final year break to see the world and experience different cultures. Jack had thought about travelling with her. Before suggesting this though, they had fallen out over her boyfriend, Jack had never liked him, he felt he treated Kim badly and couldn't understand why she couldn't see it. Things had escalated to the point where Jack punched him. Kim had refused to speak with him after that. He didn't know if it was out of pride or embarrassment, but Jack had not attempted to contact her over the last year, preferring instead to check on her via Michael. In the end Michael had snapped and told Jack he wouldn't keep telling him how she was. He made Jack agree to meet her and attempt to fix their friendship before school started.

"Ok, I'm ready to go." The Diasis they were standing before was a unique object in its own way, although commonplace throughout the world very few people had direct access to one in their own home. This was a perk of his family being on the council. Something that Jack was uncomfortable with each time he used it. Each Diasis was different but they all had the same function, if a Diasis was in a public location such as a town square, they could take you to any other location. Ones like this though could only be used by those recognised.

The Diasis was crescent shaped with words inscribed around the edge. An ancient language that had died out about the same time as Merlin. According to family legend the words inscribed read 'to fly on the wings of a dragon' Joe had often joked it was probably a shopping list scratched there by some ancient relative. Emma placed her hand to the stone, the Diasis sprang to life. Static electricity crackled, it slowly filled the room, Jack could feel the hairs on his neck standing on end. Inky blackness seemed to leak from the stone. It seemed to be drawn to the centre of the Diasis, where it coalesced into a ball that grew and grew. The darkness began to spread, seemingly enveloping all light. Emma stood quite still but Jack fidgeted restlessly as the dark came at him, he hated using the Diasis. A coldness overcame Jack as the dark swallowed him whole, it felt like a hand clamped down around him, before plucking him up from the floor pulling him inside. He was jostled from side to side as he travelled through thin air, everything turned silent, the cold dark clinging to him, making his skin crawl, a sudden explosion of light and sound threatened to overwhelm him, as he was ejected into Salisbury Town square.

Jack landed on his knee's, his ears full of air bubbles.
"Do you ever get used to that?" He said rubbing his sore knees forcing deep rasping breaths of air into his lungs.
"Yes, of course you do, it's just that you're such a drama queen." She smiled down at him. Having just landed in the middle of a busy town Jack felt he could be forgiven for feeling a little disorientated.
"We had better hurry." Emma glanced at the clock tower. "I need to go to the apothecary or you're not going to have any clean clothes." she held out her hand helping Jack to his feet,
'there has to be a better way to travel' Jack thought to himself.

Salisbury town was one of Jacks favourite places, he loved the old town feel that had become lost with newer towns and cities that had sprung up over recent years. Salisbury had barely changed since the times of Arthur; it was a mixture of wooden beams and stone buildings. Creaky windows and signs over every door which swung in the wind. The cobblestone streets that echoed as horses trotted down the road. Throughout the square stalls were setup selling a variety of items. As they walked past Jack was intoxicated by the smell of the fresh bread on display. Emma called Jack on; he had dropped behind enjoying the scent. Further down from the square and onto the main road Jack could see all his favourite shops. There was Merlin's magic all-stars sweetshop, Beasts for the Brainless where he always picked up treats for Galahad, Claudius' Coffee shop, Andersons the apothecary store, next door was Walthamstow's bookstore, a chain store popular for its spell and history books throughout the kingdom.

In the distance Jack could see Mulligan's clothing store. A line of golden windows which seemed to stretch on forever. Each window displayed the latest in witches and wizards clothing, it was the most popular clothing outlet in the whole of the wizarding world, every town in the country had a Mulligan. Clothing stores didn't normally interest Jack, but since Michael had arranged this meeting with Kim Jack had been shopping in Mulligan's every day that week, trying to find something suitable to wear, he had inwardly considered wearing his armour in case Kim wasn't as forgiving as he hoped.

At the end of the street was The Dragons Den, a shop devoted to the joker in everyone. Jack and Michael had once spent a whole month in detention because they had set salamanders loose in the teachers break room. Even Kim would occasionally join in by pranking the two of them, although she was often the voice of reason.

By far though the store that held a special place in his heart was Donovan's Armoury. Ben had taken each of his children here to purchase their wands, armour and swords. Jack remembered his father spending hours with him walking through the store looking at new items each week. They had become friendly with Donovan himself. When Ben died, he had become a fatherly figure to Jack.

After an hour had passed Jack was finally freed from his mother, she was going to go to the Claudius coffee shop to meet other parents from the council whilst Jack met with his friends.
"Now you behave, I don't want to have to come down the knights auditorium again." Jack looked at his mother sternly.
"I'm not a child any more mum, I'm an adult now if you don't remember. I can drink, gamble and do other things." Emma glared at him.
"You're also the son and brother of two council members and the brother of a Knight. That has never stopped you before." Jack held up his hands in surrender.
"I promise you I'll behave. I'm meeting Michael and Kim and that's all." Emma's eyes narrowed over him as though trying to catch him in a lie. Reluctantly, she allowed him to go.

Knowing he was still a little early Jack decided to have a quick look in Donovan's before heading to The Three Druids pub. As far away as he was, he could still see a small group of people gathered about the store, the crowd growing larger by the minute.
'What's going on? Donovan's isn't normally this busy' Jack thought. "Hey, what's up?" He called out to the crowd. One of the young boy's looked around
"it's a new Crossbow, a Merlin class." Jack gasped

'Merlin class Crossbow? there hasn't been a new one in over fifty years.' Jack ran forward hardly daring to believe. Reaching the crowd he pushed his way through to the front, it was true the Merlin was just as beautiful as he had always imagined. A pure oak handle with gold inlaid among the grains. The string made from silver unbreakable unicorn hairs. Jack had seen pictures of the old Merlin but this, was a thing of beauty. The price on the other hand was anything but.

3000 Dovans

Dovans were the highest level of value represented by a pure golden coin, then came Demoxins a smaller silver coin and finally Draxons an even smaller bronze coin. A Draxon was a hundredth of a Demoxin and a thousandth of a Dovan. Every person had only three coins. Each time that a person spent some money a number on the coin would decrease to show the value the coin still held.

Jack walked into Donovan's he wanted to know all about the Merlin. Looking around the store he saw the older crossbows along the far wall. Swords of all shapes and sizes from squires to knights were at the back, behind the counter along with the Axes and maces. Out front the less dangerous items were stored, including armour and saddles for horses. Each item like much of the world were divided into classes based on the Knights of the Round Table. In the far corner was the Galahad sword, usually used by squires whilst training, they would generally then move onto a Lancelot a larger and heavier blade. The Guinevere was a specialty for female knights, still heavier than that of the Galahad but sacrificed some of the weight of a Lancelot or Arthur classed sword for Speed. Jack had always found it preposterous that people would consider female knights to need a lighter sword. From what he knew most of the female knights of the realm could not only hold their own against the men but beat them regularly.

"Hey Donovan what's up? Are you hiding from me?" Jack shouted out into the apparently empty store.

"What, who's that there?" came the familiar voice from downstairs, Donovan's bald head popped up through a hidden trapdoor.

"Oh it's you Jack, what are you doing here? I thought that you were off today?" When a child paused their schooling they would often take up a job with a local company. Unlike Joe and Carol both of whom had modelled for the Mulligan's witches and wizards robes collection, Jack had volunteered with Donovan, it was an unusual choice for someone with his future path. He knew he would be unlikely to have the opportunity again to invest in his interest in armoury and blacksmithing.

"What am I doing here; you have the new Merlin class. Why didn't you tell me they were bringing out a new model? I've worked here every week for the last two years and you didn't feel like you could tell me?" Donovan grinned at Jack.

"Well, I wanted it to be a surprise didn't I, it's not like they bring out a new model every day." He said with a huge grin.

"Can I hold one?" Jack asked his fingers sliding over the air just in front of it.

"Well, you can do more then hold it, you can take

one." Donovan's wheezing voice added.

"Take one, what do you mean?" Jack was stunned.

"That's right, you can have one. You've been working here for the last two years and yet you have never asked me to pay you. Lets just call this a present for all those years of hard work." Jack was stunned. He walked over to Donovan and gave him a hug; he had been so kind to Jack since his father's death. Jack at times thought he would have genuinely been lost without him.

"Thank you." He gulped trying to hold in his emotions. Donovan tapped him gently on the back before breaking the embrace.

"Don't go getting soppy on me now." Donovan beamed. "Its just free advertising is all, once your new classmates see it, they will all want one, see?" Donovan was lying and Jack knew it. It gave them both a way out of the conversation without further embarrassment.

"I'll do my very best to show it off then." Jack said happily.

Jack left Donovan's in a daze not daring to believe what had just happened. He walked in hoping for just a look at the Merlin and minutes later he owned one. He was maybe the first to own one throughout the entire country, possibly even the world.

Jack slowed as soon as he saw the Three Druids pub, his stomach started to perform flips as he thought about seeing Kim again. As much as he had tried to pretend otherwise to everyone, he had missed her. To have lost that connection with someone he loved had hurt him. Like Michael, she had been a rock for him when his dad died. Whilst he would never admit it, there had been a time he had loved her as more than a friend. When she had comforted him and he had been at his most broken, he had thought there was more to them. He had never said this to her though, eventually he had pushed those feelings to one side.

Looking up Jack saw the familiar sign of the Three Druids swinging on the wind. The sign was old and faded, it depicted three men dressed in cloaks their faces hidden in shadow from the moonlight behind them. He guessed that when the tavern had been founded it may have been used by a less reputable clientele than it was now.

Jack walked in and up to the barman. He was a few inches taller than Jack, muscular and spoke with a deep gravelled voice. His dark brown eyes had appeared almost black in the low light, he seemed intimidating his shaved head reflected the candlelight into Jack's eyes.
"Hey Rob, pint please." As Jack ordered his eyes slipped around the semi empty room.
"How are thing's today?" Robin was the local barman; he too would be a pupil of Camelot when they returned to school. His uncle owned the tavern and Robin had decided to work there rather than with his mother or father in the council. Robin had been in Jack's classes at school, he was a great friend to all three of them. Jack, Kim, Michael and Robin had spent many hours in the Three Druids under Robins uncle's careful eye. Now of age though they no longer had to be observed.
Robin had been the most vocal after Jack and Kim had fallen out, he had berated Jack for how he had dealt with Kim's boyfriend. He seemed to regard Jack as having a

lack of tact. But Robin was never angry with him. Jack had always thought that Robin considered him a little slow when it came to women, Jack thought he was probably right.

"Oh, don't get me started it's been the day from hell, we had two trolls in earlier, they had stayed all night got drunk and then started a fight. We needed a dozen knights in here just to stop them." Robin's demeanour was totally different to his appearance, he was as gentle as any man could possibly be.

Jack's mind quickly drifted to thoughts on Trolls. They were the most troublesome of the magical creatures in Salisbury, most were over 8 ft tall and well in excess of 35 stone and their smell could curdle milk.

The Three Druids attracted a wide variety of clients including Wizards, vampires and the occasional werewolf. Many other humanoids also frequented the inn but most didn't have the nasty habit of tearing your head off for looking at them.

"Well at least it's not dull, has Michael or Kim been in yet? I'm expecting them." He continued looking around hoping he had missed them somehow. He couldn't see his friends anywhere inside. Jack knew that Robin wasn't really paying him any attention, he had been staring at a girl in the corner since he had arrived. Jack hadn't noticed her but now he looked closer he recognised her as a girl from their year at school. There was a rumour that she too had Elven blood, Jack had never really spoken to her. She was unnaturally beautiful and he was nowhere near confident enough to talk with someone like that.

"You're seeing Kim? That's great don't mess it up!" Robin poked Jack in the chest smiling at him.

"I'll do my best not to."

"Well, they're not here yet. I'm sure that they will be soon." Jack picked up his drink and took a sip letting the amber liquid slip down his throat.

"Cheers, when they come in, can you point them over to me?" Robin nodded and resumed his silent vigil of the girl in the corner.

Sitting alone Jack wrapped the table with his fingers, Robin threw a bar mat across the room hitting him without looking. Unable to take his eyes off the door, Jack waited eagerly in anticipation for his friends. Two elderly witches and a warlock had entered the pub and taken a seat in the far corner; they were laughing about times they had spent together in their youth. Jack could see himself Michael and Kim sitting there in year's laughing.

'Ok, keep it together, I'm sure there just late they will be here at any moment.' Jack's mind was racing, losing his nerve he jumped up deciding to leave and make his excuses when they were forced to meet up at school. Brilliant sunlight flooded into the bar as the door opened, a large group of people walked in. Jack could pick out a young handsome man with dark hair. He knew it was too late to run now. Michael was here but he could not see Kim anywhere, Jack's heart beat a little slower, at least he would be able to meet Kim with Michael at his side. As the crowd thinned Michael collected his drink spotting Jack, he walked over with his drink in one hand and an attractive girl that Jack did not recognise by his side.

'Classic Michael.' Jack laughed to himself.

"It's great to see you, how the hell have you been?"

Michael grabbed Jack's hand shaking it so rapidly he thought he was going to pull his arm off. Jack wondered if Michael was as nervous as he was, or if he was waiting for him to pass judgment on his new girlfriend. If it was the latter, he had nothing to worry about she was stunning.

"I'm great, you know me, are you not going to introduce me to this beautiful young lady then?" Michael blinked in dismay his mouth slightly ajar. Jack guessed he had said the wrong thing. The young blonde girl started to giggle.

"Jack it's me, Kim, don't you recognise me?"

Chapter 3
Reunion

Jack's jaw dropped to the floor.

"Oh my god, I'm so sorry I didn't mean to suggest." His face was bright red, feeling sick to his stomach, how the hell didn't he recognise her? Kim was laughing so hard she had to hold her sides.

"I didn't know I had changed so much." She beamed. "I mean, you've never called me beautiful before." Her smile lit up the room. Jack wanted the floor to open and have it swallow him whole.

"I'm so sorry, my god what happened to you? you used to be this scrawny little girl with long wavy dirty brown hair." The woman standing before Jack wasn't the person he remembered. Clearly full of confidence; she had blossomed in the time that they had been apart. Her petite frame that showed her feminine curves. Deep blue eyes that seemed like the depths of the ocean, her now blonde hair, flowing down her lower back. Jack's eyes bulged from the sight of her.

He felt wrong, the pit of his stomach was writhing as though a snake was thrashing inside.

"I grew up, it's been a long time!" Kim was smiling at him, talking as though nothing had ever changed between them. He felt sick, a year had disappeared and for what? look at what he had missed.

Jack and Kim laughed and joked; they discussed her

travels around the world. He drank in every word, it filled in the missing spot in their life. Michael on the other hand sat occasionally chipping in with a question or nipping to the bar for another drink. Robin had even pulled his eyes away from the girl in order to come and give Kim a hug before running back to the bar. After an hour Jack had realised that Michael was deliberately being quiet almost sinking away so he and Kim could catch up.

Most people regarded Michael as a rather arrogant and pompous young man. Those who knew him best understood differently, Michael had often been described as tall, dark and impossibly handsome, sometimes Jack thought he was too smart for his own good, he was everything most women wanted, and boy did he know it!

Jack was as happy as he could be, he had his friends, this is what he lived for.

"Is everything ok with Robin?" Michael asked, looking over they could all see him still staring, fixated. "I think I'll go have a word." Michael got up and left.

"You know why he did that, don't you?" Kim asked. Jack shook his head. He hated hidden meanings. He was oblivious to them. "He wants us to have time to really talk." Jack who hadn't been able to stop drinking in every inch of Kim's face suddenly couldn't look at her. This was the reason he had been nervous about meeting in the first place.

"I thought we had been." His voice cracked catching the lie. Kim reached over and took his hand in hers. It was warm and comforting.

"I think we really need to clear the air; I don't want to

have either of us hiding any resentment." Her voice dropped, it was soft and caring. She leaned forward so he could hear better, he could smell her perfume from this close. If asked, he would have sworn it was how angels smelled. Jack balled his courage and looked Kim in the eyes. It was hypnotising staring into them.

"I'm sorry for what I did." It was the truth, look at what their time apart had cost them, how couldn't he be sorry?

"I don't want you to be sorry Jack, I want to know why you did it?" Her hands wrapped his tighter, it was a silent plea. Taking a deep breath, he knew he had to tell her the truth, she deserved it.

"Your boyfriend had been drinking." He began, his throat suddenly dry. "He was boasting to his friends about being intimate with you." Kim's eye's narrowed but he pushed on. "he was going into detail about all the things you both had done. I told him to stop, and he wouldn't, he got into my face and started telling me everything." Jack took another breath, he hated this. Kim's hand squeezed encouraging him on. "I lost it. I snapped and I hit him. I shouldn't have done it. I should have walked away, I know, but the thought of him doing that disgusted me." He hung his head not sure if he could look Kim in the face. He could hear Kim's breathing now it was heavier and faster. He could tell she was trying to hold in her own anger.

"I should have listened to you." Her voice was soft barely audible over the buzz of the other tables nearby. The regret was stained in every note. "We were never intimate. He had tried over and over but it never felt right." Jack looked up at Kim, almost expecting her to have tears in her eyes instead, a fierce look he was all too familiar with met his gaze. "I was never angry at you for hitting him, that was part of the reason we broke up. I knew I didn't feel for him the way I should. I didn't want my first time to be with him." Jack smiled softly. "I was angry with you for thinking I needed defending. I knew what he had been doing and I was going to break up with him." Kim was strong, stronger than him, he knew. "I thought you were Jealous, I wanted you to be." She stopped looking him square in the eye. Jack said nothing, he didn't trust himself. Kim stared for a few seconds seemingly realising he wasn't going to answer, she pressed on. "I had liked you ever since we were little, I wanted you to come with me on my travels more than anything. I was scared though, about how you felt, after your father died you changed. You weren't the sweet boy that I knew anymore. You were angry all the time. When you hit him, it made me feel like you didn't trust me to look after myself. Like I needed a bodyguard." Everything Kim had thought in their time apart seemed to be flooding out of her now. Jack closed his eyes listening to every word, he needed to hear this. "he treated me like that, like I was just a little woman and needed a big strong man to support me." Jack tried to interrupt but Kim held up a hand stopping him. "I need to finish this. I don't know how you feel about me and now isn't the time for us to discuss it. I want you to know I'm sorry, but I need my old friend back, the one who believed in me. I know your protective and I understand why after your dad, but I need you to believe in me." She stopped her chest rising and falling rapidly. Jack was stunned he wasn't sure what to say. Carefully he picked his next words suddenly aware of how close they were.

"I always believed in you." His voice was barely a whisper, Kim inched herself closer to hear better. "It was never that I didn't believe in you, I cared too much to see you hurt. You said a minute ago you wanted me to be jealous, I was." They stopped, staring into each other's eyes, their faces inches away, Jack could feel her breath on his skin. His body was shaking. They both looked desperately at the other to say something. Two drinks banged onto the table next to them, making them jump apart.

"Sorry you looked thirsty." Michael said cheerfully walking away. They both sat and took a sip of their drinks, looking anywhere other than at each other. As Jack thought about all that had been said one thing sat clear in his mind. Kim had wanted him to be jealous. Despite himself, he couldn't help but grin.

Michael and Robin eventually came over to join them at the table. Both Kim and Jack didn't say a word about what had been said between them, eventually the three of them got up to leave saying thanks to Robin, Michael whispered something to him pointing to the girl in the corner, Robin nodded in agreement sending them all on their way with a hug and handshake.

"Hello Ms London, how have you been." Kim was immediately grabbed by Jack's mum and pulled into a rib cracking hug. His mother had always adored his friends, Kim and Michael were considered surrogate children. Emma had often complained about Jacks' arguments with Kim.

"How many times do I have to ask you to call me Emma?" Emma paused over Kim hushing about how beautiful she was, moving onto Michael giving him a hug and telling him how handsome he was. For hours they sat and chatted Emma positively squealed listening to Kim talking about her treks up the Amazon, or tomb diving in the forgotten mountains of the Nordic men. Jack and Michael sat back, delighted at how the day had turned out.

'She wanted me to be jealous.' This was all Jack had been able to think about since returning from his friends. He had locked himself away in his room, playing over the conversation in his head, trying to make sense of it all. Galahad was drooling on his knee, looking up at him trying to get his attention. "She said she wanted me to be jealous. To have gone travelling with her. What does it mean?" He asked Galahad imploring him to answer.
"She wants you" a voice whispered in his head.
'No, she didn't say that. She didn't mean that'
'then what did she mean?' the voice asked him reasonably. Jack couldn't answer he had been over this so many times and was no closer to understanding than he was at the tavern. 'Maybe Michael could help you?' Jack had no intention of asking Michael, as much as he trusted him, he didn't think it right to involve him. 'Maybe you love her!'
"Shut up." He shouted aloud; he was starting to lose it arguing with himself.
"What the hell are you doing up there? who are you talking to?" Jack did not realise that he was being so loud, he called back to his mother.
"Sorry, it was Galahad, he was chewing on my slippers again."
"What have I told you? if you can't control him, he

will have to go!" She shouted.

"But mum." Jack shouted exasperated. "Sorry boy, but you're taking this one for the team, don't worry she would never get rid of you." Galahad had hidden under his bed at the threat. Walking downstairs to argue with his mum Jack could not help but continue to fret about feeling the way he did.

Jack decided to go for a walk to help clear his head. Walking down one of the many country lanes that surrounded the manor he found himself at his favourite places, a small playing field lay to the east of the Henge, Jack had spent a lot of his time there as a child practicing his horse riding, whilst to the west was a woodland with low hedges and misshapen trees it was the perfect place to learn archery, by far Jack's favourite place was an old tree that he had always enjoyed climbing as a child. As he got older, he preferred to just sit underneath. That was until three years ago, when his father had died. Ben had taken him there when he was just three, that was when Jack had fallen in love with the place. After his father died Jack thought that he would never return. It hurt like a stab to the heart every time he came here, but he returned again and again just to sit and think. Maybe he would find the answers he sought here. Looking to the bottom of the tree, there was his father's grave, a cold shudder ran up his spine.

Benjamin London was a revered knight, he had been known throughout the entire world as the great and honourable warrior. No-one had been able to explain to his family how Ben had died. It had been classed as a possible murder but no-one ever knew. All they had been told was that Ben was dead. He felt the familiar cold shudder when he remembered just how easily the person from the council had told them this. He had been cold and callous, even dismissive of Emma who herself was a powerful council member. Jack had never believed the council couldn't tell them how his father had died. The council were the most powerful of government across the planet, they had information that could benefit mankind, and yet they preferred to keep it for themselves. He was sure, if they had wanted, they could have found Ben's killer in days.

Jack believed as did few others that they were keeping power for themselves, fearful of a new system of government replacing them.
"What the hell happened to you dad?" Anger filled him as always when he thought of his father, he had been such a gentle man, caring and considerate. He wanted to know what happened to his father, he wanted to punish that which was responsible for taking Ben from them. Even if it had meant taking on the council themselves. Staring at his father's grave only brought up more memories of pain and anger, turning to leave Jack looked back to his father's grave. "I swear to you, I will find out what happened to you, I will get justice!" They felt like hollow words to him, he was after all just a boy yet to complete his training, but he felt sure that one day he would honour his promise.

Over the next few days Jack had spoken to Michael and Kim for hours on his orb, he had enjoyed having the three of them back together so much, he had even stopped having nightmares. Tomorrow they would be setting off for Camelot and decided to meet beforehand.

"My, my don't we look handsome today." Joe smiled earnestly at his brother.
"Shut up Joe, I'm meeting Michael and Kim. I don't want to look like I've finished a shift blacksmithing." He eyed the torn clothes Joe was wearing after another shift at knights training. Joe continued to smile understandingly at Jack.
"Yeah, I can see why, I saw Kim the other day whilst on shift. Shes grown up well." Joe was trying to be kind, but it made Jack feel terrible.
"Yeah, she's pretty." He admitted. "She's my friend though and that's all there is to it." Joe's smile was a little too sympathetic.
"I get that, do you know what the problem with that is though?" Jack shrugged. "If not you, then it will be someone else. I know mate, I've been there." Joe walked away leaving Jack to ponder his thoughts. He had never realised Joe had cared for someone properly before, or that he had denied himself from it. When he had joined the knights, had it cost him another relationship as well Jack wondered. The horrible realisation was compounded by the other thought, he was right, sooner or later someone else would see how precious Kim was.

Stepping into the Diasis, Jack felt like his head was going to explode, The familiar tug reached Jack's stomach, his chest was restricted and the images flashing in front of his eyes made him feel nauseas. Landing on his knees once more, Jack gasped for breath, he swore that each time he went through the Diasis it got worse. Looking up, a grinning Kim met his eyes.

Jack was astounded with the light shining down behind her, she looked radiant. Picking himself up Kim helped to dust him down. Jack's heart was in his throat, beating so fast he was scared it was about to jump out of his body.

"Tha…Thanks." he stammered. "Where's Michael?" Jack said composing himself as quickly as he could.

"He's getting us a coffee at Claudius'." She told him quickly drawing her hand away, almost as though she was scared to be seen touching him.

"I never asked, how you have been since, well you know?" Jack wanted to make up for lost time, but he wasn't keen on returning to the discussion they had in the tavern.

"It was tough" Kim admitted, "Michael was amazing he was there for me when none of my other friends were." Jack looked at his trainers a brick had dropped down his throat. "When I broke up with Simon I was devastated. Michael visited me every week no matter where I was in the world, he comforted me." The brick slid further, running down his stomach, he had no idea that Kim had felt like that. How desperately she had needed her friends.

"I'm sorry Kim, if I had known how hard things had been for you, I would have been there for you too, I just never knew." He was almost imploring her to understand why he hadn't contacted her, when she said nothing but continued to look at the floor, he went on. "I didn't think that you would want me around after our argument." Kim looked at Jack as though she felt bad for him. He had always been amazed by her selflessness.

"It wouldn't have been hard to ask if you could see me, it's not like we hadn't argued before." She was right, he had been pig headed he should have gone and seen her no matter the situation.

"I did ask after you every time I saw Michael, I always asked how you were doing, I just didn't want you to know I still cared." Jack whispered his voice barely able to be heard over the laughing of passing witches and wizards.

"I wish that you had told me." Kim whispered back almost as quiet. Both fell silent as Michael approached. Jack wanted to talk with Kim alone, she should know how much he cared for her. He also wanted Michael to hurry closer almost afraid of what he would say, afraid of what he would feel.

"Sorry, I was wondering where you were, didn't interrupt anything did I?" Michael laughed passing Jack his coffee. Jack waved him away.

"Just catching up mate." The rest of the day passed without any further comments. Michael had quickly turned the conversation to Camelot and the pick for the high councillor for the student's council. For the first time in his life Jack couldn't bring himself to care about Camelot. He was in turmoil over his feelings, not even Excalibur itself could distract him.

"Jack will you get out of your bloody bed. You need to be at Stonehenge in an hour or you'll be late!" What Emma didn't know was, Jack had been up for hours already. Everything that he needed was already packed and waiting to go.

"Yes mum, I'm up, I'll be down in a minute if you could just get my breakfast ready?" Jack locked down the lid on his suitcase after checking for the seventieth time that he had everything. He was halfway out of his door when he remembered something highly valuable; organisation was never one of his strong points. The orb that had been given to him on his fourteenth birthday. It was from Ben; his death had occurred days beforehand. Orbs were useful objects they could contain a recorded message, to be viewed only by the person it was meant for, unless it was meant for a general audience. They could also be used to speak directly to another person. Most witches and wizards always carried one with them. This orb had been locked to Jack only, a private message for him. His father had recorded it for him in case the worst ever happened to him, after his death he had never watched it, an age charm prevented him until his seventeenth birthday. His birthday had come and gone, still Jack had never watched it, the time had never seemed right. He knew that one day soon he was going to have to force himself, he had to know what it had to say no matter, how unpleasant he might find it. Just as his feelings for Kim had forced a weight into his chest, it was only adding to the one of not knowing what had really happened to his father. With three years of trying, he had discovered nothing but more questions and even a couple of threats to stop looking, but if there was one place in the world that might help to yield answers, it was Camelot.

Galahad padded sadly down the stairs with Jack carrying his trunk behind him. Galahad could always tell when Jack was going away, it always made him feel terrible. Dumping the trunk by the Diasis he noticed an extra coat hanging on the holder.
"Mum, who's here?" Jack shouted into the kitchen, hearing no answer Jack walked into the room and saw

his mother brother and sister all sitting at the table. It was the first time that Carol had been inside the house since she had left two years ago. A feeling of great joy rose in Jack's chest, they were all here to see him.

"Carol, how are you? why are you here? I thought that you were training In Dublin." Jack ran over and hugged her tightly, He was taller than her now. Carol laughed squeezing him tightly.

"Hello to you too little brother. Or should that be big little brother?" She said reaching up to pat him on the head. "I took the day off, It isn't everyday that your brother starts his first day at Camelot, is it?" Jack was stunned Carol had come all the way from Dublin just to see him off. He knew how much it must have taken for her to visit him, becoming a member of the council was all she had ever wanted. "So little bro, how have you been? Worried about returning to school?"

"No not one bit. I'm really looking forward to it, I get to spend all Day with my friends. Learn lots of new spells and have no adult supervision outside school." Carol smiled warmly.

"you're not going to find it easy you know. Not with practical defensive magic, charms curses and metamorphosis, council duty and knight's training. As well as all your other lessons." He merely shrugged.

"Maybe, if I don't do well, they won't let me in." He winked at Carol. Both Carol and Emma eyed him dangerously, Joe burst out laughing.

"Why didn't I think of that?" He exclaimed.

"Don't you encourage him!" Emma and Carol shouted together. Both Jack and Joe were taken aback.

"They're like twins." Jack mouthed to his brother. Silently they laughed. "Honestly I'll do my best, I just hope I never have to take over." It was a chilling thought. He knew it would only happen if either Carol or Joe were unable to continue as a member. None of them said anything further on it. They sat as Jack ate his breakfast, Joe and Carol talking excitedly about their time at the school. Even Emma reminisced about how she had met Ben during their time, breaking down in tears and running from the room. Carol ran after her.

Once alone Joe approached Jack.
"I'm glad I got the chance to talk with you." He placed his hand on Jack's shoulder. "I just want you to know I'm here for you, things are going to be tough over the next two years, and things are going to be confusing. I know, I've been there." Jack couldn't help but remember their previous conversation. He wondered if this had anything to do with the person Joe had missed out on.

"Thanks Joe, I have Michael, Kim and Rob around. If things get too much though, I'll contact you." They smiled at each other before Joe suddenly hugged his brother.

"tell anyone I did that, and I'll whack you!" Joe laughed.

Chapter 4

Return to Camelot

The familiar explosion of light and noise hit Jack hard in the face, literally, as he crashed through the archway and straight into a queue of students attempting the long, tricky walk down to Stonehenge from Mordred's hill. The Place was named not in honour of Mordred but rather to remind people about the evils that still lurked in this world. The blackened fields that had once ran red with blood, now green couldn't hide the savagery that had plagued the land, even to this day a screaming could be heard at the dead of night as though the battle still waged. It was said that long before Arthur and Mordred had killed each other on this battlefield Arthur had died inside. When Guinevere was still pregnant with Mordred Lancelot had struck her through with a sword killing her but narrowly missing the baby. Mordred survived but many people had put this as the reason that Mordred had turned against his father. But as it was so long ago, no-one truly knew anymore. History had a way of being twisted with time, a game of Chinese whispers passed through centuries.

Stonehenge was now ancient and in disrepair, a monument gone to rot. Jack couldn't help but feel sorrow looking at it. Once, Stonehenge had been a beautiful sight to behold nothing short of the castle of Camelot came close to its importance in the history of the country. Stonehenge was the only access point to Camelot known to wizard kind, strategically it held great importance, as such, a garrison of knights were permanently stationed here, at the moment they were stood around directing the students to their assigned groups.

As his fellow teenagers piled there way down the muddy path that led to the underground caverns, Jack spotted his friend Robin again, grabbing hold of Jack's arm Robin dragged him over to Stonehenge itself.
"Come on mate, us members of the council get the VIP treatment, we get transported right to our own boat." Robins face was glistening with delight at the thought. Jack didn't have the heart to tell him that he would have preferred to walk down the muddy path rather then be paraded around like some sideshow, but as he knew, tradition was important. Robin grinned excitedly. "Let's face it mate, were far more likely to get skirt on the council than out of it. It's got to have some benefits doesn't it?" If this was Robins argument for being on the council Jack thought it was a pretty poor one, but he didn't question his friend. After all he knew Robin was interested in the dark haired girl from the three druids, and was hoping the fact he was a councillor would make him more impressive to her.

Walking up the steps to the inner circle of Stonehenge Jack could see some of his old classmates. They had changed dramatically in the few years they had been apart. It was only now Jack wondered what he must look like to them, when he left Camelot he was a short scruffy little boy, but now he was fast on his way to becoming a man. Had he changed that much?

Jack watched as some of his old friends steered clear from a group of boys he didn't recognise. From the size of a couple, he guessed they were distantly related to trolls and from the looks of them he guessed they were about as intelligent. Standing calmly at the back of the group was a tall dark-haired boy, he was giving orders to the others even telling them to shove another student down into the mud. The student was so tiny he had no hope of fighting back.

He wondered if he should go and say something, he was a member of the council after all. Robin was already rolling up his sleeves angrily.
"Think someone needs to be taught some manners." Robin, normally a gentle giant tensed his body as though preparing for a battle. Another voice came from behind them.
"Do we need to have a word?" It was Michael, he too had seen the predicament of the young wizard. Now being pointed and laughed at by the group as he tried to gather up his belongings.
"I think we should. Three on three should be fair." Jack agreed.
"You shouldn't be causing trouble you three." It was Kim, Jack couldn't look at her. He was angry and didn't want her to see him like this.
"you're all meant to be on the council." She implored them. "Kim it's not that were going out to cause trouble is it, we're members of the council as you say. And if we

don't defend the others from idiot's like that then who's going to?" It was a point well made and one that Kim was struggling to answer. Before the others could stop him he was already shouting over as he walked towards the group. "Hey, what the hell do you think you are doing?" The new boy stopped laughing at his unfortunate victim allowing his attention to drift lazily towards Jack. Kim hurried over to the boy helping him to pick up his items before cleaning his clothes and books of the mud.

"What does this have to do with you?" The boy spoke with a snarl in his voice but it was lazy, arrogant, almost bored at the intrusion into his fun. Jack's suddenly thought that this must be how people saw Michael when they first met him.

"What's your name?" Jack barked pushing aside one of the boy's henchman.

"My name, as if it is of any concern to you, is Melfice Trelane, the new high chief of the student's council." Melfice bowed deeply but never took his eyes off Jack.

"And what about the trollop?" Jack was referring to the dark-haired girl who was hiding behind Melfice. Jack felt a little bad noticing the girl didn't seem entirely happy to be in the company of the group.

"You should learn to watch your manners little boy," Melfice snapped clearly upset at the insult. Jack pushed aside his guilt, the sneer on Melfices' face made him shake with anger. "This is Louise, and she's far out of any of your leagues." Melfice grabbed Louise's hand and pulled her out from behind him, almost as though he was parading her, he twisted her arm above her making her twirl. Jack thought he saw her wince in pain.

"Yeah, that's nice does she do tricks, or do you need a

whistle for that?" Robin barked. Melfice pushed his face into Jack's. Kim tried to pull Jack away from Melfice, but he would not budge.

"Why don't you run away with your little girlfriend there?" Melfice flashed a dangerous smile his pearly white teeth visible.

"Don't even look at her again." Jack gritted his teeth his wand felt hot in his hand, sparks flew out of the end.

"Well, I suppose she might make a decent enough mistress, what do you think Louise?" Louise looked away clearly upset but Jack did not care he grabbed hold of Melfice by his top and swung his fist at his face. Suddenly a claxon sounded bringing Jack to his senses. Kim was standing with her wand pointed above their heads. A large whistle was disappearing into a cloud of smoke. "Later darling." Melfice snarled turning his back on Jack, he took Louise's arm and pulled her away.

"Count on it, sweetie." Jack bit back. He thought that Louise did not want to be there, but she also seemed content to see Melfice bully someone and that put her beyond his forgiveness. Pulling Jack to one side Kim shouted at him

"what the hell is wrong with you? why the hell did you do that? he could have hurt you!" Kim asked concerned.

"So, what should I have let him make you his mistress then?" Jack shouted angrily. Kim slapped Jack across the face as hard as she could.

"You never learn do you!" She shouted before turning and storming away up the hill.

"What was that about?" Robin asked stunned at Kim's outburst. Michael merely shrugged whilst Jack felt the sting on his face. Kim could really hit hard, something wet was in the corner of his mouth, as he dabbed his tongue, he could taste blood.

Standing in the middle of Stonehenge a voice sounded from no-where.
"School council members please make your way to the centre circle, you will all be transported to your private vessel in exactly one minute." Unhappy with himself, Jack and the others stood in the centre, he scanned the crowd attempting to find Kim, he wanted to apologise.
"Do you think that prat will really try and become high councillor?" Michael asked.
"Thought that was more your style Michael." Robin laughed.
"Guy's, do you think I have a shot at becoming the high counciler?" Jack asked out of nowhere, Michael and Robin looked at him surprised they had never known him to show any interest in the role before.
"Well maybe, You do come from the right background with your parent's being who they are and all, but I think you may have lost a couple of votes with that guy and his girlfriend earlier." Jack grinned at Michael.
Before anyone had a chance to elaborate further Jack felt dizzy, lightness was spreading throughout his body, something wet was suddenly springing forth from his nose, shutting his eyes in an attempt to stop Stonehenge spinning, he noticed what he mistook for sweat to actually be blood pouring from his nose. As suddenly as it all had started the spinning stopped. Daring to open his eyes Jack noticed he was on a ship, and if he wasn't mistaken it was The Excalibur, Arthur's own war ship. With a rising feeling in his stomach Jack leant over the

edge of the boat just in time to see half his breakfast disappear over the side.
"You know ,I don't think teleporting agrees with me." Jack said wiping his mouth on his sleeve.
He was glad it was only Stonehenge that could transport you to any destination and it was only ever used for this purpose. He would never have to experience that feeling again. He looked to his side to see Michael and half the ship still leant over the side. Faintly Michael raised a thumb in agreement.

Once his stomach had settled Jack decided to explore. He guessed that he would not have another chance to see this vessel again. Venturing around Jack could feel the old magic which still inhabited the ship. Legend had told that Arthur himself had hidden the all-powerful sword Excalibur somewhere onboard before he died, to make sure it could not be used for evil. Many people had searched but they had never found a single clue to its true location.
It had long ago been concluded that this had been a rumour passed around to hide the real resting place of Excalibur.

The Excalibur was an enormous vessel, easily three times the size of the other ships taking Jack's classmates up the river Pendragon towards Camelot itself. On the bow of the ships ornamental figureheads were engrained, the ships to the left all had a mermaid, whilst the ships to the right had a serpent which wrapped itself around the boat. The Excalibur though had a long arm protruding from the water line holding high a representation of the sword Excalibur. This could have held Jack's attention for the rest of the journey. The ship's passed through an underground cave system, stalagmites hung from the roof of the cavern, they appeared to grow and contract, as though the cavern itself was breathing. This was the only known entrance to Camelot, these caverns had held for over a hundred years before Arthur was even born, this was the darkest chapter of England's history. Orcs had taken over the country, during their invasion they killed thousands of innocent people. They imprisoned even more, Jack wished he had never read about the worst atrocities committed during this time. When Arthur was fourteen, he had led his first battle against the Orcs. He quickly grown tired of making small raids against the enemy, attempting to slowly dwindle their numbers. Arthur took it upon himself to take command of a small battalion and decimate an Orc war camp, killing a vicious Orc general responsible for the deaths of hundreds of men taken as slaves. Legend had it when Arthur took command and started raiding more war camps, the King sent forth his largest battalion to capture or kill him. The King was afraid the deaths of the Orcish generals would cause them to attempt to take Camelot itself. The battalion instead of hunting Arthur joined him. The knights had grown tired of hiding in the safety of Camelot whilst their countrymen had died. Over the next year more and more men had rallied behind Arthur, eventually he had an army large enough to defeat the Orc's, pushing those that had refused to surrender into the sea, drowning them.

These caverns had never been breached in all of

England's history; this was widely known as the safest place in the world. Every conceivable spell, curse and charm had been placed on these caves, even though miles from the ocean a giant Diasis had been built into the cavern walls. The Diasis allowed for Warship's to pass through and land anywhere with water. Arthur had used this advantage to launch surprise attack's on the enemy multiple times.

   Jack was sad to find only the top deck was accessible, it seemed that entry to the decks below had been blocked. He found Kim when he reached the stern, she was on her own. Jack knew he would have to talk with her now rather than letting their feelings simmer.
"Is it safe?" he asked walking over with his hands raised.
"I've not decided." Kim caught sight of his bloody lip, holding her hand to her mouth. "Did I do that?" she asked, mortified. Jack had completely forgotten.
"Yeah, but its ok, I probably deserved worse." Kim stared at him seemingly unsure of what to say. "I'm sorry, I know I shouldn't have done what I did." He felt as though he was always apologising to her.
"No, you shouldn't have." Kim said sternly.
"I know you don't want me to protect you, I get it. I can't help myself though. Ever since dad died, I've felt obligated to protect those I love." Kim took Jack's hand gently.
"It's not that I don't want you to protect me. It's that you think I need protecting Jack, that I'm weak." Jack shook his head.
"I don't think that at all. You are stronger than me Kim, you're as strong as anyone I know. I just can't bear

to see you hurt. Believe me, I know you are strong." Jack pointed to his lip, the dried blood still on his face. Kim half chuckled half sighed.

"One day I'll figure out how to stay mad at you." Wetting her finger, she wiped away the dried blood, her hand cradled Jacks face. Their eyes met again. There was something unspoken happening.

'Kiss her.' His inner voice shouted. It was too late though, she dropped her hand and looked away from him.

"Shall we find the others?" She took his arm in her own and started walking towards the deck.

'You idiot'.

After an hour the Excalibur sailed to a perfect halt in the harbour. The flagship, carrying the flagship pupils had arrived. Standing on the harbour seemed to be the staff of the school. At the very front was a tall grey haired man; Jack knew that this must be the headmaster, Merlin. The name had become a title since the original Merlin's death. He wasn't what Jack had imagined. Merlin had been a wizard of extraordinary power and skill, but this man before him had no presence. Jack had always thought that when he met Merlin he would be an imposing man of power and presence, a man to be respected. And even though the headmaster looked the part, he just didn't fill you with confidence. Standing behind him was the deputy headmaster, Jack had met him once before on his induction day. His name was Nathaniel Grey, but had told the group to call him Nate. When Jack had first met him he thought that he was Merlin. He was tall, powerful, with dark wrangled hair that stretched down his face, a neat goatee that he told the group covered a nasty scar that he had picked up during a fight with a troll. At the time Jack thought that he was joking but looking at him now, well maybe it was true. Unlike the others, Professor Grey looked more like a student than a Teacher. Instead of being dressed in robes he stood there in a denim jacket, black shirt, torn jeans and trainers. Yet you knew that he commanded the respect of the others around him. Another teacher stood at the very back. He seemed to radiate waves of power. He wore a high collared black robe, a trilby hat and small round sunglasses. Jack noticed some of those on the dock were attempting to give him a wide berth.

'Weird'.

The gangplank began to lower itself as though pulled by an invisible rope. Jack could see pupils beginning to divide into groups as though they were preparing for what was to follow. Kim, Michael and Robin had silently fallen by his side, where as Melfice had drawn about him a group of unpleasant looking people, again Jack noticed Louise seemed unhappy to be among the group. Jack turned to say something to Michael, he too seemed have noticed Melfice,

"Ignore him." Jack said, he knew starting a fight now would be a bad idea.

"Who?" Michael said absently. It took Jack several seconds to realise Michael hadn't been looking at Melfice as he thought, rather at Louise.

"All pupils will now disembark." One by one the students lined up. Jack thought the ship was a good idea, it felt like he was walking the plank.

When everyone had disembarked, they stood before

The Dark Heart

the teachers. Those on the Excalibur had been set apart from the rest of the pupils. Jack could see the other council members were just as nervous as he was. With the exception of Michael and Melfice, they seemed to be soaking up the attention.

"To all our new students, welcome. Please would you all wait to be called by a teacher, they will then take you to the main castle." Merlin turned and walked away.

"Oh and make yourselves at home." Shouted Grey looking exacerbated.

One by one the teachers called out the student's names. Jack, Robin, Michael and Kim had all been called over by the teacher who seemed to make the dock workers nervous. Melfice and his cronies had swaggered off towards a tough looking teacher shaking hands. Jack guessed they knew each other outside of school. The last student remaining was Louise, expecting her to be placed with Melfice, Jack was shocked when his teacher called her forward. All the other students welcomed her. Kim even gave her a little hug, something that seemed to make Louise uncomfortable. When Kim had gone to place her arms around Louise she had flinched. It looked to Jack like she had been expecting to be struck. The only upside Jack could see was the furious expression on Melfice's face. He seemed to be arguing with his teacher over the placement.

'maybe she isn't all bad then.' Jack thought.

Jack didn't know why but he felt drawn towards the teacher. As soon as they were side by side, he understood why the dock workers were nervous of him. He was unmistakably a vampire.

"All children, please line up behind me and follow in an orderly manner." He said cheerfully, he was not at all what Jack was expecting.

"Sir ,may I ask?" the teacher turned to Jack.

"Yes Jack, I am a vampire." He answered as casually as possible.

"Oh that's good I didn't want to embarrass.... Hang on. How do you know my name and what I was thinking?" Grinning the teacher seemed to think over his answer carefully.

"Well you see, certain vampires have the ability to gleam thoughts from people's minds, and please don't call me Sir, my name is Kaiba, Lord Kaiba if you must."

'Wow a Lord.' Jack thought. "So does that mean I won't be able to get away with cheating on your exams then?" He asked cheekily. Kaiba laughed.

"You won't need to cheat on my exams, I teach appreciation of magical creatures, considering the fact that you didn't run screaming from me. I think puts us off to a good start." Kaiba seemed a very pleasant teacher.

Jack followed Kaiba quietly behind, he found the idea of having a vampire as a teacher intriguing, how many times in his life was he going to be able to talk with a real vampire? Kim and Robin seemed to be holding back a little as though unsure of what to make of him. Michael on the other hand was busy engaging him in conversation about his feelings on the council. Jack knew that he was trying to win him over; a teacher's vote was worth ten students on whom became the new high councillor. Robin soon ran off to the side of the attractive Elven girl from the tavern, sensing an opportunity, Jack dropped back slowly hoping not to attract Michael's attention.

"Enjoying yourself so far then?" he asked, Jack couldn't help but notice how sweaty his hands had become, but worse how idiotic he would look if he dried them on his clothes.

"It's amazing!" Kim was looking around Camelot, the harbour itself hadn't been particularly inspiring. It had seemed like any other port in the country, housing a fleet of fishing vessels, Stacks of wooden crates had laid haphazardly everywhere. Imports and exports from around the world, dozens of exotic names had been imprinted upon the crates, Items he had never heard of. He realised it must have taken an impossible amount of resources to keep Camelot running. The harbour had reeked of fish, he was glad to now be far enough away to breathe fresh air. As they drew closer to the city, they could see the walls coming into view.

'Wow!' It was all that Jack could think, looking up Jack saw for the first time some of the beauty of Camelot; he had just sited the first tower of knights. There were twelve gleaming towers in all, each representing an original member of the round table. Each of the towers appeared as to be made from marble. The walls of Camelot were over 100 feet high, even from here Jack could just make out the trebuchet's mounted on top of the castle walls. Finally, out of the port they had just walked into what seemed the middle of an open area with no discernible boundary.

Brilliant sunshine was raining down upon them, if Jack had not known he was underground he would never have been able to guess.

"Lord Kaiba how comes we're outside? I thought Camelot was underground?" Jack asked excitedly. Kaiba laughed to himself.

"Yes, we are still inside, technically." Jack was confused.

"What do you mean?" Kaiba was clearly amused.

"Have you ever been told of the splitting of the worlds?" His voice trembling holding in a laugh.

"A little I don't really remember much about it though." Michael was paying attention now; he wanted to know everything about everything. The one thing he hated was being wrong, the annoying thing was he was hardly ever wrong.

"Throughout the world there are tears in the fabric of reality. It is generally believed these tears were caused by an intense, ancient magic, from when the god's walked the Earth." Jack didn't believe in the gods, but he didn't object to this now. "Devices like the Diasis use these tears to allow us transport between them." Michael and Kim nodded along. They absorbed information like a sponge. "Camelot exists in one of these tears, shielded from entry by magic. Only Stonehenge allows us entry here." This much Jack knew. "now where as a Diasis will take you from one location to another, what Stonehenge does is to allow for access to this pocket plane. You see, this place exists outside of the world." Jack's head was starting to hurt. Both Michael and Kim seemed to understand better than he. "Certain items like the warship Excalibur were enchanted by Merlin himself. Only items like this may use the Diasis spread around the coast of Britain to return here. I don't believe anyone else could have done this."

"but Lord Kaiba, what about the splitting?" Asked

Michael excitedly.

"Well, you see when Arthur and Mordred had their final battle it caused such a tremendous upheaval in magic that it damaged the world, creating even more tears, the only way to repair these tears was for Merlin to separate the worlds of magic and non magic forever. The effort involved took a toll on Merlin. Some say this is the reason he died. If it had been me or you, well we would have died in the attempt." Jack mused this over, it was ingenious that Merlin had been able to separate the worlds. He had allowed for two sets of people to occupy the same space at the same time.

The group continued to walk through this strange world. Jack's head was beginning to ache. He couldn't help but wonder, if Merlin had been able to separate the worlds, how many more of these chambers had he created and what could possibly be inside? Camelot was far larger then he had ever imagined, they had been walking for almost an hour and had only just reached the battlements. There seemed to be no end to the towers which appeared to touch the sky itself. Jack thought the castle itself may actually be carved from a marble mountain, glowing brilliant white. The river Pendragon ran all around the castle, it acted as an unending moat, it continued to flow into a great lake and then passing further into the distance, a forest seemed to grow from behind the castle itself spreading along the water's edge, following it off into the world. The only access to the castle was through the gate house which was large enough to fit a hundred knights side by side in full armour. Jack knew now why this was the safest place in the world. To attack Camelot, you would have to breach

Stonehenge, defeat the Knights stationed there, fight through the enchanted caverns, then past the awaiting knights, before charging across the open fields with the castle firing at you then either, breach an unbreakable gatehouse, or have swam the raging river and climbed a hundred foot wall and still get past the knights awaiting inside the castle.

Finally, inside the walls of the castle, the expanse of Camelot continued to shock. An entire city was housed within. They walked into the largest courtyard he had ever seen. It could have easily held the main town of Salisbury within the courtyard itself. Jack could hear the other students starting to mutter about being tired, but he didn't care, he was awestruck. Standing in the courtyard he could see the towers of the main castle peeking above the city in the distance. As they continued, they passed through the residential area. Small wooden houses barely big enough for a family of three were seemingly plotted at random. It still had the old town feel to it. Almost as though the walls had sprung up around the city, rather than being built purposely to maximise the space, like so many modern cities. It made it confusing to navigate but appeared picturesque. Next, they saw the main market, every shop he could think of was here. Michael saw Le Fays, it was the most famous club in Camelot, Kim gave an excited thumbs up. Jack faked a smile, the idea of dancing in public secretly terrified him. As they passed by, the residents of Camelot excitedly welcomed them all. After what had seemed hours, they reached the castle itself. It was astonishing, this was the home of Arthur and the round table. The place the council ruled from, and now his home for the next two years.

"Well, we are finally here. Welcome to Camelot Castle." Kaiba declared happily to the gathered students. "You will need to travel to your new rooms, I'm sure you will all wish to unpack, you will then have the rest of the day to do as you wish. Tomorrow you will all be in the dining hall at eight thirty sharp to hear the headmaster's welcome speech." Jack felt a bit irritated.

"I thought that we would find out what school house we are in?" Kaiba laughed out loud, some of the students backed off at the sight of his fangs.

"That's right, I forgot didn't I. Well let me be the first to welcome you all to the Arthurians."

Chapter 5
Welcome all

Like the rest of Camelot, the castle was overwhelming. Everywhere he looked banners hung; they each bore a symbol of one of the school houses. They hung from the high ceilings, the balcony's, along the railings of the grand staircase, even above the stone arches. The suits of armour were also engraved with the crests of the houses. It took a moment for him to realise but he was standing on an embossed floor, carved from granite into the shape of the round table, etchings of beasts in the place where the legendary Knights of the round table would have sat. Jack, like all the pupils, knew the houses off by heart. The Arthurians were represented by a white sword protruding from a waters edge. The Lancelot's a white mare, the Galahads a wolf. The round table represented the school council, and finally the knights crest was a suit of armour. Any student that was part of two of these houses would have a single room of their own. Jack was in three, being on the student council, a knight in training and an Arthurian. This meant he would have the second largest room available. The best room in the school belonged to the high councillor. Jack had never considered attempting to become the high councillor before. Although the idea of making sure Melfice wouldn't become it felt reason enough to put his hat in the ring. An even larger reason loomed in the back of his mind.

'imagine what Kim would think of you!' Jack smiled inwardly.

Looking around Jack could already see a small number of students wearing Arthurian badges on their uniforms. As he, Michael, Kim and Robin were all still wearing their normal clothing, Jack guessed that there must be at least thirty new Arthurians from his group. He didn't know how many pupils there were, but the school seemed far too large for the two hundred or so pupils that Jack had seen so far.

"Let's head up to the common room." Michael suggested before realising he had no idea where they were going.

"Hang on, someone was handing out maps by the door's, I'll run and grab one." Kim ran off. Robin spotted the girl he was interested in and made his excuses, leaving Michael and Jack alone. The only other Arthurian from their year left in the hall was Louise, she seemed unsure of what to do.

"What do you make of her being placed with us? I thought for sure she would be with Melfice." Jack quizzed Michael.

"You for one should know that appearances can be deceptive mate. Look at me, most would have put me with the Lancelot's." Jack could tell Michael had been secretly dreading this. He had never given it any thought. He had known all along that Michael, Kim and Rob would all be in the same house. "I feel bad for her." Jack looked at Michael slightly amazed, it wasn't often he showed any emotion for a stranger.

"Why?" Michael looked at Jack as though he had never seen him before.

"I thought I was the cold hearted one." Jack bit his lip.

"Yeah, well we didn't do anything wrong did we? it was her boyfriend that was being a dick." Jack had said it louder than he meant.

"He isn't my boyfriend." Louise walked past the two of them, Michael tried to say something, but she ignored them.

"Well done, idiot." He slapped Jack around the back of the head and stormed off to find Kim.

Jack had set off in no particular direction, he was trying to be angry with Michael, but he knew it was really himself he was upset with.

"Twat." He swore loudly.

"Now, if I heard you say that tomorrow, I would be forced to put you in detention. But I'll let you off this once." Wheeling around Jack saw the deputy headmaster.

"Oh, I'm sorry sir. I didn't see you there." Jack was in trouble; he had barely been in school for an hour, and he was about to be chastised by the deputy headmaster. At least he had done better then Joe, he hadn't even made it to the castle before getting a detention.

"I assume that you have had a fight with your friends." Grey said wisely his demeanour friendly.

"You're not a vampire are you sir? You know with the reading of my mind and all." Jack was waiting for Grey to vent his disapproval. He wasn't sure that Grey's seemingly uncaring attitude towards his harsh tongue was genuine.

"Ah, yes Lord Kaiba escorted you here, he's an

incredibly interesting man." Grey seemed jovial and caring. "No, I'm not a vampire, I'm just an incredibly talented wizard even if I do say so myself." He pointed his thumb at his chest. Jack guessed he was trying to look impressive. "I just assumed that you had an argument. Normally when someone shouts out loud to an empty room, they are not talking about someone that they have just met." Jack half smiled his acknowledgement. "Which friend was it? Kim, Michael, Robin?" begrudgingly Jack answered,

"It was me." Jack stopped and looked at Grey curiously, he had never mentioned his friend's names. Grey smiled at him.

"I must confess I know Miss Illsley's family personally. She has taken to me as something of an older brother. I believe she was rather upset by your argument last year."

'Great, who doesn't know?' He thought. The all too familiar feeling of guilt began wriggling in his stomach.

"She talked about you non-stop you know." Grey stressed. He took Jack's silence as a statement that he did indeed understand. Gently he continued. "As for being angry with yourself, all I can say is this. Every day is an opportunity to fix something broken, if only we are brave enough to try." He patted Jack on the shoulder. "Now is there anything else I can help you with?" Jack was grateful for the change of subject.

"Well actually, I was looking for the Arthurian common room." Jack still had no idea how to get there. He wasn't sure he would be able to find his way back to the main hall in order to get his own map.

"Yes, I was very happy to see you all made it into the Arthurians, not many people make it into them anymore. I was an Arthurian myself, there's only about half the number of students in the Arthurians as there are in the Lancelot's or Galahad's." He said beaming, Jack guessed he was trying to tell him it was a more exclusive group than the other houses. "Normally though, they make the best wizards, just don't tell anyone I said that." Grey said kindly. "Anyway, go back to the main entrance hall, up the stairs to the twelfth floor, turn right follow the corridor all the way down to the end, turn right and then up the next set of stairs. That will take you to the Arthurian tower. From there just follow it all the way to the top all the doors are designated, so you'll be able to find yours easily enough, now if you'll excuse me, I have a cup of tea waiting for me in the staff room." With that Grey walked around Jack and into a wall. "Ouch. Sorry, it's just to the left." Jack laughed as Grey felt along the wall a little and then walked straight through the seemingly solid stone. Jack ran his hand over the wall where Grey had just walked through. As hard as he tried the wall would not yield to his touch. It was another small, wonderous reason he was already falling in love with the place.

It took Jack twenty minutes to reach the Arthurian common room. The size of Camelot was disorientating, the entrance to the common room was exactly like that of the staff room, a seemingly blank wall. Something about the wall was different though, it seemed that only an Arthurian could sense it. The common room was unbelievable, a roaring fire with a green flame was alight in the corner. The room was kept at a constant comfortable temperature. A student had his hand in the fire, it didn't seem to be hurting him at all. His friends

The Dark Heart

were laughing daring him to try different things in the flame. Five sofa's which could easily seat ten a piece were placed around the room. A door off to the side read library. All the literature of the schools library could be viewed with in, using reference books.

'That will be good for Michael.' Jack thought deeply impressed. There appeared to also be a gym and stone mannequins for sword practice in other rooms off the main common room. The dormitories were situated upstairs from the rear of the room. It wasn't uncommon for students to share rooms. Pupils would sometimes get married during their time at the school. The walls of the common room were adorned with the Arthurian banner, Paintings of Arthur and Guinevere along with other members of the round table, were displayed proudly around the oak fireplace. The last room of to the side was a small kitchen. It wasn't a normal kitchen with any appliances. You would walk in and place an order, almost any food or drink you could think of, just ask for it and within minutes it would appear for you. Jack's room was only slightly smaller then the common room. He had a full en-suite and his own small gym next door to his bedroom. An Emperor sized four poster bed; it was ornately engraved with dragons rising up the posts. The wings falling over the bed as Satin drapes. The wooden heads seemed to breathe the smell of fresh meadows into the room. The only other items of furniture were two dressers and a wardrobe. It was up to Jack to decorate the room as he pleased. He didn't feel he required any posters or hangings. The view from his balcony window was breath-taking. Like all in the Arthurian tower, he could see clearly over the courtyard, out to the lake and down to the forest. From this high it was impossible to make out individuals, Everyone below barely bigger than an ant. He felt like the King of his own castle.

Jack stayed in his room for the best part of the day, he had been half enjoying the grandeur of his room. He was also trying to avoid Michael.
'He will come around.' Jack wasn't so sure; Michael could hold a grudge. 'Apologise!' Why should he. Michael was being unreasonable. 'No, he isn't.' They didn't even know Louise, why should it matter. 'Think.' Michael had said about appearances being deceptive. He was worried people thought he wouldn't belong in the Arthurians. That he would be alone. 'Just like Louise.' Guilt coursed through him. Michael had known how Louise would be feeling. She was alone separated from the few people she knew. Jack should have tried to be more welcoming. The more he thought about what had happened at Stonehenge, the more he realised how much she hadn't wanted to be with Melfice. Michael had seen it and he hadn't.

Hungry and bored Jack left his room. Dinner would now be being served in the dining hall. He started to make his way through the castle attempting to retrace his steps from earlier. After 20 minutes he had to admit he was lost. Frustrated, Jack leaned against the wall forgetting that door's weren't always visible. He fell straight through the wall.
"I'm sick of falling on my butt." He moaned rubbing himself. As his eyes adjusted to the darkness he was a little stunned by what he saw. The room wasn't quite like the others he had seen so far. Ancient symbols were

engraved all over the ceiling and pictures of strange creatures surrounding every corner. "What the hell is this place?" Jack stood up wiping the dust from his clothes. "What are these?" he wondered aloud looking at a picture of a great beast which seemed to be dressed in armour holding a sword.

"They are called Avatars." Jack jumped high into the air, he raised his wand with fright. A small light flickered from the end into the shadows.

"What, who said that?" Stepping out from the darkness Jack saw a tall, handsome woman, she was about the same age as his mother.

"My name young man, is Miss Levell and I am the teacher of magical creature apparitions." She flicked her wand, the air stirred. Jack felt something flutter past his ears.

"What is an Avatar then?" he asked carefully. A large eagle dropped from the ceiling stopping inches from his face. Once again Jack fell over. "Where the hell did that come from?" he asked shocked at the sudden appearance of the eagle, its claws looked razor sharp and seemed to have blades for wings.

"This is Acrista, she is my oldest friend. Every person has an animal spirit, or as we call them Avatar's inside of them. It takes practice and a great command of your peace to manifest your own." Jack stared in disbelief. "Do you feel particularly attracted to any specific creature?" Jack just sat dumbfounded. "What is your name?" Levell asked kindly. Acrista stared hungrily at Jack hovering inches above him.

"I'm sorry Its Jack, Jack London." Levell smiled again. "Thank you, so Jack, do you have an affinity with any particular animal then?" Jack thought he knew about a lot of creatures but there was only one he had ever felt close to. "Well, I suppose the animal I feel the closest to is my pet wolf Galahad, now I know it's not a terribly original name, but it suits him." Levell called Acrista away, it perched on a table for a moment chirping its satisfaction. Slowly it faded away into mist, almost as though it had never existed.

"It's a fine name; I suppose that means that your spiritual animal or Avatar is a wolf. May I also hazard a guess that you're a member of The Galahads?" she asked curiously.

"No, I'm Arthurian." Jack puffed out his chest.

"Really? how strange it's not often that an animal you are so drawn to belongs to another house. Well now I would suggest that you get some dinner and tomorrow I will begin to teach you how to make your own appear."

Exiting the room was much easier then entering, for starters you could actually see the door.

"Sorry miss, could you please tell me the way to the dining hall." Smiling Levell said

"Tell you what, i'll take you there. Please do try to remember it is a large school and extremely easy to get lost. When I first started I found myself in the men's bathroom, I was so embarrassed." Jack tried his best not to laugh.

"Ok, thank you for telling me that." He giggled.

"Do you know what's really strange about you though?" Jack was amazed at how fast she could change tack, "how little you look like your brother, but how much you look like your father?" Jack stopped dead.

"You knew my brother and my father?" He sputtered, flabbergasted.

"Well yes, I taught your brother and sister. Me and Ben were particularly good friends in school ourselves. I was very sorry to hear about his death." She added in a suitably woeful tone. "How have you been since his passing? I can understand that it was obviously a tragic time for you." There was such sorrow in her voice that Jack wondered how well she had known Ben. Jack did not know what to say he had only just met this woman and yet he felt she was kindred in their feelings for his father.

"for the longest time I was angry with him after he died. In the end I realised he would never have left us willingly. Someone enormously powerful stopped my father coming home that night." Levell patted him gently on the shoulder, she understood he was sure.

"Did they ever discover how he died?" She asked faintly.

"No." Jack didn't like talking about his father with his family let alone someone he had just met, but somehow the fact that Levell had known Ben from a young age allowed him to let his guard down. "Can you tell me Miss. What was the creature my father could summon?" He found it strangely comforting to believe maybe he and his father might share an animal spirit.

"I would, but the truth is Ben never managed to summon his spirit, neither could your brother. Carol on the other hand, well Ravid was one of the most beautiful Avatars I have seen." Understanding the look of confusion on Jack's face she continued. "Ravid was the name of her Avatar; he was a golden-haired grizzly bear, clad in shining armour. He would only listen to your sister, as headstrong as any member of your family I'm sure." Ravid sounded wonderous,

"How come then miss, my sister never showed him to me?" Jack wanted to see this Ravid.

"You saw the inscriptions in my class I presume." Jack nodded. "Well, you see without those symbols it is nearly impossible to produce an Avatar. That is why there are so many in the class, to make it easier for pupils to produce your own. Only the most powerful of witches and wizards go on to be able to summon their Avatars without need of those runes. Your sister is a mighty witch, but she still needs time to learn to control all her strength." Jack smiled, maybe one day she would show him and he in turn might be able to produce his for her. He suddenly found himself wondering if he would be able to. Was he going to be powerful enough, or was he as the youngest too weak? He changed his thoughts quickly.

"So, you knew my dad as a kid then? I take it you two were friends." Levell's face lit up.

"Oh yes, best friends." Levell positively beamed happiness remembering his father.

"I hope you don't mind if I ask a question." He felt slightly impertinent but was keen to know as much as possible.

"Ask away, you should never be afraid to ask a question. Your father certainly wasn't." Steadying himself Jack noticed his sweaty hands again.

"I was just wondering if you and my father were ever an item?" Levell suddenly looked a little uncomfortable.

"Well, no we weren't. We were more competitors for the affection of ladies." It took Jack several seconds for him to understand what she meant.

"Oh, fair enough. Sorry I don't mean to pry. I'm trying to learn as much about my dad as I can." Jack had no issues with Levell's life choice, he wished he hadn't asked in such a stupid way. The pair continued their journey in silence. After what seemed an eternity, they reached the dining room.

"Well, I'll see you later young Jack." With a slight curtsey Levell left him standing there. He was not sure, but he thought that she wanted to get away from him almost as much as he did from her, his cheeks still molten red.

Dodging his way through the crowd, Jack was trying to spot his friends.

"Finally decided to come out of your room did you?" Jack had stopped next to Kim without realising.

"yeah sorry, I didn't get a lot of sleep last night and just kind of crashed out I guess, where are Michael and Robin then?" Kim wouldn't raise her eyes to meet Jack's, when she spoke her voice was hushed and slightly broken.

"Robin is off trying to chat up that girl from earlier, and I don't know where Michael is." She almost spat his name.

"Kim are you ok?" he asked concerned.

"I'm fine, why shouldn't I be?" Her voice was cracking more and more with each word.

"Kim look at me, what's wrong?" She raised her head slowly; her eyes were puffy with tears she had obviously been crying.

"I'm fine, I just had a little fight with Michael." She wiped her eyes on her sleeve.

"I'm sure it wasn't that bad. What happened to upset you so much?" Jack asked putting his arm around her shoulder to try and comfort her. Kim shook him off and stood over him. Pointing her finger hard in his chest she shouted.

"YOU'RE what happened." Everyone in the hall turned to look at them. Jack could feel each set of eyes upon him.

"Ok, I wasn't expecting that, what did I do?" Jack was struggling to make sense of this.

"Michael told me all about your stupid fight over Louise. I tried to defend you because you're an IDIOT. And he accused me of defending you because I care about you." Jack swallowed hard. "He thinks that you defended me at Stonehenge because you love me." She blurted out her eyes still brimming with tears.

"I'll go talk to him." Jack got up to leave suddenly wanting to be anywhere else.

"Is it true?" she asked. Jack opened his mouth several times to say something. He realised he couldn't say what he wanted. He turned and left the hall whispering under his breath.

"Every word."

Walking across the fields outside the school, Jack felt distressed. Why couldn't he tell Kim the truth? There was nothing stopping him from admitting his feelings, they were both single, they were friends, why couldn't he tell her he loved her. Jack spotted Michael across at the stables. It was time to clear the air between them for Kims sake, Jack whistled loudly, Michael turned around seeing Jack. He could clearly tell Michael was annoyed by the way he had thrown his hands in the air.

'Ok, if you want to play it like that then.'

"if you're looking to join the team queue up there." A large boy from the back of the group shouted out. "Barry

The Dark Heart

Helmsley, team captain of the Arthurian Lancers." He announced,

"Sure, that's why I'm here." Jack did not care about the boy's name or trying out for the team he just wanted to get close to Michael. It was only now, standing in the queue, Jack realised what the sport was. It was the jousting team.

"Ok then, pick a lance and take a spot in the stables. You'll be called out when it's your turn." Barry ran off and grabbed his wand, he pointed it at Jack and whispered an incantation. A suit of school issued armour sprung from the corner and began attaching itself over his clothing.

The stables were full of horses of all sizes. Already fully armoured to protect them from accidental harm. Jack watched as Michael carefully chose his lance. Without paying attention, Jack plucked one from the wall, he didn't care about jousting, he had some experience as part of his education when younger. All he wanted was to make sure he was drawn against Michael. Jack saddled his chosen horse and continued to shuffle in the queue until he was opposite Michael. Finally, they were called forward, they trotted to the middle of the gauntlet run where Barry was waiting.

"Ok guys, I don't want any accidents, this is just about seeing how you ride and your lance position. No head shots, chest or shoulder only. Best of three rounds, unless you can't continue. Understood?" They both nodded towards Barry. Trotting to their ends they turned and faced each other. Both lowered their visors and raised their lances. Ben stood in the middle holding a handkerchief, raising his hand high both Michael and

Jack raised their lances higher, showing their readiness. Barry dropped the handkerchief and sprinted from the gauntlet.

   Jack kicked hard, his horse spurred forward, he could see Michael approaching fast, lowering his lance he locked it to the saddle, Michael thundered at him the hooves pounding the sand below. Gritting his teeth, he took aim at Michaels shoulder. He gripped his reigns as hard as possible, Jack's lance glanced off Michael's shoulder rocking him. Michael's crashed square into Jack's chest splintering his lance. Whilst the armour absorbed most of the impact, it still felt as though Jack had been punched in the heart. Struggling to breathe he barely managed to hold onto the reigns. Jack had taken the hit on purpose, trotting to the end and picking up a new lance he turned to see Michael struggling to lift his own.

   "Are we ok to proceed?" Barry called to them both. Taking deep rasping breaths Jack held his lance high. Jack could see Michael struggle but finally lifted his arm. Again, the handkerchief dropped, Jack charged forward locking his lance. This time he leaned forward making himself smaller. Michael seemed to struggle to lock in his own lance from the pain in his shoulder. Just before they met, he saw something fall from Michael's side, Jack's lance met its target landing squarely in Michael's chest. The sound of wood splintering filled the run. Jack could hear people cheering and screaming now. It seemed they had an audience. Michael clung on tight. As much as he hated to admit it, he was impressed. Jack had meant to take him off his horse winning the match. He still had the advantage; Michael's shoulder was hurting and now had the same pain in his chest that Jack felt.

"Third and final run, score 1-1." Jack and Michael lined up their final run, Michael rotated his shoulder, bashing the armour over it in order to regain some feeling. He was using the last of his strength to hold his lance. Jack breathed deep, the pain in his chest subsiding. The final drop, both men set off hard determined to win. This was more than a trial, any issues they had ever had with each other were being settled here.

"Come on." Jack roared at his horse. Gritting his teeth. Neither he, nor Michael locked their lances they wanted full control. Faster their horses raced spurred on by the screaming audience. Jack pulled back on his lance forcing it forward at the last second, he placed all his strength in that one blow. He heard the splintering and then felt the pain. His hands slipped from his reigns his body leaving his saddle, the horse ran on and he fell. The sickening thud as his body crumpled to the floor, a second thud telling him he too had found his target. Screams filled the stadium; some cheered others were horrified. He could hear boots running towards them. He felt the pain as he tried to breathe, but it felt good, he couldn't help It, he laughed, being helped to his feet he could see Barry shouting something at him,

"Are you ok?" Barry shouted for the third time. Jack's head was still ringing. Slowly Jack gave Barry the thumbs up. On the other track Jack could see Michael being helped to his feet he too was giving the thumbs up. The crowd roared its approval.

Both Jack and Michael were escorted to the stables. Barry helping to remove their damaged armour. One of the stable hands rushed over and gave them both a drink.

"Take it." Barry said to them both. Jack gulped his drink down in one go, the pain in his chest began to ease instantly. Michael drank his also, Jack could see him testing his shoulder clearly the potion was helping with the pain. "The bruising should go away in a couple of days." Barry assured them. "So, quite an eventful first joust." Barry smiled at them both. Neither answered him. "It was a stroke of genius to tank that first hit Jack, it gave you the advantage in the next two rounds." Jack smiled. "But Michael you showed real guts to fight back the way you did. That would have been worthy of any championship match." Michael grinned over at Jack before realising he was still angry with him and looked away. "You can both ride and handle a lance, but I only have space for one person from the council." Barry seemed to weigh up his options. "Honestly, this is the hardest choice I've had to make. Michael it's you, but Jack I would like to keep you as first choice backup." Michael nodded his approval. Jack shook Barry's hand he wasn't disappointed.

As soon as Barry left, Michael turned to Jack.

"I thought you didn't like Jousting?" His voice was barely above a snarl.

"I wanted to talk to you." Jack was calm, he had cleared all his anger at Michael in the joust.

"Well I'm here, what the hell do you want?" Michael looked like he could happily punch Jack.

"I wanted to say I'm sorry about the way I treated Louise. I don't know what is going on with you and her but I'm sorry I upset you." Jack was earnest in his apology. He heard Michael mutter something about nothing going on. "I get that your angry with me, but don't take it out on Kim." He pleaded. "You were there for her when I wasn't, she's up in the hall crying because of what you said to her." Michael seemed to be wrestling with his own guilt.

"I told her the truth." he tried to sound annoyed, but it was tinged with regret.

"You told her I love her." It was a statement. Jack wasn't interested in playing coy.

"Was I wrong?" he looked Jack in the eye, they had been the best of friends forever, but this was a conversation they had always avoided.

"No." Jack answered simply. "It's up to me to tell Kim though, not you." It felt good to finally admit the truth to someone.

"Then do it, god it's been years Jack, she won't wait forever. There are already a dozen boys sniffing around her." Michael threw his cup into the straw, his frustration boiling over.

"And what about Louise?" Michael stopped and looked at him.

"She was in the stands, and she wasn't there for me." Jack answered, Michael walked to the edge of the stable and peeked out, Sure enough in the crowd Louise was staring towards them, she wasn't paying attention to the jousting. "What's going on with you and her?" Michael took his time to answer. "What about her?" he asked.

"Nothing, today is the first time I have seen her, while I'm awake." Michael stopped himself, annoyed at what he had said.

"what do you mean awake?" Jack walked over and

started to check Michael was ok, he was worried he may have suffered a concussion.

"For years I've dreamt of a girl, the same girl always." Pointing his finger towards Louise. "Of her." Michael was scaring him, Jack had never heard of anything like this. True Kim had appeared to him in his dreams, but he had always known her, that wasn't unusual.

"How could you have been dreaming about Louise? Are you sure it's not just someone who looked a bit like her?" Michael shook his head.

"It's her. It took me a few minutes to realise how I knew her once we were on Excalibur. I can remember everything about those dreams. They are almost like memories, so vivid, but from another time." Michael sat down sinking his head in his hands. "Am I mad?" he asked Jack.

"No, but maybe we should talk to someone about this. It can't be unheard of I'm sure." Michael shook his head.

"I don't want anyone to know about this, not yet. Promise me." Taking Michaels hand, he shook his agreement.

"Don't tell Kim I love her." Jack asked back Michael nodded.

"This isn't going to be a normal year is it?" Jack didn't say a word but took Michael by the shoulder leading them back towards the castle. Looking back over his shoulder Jack could see Louise standing in the shade of a tree watching them.

Chapter 6

A Most Important Lesson

By morning everything was back to normal, Michael had apologised to Kim and she had quickly forgiven him, there had been no mention of him telling Kim Jack loved her. Jack didn't know if it had been the conversation with Michael or coincidence, but he had spent the night dreaming of Kim, he was glad that she couldn't read his mind. It certainly wasn't for sharing.

Lessons start in an hour.

"Hey, you guy's coming to breakfast, I could eat a horse?" Jack's stomach gave a low rumble.

"come on then Michael, he's obviously not going to be happy until he's fed." She tapped on Jack's stomach. Goosebumps ran the length of his body.

"Yeah alright, come on then you big baby." Jack picked up his bag, it was stuffed full of schoolbooks. When the students had woken that morning their lesson planners had been filled.

"What's today then?" Michael asked.

Some of Jack's favourite lessons were being taught today. One of the best things was on Friday, he had the last two periods off for studying. Having spent the best part of last night memorising a map given to him by Kim, Jack could now tell you almost every access way to every point in the castle. He had always been gifted with a Strong memory; sometimes photographic.

"Come on I want to go and get my sword before lessons." When a student brought a sword into school they were confiscated to check for spells and curses. Jacks had been delivered to the school a week in advance to make sure it was clear of any black magic before his first lesson. With his bag overflowing he ran on ahead shouting to the others. "You guys go ahead, I'll catch up; Grey has my sword." He was almost out the door when Kim called out to him.

"Oh, don't be late, today's the day its decided who becomes high councillor. Voting finishes after breakfast." She seemed almost as excited as Michael. Jack had forgotten, but it was ok, they would know by lunch, who had been crowned. His name would have been entered automatically, but he knew there was little chance he would become high councillor. The best he could hope for was that Melfice did not either.

Arriving outside Grey's office Jack knocked loudly, he watched as students attempted to use their maps to get around, it was clear some were struggling more than others. He knocked again, the door swung open slightly he could see clearly inside, in the corner there appeared to be a person, but the room was so dark it was hard to tell.

"Professor Grey, is it ok to come in?" He didn't hear an answer, Jack pushed the door further open. Deciding that it would be rude to just walk away, he stepped inside. "Sir are you ok?" Reaching out Jack touched the figure. The thing Jack had taken for a person was actually a coat rack and he had sent it crashing to the floor. Jack started to pick it up when something fell out of a torn pocket and rolled across the floor. Rushing over to pick it up Jack noticed it was an orb, it was filthy. The orb looked as though it had been buried for years. Dusting it off Jack noticed a name had been scratched into the surface. He cleaned the orb further to get a better look, some of the initials started to become clear. Firstly a b then an l followed by o, d, o. Jack couldn't make out all the letters. He tried rubbing even harder but in this gloom he thought he would be hard pressed to make it out. Another crash, the coat rack had fallen over again. Without thinking Jack placed the orb into his pocket to pull up the coat rack.

"Don't worry, it's always doing that." Jack wheeled around to find Grey standing there.

"oh, I'm sorry sir. I came here to see you about my sword. My first lesson is today." Holding up his hand as in an apology. Grey ran over to his desk he rummaged around for a few seconds and pulled out what seemed to be a small butter knife, he handed this over to Jack. "Sir, not to sound ungrateful but this isn't my sword?" Jack held the butter knife rather indignantly, was Grey trying to make fun of him.

"Oh yes, I forgot first years didn't know." "Know what Sir?" "First year students are only allowed their swords in their rooms and class, when not in one of those rooms it turns into this." He pointed towards the butter knife, now is there anything else I can help you with because I need to cast my vote." Jack thanked Grey and left feeling slightly upset that the school didn't trust him with a full length sword, he kicked the floor in disgust. He eventually reached his table and sat down with his friends, Robin also came over and joined them.

"Dragged yourself away from her then, did you?" Jack and Michael laughed.

"Oh shut up Jack, I don't want to talk about it." Robin said a little stung his face was drooping further by the moment.

"Ok then. So has everyone cast their vote yet?" all of them nodded. Kim handed Jack a slip of paper with thirty names on.

"Just tick the name you want, and it will be cast. You can't vote for yourself though." She warned him. Jack looked down the list, he could see all their names.

"Who are you voting for?" Michael asked trying to peek at Jacks slip. Kim smacked his arm.

"That's none of your business. Jack you vote for who you like and don't tell us. It's supposed to be anonymous." She said to Michael. Jack looked again at the names. Picking up the pencil from the table and hiding the sheet under the table to stop Michael peaking Jack ticked Kim's name. As much as he knew Michael would make an excellent high councillor, he thought that at this time Kim would be even better. Michael's admission about dreaming of Louise had worried him. As soon as he had made his mark the paper vanished in a puff of smoke.

"So, where's your sword then?" Kim asked trying to distract Michael from asking more questions.

"Oh you're not going to believe this, just look." Jack reached into his pocket he felt the orb he had placed there earlier. "Shit, I forgot I had this!" Placing the orb on the table Jack reached back into his pocket and grabbed the knife.

"That's your sword, what the hell did they do to it?" Michael said holding it up looking at it as though the school had defaced a masterpiece.

"Why do you have an orb, your mum hasn't sent you a message already?" Kim asked.

"No, I found it earlier in Grey's room I forgot to return it, weird thing though there's something scratched on it I couldn't make it out in the dark. Take a look see if you can work it out." Jack handed Kim the orb before turning back to Michael to discuss the injustice of the situation. "Yeah, look at what they did to my sword; apparently it will only change back when I'm in my room or at knight training." Robin shook his head laughing. Jack guessed that Robin also a member of the knights and council because he was an only child already knew about this rule.

"Well, just make sure it's not in your pocket when you enter else, ouch!" Michael laughed, all three of the boy's held their groins.

"better not to think of it." Robin said wisely. "but if you will excuse me, I forgot my homework." Robin jumped up leaving quickly. Jack laughed when he saw the girl Robin had become slowly obsessed with leaving just before him.

"you don't think…" Jack whispered winking at Michael.

"I hope so, maybe he can lose the fascination with her then get back to the old Robin we know and love."

"oh, you love him do you?" Michael punched Jack in the arm.

'god that hurts.' Jack shouted in his head, but Jack just gave Michael a little chuckle.

"Where are these symbols then?" Kim interrupted their teasing, paying no attention to their playfulness. Jack took back the orb.

"Look, right here." he ran his finger along the orb.

"Jack these aren't symbols it's a name, and I know what the name is. I just don't get why you carved it in here trying to pass them off as symbols." Kim seemed to think he was trying to play some game with her.

"What are you going on about? I haven't touched it!" Kim looked exasperated

"Look it's clearly, B, L, O, D, O. It's B, London. It's your father."

"What the hell do you mean it's my dad's name? it can't be no offence Kim, have you forgotten how to spell?" Jack cast her a slightly dismissive look. "Don't you think I would recognise my own father's name?" he laughed she was mistaken he knew, maybe the anticipation of the council vote later had her distracted. Michael had taken the orb and was now staring at it intently. After several seconds his eyes narrowed further until at last he gasped and suddenly started pointing at the orb excitedly.

"Jack mate, she's right this is your dad's." Michael whispered enthusiastically. Jack was starting to get frustrated, he snatched the orb back angrily.

"Look you two it say's B, L, O, D, O which doesn't spell Benjamin London. It sounds more like a medieval rock band." He snapped fire burning in his chest.

"Jack, do you know the Raizing spell?" Michael asked sounding just as frustrated with Jack's pig headiness.

"Yes Michael, of course I do, Donovan had me using it almost consistently in his shop during my first two months there. My arm will never be the same after that." He joked trying to lighten the mood. He wished he had said nothing at all now. The Raizing spell was a standard cleaning spell that most children mastered during their home tuition.

"Then use it." Kim implored him.

"What's the point? all it will do is clean off the dust." Jack hated it when the two of them teamed up against him. He knew it would only be so long he could say no.

"Yes it will clean off the dust, but one of the advantages of the Raizing spell is that it will also repair any damage done, you idiot." Kim raised her eyebrows in frustration. Just to shut the pair of them up Jack picked up the orb and drew his wand. Then rubbing his thumb over the name he whispered

"Razingdon." A little golden thread sprung out of the end of his wand entwining the orb. It began to glow brilliant gold, two small letters appeared on the orb as the glass repaired itself and the dirt faded away. Michael grabbed Jack.

"Look that's clearly an N." There was no way he could dismiss this now, the name was B, LONDON. Jack was shocked,

"This is my dad's, but why would Grey have this and not tell me about it?" Kim and Michael didn't seem to care about this small fact,

"can you watch it?" Looking around Jack decided this probably wasn't the best place to view it.

"This isn't the time or the place." Jack didn't know if he could watch it or even if he wanted to. All he knew was that he didn't want anyone else to see.

Before their first class each council member would have to undergo a test. Jack and the others had been prepared for this since their letters had arrived over the summer. Once everyone had finished their breakfast and the other students had left for their classes the remaining students sat. An excited buzz filled the hall. The usual row of tables had vanished and been replaced by a variety of objects, Jack could see from the Mannequin and targets they would be demonstrating their sword craft and accuracy with a bow. The object that caught his eye however, looked like two small stone pillars on a table. Each section was now being sealed off. From behind Jack heard a heavy breathing. Robin had reappeared, puffing out of breath.

"I forgot." He wheezed

"You're here now, that's all that matters." Kim said sympathetically. Everyone fell to a hush as Grey walked to the front of the hall.

"Good morning everyone. I hope we are all prepared for this morning's activities and for your first day of schooling." Grey smiled at them all. Jack liked Grey but the orb sitting in his bag made him nervous, why was it Grey had it? "One by one each of you will enter an area complete your test and move on. Once finished you may wait for your friends to complete their own, but you cannot interfere or enter one of the testing zones. Is that understood?" Everyone nodded. "Good, your results will be analysed and presented to you when the high councillor results are delivered. Good luck to you all."

One by one they entered each section, Jack watched as Michael and Robin started their test's.

"I'm nervous." Kim whispered to him.

"What do you have to be nervous about? You'll smash anything they have in there." Kim smiled at him.

"You'll do great too." Kim took his hand giving it a squeeze. He expected her to drop his hand any second, but she held on. She turned to watch their friends as more students started their tests. Her fingers locked with his. Jack felt he could take on any test in that moment.

"Kimberley Illsley, here, Jack London, here." Jack looked at Kim "You'll be great." He mouthed letting go of her hand. Kim puffed out her cheeks nodding. Jack watched her walk into her test before stepping behind his curtain.

It was as Jack predicted, each test was designed to evaluate their current power and skill level. As a knight he had additional elements including sword skills to those Kim would be undertaking, having completed most of the tests Jack felt he had done well except on the diplomacy test, that had been a complete failure. Maybe high councillor wasn't such a good idea, he thought. Now at the final test he was standing in front of the stone pillars, he had no idea what this could be. Kaiba stepped into the area.

"Hello Jack." He said happily. "Nervous?" Jack shrugged he wasn't that bothered.

"Not sure what this one is Lord Kaiba." Jack said honestly.

"This is a simple measure; you place your hands on the pillars. Each are calibrated to detect your magical level. The one on your left your strength in white magic, the one on the right your ability to control dark magic, its completely painless." He assured him. "When you're ready we can begin, just place your hands on the stones thirty seconds later, when I say, release them." Kaiba stood and waited. Jack wrapped his hands around the stones and closed his eyes and began to count, after 30 seconds Kaiba stopped him. "Ok, that's good thank you. Enjoy your classes today, I'll see you soon." He showed

Jack out of the curtain still smiling at him. Robin, Michael and Kim had all completed their tests and were talking excitedly about their possible results. As he approached, he gave Kim a thumbs up, she smiled happily at him. Jack knew she would do great.

Jack's first class was double charms, curses and metamorphosis. The classroom was halfway across the castle it would take him at least ten minutes to get there, he was going to be late.

"Come on guys, there's a short cut through the library." He could easily find his own way around the castle now, he seemed to know every corridor almost intimately.

'All down to Kim.' he thought.

Not paying attention to where he was going trying to allow Robin, Kim and Michael to catch up with him, he ran straight into the library door.

"Ouch, Come on inside." His eyes watering, he slowly pushed open the door, not seeing anyone they started to run through. All they had to do was get to the end of the library.

"Hey, no running in the library, come here you hooligans." A tall vulture faced woman came dashing into sight brandishing a copy of werewolf's friend or foe, as though it were a sword ready to strike at them.

"Come on, quick!" Sprinting as fast as he could Jack reached the end aisle turning left, he ran forward towards a dead end.

"wall!" Michael shouted. Ignoring him Jack carried straight on and through the seemingly solid wall. The others followed quickly Kim appeared through Just in time, pressing his ear close to the wall Jack listened.

The Dark Heart

"Where did they go? I'll find them and when I do." The vulture faced woman bellowed, Jack could imagine her giving the air a jab with the book pretending it was them.

"It's ok, she's gone. It's this way." As they went torches flared alight and faded away once they had passed. Jack could see another wall closing fast on him. He pushed his face through the wall slowly, he heard Kim muffle a squeal it must have looked odd to see him without a head. "We're in luck, its empty." Sneaking out the four of them took seats at the far back of the class.

"Jack, how did you know about those tunnels?" Kim asked looking bewildered. "Well, they were on the map." Jack explained seeing it clearly in his mind's eye. Kim shook her head vehemently though.

"no Jack, they weren't, I know that map just as well as you and those tunnels aren't on it. Look I'll show you." Just as Kim reached into her bag to retrieve the map the teacher and their classmates walked into the room, no-one spotted them sitting in the corner. "Later." Kim pushed the map back into her bag slowly so no-one would notice.

"ok, class let's talk about what you will be learning in this particular course and let me begin by saying that of all your classes this will be one of the most difficult you will attend whilst you are here. Even if you are a skilled wizard thus far, you may find that some of what we teach here is a little beyond your reach. Even so if you find you are capable of these highest levels, I must warn you to use your powers with good grace and good judgement." Jack had been expecting this; his mother and sister had repeatedly warned him about misusing curses. "My name by the way, is Mr Gerrard. Can anyone please tell me why it is that we need to be extra cautious with these spells?" Half of the class raised their hands including Michael and Kim. Gerrard went around the class asking each one by one. Michael answered.

"Certain spells are restricted to the use of council members only. Anyone who then uses these spells are then subsequently put before the council." Gerrard nodded his approval. Jack thought that he was just trying to draw attention to the fact he was on the council.

"yes, very good Mr Smith these spells are so complicated that it would be too dangerous for anyone to even try to cast them. Only those on the council are deemed strong enough to possess such magic." Jack noticed he sounded bitter. "Ok who was next, Miss Illsley I believe." Kim took a different route.

"If you're not trained well enough, the spell can backfire upon you injuring not only yourself but others around you too." Again, he nodded.

"well, that's certainly a majority of you that know the implications of a spell gone wrong, but I would have thought that one among you would have had at least one answer." He was staring directly at Jack. "Is there anything worse than what the rest of the class has said?" Jack looked blankly at Gerard, why was he pressurising Jack into an answer,

"death?" he guessed.

"Yes Jack, you are correct, death is a result of magical abuse. No-one should misunderstand what can happen if you try to perform a spell and you are not trained. You can die, and as Miss Illsley said so can others around you. Don't you agree Mr Smith?" Michael did not know what to say, so nodded his head. Gerrard turned his back on them and walked to the front of the class. Michael leaned over to Jack so that Gerrard would not hear and whispered into his ear.

"Why do all the teachers refer to you in your first name and the rest of us by our surnames?"

The class continued, they began to learn about the Revten charm, the idea of the charm was to revert an item which had been metamorphosed back to its original state. Jack thought they might have started on something a little easier, but as Gerrad had pointed out they were supposed to be the best in the school. To Jack's utter disappointment his cup now resembled a squashed looking tennis ball. Michael and Kim had succeeded in reverting their objects back to a saucer.

"Come on, next lesson will be starting soon, what is it again?" Michael puffed, putting their saucers back on the shelves.

"P E" Kim said shyly. Jack had hoped that Kim's recent transformation had resolved her self-confidence issues, but it clearly had not.

"So, do you change with us or do you get your own room?" Kim looked him over.

"Why, do you want to see me get undressed?" Kim gave Jack a wink laughing.

"No that's ok, I'll wait till later when we're alone." Jack replied grinning wildly. Kim ran on ahead smiling at their joke, all Jack could do was beam at Michael.

A small group of people had gathered outside the hall.

"What's everyone waiting for? Why don't we just go inside?" Michael asked.

"Try it." Said Robin, he had disappeared ahead of them. Robin was doing his best to look cool leaning against a stone pillar. Sure enough, the Elven girl was nearby.

"Do you even know her name yet mate?" Jack laughed at his friends seeming obliviousness to the rest of the world.

"Why do I need to know her name when I can see her for the goddess she is?" Clapping Robin on the back he wished him luck.

"Honestly, you would think that he's never seen a girl before. Her names Rachel by the way." Michael told Jack. "Come on, he told us to try the door." Jack walked over and opened the door, "ok, this must be the wrong room." The room he was staring into was no bigger than that of a standard size broom cupboard. Walking back out Jack rechecked the door it was marked sports hall.

"Can I help you?" Jack jumped out of his skin. Turning around Jack's nose was pressing into an exceptionally large man's chest.

"Sorry sir." He said backing away.

"Everyone inside now." He barked. Jack knew this wasn't going to be fun.

"But sir the room won't fit all of us." Kim was trying to be as polite as possible.

"Do you think you know anything about magic yet silly girl?" Jack's blood started to boil. How dare he talk to her like that.

"Sir, I don't think it's necessary to…" Kim's eyes had tears in them, but she grabbed hold of Jack's arm to stop him saying anything any further.

"Does it look like I care what you think? Now shut your mouth or I will give you a week's detention." A smirk had graced itself across the teachers face. He seemed satisfied with Jack's forced silence, turning his back on the class he pulled a key from his pocket; he placed the key into the door, turning it a bright light seemed to filter around the edge. "Inside now." He ordered not taking his beady eyes off Jack. Jack did not take his eyes off the teacher either; he wanted him to know that he was not someone whom he could intimidate so easily, he was Arthurian. Jack's hand fell by his side he had not realised that he had been holding Kim's shoulder; by the way she walked into the classroom, Jack could tell she was still crying all be it silently. Jack stood his ground he could not shake the anger rising in his stomach filling his lungs and threatening to break free from his mouth.

'curse him, hit him, anything.' His voice screamed in his head. Jack was brought out of his fury at the teacher by a smash to his shoulder. Melfice walked past after ramming his arm into Jack's.

"Hello Mr Bravo, lovely day."

"Good afternoon Mr Trelane, yes, it is. I believe today will be a very good day indeed." Both Bravo and Melfice stared at Jack. "Inside you moron, or do I have to drag you in?" Biting his lip so hard he felt his teeth sink into his skin, Jack entered the room. It was now at least twice the size of the dining hall. "Girls to the left and boys to the right." Jack tried to catch Kim's eye wanting to reassure her, but she was already heading into the girls changing room, a sodden tissue in her hands, Jack noticed Louise had walked over to Kim placing her arm around her.

Jack emerged from the changing room's, still shaking

with rage. Michael had repaired his cut lip after several shaky attempts. They appeared not to be the only ones annoyed by Bravo's verbal attack on Kim. A young Scottish boy and his brother had approached them,

"We're in the Lancelot's and I know were meant to be on opposing houses but what that guy said, well just let us know if you want to get even." The two boys ran off.

"Think we just found the trouble maker's." Michael nodded he too was still seething at the teacher's response to Kim.

"They might just come in handy though." Michael agreed. Throughout the lesson Bravo had made it his mission to push Jack and Michael to their limits. Lap after lap of the hall until they almost dropped from exhaustion being physically sick, he then made them lift weights far too heavy for them. Finally, barely able to stand Bravo called an end to the lesson. Melfice hadn't moved the entire time, he had spent the time laughing with Bravo and coming up with additional punishing exercise for Michael and Jack.

Kim had spent the lesson on the other court with the girls all playing hockey. Jack could tell that she had spent most of her time crying as her eyes were still puffy and swollen after class. They had a thirty minute break before their next lesson. Jack wanted to make the most of it. He didn't understand why Bravo had been so rude and arrogant, all he knew was this was a man he wasn't going to be friends with.

"Kim are you ok? you know that he's an idiot right." Kim smiled weakly, it broke Jack's heart to see her so upset. Jack tried everything he could think of to cheer her up, succeeding only in getting a small smile that looked more like a grimace.

"Don't worry, we're going to get him back. What do you think of setting his underpants on fire? Like Lancelot did to the Elven King." Michael plotted, Kim managed only a gurgled chuckle.

"You can't do anything like that, the two of you would be in so much trouble. And if you got into trouble because of me I would feel worse than I do even now." Jack and Michael looked at each other promising Kim they would not touch Bravo. Jack knew Michael was thinking the same as him. How long would they be able to keep that promise?

"But thank you both."

The end of the day was a welcome relief. Jack continued to comfort Kim; he had held her hand as they travelled around the school. Michael too, was being more caring than usual. The three of them sat in a tired silence, Jack was stonily still, his stomach filling with a vile pit of hate, all of it directed towards Bravo.

"So, are you going to tell us who you voted for then?" Michael asked again trying to distract them. Jack realised they had been talking about the vote, he had been too distracted to notice, his mind playing out multiple versions of his desired revenge.

"it's meant to be private." Jack sighed.

"well yeah, but you can tell us were not going to go shouting it about, are we?" Kim looked annoyed with Michael's constant badgering.

"Michael, he's right we shouldn't really say." Kim was as exasperated as Jack.

"Look if neither of you voted for me, I'll be ok with it I can tell you I voted for…." Jack stuck his fingers in his ears not wanting to hear what Michael had to say. Kim seemed to have done the same because when Jack pulled his fingers out, he heard Michael saying.

"Fine, we won't discuss it then, we should find out soon anyway." Michael sulked looking around the hall for any sign of when the results would be announced. He did not have to wait long. Merlin soon appeared from his usual doorway holding several cards in his long-fingered hands. He slowly walked down the innumerable aisles showing his usual nonchalance for any of the students. Jack had to wonder if he had ever really wanted to be headmaster, he never seemed to be around. He stopped directly in front of Jack.

"As you know the votes have been cast for the new high councillor." he said coldly, his eyes looking over their heads. "Well, I thought that you would like to know. My personal feelings are that due to the additional strain it would put on your time Mr London I have withdrawn your nomination and distributed any votes you received; therefore, you are unable to become high councillor." Merlin finished before turning on his heels and walking away. Michael and Kim looked at him in disbelief, but it was nothing to the way he felt.

"What does he mean the strain it would put on me?" Jack asked but his friends had no answers either. He felt a small flame of hope had been cruelly extinguished.

"Wonder what I did to piss him off." Jack muttered deflated.

Merlin returned to his podium waving his wand, scrolls appeared before every student.

"Results from the tests." Jack rammed his results into his bag. He was furious with Merlin.

"As everyone knows, this afternoon we announce the winner of the high councillor, the person whose responsibility it will be to become the head of the school council and liaison with myself and even the full council, if ever a need occurred." Merlin announced his voice still as dead as ever. "For some of you this is a dream you have been looking forward to for some time now, and for other's it is one that you will never realise." His eyes lingered over Jack for a second longer than any other. Jack's anger at his headmaster grew by the second. "Well, I shall leave you all in suspense no longer and announce the winner." He attempted to smile, but it was forced, it looked like he had never smiled in his life. Merlin unfurled a long parchment, it spilled onto the floor. Jack could see his name crossed out at the bottom.

"The person voted new high councillor is." It was as though a drum beat in their heads, everyone's nerves on end. Jack and Kim seemed unbothered by the fuss, Michael's hands were shaking with excitement, he looked like a snake waiting for the moment to strike. "Kimberly Illsley!" Merlin's voice rang. Michael had already half risen before he realised what had been said, quickly he passed it off by clapping furiously. Kim almost choked on her drink, spitting it out in amazement. The hall was silent apart from Michael and Jack's applause. No one could believe what they had just heard, there had never been a female high councillor before. Slowly at first and then loudly the hall burst into applause. She blushed furiously; her cheeks turned to a maroon colour.

"Well done Kim." Michael shouted kissing her on the cheek, Jack kissed her too and she blushed harder.

"yes, well done Miss Illsley now we have one more

announcement." The hall fell silent again, Jack, Michael and Robin beamed at Kim who was now trying to hide her face in her hands.

"All new council students undertook their initial magical testing this morning, for the first time in a generation we are able to fill the position of Dark Priestess." The hall erupted in mutterings. A dark priest or priestess was rare, able to command some of the most dangerous Dark Magic. Merlin waited for the muttering to die down, unfazed by the interruption.

"This person will also be joining the student council as an advisor to myself and the full council." Michael looked over to them

"who?" he mouthed; the others seemed to have no idea either.

"Louise Harrison." In the far corner seated almost alone Louise shrank, clearly wishing to not be in the spotlight. Jack could see Melfice on the other side of the room give a sneer at the mention of her name. A pang of guilt shot through him.

"Well done Miss Harrison and Miss Illsley, I shall see you both tomorrow!" Merlin left the podium and sat in his seat starting to enjoy his dinner. Jack thought he was more animated now shovelling food into his face than when he had addressed the students.

People from across the school had run over and started to congratulate Kim, each of them shook her hand and gave her advice on how she could make changes. Kim was overwhelmed turning bright pink. Jack couldn't be happier for her. He even saw Grey give her a little clap when he caught her eye.

"I'll be back in a minute." Michael said, he too seemed

to have noticed Louise alone. Unlike Kim, no one had gone to talk to her.

"Give my congratulations." Jack said sincerely. Michael nodded, he seemed to be resolving himself. Kim was unable to get away from the crowd to notice. Jack watched as Michael approached Louise, she seemed shocked he was talking to her. After a minute or two Michael had sat beside her. If possible, she had tried to shrink further into the corner as though hoping to become invisible.

"Do you think I should go say something?" Kim asked, the group around her had finally cleared enough for her to see where Michael had gone.

"I wouldn't now. Let Michael have this one." Kim understood.

"She's actually very sweet you know." Jack suddenly remembered it had been Louise that had tried to comfort Kim during P.E.

"Yeah, I may have judged her too quickly." He conceded.

"I don't think Melfice is happy with the situation." Kim pointed. Jack turned to see Melfice snapping at his thugs pointing to Michael and Louise, clearly angry.

"Don't worry about him, we can handle him, that's not a threat." Jack was quick to point out the sudden look of impatience on Kim's face. "I mean we can take anything he throws at us. Anyway, let's talk about you. I'm not sure what I should call you now. High Councillor seems so impersonal." Kim chuckled.

"well, best just call me your queen then." Jack broke into the biggest smile.

"Well, you always have been, so I guess it should be official." Kim blushed harder than ever.

The next day Jack was still overjoyed with Kim's news, he had even been able to enjoy some time alone with her during the evening, they had fallen asleep on a sofa watching an orb. Her smile did not fade all day all though she had talked continually about the changes she planned on making. Every time she mentioned some new idea Jack would smile telling her how great it all seemed. The final lesson of the day was Magical history; Jack had been looking forward to this lesson as it was taught by Grey, he had decided to talk to him about the orb.

"Good afternoon everyone, how are we all doing on this fine day?" Grey's frivolity seemed to rub off on the class, the only person not seeming to be enjoying themselves was Melfice. "and a big hello to our new school high Councillor." Grey bowed deeply taking off his tall hat, which had a ridiculous ostrich feather attached, and sweeping it under his chest. Kim blushed again and gave him the tiniest of waves. Jack knew he was honestly happy for Kim; she was after all like a little sister to him.

"And our new Dark Priestess also." Jack hadn't noticed but Louise was sitting next to Michael, she sank down in her seat as again Grey took a deep bow. "So, as you will have guessed by the name of the class this is magical history. Now I know it's not everyone's favourite class but still, we must try to raise our heads to their full height and our eyelids even higher." Grey tapped a blonde boy in the far corner on the shoulder waking him, Jack laughed out loud when the boy nearly fell off his chair.

"Now I'm sure you have all been told about the

The Dark Heart

responsibilities of magic, but here we don't have to worry so much, the only person who will be performing magic is myself." The blonde boy's head dropped again as though the idea of anything where you did not perform magic was useless. "So, can anyone tell me the origin of Camelot?" Jack Michael and Kim put their hands up, Grey smiled at them. "Yes, I thought that you might, so Jack," He picked out. "Please inform the rest of the class."

"Well Camelot was constructed by the first Merlin. It was originally used by a king called Uther Pendragon, the great grandfather of Arthur. The castle was positioned about a mile from Stonehenge which was used as a meeting place for other dignitaries." Grey nodded along to his words.

"All very good, correct, I must say I'm impressed. One of the other main event's in the history of Camelot was of course the splitting of the worlds, I'm sure most of you have heard of this?" The class nodded "well Miss Illsley can you tell us about the splitting please, just anything you remember dear, don't worry." Kim recited what Kaiba had told them on the journey to the castle.

"Excellent, I couldn't have put it better myself, well I could, but I didn't." The class laughed at Grey he, was excellent at putting people at ease. "Now can anyone tell me about the Kings son Mordred?" The class fell silent, even to this day his name brought up feeling's of hate and despise. Jack had never felt like that, for some strange reason he had always felt sorry for the way people had remembered Mordred. Seeing that no-one was going to answer Grey pressed on.

"Mordred had a very troubled beginning in life, what you must remember is that whilst still in the womb the most beloved woman alive, Guinevere, was killed by Arthur's best friend and closest advisor Lancelot. To this day no-one knows why Lancelot did this, all we do know is that Arthur changed, he became harder colder and more vicious towards his enemies. He became very distant from Mordred, blaming him for his mother's death." Several people stared in disbelief at Grey almost as though he was tarnishing their ideas of Arthur.

"Now don't get me wrong, Arthur was still a very noble king but things can change you, life can change you. Mordred was a very nasty piece of work, he made some of the darkest chapters in our history. Do you know it is recorded in his memoirs that Merlin wished Lancelot had killed the child?" The class gasped.

"But Merlin was a great man." Rachel shouted from the back of the class.

"He thought that the countries needs out weighed that of Arthur's. These are the decisions that leaders make, they can be awful, weighing up the lives of a few for the many. Therefore, as council members you should never take any of your responsibility's for granted." A girl from the front raised her hand.

"Yes, Miss Stapley."

"Sir, I once heard a fable that Mordred was possessed by something evil, I can't think what it was called." Jack's head began aching. He could hear and see Grey talking to the class but he couldn't take in what was being said. The pain was suddenly overwhelming, he was sick to his stomach, feeling hot and rather like he was going to throw up, he knew he had to get out of the room. Raising his shaking hand.

"Sir, may I leave? I need to use the bathroom." Grey looked over at Jack.

"You do look a bit peaky, go to the infirmary instead, I'm sure they'll give you something to make you feel better." Grey smiled at him.

Jack started to feel better the minute he had left the classroom. Not wanting to disturb the nurse he had sat down around the corner rubbing his head, why had it hurt so suddenly?

'Lack of sleep, late reaction to falling off a horse or a thousand other things' Jack thought. Waiting around for the best part of the hour seemed a waste of time, he decided to take a walk and try to clear the last of his headache.

As darkness fell, Jack decided it was best to return to the school. Rounding a corner he heard Kim's familiar voice, she sounded scared. Forgetting everything else Jack dropped his bag and ran to her. What he saw sickened him, Melfice had her pinned to a wall with three of his friends standing behind him.

"Get the hell away from her." Jack came charging through Melfice's friends. He grabbed Melfice by the throat and pinned him to the wall forcing him to release Kim. Melfice struggled against Jack but he was to strong.

"If you ever touch her again, I'll kill you." Jack roared spittle flying from his mouth. Melfice nodded this seemed to be the first time anyone had ever threatened him, all the blood had drained from his face leaving it pearly white. Jack was slightly taken aback at how badly he wanted to hurt Melfice. it was taking all his self control not to throw him through the nearest window. He settled for throwing Melfice to the floor. Jack grabbed Kim's arm and pulled her along with him. Once out of earshot Kim pulled away from Jack, she looked at him as though she was frightened. she turned and ran away from him.

'Well, you handled that well.' Jack punched the wall in anger. Blood now trickled down his hand.

'I've blown it, how could I be so stupid as to wade in there like some barbaric Troll. '

'You were just protecting her.' Jack wanted to believe this but he wasn't sure he could. Michael came rushing into his room,

'here we go.' He thought.

"Jack what happened why's Kim crying?" Michael shouted angrily.

"Ask her not me, I don't have a clue. All I did was help her, where were you anyway?" Jack hissed

"I have asked her all she did was tell me ask you." Michael's frustration with Jack was clear. "And I was busy ok. Me and Kim aren't glued at the hip you know." He was right, after all they were friends. Kim shouldn't have needed someone with her. It was no-one's fault but Melfice's.

"It was Melfice, I saw him pinning her to the wall, and I threatened him. I think it scared her." He said not looking at Michael, his stomach turning slightly at the memory of Kim's stare.

"Where is he? tell me." Michael was just as angry as Jack was.

"Probably in his common room by now."

"Next time I see him I'll make him wish he was never born." Michael snarled his hand clenched around his wand, Red sparks flittered out from the end.

"Don't worry, it's sorted now, just go and see how

Kim is we don't need her hating you as well." Michael grabbed Jack's arm as way of thanks and set off for Kim. Jack thought quickly then called after him.

"Tell her, tell her I'm sorry." Jack could see that Michael understood. He had to wonder how he always managed to make things worse.

Chapter 7

A Message From a Dead Man

"It has to be here somewhere?" Jack threw the contents of his drawers on the floor for the third time. He was searching for the orb his father had given him.

"Well, it's not under here, unless it's transformed into this?" Michael gagged as he appeared from beneath Jack's bed, holding at arm's length a pair of extremely ripe smelling socks. "You've been looking for weeks, I think it's time you face it, it's lost." He told Jack, throwing the socks into the hamper before running to wash his hands.

"It was on my dresser." Jack kicked his drawers in frustration, yelping in pain he limped to the bed and slumped defeated.

"You don't think that someone could have stolen it do you?" Kim asked, it had taken a little time, but she had forgiven him for the incident with Melfice.

"I don't think so, it would have to be an Arthurian, only they can get into the common room." Jack didn't know what to do, he was only concerned about getting the orb back. He rubbed his pained foot trying to recall when he had last seen the orb. No matter how hard he tried, he couldn't remember.

It was during a history lesson Grey had mentioned he was an avid collector of historical orb's; this had

The Dark Heart

reminded him about the one he had taken from Grey.

"Have you tried to watch this one yet?" Kim handed him the orb with his father's name scratched into it, he had hidden this one in the frame of his bed. Tucked snugly inside the mouth of one of the carved dragon heads.

"No, I had forgotten about it with everything that's been happening." He rolled the orb between his hands.

"Well, don't you think it's time?" She asked delicately. Jack considered this. If someone had taken the other orb, they may have been looking for the one in his hand. If he waited any longer, he risked losing this also.

"I suppose now's no worse than any other time. But would you mind if I watched it alone?" His friends nodded their understanding.

"Yeah, of course mate, but remember if you need anything we're just outside." He watched as they left the room. An apprehension seemed to roll like a fog into the room. Jack was unsure of what he would find, if anything on the orb, if someone had been looking for it though he knew it could be important.

"Ok dad, what do you have to say?" Jack pressed the orb to his forehead, closing his eyes, 'Play'.

His mind felt as though it was being stretched. A cacophony of sound and light washed through his thoughts. A few seconds later and the world began to form around him. He found himself standing in the middle of a cave, the walls dripped from some unknown water source above them. The only light seemed to be from a wand carelessly discarded on the rocky floor. A wet cough caused him to turn, it was his worst fear, Benjamin London lay against a rock.

His auburn grey beard stained red from the blood he

was coughing. His hand clutched over a deep stab wound in his side. This was the day his father had died. Ben was stretching for his sword with the heel of his boot, every movement caused him to cough harder. He collapsed back and looked at the orb. Jack's eyes were filled with tears.

"Whoever is watching this. I need you to tell my family something." Ben wheezed desperately struggling to force air into his lungs. Jack knelt by his father's side his body shaking. He reached out to his father trying to comfort him. Jack's fingers slipped through his father. He was after all, no more than a ghost now.

"They are in danger; the council have lied to us all. I've been searching for answers to my family legacy. I was lured here and ambushed. I don't know who it is that attacked me, I think its connected to what I discovered. My boy, Jack." Ben pointed into the darkness as the sound of steel scraping stone echoed around them. A blinding light illuminated the cave. Jack turned but he too had to shield his eyes from the intense light. He saw his father's sword raised, pointing at Ben.

"No!" He cried horrified jumping between the two. The sword slashed down pinning Ben to the rock, impaled through his stomach. His blood sprayed across the stone floor. Jack fell at his father's feet watching through tears the last few moments of his father's life.

The orb dropped to the floor and rolled beneath the dresser. Jack wept as hard as he had on the day he was told his father died. Michael and Kim rushed back into the room. They had clearly heard his distressed cries.

"Jack, are you ok?" Kim's hand covered her mouth anguished as she approached, the heartache on Jack's face, evident to them both. She reached out and held him, his body shook as though an icy wind had claimed him.

"What did you see?" Jack raised his head to Michael.

"I saw dad." His voice broke. "He didn't know who was going to see. He said my family were in danger." Jack buried his head into Kim's shoulder, his tear's felt never ending.

"What danger?" Michael seemed to be asking questions just to avoid the uncomfortable silence.

"I don't know, he didn't get a chance to say before he was...." he couldn't bring himself to say the words.

"Jack, what else did you see? surely your father would have warned the council unless," Kim stopped the realisation of what he had seen struck her, she held Jack tighter still her own tear's now falling onto him.

"It was his death wasn't it?" Michael stuttered, he too catching on.

"He didn't die, he was murdered!" Jack roared his anger exploding like a firework inside. "The council were lying about something; he was killed finding out the truth." Jack wanted to shout he felt sick to his stomach, but he was empty. "I'm so sorry." Jack sobbed harder, Michael seemed immobilised by shock. Kim stroked his head.

"Ssh, come on let it all out." She told him through her own soft cries.

"I'm so sorry, Dad." Jack wept as Kim softly rocked him, he thought the tears would never stop.

Michael left to get Jack something to eat, Jack sat in silence all he could do was to replay the scene over in his mind. He needed to know who it was, who killed his father?

"Jack, I don't want you to take this the wrong way, but do you think you should go to the council, ask them to explain what you saw on the orb?" Kim cowered slightly under his glare.

"You must be joking, they collected his body from that cave, they know he was murdered, and they never told us!" Kim tried to interject but Jack stopped her. "They knew what happened to my father. He knew they were lying to us about something. For all I know it was the council that had him murdered, run through with his own sword." A fresh wave of nausea struck him as he looked to the stone mannequin in the corner. His father's sword lay across the open palms. The item that had killed Ben, the thing he had treasured more dearly than almost anything else, lay feet away from him now. He shook the feeling away, there would be time for that later.

"You're right though, there is someone who has to see this." Jack pulled the orb from under his dresser. He walked over to Kim and kissed her on the cheek. "Thank you." They held each other for a moment.

"I'm always here for you. You only ever need ask." She whispered in his ear. He longed for her to go with him now, to have her strength to draw on. This was something he needed to do alone though.

"Hello Sir, I think we need to talk." Jack announced pushing his way into the classroom. Grey turned startled.

"Jack, to what do I owe this unexpected pleasure?" he asked warmly. Jack pulled the orb from his pocket. Grey's eyes slipped over it before returning to Jack's face.

"We need to talk about this." Jack held the orb out for him to see clearly. Grey didn't understand what Jack was talking about. It was clear from Jack's tone though he wasn't here for a friendly chat. "The first time I came into this room, I knocked over your coat rack. This came out of the pocket of a coat. I took it by accident. I meant to return it to you, but I noticed the name on it. I want to know why you had it?" Grey looked genuinely confused.

"If I'm being honest, I didn't notice it was gone. As you know I collect historical orbs. We have used them in class to explore moments of historical significance." Grey walked to a cabinet in the corner, he pulled open the double doors showing Jack hundreds of orbs crammed inside. Each orb had been neatly labelled with the memory that was contained.

"I don't understand why you're upset?" Jack stood stone faced, it was taking all his self-control not to shout at Grey. He had to be sure Grey was involved before he did anything, he did have a good reason for collecting the orb after all. It's possible he had been sent it without knowing what it contained.

"You don't? Well maybe you should watch it." Jack threw the orb to Grey. He wasn't sure if Grey did so out of patience or curiosity but held the orb to his forehead and began to watch.

Grey opened his eyes minutes later.

"My god." He had turned pure white, gripping his chair in horror at what he had seen. Jack allowed him a moment to compose himself.

"Sir, why did you have this?" he asked again, attempting to hide the anger in his voice. "Why do you have the orb to my father's murder?" The little colour in his face faded.

"You're his son?" Grey looked as though he was about to be sick. "I didn't know." Jack's temper was nearly at boiling point, his fists were shaking violently.

"You were sent the orb, who sent it to you?" Grey collapsed into his seat.

"That doesn't matter." He answered absently, looking around the room as though the answers he himself sought would spring from the darkness.

"Everything matters!" Jack growled infuriated.

"I'm sorry, I didn't mean it like that." Grey stammered.

"THEN HOW THE BLOODY HELL DO YOU MEAN IT?" Jack exploded his anger finally overflowing, he grabbed the nearest table turning it over. "ANSWER ME!" Grey tried to mutter something, but he could not get the words out. "How do you have an orb that was buried in the cave where my father died? How is it the council didn't take this when they collected my father's body? Why is it only now it has appeared?" Jack grabbed the orb and rammed it into Grey's chest.

"I don't know, how could I? None of this makes sense." Grey implored him to believe what he was saying. Whether from stress or his anger Jack began to feel strange, his head started to throb, his vision blurred.

"Jack, are you ok?" Grey reached out to him, the moment he touched Jack's arm it caused him to scream in pain. Grey leapt back dropping the orb in fright. Jack collapsed to the floor, the muscles in his body cramping. He felt like he was going to die. Grey didn't dare touch him again. Blood spurt from his nose, his vision turning red as the vessels in his eyes popped. He could feel his throat swelling, gasping for air as he clutched at his neck. With one last effort he reached for the orb as it lay feet away from him, he felt his face press to the cold stone floor. The last of his air gone, he fell unconscious.

Jack opened his eyes, he was staring at a ceiling he didn't recognise, judging by the bottles of potions next to his bed, he guessed he was in the infirmary. He tried to raise his head but felt too weak. Horrible orange and blue striped curtains were pulled around him. He reached out and pulled the curtain back. Rows of empty beds ran around the circular room, he realised he must have been in one of the towers.

"what am I doing here?" he asked the thin air.

"Ah, you're awake at last." A short middle aged lady with long platinum hair appeared at his side, she tied her hair into a bun, and squirted a small bottle of perfume. Jack noticed even from this distance she smelled strongly of disinfectant. He guessed the perfume was an attempt to make her feel less sterile.

"What am I doing here?" he repeated holding his hand to his head, it felt slightly numb, a dull pain at the back of his brain.

"You collapsed, don't you remember dear?" Jack tried as hard as he could but he couldn't recall anything like that. "What is the last thing that you can remember?" she asked, shining a light into his eyes.

"Eating dinner, I think." Everything was fuzzy. "How long have I been here Miss?" Jack asked unsure.

"A full day. To be quite honest we didn't know what was wrong with you. It was lucky that Professor Grey found you when he did." The nurse continued to fuss around him. Checking his pulse and temperature.

"But you know now, don't you?" The nurse stopped in her fussing to scratch something down on the chart at the end of his bed. He felt as though she was holding something back. "I wont be scared you know." She smiled at him.

"Yes I know, you've already proven yourself exceptionally brave." Again she seemed to freeze, seemingly weighing up if what she was about to say was for the best, or if it would cause more harm. "We think there was a curse placed on an orb. Professor Grey found you clutching one, convulsing." Jack thought that explained why he felt so exhausted.

"Why would anyone do that?" He wondered aloud.

"I'm not sure, all I do know is the high councillor is investigating personally. She seems to take your health very seriously. We should all be so lucky." The nurse tapped him gently on the knee. "Whilst we searched for a cure to whatever curse affected you, your own body must have fought it off. It's not uncommon but leaves you very weak." She handed him a slimy brown potion, "Essence of mudcrab, it tastes foul but will help you to regain your strength." She explained, Jack took the potion holding his nose he drank it all in one go. It took all his effort not to spit it out.

"Where's the orb now?" he asked between retching on the aftertaste of the potion. He didn't want anyone else to be cursed.

"The high councillor and Merlin agreed it should be handed over to the council, as far as I'm aware they have it now." Jack nodded his understanding; it was typically sensible of Kim to do that.

"Has anyone visited me?" Jack felt a little stupid for asking this.

The Dark Heart

"Yes, your mother, brother, sister and a classmate named Michael. The high councillor has barely left your bedside. I had to kick them out about twenty minutes ago, they need rest too." Jack felt if possible even worse at hearing his loved ones had seen him in the state he was, he never wanted to worry them.

"Is there anyone you can think of that would want to curse you?" asked the nurse.

"No, I'm pretty much loved by all." Jack lied.

"I'm sure you are. Well, I need to inform people of your condition. Excuse me." Walking into her office the nurse left Jack to his own thoughts. There was only a single person he could think of who would curse him. Had Melfice somehow convinced him to watch the orb, if only he could remember.

Chapter 8

The Forgotten

Two days later Jack was finally released from the infirmary. Since he had awoken no-one had been allowed to see him. The nurse insisted on the solitude, not wanting him to become over excited. She had been very firm with him almost to the point of becoming a tyrant.

Now free from confinement he wanted to find Grey, he needed to hear for himself what had really happened. When he reached Grey's classroom, he felt an odd familiarity that had nothing to do with lessons.

Jack knocked on the door, he waited a couple of minutes before knocking again. Still, he received no reply, he wondered if Grey was hiding from him. Surely not, he was being paranoid, Grey had no reason to avoid him. After all it had been him who had saved his life. Quietly, he pushed through the door. It was empty, the entire room was cleared of any item that might have proved someone had once taught there. Jack guessed that he had moved to another class, or maybe he just had the wrong one.

Everything did seem slightly different, as though seeing the world through someone else's eyes. Jack decided to enjoy his freedom instead and take a walk around the lake. He found it strange that since he had been released from the infirmary, he had not seen another person. Even when he entered the main hall it was empty.

'Where is everyone?' Jack thought. maybe he had missed a mass evacuation, or the world had ended, and no-one had told him.

Outside the castle Jack could hear the hustle and bustle of the city below, but again the courtyard was empty, it was probably for the best though, he didn't really want to be facing questions he couldn't answer.

Jack tracked along the lakeside the water was perfectly still. The only sound that of birds chirping from the nearby forest, or the occasional blip as a fish plucked an insect from the surface of the lake. As peaceful as this place was Jack felt strange, it was as though he was forgetting something important.

A reflection caught his eye. In the edge of the forest something glinted hidden between the overgrown branches.

"What's this then?" A small silver hoop seemed to have been embedded in one of the trees. He felt at the cold steel ring, it lifted like a handle. It was then he noticed a tiny crack in the bark. He realised it was a doorway.

Jack pulled on the ring with all his strength, the trunk began to move. Straining as hard as he could, the door burst open revealing a hollow entranceway. A set of step's led down into the ground. All he could see was darkness.

"Latvanta." A light shone brightly from his wand, he pointed it directly down the stairs. They seemed to go down for some time.

Excited by this hidden secret Jack descended into the gloom, his wand tip illuminating a few feet in front of him. Reaching the bottom of the stairs he seemed to be in a tunnel, Jack guessed he was probably twenty feet from the surface now. It was only now he was down here he realised how incredibly stupid he was being.

"You know what, I've seen those orbs with the kid down in the tunnels. I'm out of here." He was talking to himself as he had become acutely aware of the silence. Turning around he bumped into a wall. "What the hell?" He moaned rubbing his sore nose. The staircase he had just descended was gone. It had been replaced by a solid stone wall. "Well this doesn't look good." It seemed the only way forward was to continue on through the tunnel.

He edged his way along the wall, his footsteps echoing all around him. The old brick tunnel seemed to have crumbled over time. Here and there he could see piles of rubble and dirt where the ceiling had given way.

The further Jack walked into the tunnel the darker it got, it felt more and more oppressive with each step. The light from his wand was now virtually useless, he could barely make out the silhouette of the tunnel walls. The only reason he kept it lit was for some false sense of comfort.

"COME." A voice resonated through the tunnel. it sounded as though it came from everywhere echoing at him from every wall. Jack jumped backing up to the wall, his heart pounding like a drum. He didn't know who had spoken but he was sure he didn't want to find out.

'Screw this, I'm out of here!' He decided to turn back and retrace his steps. He hoped he would find a way to make the stairs reappear. When he turned Jack was again shocked to see the stone wall behind him.

"Come to me." The voice boomed around the tunnel. Something knew he was there, it seemed to be controlling the walls themselves. Had it made the stairs disappear, keeping him from returning to the surface?

"Shit." Thinking carefully, he decided to extinguish his light, 'maybe if I can't see it, it can't see me.' He hoped.

The further he made it into the tunnel, the less the voice called to him. Jack was glad, he didn't need it to tell him to come constantly, he was already terrified. In the distance a small light flickered catching his eye. It was far brighter than the one he had been able to produce.

Eventually Jack stumbled into what he presumed was an antechamber. He had been glad of the light when he saw it from afar, now he realised it was actually a fire, it allowed for him to see all the gruesome aspects of the room.

The chamber seemed more of a natural cavern then that of the brick tunnel, bones lay scattered across the floor, picked clean of flesh or rotten away Jack couldn't tell. Broken skulls bordered the fire, a large spit lay across the open flames. Jack didn't want to think about what had been cooked on the spit.

The cave smelled damp and musty, the air stale. There appeared to be no obvious signs of life and yet he knew he wasn't alone here. Between the voice and the fire something was living here. Edging back, he felt the empty archway now sealed, apparently this was where he was wanted.

"I'm guessing that I really don't want to be here?" His voice shook.

"Come to me." Again, the voice boomed. This time so loud Jack had to cover his ears. Panicking, he grabbed his wand, shouting obscenities and began firing spells indiscriminately. Hoping in the least to draw out whatever was speaking. His heart was hammering in his chest. With the most powerful spells at his disposal all he managed to do was break a few chunks of rock off a monolith.

He hadn't spotted it before, the only part of the room hidden in shadow. It was as large as the other monoliths at Stonehenge. He could see a red light twinkling from within the stone, stepping closer to get a better look he was barely feet away when he heard the voice again. "Come to me." Rather than echo at him, he felt as though it was whispered in his ear from behind. He turned sharply backing up to the stone, feeling safer with his back to a solid wall. There was nothing in the room. Jack half hoped this might all be some game Melfice had somehow created.

"I've got to get out of here!" He muttered.

"You're going no-where." An arm smashed through a crack Jack had made in the stone. It grabbed him around the chest, pinning him in place. What he thought was a light had in fact been red, glowing eyes. "You are mine now!" The voice echoing in his head. Jack could feel his blood turning cold, struggling with all his strength he could barely move. "Don't fight it, there's nothing you can do." Shouting as loudly as he could crying for help.

"Get off of me." Jack tried to bite the arm.

"Prepare yourself, this might sting, a lot." Another arm came through the stone grabbing Jack's head, pulling it backwards. A sharp pain pierced the back of his skull, it felt as though a needle was being injected into his brain. He screamed and screamed but the creature held him fast.

"For the love of Merlin help me?" It was no use, Jack could feel himself fading fast.

"Jack wake up, please wake up!" A voice sounded but he couldn't see who was talking.

"Help, get it off of me." The pain intensified as though trying to finish him off.

"Jack wake up, you need to wake up." His eyes opened, Jack was strapped to a bed in the infirmary, his friends and family stood over him, terrified.

Several of the straps lay broken on the side his arm was free. Michael seemed to have been holding it down, but when he awoke he let go slowly. He could see them staring at him, asking questions, but he didn't know what they were saying. The pain in the back of his skull was too intense to listen, quickly he faded back into the darkness.

Chapter 9

Le Fays

Jack had been in the infirmary for hours, not day's as he believed. The nurse had restrained him to stop him hurting himself; nothing that Jack had thought had happened was real.

He now remembered the events leading to his collapse, the memory of seeing his father's death had come flooding back to him. He felt as though he was drowning, being forced to remember every detail.

The thing disturbing him most was what he had dreamed. It had scared him more than he could say, it had seemed so real, Kim and Emma were pressuring him to tell them what had happened, Jack had refused, he knew he couldn't tell anyone, they would think he was insane.

With every horrifying moment replaying in his dreams, he could not shut his eyes at night. Every time he tried that same voice had plagued him. He felt if he could only rest, everything would be better.

Emma had been into see him everyday, Joe had come as often as possible. Jack pretended to be happy, forcing himself to smile when he felt it necessary, he knew he wasn't fooling any of them.

Emma had continued to question him at every

opportunity, she was desperate for him to tell her what had happened. Repeatedly he told her he did not remember; he could not let her know about the orb. He thought it would kill her to see what he had. His father run through with his own sword. Jack had considered showing it to Joe, he was a knight, but he knew Joe would show it to their mum. Joe, like Jack would want answers.

What were the Council lying about? He knew his mother would put herself at risk attempting to find out what her colleagues were covering up. What if she too were then targeted, he had lost one parent he couldn't lose another.

The only person not to visit Jack was the one he needed to talk with, Grey. No-one had seen him since he had brought Jack into the infirmary. Even the nurse had commented how strange it was he hadn't come to check. Grey was avoiding him, he was sure of that. Jack still didn't know if Grey had the answers he sought, maybe he had become worried by what the orb had shown. Another thought had occurred to Jack, maybe the reason he collapsed was because of Grey.

Jack hadn't stopped thinking about his father's orb. He replayed it over and over in his mind. What had his father discovered? What were the council hiding from the world? He knew it could be anything. Jack didn't know if the council would be willing to kill someone to keep a secret. Maybe he was being naive, he shuddered to consider the parents of his closest friends making that decision.

Jack's health was slowly improving, although he still looked like he had been in a fight with a mountain troll. So far no-one had been able to give him a reason why he had suddenly collapsed, Jack had started to suspect the nurse knew what was really wrong, why was she not telling him? Was it out of concern for his health or was there something more malevolent behind it? He had found himself becoming increasingly suspicious of everyone around. Jack knew his father would have told him that he was being paranoid, he also knew that Joe would have said that it was not paranoia if someone was out to get you. Was Grey out to get him? it had also been in his class that Jack had suffered his first migraine. Grey was far too involved in the whole affair for everything to be a coincidence. Jack started to record his thoughts and dreams down into a red leather book, he found he slept better when he had poured the horrific nightmares onto paper.

Another week had passed and Jack was being released, Kim and Michael were waiting outside to escort him back to his room. He was only being allowed to attend classes and minimal exercise. Jack had complained, he wasn't allowed to take part in his Knights training. The nurse had deemed it too vigorous, threatening to keep him in the infirmary if Jack so much as looked at a sword. He found it unfair.

Jack wanted something, anything to distract himself from the overwhelming feeling that someone was out to get him. He complained all the way to the common room, arguing he had started to feel flabby due to the confinement he had undergone. Kim rubbed her hand over his stomach saying it felt smooth enough to her.

Her touch was far better than any potion, he immediately felt a thousand times better, able to take on the world.

Jack's attempts to gleam further information into his father's murder were proving fruitless, Grey was missing, it seemed he had taken the orb with him. All Jack had to go on now was his memory.
He had considered asking Kim or Michael to find out through their parents if they could get any information on where Ben had been killed. But then had thought better of it, if there was a conspiracy within the council to keep his fathers murderer's identity a secret then he couldn't involve them. For all he knew it could endanger all their lives,
Whoever was behind his fathers murder, had not wanted their existence being known, he couldn't risk telling anyone else.

The nights were getting dark earlier, consequently jousting was almost straight after lessons now. Kim had promised Michael that she would attend training. Since Jack was complaining about being stuck in his room, she decided to take him along.
"Kim I've got loads of schoolwork to do; you know Bravo is desperate to get me in trouble. He thinks I put that snaggle tooth Pixie in his office." Jack knew full well it had been Ben Mclambeth. It had taken Bravo three days to capture it. "If he find's me within a hundred feet of the stables he'll report me to the nurse, I'll be back in the infirmary until I'm seventy-five." In truth he wanted to go, he was desperate for anything to do. His isolation coupled with Grey's disappearance left him feeling

disheartened.

"I've already cleared it with the nurse, as long as you don't physically ride a horse, or swing a sword then you're all clear." Kim's eye's twinkled in the candlelight. He could not help but soak in her presence, her smile was as welcome as the sunshine and felt just as warm.

"But why are you so far behind on your homework? What have you been doing?" Kim's hands slipped onto his arm. Jack blushed a little, he hadn't told her he had been investigating his father's death. He had been pouring over reference books for any hint of a clue, working deep into the night. Anytime he hadn't spent on this his mind had been distracted with thoughts of her. Rather than worry Kim with the truth, he tried a different tactic.

"Oh, I've been lying in bed thinking about you." He tickled her under her chin.

"Stop it." She laughed, before remembering to look stern and pulled her arm away from him. He wished instantly she hadn't, her touch allowed him to live the briefest world of fantasy. Jack could have lived there happily. He had to stop himself from shouting out to her, he longed to tell her how he truly felt.

"Well, if you're that far behind, I think I had best come and help you." She offered a little vexed.

"Ok then, it's a date." He greedily accepted.

"Well, I'm not sure if I would say it quite like that." Kim stuttered slightly awkward. "Could you meet me down there? I just remembered I forgot something." She turned sprinting away.

"Oh, ok no problem." He called after her. As soon as Kim left the corridor Jack banged his head against the wall.

The Dark Heart

'Stupid, stupid, stupid.' He thought,

'One day, she will see you for what you truly are.' He worried that what he truly was, would be something she didn't like.

Jack could now understand why the nurse had been so insistent on him resting. By the time he had walked to the stable, he was exhausted. He was shocked to see how many people were here to watch. The lower stands were crammed, the audience chanting towards the changing room waiting for the riders to emerge. Jack was feeling like an idiot, sat alone in one of the back rows waiting for Kim to arrive. He saw her appear at the bottom row of steps walking towards him, several of the boys stopped chanting and started to whistle at her. She had changed from her school robes and transformed the colour of her hair from blonde to black. Kim's long flowing hair flicked as she climbed the steps towards him, she wore a black sequin dress that accentuated all her features.

"Wow, you must love jousting!" No matter her appearance Jack always found Kim beautiful, when she appeared like this, it was as though another part of her was revealing herself to him. He would love this part of Kim as much as any other.

'Idiot,' the voice inside his head sniggered.

"Well thank you, it's not for the joust though." Jack didn't press her into her real meaning. His stomach was too busy performing cartwheels.

'I don't believe it.'

"What else is it for then?" Jack asked when he was able to think again.

"It doesn't matter." Kim was being evasive but had

turned slightly red. She turned her back to Jack so he couldn't continue the conversation. He sat in silence not knowing what to say,

'Someday I'll understand girl's' he thought,

'good luck' his inner voice replied.

Jack was grateful to be back in the common room. Kim had made her excuses and disappeared as soon as the joust had ended. Jack had walked back with Michael.

"What happened to Kim?" he asked having seen her disappear.

"I don't have a clue. She ran off as soon as the joust ended." Jack fell onto his bed.

"She's been acting strange all day." Michael mused. Jack could see the cogs turning in Michael's head, attempting to make sense of it. He knew Michael hated not understanding the world around him. He had once described the feeling as being like a paper cut, it wasn't painful, more a consistent feeling something wasn't right. Jack realised this was the first time he had seen Michael for more than a few minutes in weeks.

"What have you been up to lately, I never really see you anymore?" Michael shuffled his feet uncomfortably.

"Not much you know schoolwork, training that kind of thing. Barry is pushing us to be ready for the first joust of the season." Jack knew this wasn't the full truth.

"Is that all?" it sounded accusatory.

"What do you mean isn't that enough?" Michael's voice had risen to a shrill.

"Seems like a bit of an overaction mate." Why was he being so evasive.

"Have I done something to upset you?" Jack was concerned there was something he didn't know about.

They had barely spoken since he had watched the orb. Michael looked around the room he seemed unsure on answering.

"How much have you been told? From when you were unconscious in hospital I mean?" he asked, this wasn't what Jack was expecting.

"Nothing really, everyone was more concerned about what had happened. I mean I know I thrashed around a bit." Michael shook his head; it was obvious there was more than he had realised.

"You weren't just thrashing around. You were screaming." Jack was mortified. "What was I screaming?" his heart began to race, unsure if he really wanted to know. "You were asking for help, begging someone not to kill 'him'." They knew 'him' was Jack's father. "At one point you broke the restraints, it was like they were paper. You were shoving me and Joe away whilst we tried to hold you down. It was like you were fighting for your life." The red eyes flashed in his mind. "You were arguing with someone and …" Michael stopped he seemed afraid to answer.

"And what, this is important Michael, tell me?" Michael closed his eyes.

"I heard it answer you back. I laid across your chest using my weight to hold you, whilst the nurse rebound you to the bed. You were screaming in my ear. Then I heard something beneath your voice talking at the same time it told you 'you're mine now'" Jack remembered the words. They had been said just before whatever had pierced the back of his skull in the nightmare. How could it have been talking at the same time? How could it be heard by Michael? it was just a dream!

"Are you scared of me?" It was a horrible realisation

that his best friend might be avoiding him out of fear.

"No, I'm worried for you. That's why I've been trying to find out what happened to you. That's why I've been speaking with …" again he stopped.

"Who have you been speaking to?" Jack was worried now, who knew?

"Louise, she is the Dark priestess after all." Michael justified. Jack was a little relieved, he had been scared Michael had been speaking with Grey. He still didn't know how he felt about Grey, he no longer trusted him but wasn't sure if he had been the cause of his injury.

"What did she say?"

"She doesn't know of anything that could cause your injuries or for me to hear what I did?" Jack could hear the disappointment in Michael's voice. In truth, he felt it himself. "We've been investigating all sorts of dark magic, after all she is still only a student herself so she can't know all dark magics yet can she." It struck him odd that Michael would be so concerned over his feelings towards Louise.

"I don't blame either of you mate. I'm happy that you have been trying to help, I've still not found out anything myself." A new thought occurred to him. "Is that the only reason you've been spending time with Louise then?" For the first time in his life, he saw Michael blush.

"Yeah of course it is. Well, maybe not all of it. She's actually cool once you get to know her." This was the truth of it Jack realised. Michael had begun to fall for Louise, as the Dark Priestess she was outside the group of other students treated with suspicion due to her natural ability to wield the darkest of magics. Added to her previous relationship with Melfice and the

Arthurian's hadn't been the most welcoming. It had only been Michael and Kim that had spent time with her. Even Robin had tried. Jack for all his speeches about inclusivity and equal rights for werewolves and other creatures had distanced himself from Louise for no reason at all. It was a feeling in the back of his mind something he couldn't put his finger on, but she felt dangerous to him. "A few of the guys from Jousting are going to Le Fay's tomorrow, I was thinking about asking her to come with me." It was as though Michael was asking him for permission.

"You should." Jack tried to sound as happy as he could. He was being unreasonable in his feelings towards Louise, he knew that. She had willingly given up her time to help Michael to help him after all. "When you ask, tell her thank you from me." Michael nodded.

"You're going to come yeah; the nurse can't stop you and it would be good to get out of the castle for a while. Robin is coming, I think he is finally going to ask Rachel. Even Kim said she was going to come for a little." Dancing wasn't either Michael or Jack's idea of fun, he knew Michael was only going to try and help Louise to integrate with other members of the house. For Jack it meant the idea of spending time with Kim away from school and being with his friends in a relaxed atmosphere.

"Yeah, why not, if for nothing else we can buy Robin a drink if it all goes wrong." Michael laughed at this,

"Yeah, well fingers crossed it won't come to that. Honestly, I love the guy, but he needs to get this out of his system, one way or another." This was something they both agreed on, maybe it was time for a fresh start for them all.

The following morning Jack walked into the dining hall taking his normal spot at the long rows of tables. Sure enough, in the corner the person he was looking for. Sat together were Robin and Rachel, it was difficult to tell where one ended and the other began, they were so intwined.

'good for him' he thought happy for his friend. What surprised him was for the first time he noticed Michael having breakfast with Louise, cloistered in a small table almost hidden away at the side of the hall. 'Wish he weren't so secretive about their friendship' Jack was still a little sullen about how he had treated Louise. Looking at the intimate little booth they had picked he didn't think it was the best time to go over and try to change their relationship.

"I hear you are coming tonight?" A loud voice boomed behind Jack making him jump. Barry stood there grinning from ear to ear. "Sorry, didn't mean to make you jump. Just wanted to check if you were bringing a plus one. I've booked some carriages for twenty past eight." Barry was beaming, the prospect of the night seemed like a tonic to him.

"No, probably not all my friends are already going, and well, I've not had time to look for a partner." Barry looked at him sympathetically.

"Yeah, I know what you mean, schooling keeps me pretty busy. Tonight, will be my first date in a long time, still best foot forward as they say." Barry waved him a cheery goodbye. Kim was already going out with them all and she was the only one he wanted to be with.

The time to leave for the coaches was fast approaching. Jack was getting ready when he heard a knock on his door.

"Come in." he had just enough time to finish buttoning his trousers when Kim walked in.

"oh, I'm sorry I didn't realise that you were getting changed, I'll come back later." she blushed backing from the room.

"Kim, you've seen me topless hundreds of times, come in." Opening the door slowly she looked slightly coy as Jack continued to dress. "What's up?" Jack asked.

"I just wanted to check if you were still coming tonight? It's been forever since we've been out of the castle." Jack knew how Kim felt. Camelot had been his dream since he could remember, over the last couple of months it had started to become almost oppressive. His time split between classes, the constant reminder of the responsibility on his shoulder, trying to understand what had happened to him and hunting for the murderer of his father. His feelings for Kim bubbling at the surface all the time. He wanted a break, a night out just with his friends, laughing and joking would be a welcome relief.

"Yeah, I'm coming, for once I may even dazzle you with my out of this world dancing." Kim actually fell onto his bed in fits of hysterics. Jack wasn't offended she had danced with him at her cousins wedding a few years before, it had not gone well. He had stepped on her toes so often he had left scuff marks on her shoes.

"I'm sorry." She said, eventually recovering. "Well, I'm glad you're coming, I'll see you tonight in the foyer." Her smile was so warm and heartfelt Jack could have sworn he could feel it.

looking at himself Jack was for once pleased by his appearance. He had chosen a simple clean look wearing a pair of black trousers with white shirt, a jacket that tucked in at his waist but showed his shoulders. Jack had been forced to use magic to alter the suit, he hadn't realised how much he was still growing. He was starting to really fill out his shoulders broader, his chest showing definition, even his arms now barely fit inside his previous shirt straining against his biceps. The knights training and as much as he hated to admit it, the Punishing PE sessions with Bravo were paying off.

"well, I would if you wouldn't." came a voice from behind Jack, it was Michael. "it's ten to eight we had best be going to meet the others."

"yeah." Jack said checking himself once more in the mirror.

Everyone had gathered in the foyer at the bottom of the council chambers. Michael tapped his feet in anticipation, they were waiting for their dates to appear. Jack had to wonder now if he would be the only person to attend alone tonight. Maybe he should have asked someone? A noticeable change in the air occurred when the sound of giggling pierced through the foyer, Jack noticed several boys check their breath, whilst others shined their shoes on the backs of their trousers. The thing that made Jack laugh the most was one of the boys kept changing the colour of his shirt saying.

"it's horrible, it's horrible." the shirt had changed to an illuminous green when the girls reached the top of the stairs and he had been forced to stop. Standing atop the stairs was fourteen of the most beautiful girls Jack had ever seen, Rachel was stood in the middle as though it was her right, like she was the queen bee. She was stunning in a red dress that showed her curves her long dark hair seemed to dance behind her as though controlled by an outside force. Many of the boy's merely gawped at her, but she seemed to fade to grey when Jack saw Kim her now brown hair was tied neatly in a bow above her head her light blue eyes seemed to pierce the crowd, a pale blue dress that slit up the side showing her long, slender legs. She was immensely beautiful, all this hit Jack at once and he felt winded. It was then he noticed her holding hands with another girl. Barely recognisable was Louise, her dark hair curled falling over one shoulder, wearing a black sleek dress that seemed to cling to her curves. Jack heard Michael gasp beside him. He had to admit himself, she looked amazing. As the girls approached, the boys one by one stood forward taking the hand of their respective dates. Robin went first, Rachel seemed to beam almost as much as he, when he took her hand. Jack guessed that the reason she had always been there for Robin to stare at was because she had wanted to be near him to. Too shy to say anything. More partners snuck away to their carriages until finally only Louise and Kim remained. Michael smiled to Kim as he took Louise's arm and disappeared towards his own carriage. It was only then that Jack noticed Barry still standing there

'Didn't he say he had a date tonight?' with horror he realised the truth as Barry reached out his hand to Kim. Nervously she took it, smiling, as they approached their carriage. Silently Jack found the last one, alone and close to tears, he climbed inside.

They arrived outside Le Fay's a few minutes later. Jack had no idea what to do? It suddenly made sense why Kim had dressed up to go to the joust and where she had disappeared off to after. Michael himself had said he had seen them speaking.

'you had your chance, and you blew it.' He was right, Jack could have told Kim how he felt anytime, and he never had the courage to. Now he was going to have to spend the evening watching all his friends exploring new relationships and he is being left behind on his own.

A sparkling sign greeted them a well-suited troll stood outside the entrance he was the bouncer; Jack did not fancy anyone's chances against him even for a troll he was large. For some reason the sight of him in the suit mad him seem even more dangerous. The building was three levels high and backed onto the river a sign on the building read Le Fay's nightclub. Jack had never been to a nightclub before and did not know exactly what he was expected to do. The troll stared at Jack like he was a tasty morsel.

"come on, hurry up. Or you'll miss the first set." He could hear someone shout to him. Jack had no idea what a set was or why missing it would be so bad, but he hurried in anyway.

The inside was spectacular light's burst from hundreds of different candles which appeared and disappeared at random. Music pumped so loudly he could feel it pounding through his chest. The room consisted of a large booth for the person choosing the music, the dance floor was split between a large glass stage which floated above the crowd, and a second larger dance floor gathered below. Drinks floated across the room without spilling a drop placing themselves in the hands of the patrons. Above the stages were private booths for VIP members, Jack knew that some Councillors and Knights had these booked. Joe had often complained of the drunken behaviour of the VIP clientele. Once inside a tall gaunt looking man appeared, he took Jack's Jacket placing it on a hanger which floated itself away through a door. Handing him a ticket he turned away to serve the next customer, without even looking at him.

Finally, inside the club properly Jack could see his friends all on the glass stage. Slowly he started to make his way towards the wizard allowing admittance to the stage.
"Where do you think you're going?" He shouted over the music at Jack.
"I was going to join my friends." Jack answered puzzled.
"Invite only, only the best get up there mate and I'm afraid that isn't you." He pointed Jack towards the lower dance floor. "This is for you." The man grimaced his helplessness.
"Thanks." Jack was hating this, not only had the girl of his dreams been snatch away from him, apparently, he was not good enough for the elite. He didn't want to dance and thought he would be better off disappearing to one of the side booths and ordering a drink.
Jack had been sitting for an hour on his own, He had an impressive array of empty glasses on his table. He was considering leaving, it didn't appear as though he

would be missed. Suddenly a young lady sat down with him.

"Do you mind if I sit with you?" She asked breathlessly.

"Be my guest." The woman was peeking out around the dance floor as though she was looking for someone.

"Sorry some creep won't leave me alone, hopefully if he sees me here with you, he'll back off." Jack didn't object he was trying to place the girl he knew her face but couldn't think why.

"I'm sorry, do I know you?"

"Oh, you may have seen me around." She said evasively. "Oh, for goodness sake it's so loud in here." The woman tapped the table and the volume of the music in the booth dropped to a comfortable level. Outside the booth it seemed to be as loud as ever.

"How did I not know about that an hour ago?" Jack asked the ringing in his ears finally stopped.

"I take it you don't come here often then?" He shook his head.

"I'm not much of a dancer I'm here with friends." He pointed to the glass floor and everyone dancing.

"And you didn't get on I take it?"

"Yeah, something like that." It seemed that the woman had finally settled, leaning back in her seat she looked Jack up and down raising the light in the booth.

"I thought it was you." Jack had no idea what she meant.

"Do I know you?" He asked again starting to feel aggravated.

"Not really, but you're training in Camelot at the moment, aren't you" It was a statement and not a question he knew.

"Yeah, are you also, sorry I recognise your face but not your name." the woman laughed.

"We have never spoken don't worry. I'm Kestra." She held her hand across the table and shook his. "Sorry I didn't mean to suggest earlier you couldn't get up on the stage, but they are being very picky tonight. Do you see that guy there?" She pointed to a man on the stage looking out over the dance floor. "He's the creep I'm hiding from, apparently he's some big shot or something and has paid off the guy down there so he can choose who to admit up top."

"I guess I wasn't his type." Jack joked, Kestra snorted whilst laughing.

"I'm sorry, that was funny." She was holding her face embarrassed.

"Let me buy you a drink, a bottle of the 75 red please" He said to the air, if there was something he knew well, it was wine. Emma had been an enthusiast and his father had allowed him the occasional glass at dinner time when he still had been underage, but Joe had taught him the best wines to order when on a date. Jack had to remember to thank him.

"I'm extremely impressed that's an excellent year, most guy's I know would have ordered some silly girly drink. Oh, you are good." She smirked moving to sit beside him. Now he could see her properly she was extremely pretty with deep red hair and ample chest. "Hey up here." She tapped him playfully.

"Sorry I was trying to see if I can place you."

"And you thought my breasts would help did you?" She laughed.

"what can I say, I never forget a bosom!" He didn't know if it was the alcohol, but he was far more relaxed around Kestra than a lot of other girls and taking risks he wouldn't usually take. Kestra seemed to take it in her stride. For the next hour they sat laughing, looking at the people dancing away without a care. Jack thought that even he could dance better than some of the men there.

"There you are, I've been looking everywhere for you!" Michael burst into the booth. "Sorry am I interrupting something?" Kestra stood up.

"Not, at all, I need to go to the ladies anyway." She looked at Jack. "Don't worry I'll be back in a minute." As she slid across him to exit the booth, she made sure to push her chest into his face. Finally, out of earshot Michael punched Jack in the arm.

"You sly dog! how the hell have you done that? is this where you've been all night?" Jack explained about not being allowed on the floating platform and meeting Kestra. "If I'm being honest, I'm glad, when I saw Kim with Barry, I thought you might have freaked out and gone back to your room."

"Where's Louise?" Jack asked making it clear he wasn't prepared to entertain the subject. Michael seemed to pick up on his change of tact.

"Still dancing, I think it's been a long time since she's been able to let her hair down." He was half smiling, half frowning.

"She'll get there. We'll make sure of it." It was the first time Jack had said anything positive about Louise. Michael noticed. The two friends looked at each other no words were said but each knew the gratification of the other.

"Well, I had best get back or they'll wonder where I've got to. I'll let them know you're ok though." Jack waved him on and sat back in his booth playing with another drink. he watched the glass floor descend and admit Michael. The entrance floating back above to join in the merriment. Kim danced and swayed to the music, excitement burning cross her face. It pained him to watch as Barry caught her up in his arms, and suddenly they were kissing. Standing up, Jack marched from the booth determined to leave; suddenly, he heard his name being called. Looking around he could see Kestra, signalling for him to come over to her in a state of distress.

"What's the matter?" He asked as soon as he got close to her. "This is Jack, he's my boyfriend." She pulled him in front of her and directed him towards the man that had been bothering her earlier in the evening. "I told you I was waiting on him all night, well here he is!" Jack let out an inward sigh.

"You're turning me down for this guy?" The man sneered, "I'm worth a thousand of him. Come on, come home with me!" The man grabbed Kestra's arm and tried to pull her away. Instinctively, Jack hit his arm, making him drop Kestra's. "I don't know who you think you are, but it you touch me again the whole council will be down on your head!" Again, the man grabbed at Kestra and again, Jack knocked his arm away. "Who the fuck are you? You're a dead man!" Jack didn't say a word. He grabbed him by his shirt, pulling his head back and smashed forward as hard as he could, a satisfying crack and Jack knew he had hit his target. Blood sprayed out from the man's nose, broken and bleeding Jack tossed him into the corner.

"Time to leave." Kestra grabbed Jack's arm and pulled him away, heading for the exit. People seemed to be noticing the guy now laying on the floor unconscious,

Slowly the troll from the door came lumbering in, making his way to where everyone had gathered.

"Tickets please?" Said the gaunt man on the counter as they exited.

"You go, ill fetch yours, meet me down by the carriages in ten minutes!" Kestra whispered.

Jack was in trouble and he knew it, should he go to Joe or maybe speak with Emma. If the guy had been as important as everyone seemed to think, it wouldn't be long before they tracked down who had hit him. Whilst Jack was a member of the student council, that didn't make him immune from the law.

"Jack, where are you?" Kestra whispered. Standing out from the shade of the oak trees he came into her view. "Here's your jacket. I'm so sorry, I didn't mean for that to happen." Jack took a breath. He had done the right thing. If there was to be consequences, he could face them. What was important was Kestra was safe from a creepy guy.

"It's ok, honestly, I'm just glad you're alright." He smiled.

"Let's get a carriage, I think it's better if we disappear from here quickly." Kestra pulled him into the nearest carriage within moments they were back underway to the school. "I didn't expect you to hit him!" Kestra suddenly burst out laughing. "Honestly, the look on his face when you grabbed him, I think it was the first time anyone has stood up to the guy." The adrenaline that had been pumping through his veins moments ago had now gone. Tired but happy Jack laughed.

"I've never done that before, god it hurts!" Jack held his head. "I think that's why Knight's wear helmets."

"Here, let me give you some ice we can't have your head swelling or we'll never get into your bedroom." Jack was confused.

"why would we be going to my bedroom?" he asked, without a further word Kestra leaned over and kissed him deeply.

Chapter 10

The Morning After

A Nightingale perched on the balcony, its song drifting through the window of Jacks bedroom. The high-pitched notes pierced his head. Groaning, he pulled his blanket over his head to avoid both the icy breeze blowing in through the open window, and the bright morning sun which was now shining into his eyes with each flutter of the curtain.

Jack felt terrible, he could have sworn his head was two sizes larger than normal. A desperate thirst gripped him. When he opened his eyes the room around him began to spin. He felt sick to the pit of his stomach.

"I'm never drinking again!" He groaned, resisting the desire to attempt to go back to sleep. Sitting up, he could see his clothing scattered across the room. He fumbled on his bedside for a glass of water, drinking from the refilling cup until he thought he would burst.

Slowly he pulled himself to his bathroom, the mirror revealed a grim picture. Bloodshot, dark circled eyes, messy hair and a pale complexion stared back at him.

Rummaging through an overnight bag that Joe had sent him, he found a tiny vial of Watson's Elixir, he had included just for this type of situation. His hands shaking, Jack slowly extracted the top from the vial, carefully he mixed three drops with his water. Jack waited until the white elixir dissolved into the water and became crystal clear. Holding his nose, he drank it all in one, it tasted like gone off milk, making him wretch with each gulp. Once he had finally stopped nearly being sick, he noticed the soreness in his head had disappeared and the weight in his stomach lifted. Checking himself in the mirror again, he watched as the bags from under his eyes disappeared and were returning to their normal colour.

'Thank god I still had this.' he kissed the little bottle and returned it safely to his bag.

Feeling more himself, he walked back to his room, plucking up clothes as he went. He found his white shirt poking out from beneath his bed, blood spotted down the front. The memory of hitting the arrogant man from the night before strayed into his memory.

Jack waved his wand over the shirt and the bloodstains disappeared. He chucked the remaining clothes into a hamper in the bathroom. They would be cleaned and returned to his room the following day.

On his bedside he spotted two glasses and an empty bottle of wine. It was only now that the memory of last night began to surface, he remembered Kestra. She was gone, the bed empty, a letter in her place, he picked it up and read.

Jack,

Thank you for a wonderful evening. I'm sorry I could not be there this morning. I had more fun than I have in the longest time, but I don't want to be involved in anything serious right now. We had an evening to remember but I think we should leave it there, for now at least. I hope you understand.

I'll see you around

Kestra

XX

He smiled to himself recalling the events of their evening. The broken memories of the carriage ride home embraced together, up to when they had finally fallen asleep, both spent. He wouldn't have said it to anyone, but it had been one of the best nights of his life.

The breakfast hall was full by the time he arrived; the other students busied themselves in conversations about their own experiences from the night before. None of his friends appeared to have made it down for breakfast yet, he guessed, like him, they had probably drunk too much and were still asleep.

Jack piled his breakfast onto a plate and grabbed the mornings paper, he barely had a chance to read the first headline before a voice spoke behind him.

"I need to speak with you!" Startled he turned to find his brother standing there, a grim determined look on his face.

"What are you doing here, is everything ok?" Jack couldn't remember the last time he had seen Joe look so serious. He had never come to visit him at the school before and he certainly wouldn't be in his armour if this was a social visit.

"I'm here in an official capacity, grab your breakfast and we can find somewhere alone to talk." He tried to make his voice friendly, both brothers aware of the attention they were now drawing from the students around them.

'He knows about the fight.' It was the only reason that made sense for Joe to have come unannounced like this. Suddenly anxious, Jack picked up his plate and followed behind Joe to a side room where they could be alone.

Once safely away from prying eyes, Joe collapsed into a nearby chair and pointed for Jack to do the same.

"What's going on?" he asked trying to remain calm. Joe looked at him like he was stupid.

"You're not a good liar, so don't try now! You know why I'm here." Joe looked tired, he unclasped his chest plate and pulled it above his head, dropping it to the floor with a thud. He stretched out his arms and twisted his neck trying to loosen his muscles. Jack knew how uncomfortable armour was, it couldn't have been easy wearing it all day.

"So, I need to know what happened. And don't play dumb, just tell me what happened?" Joe placed an orb on the table in front of them, tapping it with his hand it turned bright red. Jack knew their conversation was now being recorded.

Jack explained everything that happened the previous evening. He only hesitated when he reached the point of his journey home in the carriage, he didn't want to tell Joe about being with Kestra all night. "What happened once you left the club? Did he follow you, threaten you?" Joe leant forward in anticipation of the answer, it was clear they were finally at the meat of the reason for his investigation.

"No, nothing happened, I came straight back here. I

never saw him again."

"Can anyone confirm that?" Jack bit his lip he really didn't want to say. "Jack if anyone can confirm this, I need to know! The man you attacked is the son of the high councillor." It felt as though the air had been sucked from the room.

"I left with Kestra, we came back here and spent the night." Joe reviewed his notebook several times, ensuring that he had what he needed. Jack realised his brother had probably pulled some strings so he could interview him privately, instead of being dragged down to the council.

"So, you are saying that once you were out of the club, you never saw him again?" Joe seemed to want this implicitly stated.

"That's right, yeah, I know I hit the guy but isn't this a bit much? He was being a real creep." Joe tapped the orb again it changed from red into a misty grey having finished recording. He chucked the newspaper Jack had started reading at breakfast in front of him.

"Turn to page 6." Jack grabbed up the paper and did as he was told, a headline blazed at him.

Man attacked in Camelot

An unnamed man was attacked last night in Camelot. Knights were called to the scene shortly after 3am. The unidentified man was found in an alley near the world famous Le Fay nightclub. Whilst little is known about the attack at this time an anonymous source did reveal that the man may never recover. The source indicated that the assault had been so severe several of the attending knights had to leave the scene due to shock.

The paper continued, but Jack couldn't continue reading,

"You think I did this?" he asked disgusted, he couldn't understand Joe's thinking. The magical ability required to harm someone to the point they may never recover was beyond him. It would require dark magic he was certainly unable to wield.

"You were the last person to be seen arguing with him. We know you hit him; you have to see why you would be a person of interest to the investigation!" Joe ran his fingers through his hair and let out a deep sigh. "The only reason I'm here instead of a squad of knights is because I called in favours." It made sense for them to talk with him he knew, he just hoped that Joe believed him.

As though he could read Jack's mind, Joe pulled a book from his satchel.

"I can't go back to the others with just your word, I'll find Kestra and get her to corroborate your story, in the meantime, I need some proof." Jack had no idea how the book would help. "This, as I'm sure you know is a reference book from the library. I picked it up on my way here. What you may not know, is everything you do in school is recorded, as a school councillor you have access to this." He placed the reference book in front of Jack. "I want you to ask it your comings and goings last night and who was with you." Picking up the book Jack felt nervous what if the book was wrong? what if it somehow showed him leaving the castle? No, he was being stupid, worrying over nothing.

"Show Jack London, location from last night and any person with him." The book gave a little shudder, the blank pages began to fill with writing. He handed it over to Joe.

"Ok, that's fine it shows you arriving back like you say. Kestra Bravo was with you until early this morning it appears." Joe closed the book puffing out his cheeks. Slowly he leant back in his chair and rubbed his temple. "That will get them off your back, do me a favour though, stay in the castle for a little and don't get in trouble!" Feeling guilty at the strain he had placed on his brother, Jack promised to remain in the castle.

"I just need to find Kestra and get her side of the story and you should be in the clear. I don't think you'll be in trouble for just hitting the guy. He had a reputation, and I don't think the high councillor will be bothered by anything other than the person that tried to kill his son." Joe picked up his armour lifting It back over his head and fixing it down. "No more knight in shining armour, right?"

He smiled at his brother and pulled Jack into a bone crunching hug. "I thought I lost you in that infirmary, I don't want to lose you to a prison. I'll let mum know what's happening, she's been worried sick." Jack patted him on his back, it had been a long time since Joe had hugged him.

Once Jack had returned to the dining hall all his friends were now gathered at the table. He felt comforted to see Louise sitting with them rather than on her own, although Barry was nowhere to be seen.

"Budge up." Jack placed his plate on the table having not taken a bite of his breakfast so far.

"There he is! what happened to you last night?" Robin slid up the bench to make room, slapping him hard on the back as he sat.

"After Michael came back and told us you had a booth, we all came looking for you, but you had gone." Kim eyed him with a small grin.

"I had a scuffle with an idiot and thought it was best to leave, besides, you guys were having fun I didn't want to ruin your evening." Jack explained grabbing two freshly cooked sausages from a nearby platter and placing them on a fresh plate.

"Was that you?" Michael laughed excitedly. "The bouncer spent all night trying to find the person that hit that idiot, I almost did myself he was groping at any woman that came within ten feet of him! Robin almost threw him off the stage at one point." Michael and Robin grinned at him.

"I wouldn't go shouting about that if I was you." Jack explained what had happened with Joe. "You could make yourselves suspects." He warned ominously.

"Not Robin, he didn't leave my side all night." Rachel implored, everyone looked at her, realising what she said she hid her face in her hands.

"So where is Barry?" Louise asked to change the subject, Jack started to play with his food he had no desire to know about Barry and Kim's exploits.

"I wouldn't know, I haven't seen him since we left the club." Kim neatly cut her food whilst paying little attention to them.

"Did you guys carry on arguing?" Rachel questioned quickly keen to continue the new subject. Jack stopped twirling his sausage his interest peeked.

'They argued.' He managed to hide his grin behind a fake yawn.

"I don't want to talk about it, if you don't mind." Kim

appeared her happy self, so Barry couldn't have done anything too bad to upset her.

'Maybe she realised he wasn't the one?' His inner voice whispered. They continued their meal chatting and joking. Jack even managed a cordial conversation with Louise. It wasn't a conversation of merit, but it was a start.

Fully recovered, Jack was back to his full class schedule. With the amount of lessons he had missed, he was now picking up classes in the evening. This influenced his time to continue to investigate his father's death, he was also constantly aware of the promise he had made to Joe. Whatever ideas he had about trying to move his investigation forward would have meant leaving the castle.

Jack had considered using the reference books to try and gleam any knowledge the council may be hiding but it would require dark magic to access the council records. Kim may have been able to help him as the high councillor, though he had barely been able to see her since the night at Le Fay's. Kim was now busier than ever due to her commitments with the council, Jack did suspect she had been keeping her distance from Barry also. Each time she had seen him since, she had suddenly disappeared.

Jack had managed to get Michael to fill him in on what had caused Kim's argument with Barry, apparently, she hadn't taken kindly to him kissing her on the dance floor. She had thought Barry had invited her as a friend, not as a date. Barry had apologised, multiple times since, to Michael for the misunderstanding.

"Good evening Jack, are you ready for our lesson?" Levell stood in the summoning circle in her room.

"Are we practicing summoning today miss?" he asked. The rest of the class had already been practising to summon their avatars for weeks, but Jack had still been readying himself. It had been Levell's opinion he would have been too weak from his injuries to risk the attempt before now.

"Yes, I thought it would be best to try the initial attempt one on one, that way if you are still too weak in the attempt, I can better help guide you." Levell placed a candle in the middle of the circle. "Now before we begin, you have read all your books on summoning and you are confident you know what to do?" she asked him,

"Yes miss." He answered nervous at the prospect of meeting his avatar.

"Now, there are a couple of things I should point out, the summoning is different for each person, you may feel different sensations than described in the books. This is a unique experience to each person." Jack understood. "The thing that often stops someone from being able to summon their animal spirit is, the connection isn't allowed to grow, have you ever felt as though someone is talking to you from within?" she looked earnestly at him.

"how do you mean? Hearing voices that kind of thing, isn't that what mad people hear?"

"It is difficult to explain, this is part of the reason why people fear the voice. Fear the union between us and our creature. Yes, they can talk to us, it is generally a feeling, or a thought emphasised. It feels like we ourselves are saying the thoughts but if you pay careful attention you can pick out the difference." He thought carefully, there had been instances he could think of. At breakfast when hearing Kim and Barry argued, at Le Fay's it had said he had missed his chance, the joust and a dozen other times, it wasn't him but something inside of him.

"I think so yes, something has been whispering almost to me. I thought it was me." Levell smiled happily.

"You have a stronger connection than I thought. Ok, well we shall try to strengthen that link today? not actually summon your creature. I would like to build a bridge in order to allow your avatar to speak more easily with you. Indeed, some of the strongest avatars are able to hold full conversations with their master. Although, for our purposes today, even a word would be an excellent start. Shall we?" the next two hours were some of the most mentally draining of Jack's life. He had sat meditating trying to empty his thoughts and allow for his creature to step through the noise.

"Well, I think we will call that a day", Levell said. Jack was exhausted and a little bitter towards his animal spirit. He also felt is Levell had told him one more time to clear his mind, he would scream. "I know it may not feel like it, but I think we made progress today." Levell was being kind he was sure, how anyone could say they had made progress was beyond him. "When you're able, try to meditate on your own, the more you practice the easier it will become to centre yourself." She handed him a stack of candles and incense. "Will there be anything else?" she asked.

"I was just wondering miss, have you seen professor Grey, I haven't caught up on his classes yet?" she looked a little annoyed.

"Yes, professor Grey hasn't been available for some time now. Apparently, he had an urgent family matter to attend to and hasn't given us a date for his return. I believe his classes are being covered at the moment. If you wait until your next class, I'm sure you can arrange it then. Now, off to bed its already late and I'm afraid I have another guest shortly." Jack thanked her and left; he couldn't help but think the meditation would be a waste of time. Clearing his mind seemed an impossibility, each time he had tried images of Kim, his father, Grey, Kestra, the pillar revolved around and around. Maybe, if he could resolve these things, he could find that peace.

Chapter 11

Frustration

Jack had grown increasingly resentful of his Avatar. Since he had first tried to contact it, he no longer seemed to have any contact at all. He began to wonder if he had somehow done something to upset Draxon? Levell's insistence that all it took was for Jack to balance his emotions was infuriating, he suddenly understood why so many people failed to summon an avatar. He felt on the verge of giving up altogether. The only highlight of the past week was Kim now had more free time from her responsibilities of school councillor.

He rarely saw Robin anymore he was so engrossed with Rachel. Whilst Michael and Louise were just as likely to be absent.

The more time he had spent with Louise, the more he liked her. She wasn't anything like he had initially thought. He found her incredibly funny when she was relaxed and enjoying herself. This had led his guilt over the way he had initially treated her to magnify. He didn't know if he should apologise or if the time had now passed and he would just be dragging up the past for no reason. Louise's confidence appeared to be her downside, as such Terry was spending all his evenings alone with her in the library, researching dark magic rituals.

The Dark Heart

"Will you put that sword down, you promised to study with me tonight!" Kim had been waiting patiently for Jack to finish his sparring, after an hour, she had finally had enough.

"I need to practice my sword skills as well." Jack towelled down the sweat running down his arms. He had been spending longer each evening training, the physical exertion had allowed him to collapse into bed, too exhausted to dream. Since the attempts to contact Draxon, Jack's nightmares had returned, this time they included the fight at Le Fay's with him too weak to fight, or of Kim suddenly deciding Barry was the love of her life and casting Jack away.

Kim had now remembered her promise to help Jack catch up on the schoolwork he missed when in hospital. It was obvious how far behind he had fallen, after their last charms class Jack had been unable to perform a simple duplication jinx. Whilst he would have preferred to have spent his time alone with her in a different manner, Jack was grateful for anytime he could spend with her. Kim on the other hand, seemed to relish the opportunity to help him, she had created a timetable of activities and had spent their entire lunch drilling this new structure into him. So far, he was already an hour behind schedule.

"Give me five minutes to have a shower and then we can settle down and read the passage on mythological beast's Kaiba gave me?"

The shower was blissful on his aching muscles, the downside to the additional training was the pain he suffered on a day that Bravo would push him past his limits. Half-heartedly, he climbed out of the shower dressing and walked back into his room, he wasn't surprised to find Kim engrossed in a book already.

"Do you ever stop reading?" he laughed pouring himself a coffee, readying for another long night of study.

"What is this?" Kim asked holding a red leather-bound book. Jack recognised it at once. It had been the book he had been writing his investigations of his father in. Everything from his dreams, his suspicions about Grey and what he had seen in the orb was written in there.

"How much have you read?" Jack asked he felt as though icy water had flooded his veins.

"Only a few pages." She pulled the book close to her chest, coddling it like a new-born.

"Then I think you know what it is." Kim walked towards him still holding the book, she placed her hand to his chest. Jack could feel his heartbeat increase at her touch.

"Why didn't you tell me all of this? Don't you trust me?" her voice was full of hurt. Slowly Jack slid the book from her grasp, he opened to a page with only a single paragraph. Handing the book back to her,

"Read this." Kim hesitated for a moment, but then took the book and started to read.

I wish I could have Kim and Michael help, but I can't ask them, if whoever killed my father found out they knew. They might hurt them or their families. If something happened to them, I couldn't live with myself. I still don't know why I was affected after watching that orb. Was I somehow targeted? If so, how did they know I had watched it? The risk is too great to my friends.

Gently she closed the book, placing it down on the dresser. She hadn't looked at him, her eyes still fixed on the red leather. Jack allowed her the time to digest what she had read.

"So, you wouldn't tell us because of the risk?" Kim eventually broke her silence, she looked like she was sucking on an unpleasant lemon. Jack could see the turmoil going on in her head. He had been through the same feelings when he decided to not tell his friends what he knew.

"After I was released from the hospital, I knew I couldn't involve you both. Not just because I was terrified of something happening to you. I was scared about what you would think of me." This was the first time Jack had admitted how he really felt aloud. It wasn't the cathartic experience he hoped, instead of alleviating the fear he felt, it had magnified. Kim fixed him with a stare, it wasn't angry or upset Jack realised it was pity.

"I know you want to protect us, but this is about more than you and what you want. Our families are involved in this too, they can't be protected if we don't know what's going on. How am I or Michael to be on our guard, if we don't know there is danger?" He hadn't considered this, he had always presumed if they didn't know, they would be in less danger.

"You say you don't want anything to happen to us, but what about you? I don't want anything to happen to you either! When you were in that hospital bed dying, I was terrified. I thought …" she couldn't finish, instead she looked out the window, the starry sky seeming to stretch on forever outside. With a deep breath, she strengthened her resolve and pushed on. "I know you're not going to stop, let-me-help-you. We can keep each other safe!" She had grabbed him by his top, shaking him to see the sense in what she said. Kim was right, Jack knew they would be safer if they worked together, now he thought about it, he couldn't summarise the reasons he was so hell bent on not telling them. Afterall, whoever had killed his father might use his friends to try and stop him, at least if Kim was with him, he could watch over her.

As much as he may not have liked to admit it, all his friends were more powerful than him. Kim and Michael were two of the smartest people in Camelot, their magical prowess almost matching their teachers already. Robin was strong also. He was the best at knights training, Louise was the Dark priestess, with access to magic that none of the others could even dream of. Jack, by their standards, was little more than a child.

"You're right." He conceded, "If we do this though, you follow my lead, if there are any signs that you or your family are in danger, you stop!" Jack wanted her to understand that he was not willing to risk her. Hesitating, Kim curled the ends of her hair between her fingers, this was how Jack always knew she was nervous.

"Ok, if that is what it takes." She finally agreed.

"Before we make any moves though, I need to study. I'm not strong enough now, I don't think any of us are. If we are going to find out who killed my dad and protect our families, we all need to be the strongest we can." Kim picked up his homework and handed it to him.

"We had better get studying then!"

The following fortnight Jack and Kim were inseparable, they spent every hour they could together. He considered it nearly a miracle, Jack had not only caught up on all his schoolwork, but ahead of most of his class. Only Michael and Kim were now ahead of him. He thought Kim could have made an excellent teacher if she weren't destined for the council.

Their studies had gone so long each evening Kim had fallen asleep next to him on the bed. Jack woke this morning to find Kim laid with her head on his chest, her hair tickled at his nose as he breathed in. The sweetest smell of vanilla filled the air. He had slept better than anytime he could remember. Whenever Kim had fallen asleep with him, his dreams were always of her, no nightmares or disturbing visions. He had considered asking her to help with his meditations to see if her company would help to calm his mind then also.

Jack lay still enjoying the moment, it wasn't until Kim began to stir, he risked moving his arm. It had fallen asleep beneath her and had now lost all sensation. Once Jack had finally got feeling back in his arm, Kim laid back down onto his chest, nudging her head into him as though he were a pillow. Jack wrapped his arms around her and pulled her tight to him, they lay there neither of them saying a word.

"Are you up? its breakfast time." Robin shouted through his door. Kim sat bolt upright as the handle became to twist. Jack had forgotten they had arranged to go for a picnic with the others.

"Yeah, I'm up ill meet you down at the hall." He shouted back quickly, they watched as the handle twisted back to closed. Kim fell back onto his pillows.

"I don't want to get up yet!" She yawned. "I was comfortable." She laid her head back on Jack's chest. "Your heart is beating awfully fast you know." Jack grunted something non comital as she brushed her hand across his stomach. "Come on then, we had best get ready. I need to brush my hair and have a shower, do you mind?" she asked peeling herself off him.

"Be my guest." It was only now that he thought about it, but Kim seemed to have moved a lot of her items to his room. When she had first suggested bringing a change of clothes, just in case she fell asleep, he didn't think anything of it. Now half of his wardrobe was full of her clothes and his bathroom looked like an apothecary.

"No peeking!" She laughed as she entered the bathroom pushing the door to.

This was the first time since their trip to Le Fay's Jack had left the castle, although he was still on the grounds, so he didn't feel like he was breaking his promise to Joe. Rachel had set up the picnic at the lake, if he squinted Jack could just make out his window in the tower. There was food, enough for two dozen people. Sandwiches, pies, fruits, cakes, meats including chicken, ham, pork and boar. An assortment of whiskey and wine overflowed from the bottomless wicker hamper. Rachel must have spent forever laying it all out on a blanket that could have happily sat twenty, it was unnaturally soft it felt like sitting on a pillow.

They spent the day laughing and eating, it was liberating to see those he cared about enjoying themselves. Robin and Rachel seemed to genuinely care about each other. Michael and Louise were slowly opening up to them all about their relationship. There was no need for Rachel and Robin to slowly reveal their relationship. Jack thought if they had been anymore intwined, they would have been a single person. Michael had pretended to gag when sitting on Robin's lap she fed him strawberries dripped in cream, something Jack and Kim playfully imitated although she had missed his mouth from laughing so hard and covered his face with cream. Jack had chased after her flicking the cream at her as she screamed laughing. It had been an almost perfect day, apart from when Melfice had found them and got close enough without them noticing to cause a sudden rainstorm soaking them all through and causing Louise to fall into a small puddle of mud covering her clothes. He and his friends had scurried off before Jack or the others could react. Louise had done her best to laugh it off, within seconds they all had her dry and clean. Rachel had threatened to neuter Melfice at the next opportunity. It didn't take long for Louise to smile again, it seemed that this might be the first time she had a group of friends ready to rally around her.

"Not that I want to end all the fun, but I have a little present." Jack declared once they had finally finished their picnic. From his pocket he pulled three envelopes, handing one to Kim, Louise and Rachel.

"What's this?" Louise asked a little suspicious.

"Nothing to worry about. Just a thank you to Kim for all her help with getting me back up to speed, to Rachel for the picnic today, and a bit of an apology to you for how I treated you at first." Jack explained sheepish at the last part. If possible, Louise looked even more shy than ever before turning pink as she looked anywhere but at them. Slowly they started to peel open the envelopes, they gasped excited as the pulled gold leaf note inviting them to a relaxing evening, overnight at the best spa in Camelot.

"Jack that's…" Rachel grabbed him hugging him tightly, soon Kim and even Louise joined.

"Enough, you're going to be late." He called trying to push them off embarrassed. It was a small gift but obviously he had chosen well.

"One day I'm going to get that smug little bastard." Michael was livid a vein pulsed in his forehead. Louise, Kim and Rachel had now left for the spa. He had been holding in his anger until the girls had gone. He vented his anger on Jacks training dummy, hitting it repeatedly with a bokken.

"We will be happy to help, if you want us to." Robin grinned. Jack knew he was thinking of several ways he could twist Melfice like a rag doll.

"Thanks, but that's something I want to do on my own. He's got it out for Louise all because …" Michael stopped himself. Jack knew he wanted to say more but guessed that Louise had made him promise not to. Robin too dropped the subject, seemingly understanding the situation.

"So, what's going on with you and Kim then?" Robin slapped Jack on the back, almost sending him crashing to the ground.

"What do you mean? She's been helping me catch up on my schoolwork, you all know that." Both Robin and Michael laughed.

"I'm often up till late in the common room and I never

see Kim leave your room, so unless you have a second bedroom in there I don't know about?" Michael was grinning from ear to ear.

"Well, occasionally Kim will fall asleep on the bed whilst I'm finishing my work. That's it though, nothing else is happening." Jack couldn't help but sound deflated.

"Take it from someone who knows, if you like someone just say, that's what I did." Robin boldly claimed. Both Jack and Michael burst out laughing.

That evening Jacks nightmares returned they had been so vivid, it felt like they had been building in strength. His father's death had played over and over. He had to watch as the light faded from Ben's eyes. Was it a punishment for not doing more? he wondered finally awake, He scratched the dreams into his book hoping someday he would have something of merit to put in. If only he could talk to Grey. It had been months now, but he was still to return to the school. Somehow, his investigation had to continue. Jack suddenly remembered that Michael and Louise had been trying to find out what had happened to him when he collapsed. Maybe that would give him a starting point. Afterall, Louise as the dark priestess should have knowledge of dark magic that could potentially help him in his investigation into his father's murder, if he could find a way to seek her knowledge without rousing suspicion.

The common room was blissfully warm winter had arrived in a flurry of snow overnight. One of the wonders of Camelot was how the seasons changed. Everything was set to a clock, the evenings grew darker earlier or later in the day, dependant on the date. Everything from snow to storms, even the fall of the leaves was pre-determined in this pocket of space. Jack looked out the window where yesterday he and his friends had been sitting by the lake barely in anything more than their summer clothes, now the spot was covered in a foot of snow. Crisp, white and clean. The lake was frozen over,

'maybe I could take Kim ice skating on the lake?' Jack pictured a romantic scene in his mind of he and Kim skating delicately across the lake. Holding hands and moving gracefully. It then occurred to him that the few times in his life he had actually been ice skating, he had fallen on his face dozens of times, graceful wasn't something he would consider himself. At least it might make Kim laugh.

Students had been pouring into the common room all morning, Jack had been waiting patiently, but so far there had been no sign of Louise. He had passed the time waiting on the sofa, rereading a book Gerrard had lent him on the known history of Excalibur. Robin and Rachel had passed through shortly before, stopping only so Rachel could gush over something called a seaweed wrap, neither Jack nor Robin had the slightest idea what it was, but didn't find it appealing. Eventually Kim had appeared and taken him for breakfast, they had spoken at length about the spa. Kim had exclaimed how she felt like a new woman after squid massage. Jack had no clue how a squid could massage but was simply happy she enjoyed herself.

"So, today is the day we make a start on your father." She looked seriously at him. Jack knew that Kim had

The Dark Heart

been building up to this.

"Ok, not that I have a clue where to start, you've seen everything I know so far." Kim chewed on her lip. "What is it?" He had seen that look on her face before she was holding something back.

"Well, whilst you were studying, I wasn't just sitting doing nothing."

"I thought you were just checking me out." He joked; Kim rolled her eyes.

"I'll have you know, as a lady, I'm capable of doing two things at once." Jack choked on his coffee. "I may have found the cave you've been dreaming of, the one you saw in the orb."

"Where my father was killed?" The place had been hidden to his family under national security. Even his mother, a council member, had not been informed. "How have you found that place?" people were staring at them whispering across the table to each other.

"Let's talk later, when people can't hear." He agreed this wasn't a conversation to be held in public.

It wasn't until after lunch they found Michael and Louise, Jack wouldn't have believed it if he hadn't seen it. They had been out in the fields making snowmen.

"Have you ever heard of a Dark Priestess using her powers to make a snowman?" he chuckled.

"There is so much more to Louise than being the Dark Priestess, you know?" Kim wrapped her arm through Jacks own resting her head against his shoulder. They watched their friends enjoying the snow, not realising they could be seen by anyone.

"Louise's is much better than your attempt!" Jack shouted once close enough. Michael turned to see the two of them walking towards him.

"Yeah, well… Shut up!" Michael threw a snowball hitting Jack in the chest.

"*War*!" Jack shouted laughing, he dragged Kim behind a snowbank to provide cover. They began forming snowballs as fast as they could, peeking out from either side of the bank to see how Michael and Louise were preparing. A ball hit Jack on top of the head as he had stayed out a moment too long, shocked to see a solid foot thick ice wall formed in front of the two with arrow slits and mini trebuchet launchers. "I think they decided to use magic. Two can play at that game!" Jack flicked his wand and a hundred snowballs formed behind him.

"You're going to need more than those!" Kim laughed creating a small snow cannon. Jack loaded up the cannon and poked it around the edge of the wall. As he was aiming Kim tapped the end of the cannon with her wand causing it to begin to glow a feint green.

"What's that?" Jack puzzled he had never seen this before.

"Ice fire, it melts anything made of ice when struck. Their wall won't stand a chance!" Kim was gleeful, beaming at her scheme. Jack fired the cannon into the wall, as the green flaming ball hit the ice shield it burst into a shower of water soaking both Michael and Louise. They screamed from the shock of the sudden cold.

Michael shivering and swearing loosed the trebuchets, a boulder sized snowball flew into the air above them. Kim and Jack screamed, jumping from their hiding place. At its height Louise flicked her wand causing the boulder to explode into dozens of small snowballs which rained down on top of them. Jack felt like he had

The Dark Heart

been pummelled by a small horse.

"Enough." He called waving his hand in the air. They all were laughing, frozen and covered in bruises "Let's call it a draw?" Jack suggested knowing full well they had lost badly. Kindly Louise agreed, even as Michael tried to protest their victory.

"Let's get in the warm." Louise suggested through chattering teeth.

"Right, I need a hot drink anyone want anything?" Michael asked once they had returned. They all told him the drinks they wanted. Kim decided to run and change, the hem of her jeans soaking through. This was the first time that Jack and Louise had been left alone together.

"I didn't know you could make such impressive snowmen!" Jack was trying to make conversation, his ability to conduct small talk was fairly awful, he knew. Louise just smiled at him, "How's your training coming on? It must be difficult Dark Priestess is some of the toughest magic I understand." Louise shrugged her shoulders.

"It can't be that difficult, if I can manage it."

"don't be hard on yourself, I've seen some of the magic you can accomplish, you're powerful!" Jack hadn't realised how short on confidence she was. Louise smiled, but it was clearly forced. "So, I have a question, in your training have you ever heard of anything that could help you to step into an orb to see it from the viewpoint of the subject?" taken aback Louise stopped and thought.

"There are way's, but it doesn't need dark magic. Why do you ask?" Jack didn't want to lie to Louise, but he had resolved at this time not to involve her any more than needed.

"I have an orb my dad recorded, as you know he died. I just wanted to see him again." It was a half-truth.

"If you like, I could look further into it. It's a difficult potion to make, one of the benefits is it can be used on memories also. So, you could theoretically use it to explore a happy memory with him. I'll try and make one if you like?" Jack was amazed, Dark Priestess or not it sounded horrendously difficult and yet she was willing to try.

"That would be… well, I couldn't thank you enough."

As the evening drew to a close, Michael and Louise had retired to watch an orb. Jack and Kim, now alone in his room, had begun to discuss what she had discovered.

"So, this cave is in another pocket like Camelot?"

"Yes." Kim pointed excitedly at the reference book she had been reading to him. She had explained to him about how when Joe had got him to show where he was in the reference books, it gave her the idea to search through the council records for records of death. As the high councillor she had access to actual council records. It was an oversight of the charm used to protect the books from being misused. As the high councillor she had the same access as the high councillor of the round table. It had only been when she had noticed the information locked to the inner council and high councillor, she had discovered this loophole.

"Why was my dad investigating a pocket though? Especially one only the council seemed to know about. Is there a way to discover what was in the cave?" he asked hopefully.

"No, it seems the charms on other sections of the book also need a specific incantation. I guess they never considered death records that big of a security concern hence, the simple lock. It does give us the exact location though." It took him a few seconds to understand why she looked so excited.

"No, you can't be serious."

"Why not" she demanded.

"Kim, we can't go there can you imagine how dangerous it will be? My father a full-blown knight was killed there. We wouldn't stand a chance if whatever killed him is still there." Jack knew it would be safe, whoever had killed his father was long gone, but he hated the idea of Kim risking her safety.

"Do you have any better ideas?" She asked indignantly.

"No." he admitted. "But I do have a different one." He explained about his conversation with Louise, about how if he could get the original orb back from Grey, he could use the potion to try and see the person his father was talking to.

"How are we going to get it back? We don't even know where Nate is." Anytime Kim had mentioned Grey, she sounded wounded. Jack had to remember that he was an old family friend to her.

"Maybe we won't need the orb. Louise said it can work on memories as well. Maybe, by exploring the cave in my memory of the orb we can see something I missed?" Kim had to agree it was the safer option.

"Ok, we can try that first but if it doesn't help, we go to the cave ok?" Grimly Jack agreed.

Chapter 12

A Friend in Need

What the hell was happening? Outside of Jacks bedroom he could hear people shouting. "What's going on?" he demanded, running into the common room. A small group of boys looked over at him.

"Haven't you heard?" asked the smallest of the boys.

"Would I be asking if I had?" Jack snapped.

"Louise and Michael have been attacked, they're in the hospital!" The boy squeaked.

"What?" everyone turned and looked at Jack, but he didn't care. "When?"

"Some time during the evening, how comes you didn't know? you're always together you lot." the boy eyed Jack suspiciously.

"If you don't want to be the next person in the hospital, then I suggest that you shut your mouth." Jack warned. "has anyone been caught?" Jack barked at him.

"no." the boy sounded frightened.

'Melfice.' Jack thought, 'it has to be Melfice.' "I need to go see them" he said as much to himself as anyone in the room.

"They won't let you in, they sounded lucky to be alive. Apparently, Merlin has called Elves in to guard them." The boy squeaked.

'lucky to be alive, how could this have happened?'

Jack banged on Kim's door,

"Kim, Kim are you awake?"

"She's not there." A teary-eyed Rachel had appeared from next door.

"Where is she?" He asked desperately.

"She was the one who found Michael and Louise apparently. I saw Merlin escorting her to his office last night. I've waited up all night, but she hasn't come back." Rachel burst into more tears. Why had Merlin taken Kim away?

'to question her, she was the person who found them.' It made sense but why hadn't she come back yet? It shouldn't have taken all night to find out what she knew, surely.

Not knowing what else he to do Jack ran to see Levell, he hoped she might be able to give him some answers. Robin had offered to accompany him, saying it wasn't safe for anyone to be alone. Jack had refused, insisting he stay with Rachel, she right now was Robin's number one priority. He promised to let his friends know the moment he discovered anything.

Rapping on the door, he waited listening to the sounds of scurrying within the room. Levell popped her head around the door.

"Jack this is unexpected, what can I do for you?" she asked breathlessly it was clear she had been in a hurry. Jack had the impression that he had just interrupted something.

"I'm sorry miss, I was hoping you might be able to tell me what was happening with Michael and Louise? I'm worried and don't know anything. There are so many crazy rumours flying around, I don't know what to believe." Levell looked behind her.

"Just wait here for two minutes. I'm… finishing a consultation with a teacher." She shut the door before Jack could see inside. He waited patiently for five minutes before the other teacher appeared,

"she is ready for you now." the woman smiled at Jack.

"ok, thank you Miss err?" Jack suddenly realised he had no idea who this teacher was.

"It's Mrs Bravo." Jack smiled thanked her and entered. He would admit he was surprised anyone like Bravo would ever be able to marry a woman like his wife she was a stunning lady, and yet oddly familiar.

"I'm sorry I interrupted miss."

"It's fine, this is an important matter, and the consultation could wait. What have you heard about the incident with Mr Smith and Miss Harrison?" she patted a chair for him to sit.

"I've only just heard that they were attacked, apparently they are in the hospital wing?" Levell nodded solemnly.

"Someone assaulted your friend's late last night. It was a serious attack. If I am to be honest with you, I think whoever did it intended to kill them. I personally feel it was only because they were interrupted that the assailant didn't have the opportunity to finish." He felt sick to his stomach, it wasn't possible who could attack them in the middle of Camelot?

"Do they know who it was?" Jack asked.

"We don't know yet but whoever it is, they were they were far more powerful than any student." Levell seemed genuinely afraid.

"They're going to be ok though, aren't they?" Levell paused before answering.

"We won't be sure for a while yet… as I say, it was a serious assault."

"Do you think I would be able to see them?" Jack had been praying it wasn't as bad as he feared. If anything, it was worse.

"I'm not sure if that will be possible. They're under tight confinement, we don't want the person who did this to be able to finish what they started." Jack could feel his body trembling; he wanted to see his friends. He needed to see with his own eyes they were alive.

"Miss please, if there is anything you can do to get me to see them, I will be forever in your debt." She smiled softly and patted his hand.

"I'll see what I can do, stay here and I'll speak with the guards." As she left the room, she collected her wand and a small knife for protection. Jack wondered if Levell was right and it wasn't a student, then who could have done this and why would they attack his friends?

Levell walked back in through the hidden door posing as a solid wall, Jack lowered his wand startled by her sudden appearance.

"Jack, I have been able to convince the other teachers to allow you in the hospital, only under a couple of conditions though."

"Anything." Jack agreed eagerly.

"Well firstly, you will only be able to see Michael not Miss Harrison, she is still too weak to see anyone." Jack nodded feeling horrendous for Louise.

"Secondly, you won't be able to take your wand with

you." Jack did not care if they took his wand, if he could see Michael, they could have made him go naked.

"Let's go then!" Jack went to hand her his wand.

"Hold on to it until we reach the infirmary, we do have an attempted murderer on the loose." Jack's fear of what he would see when he saw Michael hit a new high.

"Miss, has Merlin finished talking to Kim yet? I don't understand what's taking so long." Jack had withheld from asking about Kim until now. He had been worried about asking to many questions in case it stopped him seeing Michael.

"Merlin is still interrogating her in case she was the one who attacked your friends." Levell seemed dubious about the reality of this.

"Are you saying she's been arrested?" Jack was aghast it didn't make sense Kim was the one who found them.

"I'm afraid so, don't worry though she is being treated well, as far as I am aware, she is in Merlin's private quarters, one of the safest rooms in Camelot. By tomorrow she will be back with you all, I would stake my life on it." Levell knew how ridiculous it was to hold Kim. Jack knew there was no way she would have any hurt Michael or Louise. He was glad she was safe and not in the dungeons like he had feared.

"What about Melfice, has he also been taken in for questioning?" Jack thought Melfice was probably the most likely suspect in the whole school for any misdemeanour, but when it involved Louise however, he should be at the front of the queue.

"No, I know he was considered by some, but he has an alibi in the shape of Mr Bravo, apparently they are having extra training sessions every night."

"Oh, how convenient." Jack spat.

"Yes, I have heard that you three aren't what we would call the best of friends."

"Bravo hates me, I don't know why, and as for Melfice well let us just say, I've known rats with more charm." Jack said with a shrug of his shoulder's.

"I can't say about Mr Trelane but Mr Bravo, I would have my suspicions, but I don't think that I should say."

"You have to tell me now that you've brought it up?" Jack said intrigued.

"What you must understand Jack, is that when you were young, and your father was still with us. Francis Bravo was a knight."

"A knight?" Jack said shocked

"Yes, a knight he was in fact good friends of some incredibly important council members. Your father on the other hand had always been a little suspicious of Francis and for good reason, Ben found out that he had been taking bribes from criminals to allow them to go free. Obviously, Ben did not like this and reported him to the council. Where Francis was Tried and convicted. But because of his friends on the council, he was spared jail and ordered here to work as a teacher as part of his rehabilitation, he has stayed ever since. Believe me he was no easier on your brother or sister, if there is one thing I can say about the man, it's that he knows how to hold a grudge." so that was why he didn't like Jack, he understood now, not that it made it any easier to stomach. "come on, you won't have long with Michael we had best hurry, or they may not let you in."

Standing in the doorway were two elves in full battle armour. Even though Elves were beautiful creatures, they were also some of the fiercest of all inhabitants of this world. A long time ago, humans and Elves had battled for control of Earth, Arthur's great grandfather Thangar Pendragon had made a pact with the Elves, and humans and Elves had lived together ever since in relative harmony.

"Is this the one named London?" the Elf asked in a cold voice.

"Yes." Levell said she sounded a little panicked. The Elf looked Jack over giving him an approving nod, he held out his hand, Jack guessed he was asking for his wand, he handed it over. As much as he didn't like the idea of being defenceless with a madman on the loose, he was willing to do anything to get through the door.

"Thank you, young London, you remind me of your father!" Jack looked at the elf.

"You knew my father?" he asked.

"I don't think now is the time, do you Nefarios?" Levell scorned.

"No, you're right, enter London and be quick, you have ten minutes." Nefarios turned and ran his long finger down the doorway, it sprang open allowing Jack access to the infirmary.

"Thank you." Jack nodded and stepped inside.

There were two beds in the infirmary with curtains drawn around them, Michael's was at the far end, Jack approached cautiously, he drew level with the bed and took a deep breath steadying himself for the worst. He stepped in between the curtains and saw him.

"My god." Michael was in far worse condition than Jack could ever have imagined. His entire face was covered in bruises and dried blood had matted his hair.

His body looked like it had been used as a sharpening stone, everywhere he looked Michael was covered in cuts. "Why hasn't anyone cleaned you up?" Jack asked the unconscious Michael. Tubes had been placed into his body with what looked like every conceivable health potion pouring into him. "Who did this to you?" Jack looked on despairingly at him. He sat on the side of the bed, trying to think who had the power to be able to cause this much damage? and how had he survived? Secretly, he was glad he couldn't see Louise. If she were considered in a worse condition he would have been completely overwhelmed. Jack gripped Michael's hand. "I'll get the bastard that did this!" He promised. Pulling his hand away from Michaels something dropped to the floor. A piece of paper that had been scrunched up. Jack unrolled it quickly and there written in Michael's own blood was one word. Devaldros.

Chapter 13

Tell No Lies

It had been the longest day Jack could remember. The wait for answers had been excruciating, he couldn't remember the last time he had felt so anxious. It was as though there was something inside him squirming, unable to settle until he knew. Levell had finally got the news Michael and Louise were expected to survive their injuries. The vipers in his stomach had stopped squirming but the anxiety still flooded him over Kim. Now that Michael and Louise were safe Jack had turned his attention to her. He had asked Levell if he would be able to see her, or if he wasn't allowed if she could attempt to, just so they could see she was ok. Levell had spoken to Merlin but was refused outright. He had mandated Kim was to have no contact with anyone, and if Levell asked again she would be fired. Levell had been shaken by the severity of his reprimand.

The next idea that occurred to Jack was his brother. Joe as a knight would surely be able to sway Merlin into seeing Kim. The knights would be investigating the assault after all, it was possible he already knew. Joe had agreed to meet him in his room at school, he still didn't want to risk Jack leaving the castle. When Joe entered Jacks chambers, he looked exhausted, dark circles around his eyes and shoulders slumped. He seemed glad to be in normal clothes and out of his armour.

"Sorry I'm late, as you can imagine things have been nuts." Joe laid his jacket over the chair and ran his hands through his hair.

"Do they know who attacked Michael and Louise?" Jack blurted out, he wanted to know if there was someone to hold to account for the horror he was feeling. Joe shook his head, he was agitated pacing the room, stopping suddenly and resuming his pacing over and over.

"I don't know, the attack happened on school premises its outside our jurisdiction." He shouted with spite in every syllable. "Merlin has total authority here. Unless he asks us for our help we can't interfere. My boss has been attempting to offer our support since the attack, Merlin has refused to even speak to us." Joe was ranting at the stupidity of the situation. They were knights charged with protecting the kingdom and its citizens, now their hands were tied by some ancient law.

"I thought that you could tell me how Kim was coping, they've been interrogating her all night and day." Jack explained now hopeless, if the knights couldn't investigate then he knew they wouldn't be able to get him in to see her. Joe kicked over the chair, slamming his fist into the wardrobe splintering the timber.

"Bastards." He snapped. "I didn't know about Kim. I'm sick of this. Our hands are tied behind our backs, whilst Merlin and the council seemed determined to stop us doing anything!" Joe poured himself a coffee, it was the oldest Jack had ever seen him look. He seemed to be carrying the weight of the world on his shoulders.

"What's going on Joe?" pulling a flask from his

pocket, Joe added the contents to his coffee.

"What I'm about to tell you cannot get, out do you understand me?"

"Of course." Jack agreed.

"The council forced us to stop our investigation into the attack on the high councillor's son." Joe whispered furiously.

"Can they do that?" Jack asked appalled.

"It's the council, they can do what they want. I got into a huge argument with mum last night about it."

"She can't be happy they are stopping the knights investigating, surely?" Jack had never thought Emma would be party to the corruption within the council.

"No, she's not happy about it either, but she doesn't want me kicking up trouble like dad did, she's worried something will happen to me like it did him." Something occurred to Jack that hadn't before. Louise had been working on his potion, had she been attacked because she was helping him?

"Why would they stop you investigating that attack? it doesn't make sense." Jack was talking to himself more than Joe.

"If you can work it out, you can explain it to me." Joe took a swig of his drink, he coughed from the strength of the whiskey he had added.

"If I tell you something, do you promise you won't say to anyone else?" Joe sighed, it seemed to be the last thing he wanted to hear right then.

"As long as it's nothing illegal." He answered exhausted. Jack pulled the paper Michael had been holding from his pocket. He explained to Joe about how he had found it when he had been in the infirmary.

"I'm trusting you with this because I don't trust

Merlin or the council to find this Devaldros. They are all hiding something Joe, I can feel it. Four people have now been attacked and no one knows by who. Me, the high councillor's son and now Michael and Louise. Luckily, no one is dead yet." Joe handed the paper back to Jack.

"I've never heard of the name and there is no way they will let me see Michael. I'll do what I can my end without raising suspicion, the knights, like the council have records going back centuries, there might be something in them. If you find out what Michael knows tell me, got it?" Joe threw the remainder of his coffee down his throat. "I'll try and find out what I can about Kim, Ill speak with a contact and see if they can get me in with her." They had never spoken of it, but Jack thought his brother knew of his feelings towards Kim, if he was being honest Joe had probably known longer than himself.

News reached Jack the following morning that Kim had been released. He had waited for her in the common room rushing over and hugging her as tightly as he could the moment she walked in the room.

"how are you?" Jack asked cautiously.

"well, I haven't been arrested yet if that's what you mean." Kim spoke into his chest. Jack guessed she had spent most of her time crying.

"Kim, I know that you didn't attack anyone." He released her from his grasp. "Did Joe manage to see you? He promised me he would try. They wouldn't let me." He stressed this to her. Jack needed her to know he had tried.

"No, Merlin wouldn't let him; I could hear the two of them arguing outside the room." She took Jack's arm unsteady on her feet.

"Come on, let's get you some rest, we can talk later." Jack took Kim to her room helping her into her bed. He made her a camomile tea.

"Please stay, I don't want to be alone." Jack could see more tears in her eyes.

"Wild horses couldn't drag me away." Sitting next to her on the bed he wrapped his arms around her holding her close to him.

Jack and Kim stayed in the bed for hours. Kim had been exhausted. Jack didn't know what she had been through. How hard they had questioned her? It was clear to him they had stopped her sleeping during the interrogation. Had they really considered that she had committed the attack, or more they had to be seen to be doing something?

"I can hear you thinking." Kim's voice drifted up to him.

"It's nothing, how are you feeling?" Kim looked up at him.

"tired, but physically ok. Have you heard anything about Michael and Louise, I only know they are alive."

"I was allowed to see Michael once, he's alive but in the best place. There are Elves guarding him and Louise and the nurse is one of the best in the business. I've told Joe only, but I found this when I saw Michael." Jack pulled the note from his pocket handing it to her.

"what is…." she saw the blood written on the paper. "Devaldros." Kim muttered to herself. "I've heard of him; I think that he has something to do with Arthur." Kim was concentrating hard trying to remember where she had heard the name before. "I have no idea how it could be. Arthur died centuries ago." They both sat and pondered for a moment.

"All I know is no-one has any idea of who did this, Levell thinks the person responsible is too powerful to be a student. I don't know who or what Devaldros is, but I'm going to find out!" A grim determination had fired inside of Jack, it was the same determination that was ablaze in his chest in trying to find his father's killer.

"fine, but you're not doing anything without me." Kim glared at him.

"We will do this together. When Michael and Louise are better, they will want to be involved I'm sure."

At that moment, a loud thunderclap reverberated around the room. Merlin's voice echoed through the castle.

"I would like everyone's undivided attention; all students must report to the dining hall at once. Any student or member that does not report here within the next 15 minutes will be expelled. Further explanation will be provided once all are in attendance." Jack had to wonder if anything else had happened. Looking at Kim he knew she was thinking the same thing.

"Thank you all for coming." Merlin announced once it had been confirmed all students were in attendance. "As I'm sure you are all now aware two of our students have been attacked, this is such a hideous crime that I have decided to enact my right as headmaster to conduct interviews under the influence of the Serene potion." Jack looked quizzically at Kim; she shrugged her lack of understanding. "the Serene potion is in effect a truth telling potion, anyone under its influence will be unable to lie. I, Lord Kaiba and professor Grey will all be taking you one by one to the back to interview you. Please stay where you are and wait to be called." Jack had not noticed before, but Grey had appeared on stage, this was the first time that Grey had been back to the school since he had been in hospital. One by one, the room began to empty.

"do you think Melfice could have done it?" Kim asked.

"My ears are burning." a snarling voice came from behind the pair,

"I know that voice isn't it the tooth fairy." Kim said with a smirk. They turned to see Melfice standing there looking as though someone had hit him. Quickly regaining his composure,

"you should not talk like that not with an attempted murderer on the loose, who knows who he might attack next. After all we know he has a taste for weak men and their dogs." Jack lunged at Melfice, but Kim jumped in between them.

"Jack leave him, think about where you are. If you hit him everyone will see, and they will start to think it was you." Melfice continued to laugh at them as he walked away. Even if Melfice wasn't directly involved in the attack, Jack knew he had his hand in it somehow.

Kim had been called for her interview leaving Jack on his own he sat pouring over everything they had discovered. It was difficult to take in,

"Jack, I need you to come with me." Jack turned around Grey was standing over his shoulder.

"good to see you again." Jack said with more than a little sarcasm in his voice.

"I am glad to see you have recovered, please come

into the back and sit on the chair provided, I will return in a minute." Jack entered the room and sat down; Grey was acting as though nothing had happened. Maybe he believed he wouldn't remember the orb due to his illness, or even that he would be too scared to continue to investigate his father's death.

The door opened and in walked Grey with Kaiba and Merlin, "Jack, It has been decided for all three of us to be present during this interview." Grey said, Jack thought he saw glimpses of anger in their faces as they looked towards the headmaster.

"that's fine, let's just get this over with." Merlin strode forward.

"very well." he sat in Front of Jack "drink this." Merlin produced a potion from thin air. Jack downed the drink in one, wanting to get the test over with quickly. A warm feeling trickled down his chest, reminding him of the first whiskey his father had given him at dinner. His head began to swim a little struggling to gather his thoughts.

"I feel drunk." He was surprised to find his voice steady.

"That is a normal side effect, don't worry, it will pass soon." Kaiba explained.

"What is your full name?" Merlin asked without pause.

"Jack London." he said without thinking.

"where were you born?" Merlin pressed.

"At the henge Manor." It appeared Jack did not have a choice in answering.

"how did your father die?"

"really Merlin, I don't think that's…" Merlin held up a

hand to silence Kaiba. Jack held his lips tight shut he was not telling them that.

"How did your father die?" Merlin repeated. Jack was fighting as hard as he could. But it was no use he could feel the words slipping out.

"he...he was...murdered!" Jack spat no longer able to suppress the words.

"Do you know who murdered him?" Merlin continued leaning into Jack's face so close Jack could smell the tobacco on his breath. He shook his head feverishly. Merlin considered him for a moment before sitting back and continuing reverting to his bored persona.

"Did you attack Michael Smith and Louise Harrison?"

"no!" Jack shouted at Merlin he had never felt angrier.

"where were you at the time of the attack?"

"In bed." Jack felt humiliated. As though he was some sort of circus animal being forced to do tricks."

"very well, you can leave." Kaiba and Grey looked horrified at what they had just seen. Kaiba grabbed Jack's arm.

"here, take this it will take away the effects of the potion." He handed Jack a vial containing a clear liquid. Jack drank the potion and threw the empty vial at Merlin's feet; he paid no attention to the shards of broken glass as he walked past Jack.

"You two may finish the rest of the interviews." Merlin said lazily to his colleagues leaving the room behind.

"Jack, I think its best if you return to your room. Try not to speak to anyone for the next ten minutes or so." Kaiba gave him a little nudge out of the curtain.

'What the hell is going on?' he thought.

The Dark Heart

Two days had passed since the interview, no-one had seen Kaiba or Grey since. And none of the students had been told if anyone had been arrested. Jack had tried to concentrate on the piece of paper that he had pulled from Michael's hand. So far no-one had updated the students on the condition of Michael or Louise. Even Levell had not been able to tell him, as she herself had stopped being informed of their condition. Jack knew this was a punishment for helping him to see his friend. Merlin it seemed, didn't wish for Jack to know anything at all.

"Jack, Earth to Jack."
"what?" Jack said as though he had just woken up.
"I was saying, could you please pass me Arthur Myths and mistakes?"
"oh, yeah here you go." Jack handed Kim a large leather-bound book returning his head to his hands and rereading his own book. Genealogy of the Roundtable.
"Jack, if you're tired, why don't you go to sleep?" Kim asked clearly concerned.
"I can't sleep, I need to know how Michael and Louise are. Plus, it would help if we could narrow down who or what this Devaldros is."
"Jack, there's nothing we can do for Michael right now, please get some sleep you're not going to be any help to them like this!" Kim implored him.
"maybe your right, a couple of hours might do some good." Without thinking Jack leaned over and gave her a kiss on the cheek. "night." Jack was at his bedroom door before he realised what had just done, he smiled to himself and went to bed.

"so, what are you attempting to teach me then?" a deep voice boomed. Jack was astonished to find the voice was coming from his own mouth.

"sire, as I have told you many times, I attempt nothing, I succeed at everything and even if it takes me seven lifetimes, I will make a fine potioneer of you." the figure that Jack seemed to be inhabiting looked up to see the man talking, standing there in all his glory was the original Merlin.

"My dear Merlin, we have been ATTEMPTING," he put an emphasis on these words. "to make a poor potioneer out of me, for almost two years. I can barely make a weak soup. You know Galahad was always the potioneer." Merlin smiled.

"sire, I would never think to waste our valuable time, so today I want to see if you can make a far more difficult potion than we have ever tried before." Jack could feel anxiety rise within the person.

"if it goes wrong, it won't hurt anyone will it?"

"my lord I am here, nothing is going to go wrong."

"Are you sure?" kindness feel upon Merlin's face.

"Arthur, have I ever led you wrong?" Jack realised this was Arthur's body.

"alright, what are we making?" Arthur finished.

"an invisibility potion." Jack jerked awake, the dream vivid in his mind, He could remember every detail including the method for making the potion.

'but it can't be an invisibility potion, they don't exist!' he lay there reciting the method over and over. It had been a dream, but it was so real. Could it hurt to try to make the potion he wondered. 'this could be my only hope of getting in to see Michael again.' he thought.

The clock rang midnight, the castle corridors would be pitch black now. Jack knew it would be difficult to find his way around at this time of night. Though, considering what he was about to do, it wouldn't be sensible to try in during the day. Whilst it was not against the rules to be out around the castle after dark, Jack didn't think it would be a good idea to be caught wandering the corridors when an assailant was on the loose. Slowly, he cracked the door to the common room peeking through the open sliver, he couldn't see anyone inside. Snatching up his bag, he snuck out determined not to be seen.

"Going somewhere?" Kim asked staring up at him as he passed the sofa. He hadn't spotted her laying down book in hand.

"I need to get something." He remembered his promise not to lie to her. Jack had hoped to avoid telling Kim, to keep her out of this if he got caught.

"I'll come with you; I need a walk. I'm finding sleep a little difficult." She stood up stretching out stifling a yawn.

"It may not be a good idea, what I need is against the rules, but I think it will help us in what we are doing. I don't know what Merlin will think if we get caught." Kim moved towards the door.

"Well, we had best not get caught then." She smiled at him, it was infectious and warm. Jack always felt he could achieve anything when she smiled.

"Are you sure?" he needed to give her the opportunity to back out.

"If whatever it is your about to do is that important, and it can help us, then yes, I'm sure." Kim pushed open the door waving her arm for him to go.

"so are you going to tell me what we are doing then?" Kim asked Jack place his finger to his lip Kim understood. Jack was weaving his way through the castle without a problem Kim on the other hand was having difficulty.

"Jack, I can't see, the castle it's different somehow,"

"what are you going on about it's the same look, there's the courtyard, thats me and Gerwaine...." Jack stopped dead.

"what did I just say?" Jack asked Kim confused.

"you said something about you and Gerwaine, but there hasn't been another Gerwaine since the time of Arthur, the name was made sacred after he died on Mordred's hill," Kim stared at Jack. He had noticed what Kim was talking about, the castle was different at night.

"I guess I'm just tired, come on let's get this over with." Jack knew where he was going, he just wished he knew why.

They reached the storeroom without meeting another person,

"Wait here and keep an eye out." Jack pulled his wand from his pocket knowing that the room would be secured, anything could happen. Inside the room hundreds of different bottles and herbs filled row upon row of shelves. The room seemed to stretch into the shadows. Cobwebs and dust filled the storeroom. From somewhere in the back, he could hear something scratching away, inwardly he hoped in was just a rat. He could see an assortment of magical creatures suspended in a clear liquid in jars on the shelves. He hoped that a gremlin hadn't gotten loose in the cupboard.

Three steps into the doorway Jack felt a strange sensation around his feet, looking down he had stepped into a puddle of water. The water started to turn colour as it rose around his feet, over his shoes and up his shins. Now the silver water clung around him as though suspended in air.

"What the hell!" He exclaimed when he tried to step forward his feet would not move; the liquid was holding him in place. "ok, this could be a problem." a clock face appeared on the wall in Front of him showing thirty seconds and began to countdown. "ok, not good. Solas." he whispered a flair of intense heat shot forth from his wand hitting the liquid nothing happened. Twenty seconds remained, 'ok let's try just removing it?' "Syphinious." again nothing happened only ten seconds remained, there was nothing he could do, he was going to be caught five seconds four seconds three seconds. 'bugger!' was all that he could think. A bottle flew off the shelf hitting the liquid around Jack's feet dissolving it. The clock stopped on one second and slowly faded away, Kim was standing behind Jack. "wow, I thought that only happened in orbs, you timed that well."

"not really, I was here all along, I just wanted to see you sweat." she grinned. "Living sand from the banks of the Nile. It's not really sand or water of course, when I was in Egypt, they told us how it was used to hold prisoners in place until the tide came in and drowned them. Crushed King Scarab carapace mixed with frankincense and myrrh is the only way to remove it."

"How did you know it was that bottle though?" Jack asked, out of the thousands in the room how on Earth did she know.

"It was the only one without dust on it near to where the person trapped would stand." It was stupidly simple, in is panic he hadn't considered what would be on hand. Something the teachers would expect of a student. They had never counted on Kim though.

Within an hour Jack had managed to get all the ingredients back to his room. They had nearly been caught on the way back, but it had turned out to be a couple on a moonlight stroll luckily, they had been paying too much attention to each other to notice Jack and Kim.

"so, are you going to tell me what we need all this for now?" Kim asked for what seemed the hundredth time.

"I told you it's going to help us see Michael."

"why didn't we just sneak in there instead of you making Merlin knows what?"

"that's right, he does." Jack muttered to himself.

"what was that?"

"I was saying there is no chance of getting past those elves without this, and even then, it's going to be tricky." Jack had no idea if this potion would even work, it had after all come to him in a dream, a dream that wasn't about him, but the fact that it had been Merlin teaching Arthur made the notion seem possible.

Jack poured over the cauldron tipping in ingredients, he didn't have a clue how long it would take to make the potion, but he knew that it was going well, the liquid had turned from green to red, to a light brown finally Jack added the final ingredient a unicorn's hair, there was a silent explosion of steam, the liquid turning so clear that he could have been forgiven in thinking that the potion had disappeared altogether.

"finished." Jack puffed,

"well done, now what exactly have you finished?" Kim asked sceptically.

"if it works, trust me, you'll know."

"Jack, that doesn't sound very promising, is this dangerous." Jack said nothing, he steadied himself and drank the potion.

"I guess we'll find out." Jack's insides convulsed a blinding pain but also a lightness Ran through his body.

"Jack?" Kim screamed so loud Jack thought she might have woken the castle.

"I'm fine, just need to get over the initial effects." he lied he was far from fine, Jack had made a mistake he remembered now, he had forgotten to add in the manticore blood, to lessen the pain.

"Jack, what's happening to you? why's your body disappearing?" Kim Ran over and tried to grab Jack but his body convulsed again sending her away. By the time Kim had gotten to her feet, he had disappeared completely.

"Where are you? what's happened?" Kim rushed over to where Jack had been, she felt around on the floor, there was nothing to feel. Kim rushed at the door, intent on getting help, but she could not open the door.

"come on, come on." She screamed at the door but still it would not move.

"Kim, if you keep shouting, you'll wake the castle, and we wouldn't want that now, would we?"

"Jack is that you where are you."

"I'm right here." Jack brushed his hand up the side of Kim's face.

"my god, what's happened."

"I forgot to add an ingredient, that's why it hurt but for all intents and purposes it works, the invisibility potion works!" Jack could tell Kim was stunned but he did not have time to explain everything. "Kim, I don't know how long this potion will last it could be an hour it might be five, now your choice, I can add the Manticore blood, or you can stay? but you need to say now." Jack would have preferred it if Kim stayed behind, but he thought that she deserved the choice.

"but Jack this is impossible, there's no such thing as an invisibility potion?" Kim said aghast.

"Kim, I haven't time to argue, what you're seeing, or not seeing I suppose. Are you coming or not?" Kim seemed to steel her resolve

"fine, add the blood to the potion and then let's go." Jack nodded.

"This is so creepy." Jack laughed a little.

"I wouldn't have let you drink the potion if there was any chance of you being hurt. I must admit though, I didn't think I would be able to see you once you had drunk the potion." for reason's Jack didn't understand he was able to see Kim and her him.

"I guess it's one of the effects of the potion." Kim said.

"I still can't believe you know how to make an invisibility potion Jack, who taught you?" Jack did not think that Kim would believe him, so he said nothing.

"we had best be going."

Finding his way around the castle was child's play now he did not have to worry about being seen. They ran to the infirmary, reaching It quickly and only stopped when the elves came into view.

"how do you suppose to get past them?" Kim whispered in his ear.

"I was hoping a moment of inspiration would come to me, so far not a lot has."

"you don't have a plan?"

"well, I'm sorry but Michael was always better at this sort of thing than I was. He used to plan all our delinquent behaviour, like the time we…" Jack had an idea. "wait here," Jack whispered.

"what are you going to do?" Kim asked.

"just stay against the wall, when they leave unlock the door, I won't be far behind." Jack slunk around the corner. Kim was wondering just what it was Jack was up to when she heard a crash. The two elves jumped at the sound before running to investigate, Kim saw Jack come around the corner, he waved at her furiously to get the door open.

They had made it safely inside, Jack pressed his ear to the door, he heard the elves return complaining about a windy castle.

"Child's play." He took Kim by her hand walking down to Michael's bed. Jack was glad to see that the tubes had been removed and the cuts across his body had healed.

"I thought that he would look a lot worse." Kim said.

"he did." Jack stated simply. Louise was in the bed opposite the curtains removed from around her. She too seemed to be healed, although Jack had never seen the results of her injuries. He reached down to the end of Michael's bed he had hoped that his friends would have recovered by now. Michael opened his eyes.

"who's there?" He snarled pulling his wand from beneath his blankets.

"Jack, he's awake!" Kim squealed excitedly waving happily, before remembering Michael wouldn't be able to see her.

"Kim is that you?" Michael was looking around the room, trying to find the source of the voice.

"Yes, me and Jack are here, don't worry were invisible."

"you are what? What are you going on about?" Jack quickly explained about the potion leaving out the part about the dream.

They spent the next hour whispering, so not to wake Louise, Michael explained they had now both recovered. Louise had been as injured as he was. Jack could hear the pang of regret in his voice, He knew that Michael was blaming himself for not being able to protect Louise.

"I found a note in your hand, written in your blood. What's Devaldros, is that who did this?" Michael looked at him bemused.

"I have no idea. Neither me nor Louise can remember a thing. The last thing we remember is from hours before the attack took place. The nurse thinks it was caused by head trauma, but me and Louise reckon a part of our memories were wiped."

"Why?" Jack didn't understand why Michael and Louise had a differing opinion.

"Because its exactly the last thing we both remember. If it were head trauma surely one of us would remember something later than the other? Ours both stop at the same moment." Jack had to agree that was suspicious.

"Do you think you knew the attacker then? That's

why they removed the memory?"

"It's the only thing that makes sense to us." Michael agreed. "Have you found out anything on a Devaldros then?" he asked. Jack shook his head, but Kim spoke.

"After you went to sleep, I found a reference to him in a child's nursery rhyme it was meant to have been written Just after the battle of Mordred's hill. He's a boogey man type, he will steal your soul, eat naughty children, that kind of thing. I can't see how it connects" Jack had been so happy at the thought that Kim had finally found something, but again his hopes burst, this couldn't be the connection they were looking for.

"Didn't Grey mention the name in class? something about him being a myth, it was in out very first lesson with him." Jack racked his brains but could not remember anything like that. Quickly, he remembered that he had been ill during class suffering a nauseating migraine. Kim looked ecstatic though, she seemed to have remembered what Michael was talking about. Light starting to pour into the room, morning was fast approaching. "You had best get going, they will change guard soon and your potion looks like it's starting to wear off I can just about start to make you out, if I concentrate." Kim and Jack hugged him and made for the door. They waited and like Michael had said they heard the guards leave their post for a moment to change over. Silently they let themselves out and hurried back to the common room.

Chapter 14

Draxon

Michael and Louise had been released from hospital with a clean bill of health. They had been hounded constantly about the attack, the pair had repeated over and over they couldn't remember. Michael had snapped at the last person to ask him. Sick of the celebrity status the attack had given them.

The four of them had continued to research into the meaning of Devaldros' name but had kept on coming up with the same thing.
"I can't find anything other than this bloody nursery rhyme." Michael threw his reference book on the floor in frustration. It had been another night's fruitless searching. Jack and Kim had become just as angered in their search.
"maybe we're going about this the wrong way, maybe we shouldn't be trying to find out about other people or creatures named Devaldros, maybe we should concentrate on the only Devaldros we've all been able to find?" Kim stretched stifling a yawn.
"but Kim," Michael started, "that Devaldros never existed and even if he had, he was apparently destroyed in the story, and even if he hadn't of been then. The law on immortal being's would have had him destroyed,"

The Dark Heart

Michael finished as though it settled the point. Kim was not buying it though.

"like you said Michael, everyone thinks it's a myth, if he had managed to survive then no-one would have been looking for him because they didn't think he existed, and if he was as powerful as he was said to be then he could have easily avoided the knight's and the council."

"And what would this apparently powerful being want to with two students?" Jack could see both points of the argument, the clock chimed in the corner.

"I need to go, Levell is going to try and speak with my avatar directly tonight, find out why I'm having difficulty in summoning him." If he was honest, he thought it was probably his fault. He hadn't meditated in weeks and his mind was all over the place with everything that had happened.

"Good luck." Kim squeezed him hand gently. Before turning back redoubling her argument with Michael.

Jack arrived at classroom; he was hoping to have arrived at a better time than he did the last.

"Jack, how pleasant your right on time." Levell was always a little too excited when it came to avatars in Jack's opinion, whenever they had held these extra classes, she positively bubbled with happiness. "Come in, come in." Jack stepped inside he had little expectation tonight would wield any greater success than his previous attempts. "Have you decided on a name by the way?" Levell asked.

"I'm not sure, I thought he would tell me his name."

"well, that might explain a little of your difficulties. You are not showing any dominance over your creature.

What you must understand Jack is that your creature is like a child, you must teach them with love and understanding, but they also need boundaries they need to know that you are the one in charge. Can you think of a name?" Jack thought hard he needed a name that would reflect well upon his creature and himself that would command a respect of any his other.

"Draxon." Jack said finally.

"That's a fine name." she said sounding a little proud. "your father had a name for his apparition, if he had ever been able to conjure one you understand."

"really, what?" Jack interjected.

"Reven, apparently in his final year he had begun to master his creature, he had told me he could hear his voice at night." Levell became noticeably quiet, Jack could see that his father's death had impacted the life of many people. "well, I suppose we should try to speak with Draxon so he can tell us what disturbs him. so, Jack please sit at my desk."

Jack sat whilst Levell place candles around him, he sneezed when Levell threw powder in the air.

"ground ginger and pixie wings, it acts as a spiritual conductor." she answered Jack's inquisitive look. He was starting to feel nervous. "ready?" Levell asked. Jack nodded

'here we go.' he thought.

"to the spirit within, we beseech you, please come forth, tell us your fears, tell us your sins."

'what the hell does that mean?' Jack thought. A pain shot threw his side as though it had been pierced by a sword.

"come forth, I command thee!" Levell shouted.

"it hurts." Jack was barely able to speak through the pain. He clenched the desk for support, images flashed in his mind, it was like watching a broken orb. A cave, blood, an armless corpse laying on the ground, Kim in strange dress, laying on the floor screaming in pain, the cave again. "stop it!" Jack screamed aloud. "stop it, please!" more and more images were flooding not only his mind but the room. A darkness had spread across the room, the images flashed through the darkness. Levell looked horrified "please stop it." he cried his voice barely heard over the screaming in the room. Michael lay on the floor cut in two, a dragon on fire. Jack thought his head was going to burst. Levell Ran over to the candles kicking one over, they all extinguished the darkness left as suddenly as it had arrived.

"Jack, are you ok?" Levell shouted running over to him.

"who ever invented pain should be stabbed." Jack groaned holding his head. Levell let out a small, forced laugh.

"Come on, to your feet let's have a look at you." Levell gave Jack a quick once over, apart from a bleeding nose and a headache Jack was perfectly fine.

"what went wrong?" Jack asked ruefully.

"well, it appears that Draxon is a very strong creature and not very talkative, well not to me at least."

"do we know any more than we did at the start?"

"well, we do know that he's a lot like yourself and your father."

"how do you mean?"

"that all three of you are as pig-headed as each other." Jack laughed a little.

"are we going to try again Miss?" Jack asked hoping

the answer was no.

"not tonight, your too weak to try again, in a week or two I'll add some more protective measures for both our benefit's, I would suggest that you go and get some dinner and then sleep. But before you do can I ask you one question?"

"sure."

"those images we saw, have you seen them before?" Jack thought hard, he didn't want to remember what he had seen

"a couple in my sleep, the dragon and the cave. why do you ask?"

"no real reason, just thinking that's all."

Jack was exhausted the ritual had taken more out of him than he had thought. When he arrived back at the common room Michael and Kim were still up waiting for him, Louise had gone to bed.

"How did things go?" Kim asked looking slightly worried at Jack's shabby state.

"not too good. I don't think Draxon was in the mood for talking."

"who's Draxon?" Michael asked.

"oh, he's my avatar. How's it been going here anyone decided on how we should continue?" Michael crossed his arms clearly a sign that Kim had won.

"I take it were going ahead with the nursery rhyme then?" Michael clicked his tongue.

"*Yes*, Jack, we are." Kim said looking over at Michael impatiently.

"Have you found anything since I left?"

"Well, if we take the rhyme literally, Devaldros was a powerful being who inhabited the most powerful wizard of the age, he possessed Mordred, that's why Mordred turned on Arthur." Jack looked on disbelievingly

"But obviously Arthur defeated Mordred, killing this supposed Devaldros, so he's dead, he can't be the guy were looking for!" Jack stated.

"well, there's a scripture at the beginning of this book, but were having difficulty translating it I'm hopeful that will give us some more information."

"fat chance." Michael said.

"why?"

"it's say's underneath that no-one has ever been able to translate it, it's the same symbols that are etched on the Diasis. You know the language that died at the same time as Merlin?"

"ok, that is a problem." Kim admitted.

"but we're in Camelot, with a boy who knows more about the history of this castle then almost any other man alive, that means we have a good chance of translating it." Kim said optimistically.

"I'm sorry Kim, I think that you're giving me far too much credit, everything I know about Camelot I learned from books and other people. I haven't ever read anything that would tell me how to read an ancient dead language." Jack shrugged.

"Jack, do you remember me asking you about the secret passageway in the library and you said it was on the map?"

"yeah, of course I do."

"well here." Kim searched in her bag and pulled out a crumbled map. She opened it revealing the library.

"what am I supposed to be looking at?"

"where's the secret passageway?"

"right here……." there was no passageway on the map, none of them were. "ok, that's weird." he said.

"Jack, I don't know how or even if I'm right, but I think that you have some connection to this place."

"what are you going on about Kim?" Michael asked almost as exhausted as Jack.

"think about it, Jack knows these secret passageways he can make his way around the school at the dead of night without any trouble, even though the hallway's change, he knew how to make an invisibility potion."

"well that just proves he's smart, not the reincarnation of Merlin or something." Jack felt hot under his collar, Kim was right there was something happening to him.

"I'm not sure Michael, but Kim might have something I've felt like I've been changing ever since we came here."

"Jack can you hear yourself, I know that your life's been difficult since you've come here but you're not talking sense mate. Maybe we should all just get some sleep, come back to this in the morning when were all a little fresher yeah?" the trio for once were all in agreement, and even though they hadn't really discovered anything Jack felt better as he went to bed that night.

Chapter 15

A clue, a clue my kingdom for a clue

Jack and his friends had poured over every text in the library and cross referenced any result in their reference books for Devaldros. They had found no other references. Louise had searched through the dark magic vaults also but had found no mention. She had explained that her access was severely restricted as she was still a student. Jack now felt like he would be unable to discover anything else for the time being. Joe was still investigating, but so far hadn't found anything either. He had promised to let Jack know the second he found something. Jack felt hopeless. He knew he was running out of options. He now had to hope either Louise would be able to produce the potion to help him invade the orb or confront Grey.

It took until after lunch for Jack to get to speak with Louise alone.

"Louise, may I have a word quick?" They both moved into a hidden passage once the coast was clear. "Don't worry this takes us to class, so we won't be late." He assured her.

"What's the matter?" she asked. "If it's about Devaldros, I haven't been able to find anymore yet."

"No, I was wondering if you had any luck with that

potion you were going to look into for me?" Louise stopped dead in her tracks.

"What potion? What are you talking about?" she was confused a result of her attack he was sure.

"I asked you to create a potion to help me move about in a memory of my father?" Louise just stared blankly at him.

"I have no idea what you're talking about." She was being earnest.

"A few weeks before the attack you told me there are ways to get inside a memory and walk around it. You were going to look into how the potion was made. Are you ok?"

"I don't know, I found a potion in my room and had no memory of it, but it is one that will do exactly what you describe. I just thought I had picked it up by mistake somehow." It was with a sickening realisation now of why Louise and Michael had been attacked. It was due to Jack's request. How had anyone heard though? they had been alone like now. "Someone really doesn't want you to see what happened." Louise was scared.

"I'm more concerned about how they knew. Are they listening in on us somehow, do you think?"

"They can't be, I can't sense any dark magic on either of us. I'll sweep the rooms later, see if I can sense anything. Come on we had best get to class. You can have the potion after school finishes today." She was right, being in a dark secret passage suddenly seemed far more dangerous now.

Once classes had finished Jack had escorted Louise back to common room. She had disappeared and

The Dark Heart

returned with the potion. Jack hoped now it was in his possession she would be safe from any further attack. He now had a plan with the potion, he would be able to explore his memory of the attack. It may reveal to him something he had missed the first time. He also needed the original orb for his plan to work though. Now Grey was back, he may have bought the orb with him. Tonight, he would break into his office and steal it.

Jack waited until the castle was asleep. He stared at the clock every few seconds.

"Jack stop it, you're making me nervous." Jack and Kim were the only two people awake in the whole castle.

"Jack, let's go over the plan one more time." The two of them had spent the last hour planning on how they were going to get into Grey's room. Eventually it had been a simple plan that had shone through the others.

"Kim you know the plan, we walk down, I go in whilst you keep an eye out. It's simple." Jack knew it wasn't going to be so simple, that's was why he had asked for Kim's help. He couldn't risk taking the ingredients again to make another invisibility potion, he just hoped Grey would be out tonight rather than in his room.

The corridors were in perpetual darkness a full moon was cast, but on the wrong side of the castle, Jack preferred it that way there was less chance of being seen. He again, had no trouble negotiating his was around the school in the dark, this time he held Kim's hand to make sure that she was able to keep up.

"Jack, do you know where were going?" She asked

him.

"of course, I do Kim, we'll be there in a minute just keep quiet." he whispered. Jack walked past the same cloister that he had done a few minutes before.

"Jack, we're lost, aren't we? that's the third time we've been past this cloister."

"we aren't lost the halls constantly shift, I had Merlin do it." Kim grabbed Jack.

"what did you say?"

"I said, I read that Arthur had Merlin do it, you know to disorientate the enemy, if anyone had ever managed to break into the castle," he answered.

"no Jack, that's not what you said, you said I had Merlin do it."

"did I? oh well." Jack was not paying attention he was waiting for the next hall to shift.

"Jack." Kim continued.

"Ssh, someone's coming." Jack pressed himself hard against the wall it was not any good really, he would be clearly visible as soon as they walked past with their torch. Kim grabbed hold of Jack kissing him hard on the lips. Jack wasn't sure what was happening, his mind had gone blank. He felt Kim grab his hand placing it on the back of her head. Her hair, like silk, ran through his fingers. Her lips as soft as velvet. He heard the footsteps fading away. With his free hand he pushed a suit of armour making it clatter loudly bringing the footsteps backwards so he could remain with her a few lips pressed to his for a few seconds longer. Jack's heart was beating so fast, he feared it might pop out of his chest. A cough behind them broke the pair apart, Jack was glad it was dark, he did not know if it was possible for him to blush any harder.

The Dark Heart

"May I ask why you two are out of your dorm room at this time of night?" It was Gerrard clearly amused. Before Jack could speak Kim jumped in, he was glad though, he wasn't sure he could say anything at all.

"I'm sorry sir, but we're out on a moonlight stroll, it is allowed isn't it?" Kim fluttered her eyelids cuddling up to Jack.

"no, that's fine but do remember that there is an attacker on the loose, and some of the other teachers may not be so forgiving of the situation that I just found you in." he laughed, "well, carry on," he grinned walking away. Jack and Kim stood there in an awkward silence before Jack finally said.

"That was quick thinking." he sat back onto a wall thinking about the kiss.

"well, men always fall for that trick." She blushed.

"do you do it often then? just kiss random men." he grinned.

"no, I don't, now come on let's get going."

"just a second need to catch my breath, we were kissing for a little while there or did it just seem that way?" she smiled slightly. His breath returned but his cheeks still burning he grasped her hand softer than he had before allowing his thumb to brush over skin before setting of again. They rounded the corner and found themselves outside the Grey's room.

"ok, we are here, remember keep an eye out, I should only be a few minutes." Kim nodded Jack was surprised the door was slightly ajar. Unsettled he pushed the door open stepping inside and closing the door quickly again.

"My dear Jack, I was beginning to worry!" A light pierced the room so Jack could see all. Grey was sitting at his desk. resting on his desk were two orbs', the one

Ben had given Jack and the other of his death.

"Did something happen to detain you?" Grey had been expecting him.

"Nothing has happened, yet."

"Jack, you make it sound as though you don't trust me?"

"why should I? the last two times I've seen you I was put in a coma and asked a rather disturbing line of questioning concerning my father." Grey winced slightly.

"You've been having elocution lessons from my dear Kim I see?" Jack pointed his wand at Grey who recoiled slightly but settled again.

"*Don't even mention her name.*" Jack hissed.

"Paranoia is an ugly thing." he said still with the infuriating air of humour.

"it's not paranoia if someone's out to get you." Grey stared at Jack almost as though he was weighing what he was about to say to him.

"Jack, if you want to know the truth, you're going to have to trust me." Jack looked at him his fear raging against his desire to know the truth.

"which truth? no offence but there is a lot being lied about." Jack asked warily.

"the truth about yourself and your father." Jack did not understand.

"don't play games with me, if you have something to say then say it."

"Jack there are things in the world that you don't understand things about yourself as well, and I don't blame you it's taken me more than a lifetime to learn." this was just ramblings Jack was sure.

"is this supposed to mean anything or are you just

going to continue to piss in the wind?" Jack snapped. Grey responded by throwing him an orb,

"do you remember when you rather ordered me to watch that orb of your father? Well, I think that you need to watch this one and things will start to become clearer for you." Jack did not trust him.

"this is the orb your father left you, I assure you no curse is placed on it." Jack's curiosity overcame his reluctance to close his eyes in Front Grey. He placed the orb to his forehead, the familiar fast paced scene flashed through his mind, before returning to the beginning and there he stood in all his glory Benjamin London, Knight of Camelot. Jack's eyes watered at the sight of seeing his father, standing so proud, in Front of him.

"play." the scene began to move

"Jack if you are watching this it means the worst has happened and I have died, I'm sure there are a great many things that I never said to you, like how much I love all of you and now I never can so please hear me Jack, I love you all. I also remember treating you as a friend rather than a son, again I am sorry for this, I guess I was not the most responsible father in the world. But Jack, there is something you need to know something that has been passed down through the youngest member of every generation of London, and it is something that you and you alone can bare," Ben stressed this. "do you remember me telling you that you are a descendent of Mertous the Knight of Lower Gaulsden? Well, I lied, there never was a knight by that name or land, that is why you have never been able to find a reference to him, you see we are descended from the great king Arthur himself." Jack spat in disbelief. A hand reached in Front of Jack pulling the orb from his head.

"I believe that's enough for the moment." Grey placed the orb back on his desk.

"what the hell has this to do with you? my father left this orb for me not you; I decide when I've seen enough." Jack shouted he was so angry with Grey how dare he watch the orb. "what gives you the right to watch this orb?" Jack screamed a fury filling his body.

"national security!" Grey said simply.

"national security, national bloody security?" Jack said in disbelief. "what the hell does this orb have to do with national security? and you don't have the right to view it anyway, you're not a council member, you're a teacher." Jack berated him.

"I have a higher power than the council, but that's beside the point, I understand that you are trying to discover the reason behind your friends attack and the murder of your father?"

"how the hell do you know are you spying on me?" fear was overtaking his anger, had Grey been the person to attack Michael and Louise?

"I would never be so blasé about someone's personal life."

"what do you call stealing a personal item and then watching my sealed orb then, if not an invasion of privacy?"

"as I have said, a matter of national security. You know the name Devaldros of course?" Jack's heart seemed to stop.

"what about Devaldros?" all of Jack's anger and fear had been replaced by a desire to know more.

"he or more appropriately, it, is connected to all the things you are investigating. That is why I needed to see that orb, and what your father say's about your family's true bloodline only confirms my fears, when I first saw the other orb, I knew that the man in question had some connection to Devaldros. Unfortunately, I never knew the man's name." Jack did not know what to say,

"you're crazy……it's not possible for all this to be connected. Devaldros is just a myth and even if it wasn't a myth Devaldros was destroyed on Mordred's hill!"

"All myths begin in truth. And the legends don't say that Devaldros was destroyed, they say that he was killed."

"that's the same thing isn't it? I mean, dead is dead?" Grey openly chuckled at this.

"death isn't a final end for one such as Devaldros, it's more of a pause." For the first time Jack heard a flicker of fear in Grey's voice.

"then, how do you destroy him forever?" Jack scoffed.

"to be honest with you, well, we don't know." Grey said shrugging his shoulders.

"Who's we?" Jack asked.

"what?"

"you said we, not I don't know, you said we don't know." Grey seemed annoyed with himself.

"that isn't something that you need to know about at the moment."

"how do you expect me to trust you, if you won't tell me everything?" he asked stubbornly.

"Jack, there are things occurring that are far more important than your comfort."

"What is it you want from me?" Jack was trying to keep his temper in check.

"I want to keep an eye on you, maybe remove you from the school, in the hope to protect the other students."

"protect them from what?" Jack could not understand why him being removed from the school would protect the other pupils.

"I need to protect them from you Jack, don't you see yet? you're the danger." Grey stopped in mid-sentence Kim had just walked in the room.

"Jack is everything ok?" she spotted Grey at his table she gave him the smallest of waves which he responded. Jack stared at Grey; he was seething inside.

"yeah Kim, everything's fine, I was just leaving." Jack turned taking Kim's hand just as he reached the door Grey called out.

"later Jack, we need to finish this." Jack continued out the door, he could not believe what he had just been told but he needed time allow it all to sink in.

Jack sat on his bed trying to put in order everything he had just seen and heard,

'is it possible that I am a descendent of Arthur? am I somehow a threat? So far, he had not told Kim what had been said. He suddenly felt unclean, dangerous. 'Grey is lying.' It had to be the case. 'The truth potion' he was right, he had said under the truth potion he had not attacked them. It was impossible to lie under its influence. 'Grey had no right to take the orbs, no right to accuse! He cannot take Kim away' He wouldn't lose her, no matter what. She was his lifeline, the thing that kept him sane. 'he cannot take away that kiss.' The scent of vanilla seemed to fill his being. The memory of her lips the feel of her body pressed against him. No one was going to stop him being close to her.

Chapter 16

Old Flames

In contrast to Greys absence over the past few months, he now appeared to be everywhere. Wherever Jack turned he was there watching, waiting for his moment to strike. Jack hadn't been able to talk through what had happened with Michael and Kim. On his walk back to the tower that night, he had been too much in shock to explain to Kim what had transpired. She had since been in meetings every night with the council representing the school. Michael had been willing to listen, but Jack only wanted to go through the situation once. They had agreed to wait until Kim was available to talk.

"Ok, are you ready to do this?" Kim sat down on the sofa, the four of them now alone all the other students having retired to their rooms.

"I don't know where to begin really." Jack was nervous he had been worrying constantly about how his friends would react.

"Tell us the worst and we can go from there." Louise offered delicately. He tried to look at them all gathered around him, concerned for what he was going through. How could he tell them he was considered dangerous? It may have been him that attacked them, almost killed them? It didn't matter though, to lie would only compound the horror, his friends deserved the truth.

"Grey wants to remove me from the school. He thinks it would be safer for the other students." The expression on their faces were a mixture of confusion and disbelief.

"They're not removing you from anywhere." Michael eventually said.

"Why does he want to remove you? it doesn't make sense. Do they think you're a target?" Louise asked concerned.

"A target or a threat, Grey thinks I'm a danger to the other students somehow." Kim placed her hand on Jack's shoulder. It sent chills down his spine.

"the only danger you are, is to them." Louise answered for his friends.

"Yeah, think about it. When you were under the Serene potion, they asked you about your dad barely anything about us." Michael pointed out.

"And Grey took the orbs, something that might have given you answers." Kim continued. He couldn't tell them how much it warmed his heart to hear his friends defend him like this.

"Thank you." His voice broke as he wiped a tear away from his eye.

"Why don't we stay up, watch a film?" Kim asked him delicately. Jack guessed that she was feeling bad for him.

"yeah, that would be nice." Louise squealed happily.

"oh, I have a new one its really good we could all watch it to…." Michael squeezed her hand making her stop.

"Sorry mate, we would watch it but me and Lou have a couple of things to do tonight." he was speaking more to Louise than Jack.

"oh yeah sorry, I forgot, but you can have the film, I'll

be right back." She ran away returning a few minutes later with the orb. As soon as she had handed it to him Michael pulled her to bed.

"night you two." his voice was shaking Jack knew that he was trying not to laugh. Kim pulled him over to the sofa, placing the film onto the orb display a small circular stone basin sat on the mantle when Kim placed the orb on it a large sheet descended from the ceiling and the film began. He watched her cross the room picking up a nearby blanket. Snow was falling heavily outside; December had come at last.

"is it ok if I snuggle up to you? it's a little cold." she asked him. Jack nodded his brain frozen by the question. She sank down next to him placing the blanket over the two of them her head slid onto his shoulder.

He should have been asleep, he was exhausted and yet he could not take his eyes off her, she had laid her head on a pillow over his lap watching the film. When it had ended, he was amazed to find his own hand in hers and the other stroking her hair. He had been doing it without thinking. He stopped stroking her hair, she stirred a little, he knew she must have fallen asleep. He was happy, so incredibly happy and yet he knew that when she awoke this happiness would be broken forever. He clung to her a little tighter and prayed for time to stop.

He awoke, still tired and cold the blanket was laid over him tucked in tightly, but Kim was gone. A small note lay besides him.

I didn't want to wake you. I've gone to breakfast with

the others, see you soon.

Kim
X

Jack found his friends already seated at the table halfway through their breakfast.

"Morning, sleepy head." Kim moved around so he could sit next to her. Robin put a plate of breakfast in front of him.

"You look exhausted. Didn't you sleep?" Jack muttered something indistinguishable to his friend. He didn't want to explain he had been up all-night watching Kim sleep. Jack was happily eating his breakfast and joking with his friends, that was until a pupil came around with several leaflets, Jack hadn't even glanced at his, but Kim and Louise let out a scream of excitement next to his ear that shot through head like an ice pick,

"oh, I'm sorry Jack." Kim stroked his head.

"yeah, I'm sure that will make him feel better." Louise laughed.

"so why with the screaming?" he grunted

"well, it looks like because of the trouble that's happened the school has decided to put on a Christmas ball to try and raise peoples morale. It has a formal dance and everything" Louise answered him, she Kim and Rachel were positively bouncing in their seat

"Well, it lowers my morale, I can't dance, formal or otherwise." he joked.

"You dance wonderfully, don't you Michael?" Louise cuddled up closer to him.

"Imagine a one-armed, one-legged werewolf that's

drunk a vat of round table ale and that pretty much describes the way that both me and Jack dance, we taught each other." Michael and Jack grinned.

"well, you had better learn quickly, because I'm fantastic and I'll want to dance with you." Louise leered at Michael.

"unlucky." Jack pointed at Michael howling with laughter at his friends face that had dropped like a stone.

By that afternoon, the news of the ball had spread all over the school. Girls had begun to travel in larger groups than normal, Jack thought they looked like packs of animals searching for weak prey. He could see the way they would surround a boy on his own, the girls seemed to break him down and he had been roped into taking one of them to the ball. Jack laughed out loud at the boy's misfortune, that was until he turned around to leave. A group had gathered behind him without him noticing.

"wow, I need to get you a bell!" Jack said to the girl standing at the front.

"Jack, how are you?" the girl said sweetly. Jack was not sure what he could do to get out of what was about to happen.

"I'm fine, Amanda but I'm running late for something I'm going to have to leave you, sorry." Jack tried to leave but it was no good the girls had blocked off all the exits.

"oh, I'll just keep you two minutes." Seeing no way of escaping without injuring one of them, he decided he would have to listen.

"yeah, sure just please be quick, I really do have to be going."

"well, we heard about the awful news of you being single at this time, it's a tragedy really." Amanda's smile was sickly sweet.

"It's a ball, not a funeral." Jack said coldly not trying to hide the fact he didn't like the way the conversation was going.

"I understand that, but it can still be hard. So, we thought it would be a good idea if you took our friend here."

"you do, do you?" he was starting to get annoyed now.

"yes, we do." Amanda grabbed Jack and pulled him to a girl at the back of the group, she was clearly a shy girl, Jack had seen her once or twice around the school, Jack thought she could be pretty, if she tried, but he thought that she might not try on purpose, so she could hide easier.

"this is Becky, she is very keen on you Jack. We all think that you should take her to the ball." Becky blushed furiously. Jack shook her hand and she blushed even harder,

"Hello Becky, it's really nice to meet you, but I'm sorry, I can't take you, you see I'm already taking someone else." he lied not wanting to upset the girl it wasn't her fault her friends had set up a kidnapping ring for men, or so he viewed them.

"what?" Amanda screamed. "but I haven't heard that?" she seemed livid with not knowing this new piece of gossip.

"why should you have? My life is my business." Jack shook Becky by the hand again. "I'm sorry again Becky, If I had seen you a few hours ago the answer would definitely have been different." Jack gave her a wink she smiled at him sweetly leaving him a little guilty as he left.

He didn't like lying to the girls, but he didn't think it fair for them to try and pressure him into dating someone either, the truth was Jack didn't have a date for the ball. His mind had kept drifting to Kim and the previous night. The ball was held on Christmas night, that was only three short weeks away. Jack had been concentrating so hard on Devaldros and the meaning behind all his recent troubles that he had not noticed that Christmas was coming so soon. His family did not really celebrate Christmas, they shared presents as did most other families, it was the one time of year that Joe was nice to him. Christianity had only come to the shores of Britain with the arrival of the Romans, but Jack's family had stuck with their original religion as Pagans, he hadn't ever been a religious person, but he had always enjoyed the holidays that came with them.

Jack was amazed at the excitement that the ball seemed to have raised even during lessons there was an unmistakable amount of interest in it, Jack had begun to find it annoying, his favourite lesson had soon become PE, even with Bravo doing his best to punish them with whatever he could come up with, but at least he couldn't hear the girls silly giggling in the far corner. The only thing that annoyed Jack was the fact that the boys were clearly doing their best to impress the girls and quite often falling flat on their faces, Jack and Michael on the other hand were trying to ignore it all, and for some reason it seemed to be impressing the girls even more.

"it's because you don't care, it adds a coolness factor

for you," Kim explained.

"You need to be careful though. I think they have worked out you lied to them about taking someone." Michael said pointing out Amanda's group in the corner.

"I don't want to take someone, unless it's someone I like." Jack said.

"Well, you had best work out who you like because most of the couples are now sorted." Kim blurted out quickly.

"well, I guess I had better find a date then."

"Think fast, most of the best-looking girls have already been snapped up." Michael warned him. Jack thought hard there was only one person he would like to take, and he was not about to ask her in Front of Michael.

"are you going to the ball then?" Jack asked Kim once they were alone.

"yes, I like to dance." she gave a little pirouette.

"well, I was wondering, if you wanted to, maybe I could take you?" he said quickly seeing the look on her face.

"Oh, Jack I'm sorry but I have already said that I'll go with someone."

"excellent." Jack fawned. "who might I send my thanks to?" he sounded honestly happy for her when really, he just wanted to know who to jinx repeatedly until they resembled a sea lion.

"what do you mean thanks?"

"the person who has managed to cheer you up, make you love again."

"I wouldn't go that far; all I'm doing is going to a ball

with him." Jack was upset but he had no intention of showing it.

"So, who is it then?" His voice was unnaturally high.

"it's Ben Mclambeth, from the Lancelot's." he nodded

"oh yeah, I know him, he's a nice guy." Jack wanted the conversation to end. He could feel his blood boiling. "I suppose I need to go and find someone else then?" Kim caught him by the arm as he turned to leave

"Jack I am sorry, if I had thought..." Jack waved as a way of saying he understood and left Kim standing there.

Jack stalked the castle, his temper foul. Around him he heard his fellow students in high spirits. Laughing and cheering as another boy had plucked the courage to ask the girl he cared about to the ball.

'I was too late.' He thought. He sat in a window on the far side of the castle, students usually did not come here as it was currently not in use for classes. It provided the most spectacular views of the lake and forest beyond. If you squinted, you could see over the wall and down to the harbour. He wished he had the courage to do what he wanted more than anything in the world. Even if Kim had guessed at his feelings for her, he had left it too long to tell her she had grown tired of waiting or maybe this was her way of showing him politely that she wasn't interested.

As he sat there, he heard the approaching sound of heels on stone.

"Hello you." The voice was strikingly familiar.

"Kestra!" she stood there in a tight-fitting suit, peeking over at him, atop of her glasses. Her Auburn hair tied into a bun on top her head. She was holding several large volume books to her chest. She almost looked like a teacher. "What are you doing here? I haven't seen you since…"

"Since our night together?" She finished blushing slightly. "I'm doing some work in Camelot. It's nice to see you again." Kestra sat beside him. Jack hadn't realised she wasn't a student anymore.

"Is that why I haven't seen you around? You've been working then. Sorry, I thought you were a student still." She laughed.

"Last year was my final year. Does it bother you I'm older than you?" She asked him.

"Not at all."

"Well, I'm afraid I'm only around until Christmas, then I'm travelling away again for work, so I won't be seeing much of you this time." She made a point to look him up and down smirking.

"How would you like to go to the ball with me?" Jack asked without thinking. Kestra seemed shocked but happy at the question.

"Why not? it could be fun I guess." She gave him a kiss on the cheek and stood up. "I'll see you tomorrow then." She waved him goodbye setting off with a little skip in her step. Jack smiled to himself, maybe it wouldn't be so bad after all.

Chapter 17

The Christmas Ball

Jack woke early on Christmas morning; the end of his bed was crammed as his presents had arrived from his family and friends. He immediately tore into them. The wrapping paper was sent flying into all corners of the room. Joe had given him the latest Merlin's madness tour live orb. Michael a Dragon embossed scabbard for his sword. Kim a book on ball room dancing. She had written a note inside.

Have a wonderful Christmas,

Please save a dance for me later.

Hopefully, this will stop you stepping on my toes again.

Love Kim

xx

He stared at her note. The nook containing her love he would treasure he knew, forever. He continued to open the rest of his presents. Carol had given Jack a full encyclopaedia of council rules and regulations, stuck to it a promise to see him soon. His mother a new suit that

Jack thought he could wear to the Christmas ball. Whilst Louise had procured him a book on the life of Camelot pre-Arthur. He was grateful to them all, even Carol's books on council rules. He knew she meant well even if he never actually read them. He hoped his presents to his family were as well received as his own had been. Jack got up, he wanted to see the look on his friends faces after they had opened his presents.

"Excellent just what I wanted!" Michael screamed aloud, after hours of nosing around the shops in Camelot, Jack had found Michael a pair of around the hand Sycle's, he had got them cheaper through Donovan but didn't think he needed to know that. Louise was happy with her new silk coat. Kim had been a lot trickier shopping for though. Jack had been through every shop a dozen times over, every time that he found something that he might be able to give her, it wasn't available or when he found something it seemed far too romantic to give to a friend. He had eventually decided on a diamond necklace which said Kim.

"this is a bit extravagant don't you think Jack?" she asked in awe clutching onto them tight.

"hey, do you have any idea just how hard it is shopping for a girl, it's just diamonds perfume and lingerie, that's all you can get. And you have enough perfume." he pointed to a large pile of bottles in the corner of her room. "and as for the lingerie, I wouldn't have got to see you in it so what's the point?" Kim hit him laughing.

"well, thank you anyway. You have excellent taste for a boy. I am a little sad you didn't get the lingerie." she grinned.

"what?" Michael spluttered, Kim and Louise looked over at him dolefully. "and thank you, for your present as well Michael." she held up a cashmere sweater.

"think nothing of it, fashion has always been a strong point of mine." Jack almost chocked on his coffee.

"what's that supposed to mean?" Michael asked.

"nothing, I'm just remembering that Viking outfit you wore one Halloween." Jack laughed.

"What? Vikings were cool." he said a little hurt.

"yeah, Michael they were, but they never wore skirts." the four of them laughed heartily enjoying the Christmas spirit.

The whole day was spent with the trio laughing together, Michael was missing Louise she had gone home for the day, until the ball was due to start. All in all, the group had a great day Robin and Rachel had joined them at Christmas dinner.

"oh, thanks for the new aftershave." The only thing that was weighing on Jack's mind now was the thought of dancing with Kestra. As Michael had so rightly said before Jack was not the best dancer in the world. Through the day he had been reading the book Kim had got him hoping to pick up tips. He had even confessed his fears to his friends not wanting to make an idiot of himself.

"I mean it's not exactly like it's a date, it's a ball, we need partners, right?" Jack asked his friends.

"No, Jack it is a date that's sort of what you do, you ask someone there as a date, it's not like you're asking them if you can join them at breakfast is it? Even if you hope it leads to breakfast." Michael nudged him in the ribs

"I think what Michael is trying to say." Kim looked at Michael dangerously. "is that this girl, whomever she is, would be most disappointed if you didn't treat this as a date."

"well yeah, I guess so." he scratched his head hoping to find a way out of dancing. "come on Jack, you must fancy her otherwise why would you ask to take her?" Michael said, Kim stared at Jack.

"Is that why you asked her to the ball, because you liked her?"

"sure." Jack answered, "I mean why else would I ask someone?" He did not think about what he was saying. Kim blushed but said nothing.

"Jack, look at the time, we had best be getting ready."

Jack had already chosen what he wanted to wear; he had decided on the suit his mother had gotten him for Christmas. The suit was a three-quarter length black Jacket with a folded-up collar a small slit by the throat under which he wore a white t shirt, Jack was beginning to think he looked like a priest.

"I must be insane to be doing this," he was nervous again, the idea of dating wasn't new to Jack he had girlfriends before, it felt as though this was another level.

Michael was with Jack in the common room they were both waiting for Kim.

"come on Kim, just how long does it take for you to get ready? we've been waiting for hours." Michael screamed through her door.

"well, you can wait five minutes longer then." she screamed back.

"why does it always take women so long to get ready?" Michael asked.

"This coming from the man who started to get ready probably three days ago, if not longer." Michael held up his hands.

"hey, there's nothing wrong in wanting to look beautiful. If there is a god and he made me in his image, who am I to disappoint?"

"if vanity was a person, it would be named Michael."

"thank you." Michael laughed giving Jack a curtsey.

Kim poked her head around the door,

"ok, I'm ready."

"well come on then, let's have a look at you." Jack said, as Kim stepped out, he was again stunned at just how breath-taking she was. She was wearing a long silver dress with a slit up the side, it tied around the back of her neck. Her hair had returned to its familiar brown she had straightened it laying down to the small of her back. The diamond necklace he had gotten her for Christmas lay around her neck, sparkling gently.

"you look amazing Guin." Jack suddenly thought that his jaw had hit the floor.

"thank you, but who's Guin?" Kim asked him. Jack had done it again, saying something without thinking about it, something from the past.

"Don't worry about it, come on let's get going or my date is going to have a part of me on a silver platter that I rather she didn't." Michael winced.

"ouch, so who is she again?" he tried to weasel the answer out of him.

"I'm not telling you."

"why are you always so secretive about these types of

things?" Kim asked linking her arms through the two of theirs.

"I just don't want people to go shouting it around. Just wait for another couple of minutes and you'll see."

The ball was being held in the dining hall, it was the largest room in the castle and so best suited to hold the ball. The trio arrived and Jack spotted Kestra,

"so, where is this mysterious beauty then." Kim asked sounding a little bemused.

"wait here." Jack trotted off to grab Kestra.

"hi, you look amazing!" Jack gave a deep bow and kissed Kestra on the hand.

"such a gentlemen." Kestra flickered her eyelashes at him. Her deep green eyes splashed over Jack like waves of water, she seemed highly sophisticated in a long green dress, it was same as the one Kim was wearing. Her Auburn hair tied together and allowed to dangle down her shoulder. Kestra was drawing rather a lot of attention.

"Jack who is this then?" Jack closed his eyes praying for patience. Michael and Kim had snuck up behind them.

"Michael, this is my date Kestra. Kestra these are my friends Michael and Kim."

"it's really nice to meet you Kestra, I don't mean to sound rude." her voice warned of rudeness in almost every syllable. "but what house are you in? I don't think I've seen you around before." Kim asked sounding slightly aggressive.

"I don't attend school, I finished last year." A boy passing by walked straight into the nearby doorframe due to staring at the girls.

"oh, what class were you in when you were here then?" Kim asked a little unnerved

"I was in Lancelot." Kestra was clearly defensive. "well, shall we go inside then." She grabbed hold of Jack's arm pulling him away from his friends.

Once inside Jack was amazed the hall had been transformed from a dining hall into what looked like a palace of ice and snow.

"this is magnificent." Jack gasped trying to take in all that he was seeing. Icicles hung from the ceiling long and short whilst snow fell gently from the air never leaving itself on the gatherers below. The largest Christmas tree Jack had ever seen stood in the middle of the floor, ornately decorated with what appeared to be real dragon flies inside to provide the lighting.

"thank you, but I can't take all the credit."

"what?" Jack whispered in awe.

"I designed the décor for tonight, it's my job I'm a trainee architect. Merlin asked my father to talk me into it." it suddenly made sense to Jack why an over aged woman would have been at the school.

"so that's why you were here then? you were checking the decorations."

"you got it." she squeezed Jack's arm tight.

"so, who is your father then?"

"oh, here he comes now," she sounded a little worried. Jack looked around and to his horror he saw the one man he would never have wanted to see stare at him the way he was.

"Kestra, my darling, the hall looks wonderful, but I didn't realise you were bringing." The man looked Jack up and down disgust in his eyes. "a date." He finished.

"hello Mr Bravo, I must confess I didn't realise that Kestra." Jack was trying to sound polite and happy at the news she was Bravo's daughter,

"that's Miss Bravo to you." he snarled

"I'm sorry, I didn't realise that Miss Bravo was your daughter."

"How I believe you." Jack knew Bravo thought that he was lying and yet he didn't care. "Kestra dear, allow me to have a gentle word in the ear of young Jack here."

"oh no you're not, you're not scaring him away like every other boy I've ever been interested in." She pulled Jack away from Bravo he was rather relived he did not know how long he could keep in check if Bravo had tried to berate him again. "don't worry, you won't have to go around calling me Miss Bravo all night." Jack laughed thanking her. "well, shall we dance?" The four words Jack had been most dreading all night rang through him,

"sure, but let's grab a drink first ok?" Kestra agreed Jack was going to need as much Dutch courage as possible.

Jack danced as well as he could have possibly imagined. Even Kestra had complimented him on his moves.

"hey, I didn't know that you could throw shapes so well?"

"throw shapes? why is it that all intelligent girls seem to want to speak like some demented druid. It's called English people, let us speak it properly." Kestra smiled.

"I'm sorry, I guess it's just our way of trying to be cool." Jack held Kestra around her waist swaying gently to the music.

"see that's another thing, I don't understand why everyone wants to be cool, look at Michael he is regarded as one of the coolest people around, and yet most people also think he's an arrogant jerk. If that's what cool is meant to be, then I'm happy the way I am!"

"I'm happy the way you are too." she said giving his bum a cheeky squeeze.

Jack spent the next hour with Kestra dancing, finally almost exhausted they sat at a table with Kim and Michael, their dates nowhere to been seen. Kestra made her excuses saying she wanted to say hi to her mum leaving the trio alone.

"where's Lou and Ben then?" Jack asked,

"Ben is with his brother," Kim answered rolling her tongue.

"ok, what about Louise?" he turned to Michael

"oh, she's running late she shouldn't be too much longer; she met an old friend on the way back from her parents and is giving them a lift in." Michael was concerned with Kim. Jack felt guilty, it hit him like a lead balloon.

"are you ok Kim?" Jack gently stroked her arm.

"yeah, why shouldn't I be?" she answered glumly.

"well, I just meant with Ben being with his brother rather than you,"

"Jack, leave it." Michael said.

"no Michael let him finish, what do you mean Jack. Tell me are you saying that I'm not good enough for him or that I should be upset with the fact that he would rather spend time with everyone who isn't me?"

"Kim, calm down, I didn't mean anything like that, I'm sure he will be back in a second."

"oh, just shut up Jack you can never do anything right can you?" Kim stormed off.

"just how big is your mouth Jack?"

"big enough for my foot and yours I'm starting to think." Michael sniggered.

"Hello." Jack spun around, Louise was standing there. Michael eyed her hungrily. She wore a full-length dragon patterned red dress. Her hair blacker, than black seemed to highlight her eyes, drawing you in.

"Hi, would you like a drink?" Michael said standing up pulling out a chair for her to sit. With a slight bow of her head, she sat down.

"I'll leave you guys to it. Louise you look wonderful." She smiled at Jack before he disappeared into the crowd.

Jack sat alone at a table waiting for Kestra to finish with her mother, he could see Michael and Louise now on the dance floor. Michael had clearly been practicing in private. Kim had joined Ben and his brother her smile was clearly strained. Jack didn't know what Kim saw in Ben Mclambeth, true enough him and his brother were both good boy's, kind natured but the constant joke breaking and rule bending which had landed not only them but Michael and Jack in detention could become a little bit wearing. Jack waited for another half hour Kestra was nowhere to be seen tired of waiting he decide to see Kim and try to straighten things out between them.

"Kim can I have a word please?"

"in a minute, I'm finishing a conversation, wait over there and I'll come see you." she pointed to the furthest corner away from her.

'ok so she's still annoyed with me.' Jack thought. Kim

came over after a few minutes sitting down she pursed her lips making clear that she was not going to be easy on him.

"so, what did you want to talk to me about?" Jack turned around to face her with his shoe in his mouth. Kim let a grin cross her face.

"hang on just let me take my foot out of my mouth." he muffled.

"Jack you're such a bastard, here I am trying to be mad with you, and you make it impossible." she laughed

"I'll take that as a compliment. I just wanted to apologise to you, my choice of words earlier was poor to say the least."

"you shouldn't apologise for what you said, you're an idiot it's not your fault."

"is that a compliment I can't tell?" Kim laughed.

"so why are you on your own then where's Michael?" He pointed out their friends on the dancefloor.

"I think you asked me to save you a dance?" Jack asked holding out his hand. Ben Mclambeth walked over before she could answer. Jack could have strangled him for interrupting them.

"Hi Jack, great evening, Sorry but got to steal Kim for this dance." Kim smiled at Jack rolling her eyes.

"Save it for me please." She seemed a little sad as she left him, maybe he was just imagining it, wishful thinking.

"waiting for someone?" Kestra had come back.

"yes, a rather attractive young lady, I can't remember her name, don't suppose you've seen her, have you?" Kestra Laughed.

"I'm afraid I haven't, will I do instead?" Jack pretended to way up his options

"why not."

"charming." she laughed sitting next to him.

"it's a shame you know." Kestra sighed

"what's that then." he asked, "the fact that after tonight I'm not going to see you again." Jack smiled.

"I know, the time we have spent together I have really enjoyed, I would have liked to have spent more than tonight with you, but I suppose it wouldn't be a good idea to get to close now would it?"

"no, I suppose that it wouldn't be a good idea. But at least we still have the night, don't we?" Jack blinked unsure he had heard right.

"Jack, I'm a woman and you're a man. or at least so I remember" Jack grimaced.

"And I do like you so let's not waste what little time we are going to have together." she ran her finger in circle around his chest clasping his hand and lead him from the hall.

Chapter 18

The day after the night before

Jack awoke a beaming smile on his face, he rolled onto his side wanting to see Kestra, even if it meant risking her now un-brushed teeth. But she was not there, again a note was left in her place.

Jack

I hope that you are not disappointed to find
This note and not me, but I felt it best if we did not
See each other again after last night. It would be
Be better if we remember each other the
Way we were last night, rather than the morning after,
I hope I will see you again one day and thank you for a
Wonderful evening and an even better night.
until we speak again.
yours

Kestra
XXX

Jack folded the Letter carefully, he placed it on his desk not wanting to taint the memory of last night.
"Is there anyone more perfect than me?" Jack gloated to himself.

"Careful or you'll begin to sound like Michael."

"What the hell?" Standing in his doorway was Kim.

"Don't you ever knock?" Jack shouted pulling the duvet up to his neck.

"I've seen you topless before, and why should I knock it's not like you have anyone in here is it?" she asked looking around.

"No-one is here." Jack sat up straight in his bed.

"Are you sure, I don't want to interrupt anything." she said walking into his en suite.

"Kim, I'll save you the trouble of actually asking me, yes, I did bring Kestra back here, she has also left now ok?" He waved his arms around the room to demonstrate it was empty. Kim chewed on her bottom lip.

"I'm sorry, I didn't mean to upset you." She seemed to accept they were indeed alone closing the bathroom door.

"You haven't upset me? I just find it a little strange that you want to know about my sex life."

"Can't I take an interest in all aspects of your life, not just the life and death part's?" It was a good point they were after all friends. She should hold an interest in potential partners.

"ok, I didn't mean it like that. What about you did you and Ben..."

"No." Kim answered forcefully before he could even finish his sentence. "We didn't do anything like that." A relief spread through him, it felt like letting air out from a balloon.

"Why don't we go and see if the others are awake?" Jack wanted to get away from this line of conversation, Kim to seemed keen now that they had begun to discuss her evening with Ben.

Kim rapped on Michael's door,
"WHAT?" Came the groggy reply from within.
"We wanted to know if you wanted breakfast?" Kim asked. Inside they could clearly hear Michael and Louise discussing the situation.
"Yeah, all good, I'll meet you down there. After getting Louise from her room." Jack held back the laugh that had choked his throat.
"Ok mate, see you soon." Jack said shakily. Kim nudged him in the ribs.
"leave them to it, they both deserve to be happy." Jack couldn't agree more.

Louise and Michael eventually joined them for breakfast.
"You look like you didn't get much sleep." Jack ribbed Michael who glared at him.
"How was your evening then, I saw you disappear before the end?" Jack took the hint. Robin and Rachel joined then shortly after. They were still falling over each other at every moment. Jack had thought they would have settled down a little by now. Maybe they were the one in a million for each other.
"What's everyone's plans today then?" Jack asked, he was hoping to spend the day with his friends.
"I'm returning home for the holidays." Louise said a little sadly. Jack saw Michael clench her hand tightly. He still didn't know the full story behind her family, other than they were council members, but she had never appeared to regard them warmly.
"We are going to the theatre in the city later." Rachel

said excitedly.

"I've got Joust practice once Louise has gone." Michael groaned.

"What about you Kim? Doing anything. Meeting Ben?" Rachael squeaked as Robin was tickling her.

"No, he's a boy still, he got caught last night trying to set up another stupid prank. I would prefer to spend time with a man, not a child pretending to be one."

"I could loan your Robin for an afternoon. I just need him back before the play." They all laughed.

"Well, why don't we spend some time together? I'll even do my best manly impression for you." Jack flexed his arms dropping his voice to a deep growl. Kim laughing took his hand under the table.

"Well, I suppose I could lower my expectations for one day."

The group wished Louise goodbye; it would be a few weeks before they saw her again. Michael had soon disappeared off to the joust practice, he looked sullen. Jack felt sorry for whoever his training partner would be today. Robin and Rachel had decided to take a stroll around Camelot before the evening's entertainment, leaving Jack and Kim alone.

Jack suggested they spend their evening down at the boat house. Kim had gleefully agreed as the night sky would be crystal clear that far from the city lights. She told Jack to meet her down there as she wanted to grab something warm to wear.

The grounds were beautiful in the fresh snow. The Lake had frozen over, and the boat house resembled more of a log cabin with the roof covered in snow. Icicles stretched to the ground. On the lake Jack could see a couple ice skating. He could hear their laughter as they fell over again and again. On the edge of the forest a deer ate berries from a bush, its fawn nuzzled at the lowest branches. It was so tranquil this was the Camelot he had dreamed about when he came all those months ago.

In the distance Jack could see Kim walking through the snow towards him. He cleared the sheltered pods of snow and lit a small bonfire close to the seat. Two steaming mugs of hot chocolate sat on a table close by.

"Took you a little longer than I thought." Jack shouted playfully, warming his fingers over the fire. Kim was wrapped in a large woollen coat its hood pulled over her head so he could barely make out the person beneath it.

"It's freezing." She shook from the cold. Jack could have sworn he could hear her teeth chattering.

"Here." He handed her the hot chocolate as she stood by the fire warming up.

"You're always my knight in shining armour." Jack wrapped a heavy blanket around her shoulders.

"I told you a long time ago, you're my queen." He led her to the tear shaped pod, it was just big enough for the two of them. If they sat to the back the sides shielded them from the cold breeze. Kim snuggled in as far as she could, the red, velvet cushions were soft and inviting. With the fire stoked and plenty of wood chopped Jack sat back with her. She placed the blanket over them both and they sat in silence enjoying the warmth from their drinks.

Kim had cuddled into him their drinks long since

empty. They had talked at length about nothing at all. Jack was content with her company. Kim kept looking at him, there was a question in her eyes. She was searching his face for recognition of something, he could tell.

"What do you think of love?" The suddenness of the question caught Jack unguarded.

"Where did that come from?" he stalled.

"I see Michael and Louise and Robin and Rachael, they are happy. I just wondered why we can't find love. Unless you love Kestra, that is?" Her eyes narrowed watching his reaction like a hawk. "No." he conceded. "I don't love her. If I'm being honest, I think I was filling a need for her, she doesn't seem to want anything meaningful." He had never considered this. The two evenings they had spent together had always ended with her leaving so abruptly he hadn't time to consider his feelings.

"I thought that was the case." Kim was sad, she wrapped her arm around him more tightly. "Why do we never seem to find love?" she sighed. Jack watched as the deer from earlier edged their way towards the boat house to drink from the unfrozen rain barrel. Gerrard jogged past waving as he went.

"Who say's we haven't? maybe we are just afraid to be honest." Kim sat up straight her hawk like observation of his face resuming.

"Why would you be scared to tell someone though?" Kim had pulled away and was pressing against the wall of the pod. Her attention focused solely on him.

"When you're in love, just the sight of that person is enough to make you lose yourself. It feels like the air has been sucked from the room. You feel breathless, it leaves you shaking from just a touch. Men are taught to be tough, show no emotion. When a man say's he loves you and he *really* means it, he is giving you not only his heart, but his ego, pride and his devotion. They may not sound like the gifts you want, but these are ways to hurt him deeply. He is trusting you with his soul. I would sacrifice everything for the one that I love, without hesitation. What if you confessed that to someone and they laughed at you? if you then knew it would never happen. That's why I'm scared." He looked her in the eyes and could see the tears forming in her beautiful eye's, a sad smile on her face.

"Who do you love like that?" she quivered unable to look back at him.

"That's not something I want to talk about." Jack was desperate to tell her the truth, he ached from the weight of his love. He was tired from hiding this secret.

"why? not it's not like I don't know about everyone who you have ever dated." The stars had now come out, the light from the fire and the moon half white half fire illuminated her face. An ironic reminder of the heaven or hell of his possible future.

"I can't say, I promised you I wouldn't lie anymore." He could feel his body tensing, his leg was shaking uncontrollably.

"Why would you have to lie to me? I don't understand." She reached over and held his hand. Jack pulled his hand away his whole body now shaking. He felt like he was fighting himself, desperate for the words to come out.

"*Because it's you.*" He shouted, jumping from the pod. He lashed out at the fire kicking the embers scattering them across the snow. His breathing had become ragged and heavy, the pressure that had been building inside him now gone replaced by a numb fear. What had he done?

"Jack I-" Kim started, but was interrupted by a shout nearby.

"London." It was Melfice. Jack looked over at him, He was with about ten of his friends. Inwardly he prayed for the strength to hold his tongue.

"What do you want?" Jack could see the goons clenched and unclenched their fists, they were either getting ready for a fight or trying to intimidate him. Jack wasn't afraid of them; he was angry they had interfered at that moment.

"All alone are you, how romantic." Melfice was laughing, his friends laughed as well happy at the snipe.

"Well, you seem to be on a date yourself?" Jack pointed at his group. It wiped the smile from Melfice's face.

"You think you're so great, don't you?" He pushed himself into Jack's face, he didn't flinch. Jack could see from the corner of his eye the others beginning to surround him.

"I wouldn't say great, just better than you." Carefully Jack slipped his hand to the log pile feeling for a suitable branch.

"Melfice, just get lost." Kim had moved out from the pod her wand drawn.

"She's got more gut's than you. I think we will have to teach you both some manners." The smile on Melfice's face was pure malice. Jack understood why they had waited until now. It was dark, they were far from the castle and all their friends were either busy or away.

"Touch her and die." His hand was clamped on the log now, ready for the moment.

The Dark Heart

"Grab them." Melfice ordered.

Kim screamed behind him, a flash of light and a grunt of pain. One of the men lay crumpled on the floor. Jack swung the log as hard as he could. Melfice didn't have time to react, it landed square on his jaw. There was a satisfying crack and Melfice fell to the floor unconscious. Jack turned to Kim. One of the men had grabbed her from behind. Jack saw as she tried to pull away, the man ripped at her top tearing it. She fell in slow motion to the floor, her head bouncing off the ground. She lay still unconscious her wand had been sent flying from her hand; the man stood over her a disgusting look of desire on his face. Jack could hear the others rushing towards them hollering their delight. Something inside him snapped at the sight of Kim defenceless the men baying like animals. He could feel his rage swell inside like a storm, it built until he could stand it no longer bursting out like a shockwave. It threw the men to the floor, the boat house shook the snow from its roof. The windows blowing out. The men shielded their eyes from the snow and debris flying at them, only Kim remained unaffected her hair didn't even flutter. Jack's eye's had turned red and blue flames seemed to burn from his hands. The man that had grabbed Kim lay curled in a ball at his feet. Jack reached down and lifted him by the hair from the floor with one hand. The man screamed in pain thrashing around against Jacks grip. He could feel the hair tearing as the man swung helpless against him.

"You'll never touch her again!" He shouted over the swirling wind around him. Jack grabbed the man by the face and pushed him through the boat house wall. The roof collapsed down on the man. Anger had overtaken Jack these men had crossed a line and now they would pay. Behind him one of the other men had managed to battle against the storm raging around Jack, he smashed the log he had dropped across his back. It snapped in two like a twig. Jack turned to face him, his face a picture of horror.

"What are you?" he screamed. Jack grabbed him by the throat squeezing the life from him. Veins of black were crawling up his arm. He could see those still standing start to run away terrified by what they saw. A stuttering cough behind him made him drop the man. He didn't know if he was alive or dead, it didn't matter. Melfice had awoken, he knew what he needed to do. To protect Kim and Louise and everyone else. He walked over to Melfice grabbing him by his jacket pulling him upright. Melfice gurgled a scream at the sight of Jack. The black veins all but covering is skin now. The blue flames danced in the wind. Melfice's jaw was broken it hung limply. The sight would have normally horrified Jack, but now it filled him with a perverse thrill. He dragged Melfice to the end of the dock. Melfice kicked and punched each step of the way but it had no effect. Stomping down hard on the ice, it broke apart. Jack forced Melfice onto his knees his head inches above the frozen water.

"You will never touch our queen again!" Jack whispered into his ear. Melfice eyes bulged desperately pleading the words he could not say. Jack grinned teeth barred before thrusting Melfice's head under the water. He watched as Melfice thrashed his arms beating against Jack, trying to free himself.

"Jack stop!" Gerrard had appeared pointing his wand at him. He was horrified by Jack's appearance. "You're killing him, stop!" He ordered. Jack wasn't listening, he needed Melfice dead. It burned in him.

"Jack, please stop!" Kim's voice pleaded he turned to see her awake a cut above her eye. The black veins disappeared, and the flames died, his eyes returned to normal. Shaking, he released Melfice running to Kim, she recoiled as he touched her face. Was it from pain or something else? Gerrard pulled Melfice from the water he was barely breathing spitting out water, alive. It was then he heard the spell, he felt it hit him in the back and the dark descended on him.

Chapter 19

Solitary

Jack was taken to one of the schools unused towers and shut inside at the very top. Two knights had been sent to guard outside the thick wooden door. Heavy bolts were inset within the timber, each time it had been unlocked Jack could hear the metal grinding against the stone. They seemed to stretch into the wall, at least a foot. This was definitely a tower used for imprisonment, in the past. On the walls high out of reach torches lit the room. It was clear they hadn't been used in a long time. The metal brackets were rusted and broken, one of the torches was barely hanging in the cradle. The stone floor was broken in places, Jack guessed the previous occupants had spent time trying to break the floor to escape to the next level below. The walls had manacles attached at intervals, but again these had rusted to the point of being useless now.

One of the knight's told Jack that Melfice had been rushed to the infirmary, his jaw had been fixed and was expected to fully recover soon. Jack didn't care about Melfice recovering, he felt justified in defending Kim. What was worrying him was what happened to him during the fight. It was a little hazy, in his mind, he recalled the veins and fire. He had never felt hatred like that before and the power that had come with it.

"Jack London, stand." a knight shouted in through the bars in the door. Jack did as he was told, backing away into the shadows. The door opened slowly, and Grey walked inside.

"Close the door and go for a walk for two minutes." He told them. Reluctantly, the knight nodded. As soon as the door closed, he pulled Jack's school bag from behind him. "Your sentence has been decided." Grey threw the bag to the floor between them.

"Didn't the council want to hear my side of the story then?" Jack asked coldly.

"You nearly beat a group of men to death, and then in front of witnesses, tried to drown the son of two council members. From what Professor Gerrard tells me if it hadn't of been for Miss Illsley, you would have succeeded. He also reported you had a strange appearance, your hands were on fire, covered in black veins, strength and magical power that frightened him. You have no side of a story." Grey seemed wary of Jack now.

"What about Melfice? Have a punishment been decided for him?" Jack spat his anger flaring.

"Mr Trelane will not be punished…." Grey started to explain.

"What do you mean he wont be punished." Jack roared loudly. He heard the scuffling of boots heading back up the stairs.

"If you would listen for a moment instead of acting rashly, which was exactly my fear by the way. There is little evidence of wrongdoing by Mr Trelane or any of his apparent friends. All we have is your and Miss Illsley's word, they are telling a vastly different story about how you attacked them unprovoked. The fact you almost killed Mr Trelane and his associate has been taken as punishment enough." Grey tried to sound indifferent to the news, it was clear he didn't like it any more than Jack.

"What has the council decided for me then?" Jack wanted to speak of anything other than this, he knew Grey wanted to tell him he was right. He should have removed him from the school. How Jack was clearly a danger to the other pupils.

"They haven't, as the incident occurred at the school it is up to Merlin to decide your punishment. He was inclined to expel you and turn you over to the council. Thanks to Miss Illsley's testament though, I managed to talk him into reducing your sentence, you will spend the next six weeks in solitary confinement within this tower. I have taken the liberty of bringing some of your items, you will only have basic equipment and books, your lessons will appear in the centre of the room, as will your food each day. No one will see you and no one will speak to you for the next six weeks, do you understand?" Jack nodded he could see Grey keeping his distance from him, it was unnerving to realise people were now afraid of him. "Your sentence will start as soon as I leave, there is no point in calling out, no one will come." Grey backed away as Jack took a step forward. "I will try to help see if I can get the sentenced reduced, I can't be responsible for Arthur being locked away in his own castle. When this is over though we need to talk, when your released things can't go back to the way they were now." Grey turned to leave but Jack called out after him.

"Professor one minute please." He had this one

chance he knew he had to take it. "Please watch over Kim, make sure she is safe." Grey smiled sadly.

"I will watch over her, don't worry she will be safe." Grey left, bolting the heavy door behind him. Jack could hear as he and the two guards started to descend the stairs leaving him alone.

Grey had filled Jack's schoolbag with a few items from his room. It appeared he hadn't taken the time to empty its prior contents beforehand. Jack poured the contents of the bag onto the floor, he found two of his reference books, the orb of Merlin's Madness given to him at Christmas, his outstanding homework, his exam results he had never looked at, screwed up at the bottom of the bag, and a picture of his friends and family. Every time Jack looked at the picture it made him feel lonely. Somehow, the pictures of Kim made him more afraid. What was happening to him? what would happen when he saw Melfice again?

As each day passed Jack was increasingly eager for his schoolwork to appear, he had already spent hours listening to his orb and now knew each song by heart. Thanks to his studies with Kim, he was far ahead of his classmates and was learning advanced magic. Without his wand though, all his learning was theoretical. The silence of the tower made it perfect for meditation. There was nothing to disturb him here other than his own thoughts. The only other way he could occupy himself was with his reference books. He had taken the time to read about Camelot and the history of the tower. It seemed that Arthur had imprisoned many of his enemies in the same room. Jack felt sympathy for them, as horrid as his situation was, he was hardly in the discomfort they would have found themselves.

Jack threw down his schoolwork, in a moment like every day before, it would soon disappear along with his writing supplies. He looked to the reference books stacked beside the thin blanket he had been using as a mattress. The stone floor uneven, broken, cold as ice made sleeping impossible. He felt exhausted and irritable, the idea of returning to his research of Camelot only increased his annoyance. Instead, Jack found the only item he had not read so far. He grabbed up the scrawled piece of paper that was his exam results from so long ago.

Examination Results

Jack London

Scores are recorded out of 100

1 is the lowest score possible
100 is the highest possible.
Archery 87
Swordsmanship 88
Politics 20
Diplomacy 10
White Magic 100+
Dark Magic 100+
Charms 62
Curses 67
Metamorphosis 54
History 94

You are indicated to be in the top 0.1% of students for White and Dark magic. Your scores are recorded with a + as they went beyond what we were able to record. You are exceptionally strong in these attributes. You will benefit from advanced study in these subjects and should seek support immediately.

You are indicated to be in the top 5% for History. You are strong in this subject and would benefit from advanced study.

You are indicated to be in the top 10% for Archery and Swordsmanship. You could soon need advanced lessons to support your development.

You are indicated to be in the top 50% for Charms, Curses and Metamorphosis, given your indicated score in White and Dark magic it is likely, due to a lack of education in these subjects. Please arrange additional support from your teachers in order to progress to you expected top 10% level.

You are indicated to be in the bottom 10% for Politics and Diplomacy. This should be carefully monitored; you may wish to add additional study for these subjects if your score does not improve rapidly.

There must have been a mistake, he had expected high scores for Archery and Swordsmanship. Ben had spent hundreds of hours training them from the moment they were able to hold a weapon. History was a little higher than he had expected, although Politics and Diplomacy were about as bad as Jack had believed they would be. The scores for his magical power had to be wrong, none of his friends scored above 80 in white or dark magic. If he was so strong, how was it possible that Michael and Kim were so much better than him? Why was Louise the Dark Priestess and not he who was the Dark Priest? It didn't make sense the results had to be wrong.

The next two weeks dragged for what felt like forever; time seemed to have stood still. Jack felt like he was losing his mind. Between the revelation of his powers, his actions, attempting to kill Melfice and the isolation he felt that at any moment he would lose his final sense of rationality. When the sun faded through the tiny, barred window high above him Jack settled down to his meditation. He had managed to dislodge the torch from the broken cradle and was using it to keep warm.

Attempting to calm his mind, Jack closed his eyes. He could feel the warmth of the flames near to him. The orange glow of the flames danced through his closed eyelids. In his mind visions of blue flames and black blood formed. It had been the same as his dreams every night now. He shook them away.

'Calm your mind.' Jack reminded himself stern. He allowed himself a moment to think of Kim. Her blonde hair dancing as she walked. The sweetest smell of vanilla when she leaned into him. The eyes that seemed to capture the essence of her soul. All other thoughts faded away, the beacon of his calm and tranquillity held like a torch keeping the dark at bay. He allowed for the image of Kim to fade away into a velvety blackness. He could feel the cold lifting from him. The feeling of the stone floor was now forgotten. He felt like he was floating in a dark void, seeking out an inner light. He knew, if he could find it, there would be Draxon waiting to talk with him. Jack breathed deeply focusing for the light. In the distance of his mind, he felt a tug something pulling at him. Concentrating harder on the tug he could feel it moving closer to him. He was excited now; it was

The Dark Heart

so close. Soon he would hear the voice of Draxon he knew it.

'Please speak to me.' Jack pleaded inwardly, then it happened a voice close to his own answered him back.

'Hello.' It was the same voice that had spoken to him before.

'Are you what has been speaking to me?' Jack was concentrating as hard as possible.

'Yes, it is me. I haven't been able to talk to you in what has felt forever.' The voice sounded happy to be heard. Jack couldn't believe it. He had wondered if he would ever truly get to this point. He was speaking directly to his avatar. Only the strongest of wizards were able to do this. Something that had evaded all his friends so far.

'What stopped you from talking to me? Did I upset you?' Jack wanted to know why he didn't want to lose this connection now if he could help it. This was the first time he had spoken to someone in weeks even if it was technically himself.

'You didn't upset me.' The voice laughed. 'No, you interfered with our connection when you tried to summon your avatar.' Jack was confused.

'I thought you were Draxon?' If this wasn't his avatar what the hell was talking to him?

'No, I'm not an avatar. There is no need to be anxious. I can feel it swelling within you. I'm a part of your life from long ago. I'm the piece of Arthur you hold within you, passed down within your bloodline.' The voice was calm and soothing. 'I have passed down through your family, I have existed in all of them, I know all they know.' Jack could almost feel the voice smiling at him.

'This isn't possible, why are you in my mind? does everyone's previous lives pass down their bloodline?'

there were so many questions.

'I'm afraid not, the members of the round table were bound to their descendants. Merlin realised that one day they may need to return. Your friends contain the memories of their former lives, as do you. They may have begun to remember details through their dreams. Only you though, hold inside your former spirit.' Jack suddenly remembered the conversation about Michaels dreaming about Louise. The voice of Arthur was telling the truth, how many others were there.

'Why can I hear you though? my father didn't hear you.' Jack needed to understand, with the recent transformation during his attack Jack was terrified his dark heart was taking over.

'That is a reasonable question, one I think you know the answer to already.'

'Devaldros.' Jack felt a chill run through his body almost breaking his concentration. He had started to feel the cold air sweep back into the room.

'We are connected now, there is no need to meditate anymore to speak with me. When you attacked that boy and his friends you broke through barriers in your mind. Before this I was only able to whisper to you. Now with that barrier gone, we can talk freely.' Jack opened his eyes; he was in the tower the torch burning before him.

'Are you still there?' He thought.

'I am here, like I said we are connected now.' Arthur's voice carried through his mind. 'I know you are afraid, and I know why, being strong in dark magic's doesn't mean you are a bad person. Look at your friend, you don't believe her to be evil' Arthur was right Jack knew Louise was a good person, she had been just as afraid of her dark magic as he was.

'Louise has never had flames cover her, and wanted to kill someone though.' Jack reasoned.

'What you did whilst unorthodox was understandable. If I had to guess I would say in your anger you tapped into some primal magic, it isn't an unheard of. On the battlefields, I saw some truly shocking moments of magic, when someone was at their most desperate. Afterall how do you think avatars were first discovered, it was someone in a moment of desperation calling upon something inside to protect them. You were desperate in that moment, that boy wanted what was yours, all you did was to protect her.'

'Kim isn't mine; she doesn't belong to me.' Jack snapped.

'No, she doesn't belong to anyone, but you wish she were your queen. You may not consider her yours; he obviously does, he thinks that she is yours, and that is why he wants her.' Arthur seemed to know what Jack wanted better than he did. It was as though being inside Jack's mind allowed him access to all his thoughts.

'Yes, I do want her to be with me. I love her and won't let that scum near her again!' He vowed.

I'm afraid it isn't as simple as you think. Dark forces are returning, you have seen it for yourself.' Jack remembered Michael and Louise laying in the infirmary lucky to be alive.

'You're talking about Devaldros.'

'Yes, I am needed again in the world. You may not realise but as you grow stronger so do I. I fear there will come a point when we can no longer inhabit the same body. If you do not summon me, we will both die.' The wind blew hard around them causing the torch to spit and crackle.

'What do you mean summon you? Do you mean like an avatar?' Jack didn't understand, an avatar would still be bound to its owner. How would that stop them from dying?

'No, as I have said, I'm not an avatar.' For the first time Arthur sounded annoyed. 'We can work together to remove my soul from your body. We can use ancient magics to recreate my body. We will be separated no longer sharing your body. I can ensure that your queen is never hurt again. You will not need to be King. I can take the weight of the crown from you. I can finally finish the war that started centuries ago. Together we can find your fathers killer.' It was exactly what Jack wanted, none of the responsibility of the crown. The woman he loved protected and justice for his father.

'How can I summon you? I have no wand no wand. Even if I did, I don't know how to summon you back into the world.' Arthur laughed.

'Whilst certain words hold power in ancient rituals, most magic is not dependant on words or wood. Wands are not magical. They do not produce magic; they were a training tool Merlin devised to teach children to focus their abilities. Let me ask you a question, does everyone around the world use the same word to produce a spell?'

'Well, no, they all speak other languages.' Jack conceded he had never considered this before.

'Exactly magic comes from within, words and wands are to help you focus your own ability. Once you have done this, you have no need for either. I can teach you to not need a wand to access your magic. I can teach you to summon me. For that you will need to remember the ancient language, to speak the incantations, but the magic to perform the spells are within you, always. Help me to protect this world and your queen.' Jack plucked up the torch from the floor and stood. He didn't have an option, Arthur needed to be reborn. He knew that only he could face Devaldros.

'Ok, please teach me.'

The next week Jack had spent either meditating, trying to centre himself or practicing magic without a wand. So far, he had been able to perform magic he would have considered almost impossible. He had managed to duplicate his blanket several times. Enough so that he now had a suitable thick mattress and blanket. Create fireballs from his hand. Transform a broken piece of the stone floor into a diamond and repair the torch bracket above him. Arthur seemed pleased with the progress they had made so far; he had tried to teach him levitation but so far that had only resulted in Jack falling on his face several times. He had begun to remember spells which he had never heard of. Battle tactics for knights, long lost to time. His memories of being Arthur were now starting to intermingle with his own, the ancient language of the gods had begun to make sense.

For the first time in his life, Jack could sense his strength, his power was focused like never before. Arthur seemed a far better teacher than the professor's, everything stuck in his mind. Jack believed that he could do this, he could summon Arthur.

Sleep had become a welcome relief from the efforts of the day. Jack had collapsed onto his newly comfortable bed. A night of dreams filled with scenes of balls and

Kim beckoned to him. He had barely drifted off before a scraping outside the tower door awoke him. A shaft of light illuminated through the bars for a second before disappearing.

"Who's that?" Jack shouted his voice cracked, barely audible through lack of use. No one responded, tentatively Jack looked through the small window into the tower's hall. He could just make out two people standing in the shadows, but it was hard to make out who in the din.

"Enjoying your little holiday?" The sneer in the voice was unmistakable it was Melfice. The figure standing behind him moved closer, whispering something in Melfice's ear, before sneaking away under the cover of shadow. Stepping forward, Jack could now make out the features of the face he loathed so much.

"It's great." Jack coughed clearing his throat. "I was enjoying the peace. What do you want?" Melfice pressed his face to the bars a smile curled on his lips.

"I wanted to let you know what's about to happen. I want you to sit here and know there is nothing you can do to stop it." His smile drawn broader still.

"What are you on about?" Jack could feel his pulse beginning to race. Melfice had a plan, and he was right, in here there was nothing he could do to stop him. His wandless magic wasn't strong enough to get him out from here yet. "Let's just say, I have some unfinished business with your queen."

"*Leave her alone.*" Jack shouted so loudly he was sure it would wake the castle, he rammed against the door it didn't even shake. Melfice seemed unabashed.

"Not now. Now, I know it kills you I'm going to make sure you know and remember every detail of what I

The Dark Heart

have planned. Don't worry, it might even make an orb. Goodbye for now." Melfice mocked laughing, Jack reached through the bars grabbing Melfice by the throat. He could feel Melfice struggle against his grip, his eyes widening at the shock, gasping for air. Melfice desperately grabbed for something out of sight. Too late Jack realised it was his wand, Melfice managed to hit him with a spell, knocking him unconscious on the floor.

His head ringing Jack was woken by Arthur screaming in his head. Sitting up straight Jack ran his hand over his forehead a little blood had seeped across his hand.

'I should have killed him.' Jack groaned.

'You have more important things to worry about, you have been unconscious for at least twenty minutes now. And he will probably be about to set his plan for your queen in motion.'

'*Kim*' Jack shouted remembering Melfice's threat, but it was no good there was no way he would be able to get a warning to her, stuck in solitary confinement unless. Panicking he formed a fireball in his hand throwing it at the door. It didn't even scorch the wood.

'It's no good, this tower has powerful enchantments to stop such things.' Arthur tried to calm down Jack.

'Do you think I can summon you?' Jack asked desperately.

'Maybe, but the effort involved might kill you, we need more time to train you.' Arthur warned.

'I don't care.' Jack pleaded; death was a price he was willing to pay for her. 'You must protect Kim!' Jack was not sure if he could pull this off but if there was the smallest chance that this could help Kim then he would take it.

'Very well.' Arthur seemed unsure, but agreed to Jacks condition. This was the only way it could be.

Jack's heart was racing, he needed to calm down. Sat on the stone floor, a chill ran up his spine that had nothing to do with the cold. Slowly he began to whisper the incantations taught to him by the spirit, his voice barely audible over the howling wind now ravaging the outside of the tower. Louder and louder, he spoke the words. Jack did not understand the meaning of what he spoke, his memory of the language still not perfect. The pace increased as Jack fretted that he would not be in time. The louder Jack said the spell the fiercer the storm became the tower slowly began to rock; the walls seemed to whisper back to Jack giving him the feeling that he was not alone. The spell was working though he knew. He continued to shout as the wind whipped around the tower, it felt as though it was about to tear from the castle itself, swaying dangerously in the wind.

'It's working I can feel it.' Jack ignored Arthur he knew it would. Lightning struck the tower a shower of sparks poured down on Jack. Parts of the roof having been lifted away from the stormed raging outside. He ignored them, not letting anything distract him. Jack Screamed to be heard over the roaring winds and crashing thunder. Another bolt of lightning struck the tower, this time instead it passed through the ceiling, striking Jack's chest.

Pain a thousand times over passed through Jack in a second his mind felt as though it was being torn in two.

'This is it, concentrate.' Arthur shouted jubilantly. Jack

was trying but his mind seemed to be scattered. He was attempting to pull the fragments together, but it was difficult just to keep the remaining intact, it felt like he was trying to catch water with his hands. Another bolt hit Jack, his mind was even more disarranged, but now it was his body that was being torn and not just his mind. Jack gasped for air, he could not breath. He punched the floor trying to regain a sense of reality. His hand sunk into the floor an inch. There was so much power escaping through his body the entire castle shook from the punch.

'Help me.' Jack screamed inwardly the pain all consuming.

'Just hang on, a few more seconds.' Arthur shouted back. Jack gritted his teeth he did not know how long he could hold on, but if it meant saving Kim he would die trying.

The storm outside faded, the tower stopped swaying. Broken timber cracked and the tower settled once more. Jack lay on his face, his breathing shallow. He felt like he would die any moment. Had he succeeded had he managed to accomplish the impossible. Slowly he opened an eye and watched as a blue flame seemed to crawl from under his skin onto his hand, he could feel the heat but there was no pain. Flames were now engulfing his entire body, he thought he would soon burn, but then they began to spread from him. The heat becoming unbearable, the more it was removed from him. Slowly the fire began to coalesce just feet away from him. Jack slumped onto his face the cold stone stinging against his skin. Exhausted, body aching, he could barely keep his eyes on the blue flames that seemed to be forming into a body. He watched as it stretched out its arms, stretching fingers that hadn't existed for centuries. Jack felt relief he had managed to summon Arthur. Kim would be safe; he had even survived the effort if barely. The figure leaned over Jack placing his blue flamed hand onto his back, it burned.

'Thank you, Arthur, for releasing me from my prison.' He hissed coldly. Jack coughed barely able to make out what was being said.

"What do you mean Arthur? You are Arthur." he panted coughing blood as his skin hissed from the heat.

"Yes, I am, but I also go by another name." The figure forced Jack flat to the floor pinning him. His mouth broke into a grin showing fangs rather than teeth. Its dark red eyes seemingly piercing into Jack's soul. 'I'm sure by now you are realising who I really am." Panicking Jack couldn't think straight.

"You are Arthur, you're going to save Kim, you said." The figure laughed at him; Jack tried to fight against he, but he had no strength left.

"I told you I am the part of Arthur that passed down through your family. I'm the dark heart of Arthur, the side of him he tried to remove. I'm Devaldros." What was happening? how could he be Devaldros?

"No, that can't be true." Jack desperately wracked his brain he must have heard wrong. The ritual messed with his mind. It was Devaldros that had attacked his friends how could he have done that if he were within Jack?

"Are you starting to understand now? I have been imprisoned within your mind all this time. Only occasionally able to take control. Your father wanted to warn you, he knew you had the strength to bring me

The Dark Heart

back. So, I had you kill him with his own sword. I made you attack your friends; Le Fay's potion could have ruined everything." Devaldros leaned in and whispered into Jack's ear, he delighted in revealing to him all his involvement. It was as though Jack's pain and anguish tasted delicious to him, an appetiser to be savoured.

"How did you know about the potion though?" Jack watched through tear-stained eyes, as the veins on Devaldros' face began to engorge, black blood seemed to be filling them. It was with horror, he recognised the sight as how he had appeared when fighting Melfice.

"I knew, because you knew, I know everything that you know. You don't yet realise how involved I have been in your life." Devaldros shoved down hard pushing himself up to stand. Jack felt a rib snap against the stone floor. It was nothing to the feeling of the searing heat slowly leaving his back. His hands and teeth clenched in pain, he screamed in agony. Jack couldn't resist, he had no energy to do anything, even move.

"I don't believe you. I would never have hurt my friends or my father. You're lying." Jack spat with what little energy he had. Devaldros growled his displeasure the blue flames surrounding him burned a little brighter.

"I haven't lied to you once, if you don't believe me, let me tell you more then. It was me that nearly killed the Councillors son, I took control of you whilst you and that girl slept. A simple message to those in the council. I forced you to collapse when you and Grey were discussing your father, I couldn't risk him revealing too much to you at that time. I lead you to prison in your dreams, you broke away at your own protection giving me even greater control, you remember that dream I told you then, you were mine." Jack did remember the horrible nightmares that had followed. The red eyes in the pillar staring at him. The feeling of something piercing the back of his skull. "All I needed was something to really push you over the edge, break those final barriers in your mind. Talk to you, rather than whispers in your ear. And then it came, you attacked that boy Melfice, you wanted to kill him. That moment born of hatred broke the last barrier it was me who gave you that power. I was the one who allowed you to protect our queen."

"No." Jack groaned, what had he done? "Why?" It was a childish question and Devaldros laughed at it.

"Why? To be reborn, to rip away everything you hold dear. To take your queen as my own." Jack stared into the face of Devaldros, long black hair hung across his red eyes, but it was his own face staring back at him.

"Leave her out of this. Kill me and be done with it. But leave her alone!" He begged, but Devaldros put his foot on Jack's head, pinning it between the floor and the tread of his boot. Jack cried out it felt like he was breaking in two.

"I haven't decided what I want to do with you yet. Don't worry our queen will be safe, no harm will come to her." Jack could hear a sudden strain in Devaldros' voice. It was as though he was weakening, the flames, which had burned so brightly and hot had begun to fade. "Merlin's magic at play." Devaldros said to himself looking at the fading flames. It appears, outside of your body, I can only be in this place so long. The fool, he should have known better than to think that would stop me. We will see each other again soon Arthur, I promise you that." Devaldros turned passing through the door as

The Dark Heart

if he were made of mist, Jack was left alone on the floor broken.

Chapter 20

It Begins

Jack crawled across the broken tiles and stone floor to his bed. He was showered in dust and rubble, his skin scorched from Devaldros' touch. He lay in shock at what had just happened his breathing shallow from his broken rib. Was it all true, had he killed his father? Had he attacked his friends? Deep down he knew it was. Everything made sense now. He was terrified by what could be happening as he lay there powerless to stop it. No one knew Devaldros was back. None seemed to know anything about him. How dangerous he was. Right now Kim and his friends would be sitting there unaware they were in terrible danger.

His only hope was in what Devaldros had said about only being able to stay so long in Camelot. Perhaps here they were safe, but what of his family, Carol was in Dublin and his mother may be home at the henge. Who knew where Joe was stationed now? He has no way to alert anyone. It would be a week before he could say anything or check on Kim.

Had Melfice been lying when he had come to his cell. Was he involved with Devaldros somehow? Jack thought it more likely not, he couldn't imagine Melfice would have allowed himself to be beaten almost to death as part of some grand plan. Devaldros had used

The Dark Heart

the situation to his advantage. He had said no harm would come to Kim though, could he believe that? He lay back attempting to concentrate on his rib, hoping what Devaldros had taught him about wandless magic still worked.

Jack counted down the minutes until his release. He waited, coiled ready for the moment his time would be up. It had taken several days but eventually his rib had healed. It seemed the power he had felt when training was indeed his own, not supplemented by Devaldros as he had feared. The door clicked open, and Jack sprang up, running for the Arthurian common room. He raced down the steps of the tower three at a time crashing against the walls barely maintaining his footing. He burst through the heavy wooden door at the bottom and ran straight into Michael.

"Finally." He pulled Jack into tight hug. Kim was stood beside him, as soon as Michael had released him, she launched at him holding him tightly. Jack held her tighter than he ever had before, she was here safe. He looked at her beaming smile,

"Are you ok?" he asked desperate for her to tell him what he needed to hear.

"Of course, we've been waiting for you all morning." She clung back to him. It seemed Devaldros had kept his word.

"I need to speak with Grey, and you guys need to come with me." Jack said once he had finally allowed himself to let go.

"Don't you think it can wait, maybe have a shower and get changed first." Jack looked down at his clothes they were tattered and ripped. Blood stained his top; he knew that he smelt horribly also.

"It can't wait Louise. We need to go now." They could hear the fear in his voice.

"Ok, let's go see Grey." Kim waved her wand over him the dirt lifted off his skin, for the first time in six weeks the smell of soap filled his nostrils. Normally he would have enjoyed the sensation but now he just needed to get this over with.

"Professor, are you in?" Michael called knocking on the door. Jack clutched at the wall for support he felt disoriented from the noise of the castle. Students passed by the group whispering as they saw him. Someone spat at him as they passed.

"Come in." Grey called. Kim pressed Jack inside first. Michael followed, Louise pushing him in as he shouted at the student who spat at Jack.

"Jack, I'm surprised to see you so soon. I thought you would have wanted to get some rest?" Jack sat in a chair by the fire, and turned his back to them all, he wouldn't be able to look at them whilst he did this.

"We all need to talk. You need to send for our families immediately and bring them to Camelot." He could feel their silent eyes on his back.

"What's going on?" Kim placed her hand on his shoulder.

"Please don't." he said. "I don't deserve your sympathy." Kim didn't remove her hand.

"Jack, I know why you did what you did to Melfice, what I don't understand is how you did it?" Michael said.

"It was Devaldros, he gave me the power." He felt Kim's hand tighten on his shoulder.

"I think it best if we continue this alone." Grey said quickly.

"No." Jack said with a finality. "You all need to hear this. Devaldros is back, I released him, everything is my fault. You need to bring our families here now. Everyone we love is in danger."

Grey had reappeared moments later, he had rushed off to send word to bring their families to safety within Camelot. None of his friends had said anything.

"Do you understand what you have done?" Jack understood and did not need Grey telling him.

"Yes, I know." Jack replied.

"I don't think you do Devaldros is a creature of pure evil, only at the cost of his own life did Arthur defeat him. Humanities only hope was to keep him contained and you've let him free." Grey's fury was palpable, it was nothing to what was building inside Jack. He swallowed hard keeping it in check.

"Is he connected to me still, would killing me help?" His friends gasped horrified.

"No, it wouldn't do anything to him now." Grey admitted.

"You should have killed me the moment you saw me. Because you knew all along." Jack wasn't accusing Grey he already knew the truth.

"I had my suspicions. You're right I probably should have killed you." Grey leant on his desk and rubbed his eye's he suddenly seemed old. Older than Jack had ever seen him before. Michael roared in anger at Grey's admission.

"What the hell are you talking about? Killing Jack, are you mad?" Louise held Michael back as he had jumped at Grey.

"We will get through this together." Kim shot at them both. Grey shook his head in despair.

"It's not that simple."

"It is that simple we are stronger together." Louise held Michael tightly.

"You are all so different now." Grey muttered despite himself. They looked at him confused but Jack understood. Finally, freed from Devaldros' influence his dreams had stopped trickling memories to him, they had come like a flood. Arthur's life was almost entirely entwined with his own.

"Why was Devaldros in Jack that's what I want to know." Michael asked.

Someone knocked on the classroom door. Grey opened it speaking the person outside.

"I have been summoned by the headmaster, wait here, I shall be back soon."

Grey returned within the hour. It had been a horrible silence the whole time. Jack could feel the questions burning on his friend's lips. Too scared to ask him, was it fear of upsetting him or of what the answer might be that kept them from speaking? he didn't know.

"Jack, there's something I need to tell you." He looked up at Grey who had a determined look on his face.

"I'm not leaving, the damage is done now. I can help, I need to help correct this." Jack pleaded. Grey closed his eyes he seemed to be preparing himself for what he was about to say.

"Jack, it has nothing to do with your staying or leaving, it's about your sister." he jumped to his feet.

"What about Carol?" The familiar feeling of nausea

The Dark Heart

swarmed him.

"I have just been informed that she is missing." Grey explained, his voice tinged with regret.

"For how long has she has been missing? What's happened." Jack's voice broke and the tears poured freely, it was as he feared.

"The council training college in Ireland was destroyed a few hours ago, your sister's body hasn't been found." Michael fell into his chair; Jack knew he also had family at the college.

"What do you mean by body?" Jack felt sick, his chest tight barely able to breath.

"Fifteen bodies have been dragged from the rubble so far, I'm afraid they were all dead." Louise let out a small shriek of horror. It was nothing to what he felt at that moment.

"Do they know who has died? How many in total?" Michael was on the verge of being sick. Louise held his hand's her face buried into them.

"I don't know." Grey was just as agonised as any of them. Kim was silently crying in the corner, Jack wanted to run and hold her, but he was unable to move. He felt locked in place like a statue.

"How though? The college is one of the most well protected buildings in the world. It can't be true." He looked at Grey longingly he was desperate for him to tell him it was a lie. He knew he couldn't Devaldros had come to the college had come for his family. "Have the rest of our families been brought here like I told you?" Grey shook his head.

"Not yet, they are still being gathered, some like your mother are refusing to come. She told my men she will wait at the house in case Carol appears." Jack opened his mouth to object but Grey cut across him. "I have powerful people watching over her as we speak. I promise they would die rather than let Devaldros near her." Powerful people Jack scoffed inwardly.

"Devaldros is more powerful than anyone, you said it yourself." He doubted they would be more than an irritant. Grey had been afraid of Jack when he had a small portion of Devaldros' strength.

"He is strong, but I doubt he will be at full strength yet, and there are people far more powerful than this school's Merlin and they're protecting your family now." Grey tried to sound confident, but his face betrayed him.

"Who is more powerful? Stop this cloak and dagger crap." Jack ordered he was tired of the games. Grey scratched at his chin he peered at them all before relenting.

"Maybe it is time for you to know, Jack there is a group called the Elders they were founded by the one true Merlin. We have lived since the time of Arthur. It was our duty to stop Devaldros at all cost. But as you now know we have failed." Grey was mournful, he summoned a drink to his hand and offered one to each. Michael took his swirling it around absently. Jack without thought held out his hand. The glass flew across the room into his open palm. The group looked at him in amazement but didn't say anything. Again, Jack had turned to the fire considering what Grey had said.

"Why haven't we ever heard of these elders?" Kim snapped bringing the group out of their reverie.

"The council would need to know of our existence. Merlin created our group in secret from the council and from the Knights. He knew that overtime they could become corrupt." Grey couldn't hide the bitter tone aimed at the council. Jack guessed he thought that if they hadn't been corrupted then they could have helped stop Devaldros.

"Are you as a group powerful enough to stop him?" Louise asked hopeful.

"No." Grey admitted, he wanted them to understand this before speaking again. "Jack we may be able to hold him back for a while, but you must understand that he is more powerful than any of us, he's going to be stronger than he was at the time of Arthur, and he's going to be coming for you." All eyes fell upon Jack, Kim seemed to pull further away from him. He felt contaminated by Devaldros.

"Why though. If you can't stop him why am I important enough for him to bother with. I'm not Arthur." Jack threw his glass into the fire it roared higher than before. Quickly he calmed himself afraid of what the others would think now of his anger.

"I think and you need to understand I am alone in this, that you may still be a threat to Devaldros you are after all, of Arthurian blood and you were connected in spirit, maybe our only chance." Grey's voice was drawn quiet he had not real conviction in his tone.

"I guess were thinking the same thing. The world is screwed."

Chapter 21

A Loved One Lost

Jack paced the floor tormented over the fate of his sister, two days had passed since the incident at the college and the last of the bodies had been dug out of the rubble, a news orb had said that several of the bodies found appeared to have been murdered before being buried in the explosion, twenty-six bodies had been discovered in all, three were official council members who had been visiting the college. Grey had told him it had left a weakness within the council that Devaldros would look to exploit.

Jack was to return home to see his family that afternoon. He wanted desperately to see his mother and brother to make sure they were indeed in good health physically if not mentally. Michael had come to see him before he was meant to leave to see how Jack was coping with everything.

"How are you?" He inquired tentatively. The news of Carols apparent abduction spread quickly throughout the school. No-one other than themselves knew who was responsible.

"I'm coping what about yourself?" Michael's cousin had been in the college at the time of the explosion, he had been confirmed as one of those that died. It had hit

Michael rather hard as the two had gotten on very well.

"I'm ok, just finding the last few day's a bit difficult to take in you know?" Jack could not bring himself to look at Michael, so many people had already suffered because of him. He wondered how many more would have to.

"Do you know how Kim is?" Since they had left Grey's office, she had locked herself away in her room. Jack longed to talk with her.

"No-one knows, she hasn't come out of her room since we came back. I asked Louise to try and speak with Kim, but she didn't have any luck either." It was as he had feared, she rightfully blamed him. A feeling of inward dread crashed over him like a wave he felt like he was drowning in the guilt. "I need to ask you something." Michael mulled over his wording. "Did I see you use magic without your wand?" Jack remembered back to taking the drink in Greys room.

"Yeah, it was something he taught me." Jack closed his eyes disgusted at how he had considered Devaldros his teacher. "You don't need a wand to perform magic, although ill be keeping mine for now. Its just more natural at the moment." Jack explained, with effort he managed to make his bed by rolling his hand over it. He knew it was stupid to continue to use his wand now he knew the truth, it somehow felt more natural though. Until he was fully in control of wandless magic he would still rely on his old methods.

"Take care of Kim for me." Michael shook Jack's hand.

"I will do, but we should be safe here in Camelot from what you say. If you need me, I'm here for you. As soon as you hear anything about Carol let me know."

A bell rang inside the room it was time to leave for home.

"I have to get going mum needs a lot of support at the moment." he turned to Michael and shook his hand. "I'm sorry Michael." he smiled softly at Jack

"it's not your fault mate, no matter what I know you think you didn't do this." Jack's stomach dropped like a stone, no matter what Michael said he was wrong. This was Jack's fault and nothing anyone said otherwise would change that.

Grey had convinced Merlin to allow Jack to use his personal Diasis to travel home. As he walked the length of the school people stopped to stare at him like he was a leper. Most did not even bother to disguise their interest. By the time Jack had reached the corridor outside Merlin's office he had had enough, half the school seemed to have followed him into the corridor. Finally, sick he turned on them.

"Take a picture, it will last longer." He shouted most of the group turned away pretending they had not been following him. At the back of the group, he could see Melfice smirking at him. He longed to go and take out his anger on him, but he knew what would happen if he did. Right now, it was more important to get home. He needed to protect his mother however he could. Devaldros would be coming for her he knew it, and he couldn't do anything to help if he was behind bars.

The familiar sensation of the Diasis pierced Jack as he collapsed on his hallway floor his first sight was a little shocking his house normally exemplary kept seemed to be in a state of disarray, his house looked like a war

The Dark Heart

zone, chairs, plates, even a mirror lay broken on the floor.

"*Mum.*" Jack shouted worried.

"oh god Jack." Emma came running out almost tripping over the broken chair. "Jack is that you?" she grabbed him hugging him as hard as she could, she kissed him several times on the head before she let him go. "how are you?" she said through a well-used handkerchief. Jack could still see the tear stains on her face.

"I'm ok." Jack lied. "what's happened here?" he gesticulated around the room.

"It doesn't matter," Emma tried to remove Jack's attention from the mess.

"No, it does matter you have enough on your mind without this, who did this?" Jack pressed her.

"I don't know." Emma broke down in tears for what was clearly not the first time that day.

"When did it happen mum? it's very important." Jack was trying not to arouse her suspicion.

"Sometime today, I got back a few minutes before you arrived, I had taken Galahad to the neighbours. They won't let me bring him to Camelot." Emma seemed different to Jack all the fight that she had always been renowned for seemed to have been sucked out of her.

"Mum, wait here I need to speak with someone I'll be just outside don't worry ok, put the kettle on and we'll have a cup of tea. And then I'll tidy up you would be amazed at what I can do with a broom these days." she chuckled wetly as Jack held her shoulder trying to share the responsibility that she had taken on for so long.

"Ok, just don't be long." she sniffed.

Jack walked into the field next to the Henge, he pulled a strange looking whistle from his pocket he placed it in his lips and blew hard. Two hooded figures appeared from the hedgerows. One of them was shaking his head trying to quieten the ringing in his head.

"Jack, there is no need to blow that hard." it was Kaiba how could Jack not have guessed that he was one of the elders.

"I suppose I shouldn't be surprised to see Levell under the other hood." the figure removed their hood it was in fact Nefarious, the elf that had been protecting Michael when he was in the hospital.

"I'm afraid Levell isn't one of us young London." he said as though it ended the conversation.

"Why did you want to speak with us anyway Jack? You should know that we need to remain inconspicuous" Kaiba said.

"I want to know who the hell took a hammer to my house whilst my mother was out in town when your meant to be protecting her?" Jack said in anger.

"Jack what do you mean no-one has been near your house we've kept an eye out the whole time." Kaiba and Nefarious looked worried.

"*Mum.*" Jack shouted he turned running as hard as he could back to his house, he didn't stop to open the door but just slammed straight into it opening it. Standing before him was Devaldros, the blue flames lighter as though fading away. Emma lay unconscious in his arms.

"Let her go now." Jack shouted. A long Black cloak bellowed around Devaldros even though there was not the faintest whisper of wind his red eyes pierced through the long bedraggled black hair that flittered across his black veined face.

The Dark Heart

"Arthur, how pleasant to see you again and after so short a time apart." a cold gravelled voice rang fourth.

"*Let her go.*" Jack shouted. Devaldros laughed.

"Why should I? she's just as much mine as she is yours." Jack raised his wand pointing it directly at Devaldros.

"You can't hurt me Arthur. no more than you could before, and if you ever want to see your mother or sister again then I suggest you do exactly as I say." Devaldros warned him.

"What is it you want me to do?" Jack asked trying to keep the panic out of his voice his eyes flicked between his mother and Devaldros he could not see if she was breathing.

"Join me, be at my side we can rule this world together you and I. we can bend it to our will. Anything that you want will be yours, except for your queen." in a heartbeat everything changes Jack's fury was released in a single burst of rage. All his energy exploded outwards windows shattered the stairway collapsed the wall and ceiling blew outwards away from the three of them.

"You leave them alone; I'll never join you." Jack shouted in the ensuing chaos Devaldros seemed unaffected by this show of power. The entire building was coming down around them but Devaldros carried on as the floor broke beneath his feet.

"We'll see." he said ominously. "Meet me tonight at the stone circle, if you ever want to see our family again." Jack rushed forward trying to grab his mother, but it was no good Devaldros with a thought threw him backwards through the front window, Jack crashed into the floor sliding up the drive, he picked himself up but by the time he managed to get back inside they were gone.

"Jack." Kaiba screamed over the sound of falling debris, the henge collapsing in on itself. The wall close to where the front room had before stood blew apart as Jack stepped out from the rubble. Coughing from the dust he bent over to catch his breath.

"Where the hell were you?" Jack asked them.

"We were trying to get to you but there was something blocking our way as soon as you came through the window whatever it was disappeared. What's happened?" Nefarious answered remaining completely calm looking at the destroyed manor.

"He's taken my mum." Jack looked at the wreckage of his home.

"Devaldros was here?" Nefarious drew his sword and walked around what was left of the Henge.

"It's a little late for that." Jack shouted after him exhausted and panic stricken. "where's Joe?" he asked.

"I don't know, Nate was over seeing his protection personally." Kaiba said not looking Jack in the eye.

"How the hell did Devaldros manage to get here without you noticing, aren't you meant to be nearly omnipotent? He couldn't have used the Diasis to enter the house directly it wouldn't have recognised him." Jack said thinking aloud.

"Jack were not omnipotent were powerful yes but you're talking about the strongest being ever known, he must have somehow tricked the Diasis into allowing him entry. It's possible that he doesn't even need a Diasis to travel." Kaiba Grumbled.

"You're telling me this now, can you do it travel without a Diasis I mean?" Jack asked. Kaiba shook his head.

"No, we're limited by our own magic, something like that would be beyond us."

"Then teach me black magic, Elven magic, any bloody magic there is. I need to rescue my family." Jack implored even though he could barely stand.

"Jack, I don't think we're going to be able to save them." He spat at Kaiba's feet. "Don't ever say that again, just get me to Grey." Jack did not want to hear anymore from Kaiba he was going to do anything that was needed to get his family back safe.

"Jack, Joe is being looked after by Nate he is the most powerful of all us Elders. He can look after Joe." Jack eyed Kaiba.

"I trusted you with my mother's safety and you couldn't protect her I'm not going to make that mistake again, get me to Grey now!" Jack commanded Kaiba. He looked as though he was about to argue his point but conceded.

"Wait here, I will contact Nate. To check on your brother I will not be able to take you to him, you must be returned to Camelot for your own protection. And that is final." Kaiba told him he understood Jack's apprehension, but he could not allow him to remain in danger being out in the open.

Jack returned to Camelot, everyone stared at him. He was covered head to toe in brick dust and thatch, he had cut to his face and arms, his eye swelling his face now a large bruise. His clothes were torn, he held his arm to his sore ribs. He could barely breath from the pain. Kaiba had contacted Grey, Joe was indeed safe, he had promised to contact Jack immediately if anything happened.

"Jack, what the hell has happened to you? I thought you were going home." Robin ran over and helped him to a seat. Jack looked Robin up and down.

"How Strong are you? magically I mean not physically, we all know you're an ox." Jack was trying to formulate a plan.

"I'm pretty Strong I've never had any difficulties performing any of the spells we've been taught, well so far." Robin shrugged still looking over Jacks sorry state.

"Rob, there's something I need to speak to you about can you help me find Michael and I'll explain everything?" Robin agreed he helped Jack stand, but he had refused. Jack needed to talk with Michael if he could convince him then he would stand a better chance of convincing Robin as well. He felt sick to his stomach that had nothing to do with the pain he was in. An idea had started to form in his head, it was madness, but it may be the only possible way he could get his family back safely.

Robin had helped Jack back to his room before running off to find Michael. Jack saw himself in the mirror, he looked like death warmed up.

"Jack he's here." Robin had returned with Michael; he had brought Louise he hadn't been expecting that.

"Oh my…" Louise gasped looking at Jack. She ran over to him examining his cuts.

"What's going on? I thought you went home, what's happened to you?" Michael like the others was shocked at his appearance.

"That can wait, take a seat." Louise said. Jack tried to brush her away, but she wouldn't listen forcing him to take a seat.

"It's quicker if you just do as your told." Michael said. Louise busied herself around him. "She's an excellent healer now." Michael explained. He was right. Jack could already feel his ribs healing and the swelling from his eye going down.

"Devaldros has my mum and sister." Jack explained whilst Louise continued to work. "He was at my house, waiting for my mum to get back. He took her and there was nothing I could do to stop him." They all looked horrified.

"Who the hell is Devaldros?" Robin asked. Michael explained everything that had happened since Jack had been released from his isolation, how everything that had happened to them was all connected to Devaldros. "And this guy, this evil version of Arthur, has Emma and Carol?" Jack nodded. "What are the council doing, the knights?" no one answered. Jack didn't even know if Grey had told them, now he came to think about it. Although, he thought he must have, if Joe had gone with him.

"Why does he want them though?" Michael questioned.

"I don't know if he does, he wants me to meet him tonight at Stonehenge or he will kill them." Everyone stood in silence looking at him like he was mad.

"You're not going? You can't go you must know that. He will kill you all." Louise was right and he knew it.

"I'm going, it doesn't matter if I die but I must rescue them somehow." He looked at them all.

"If you're going up against this guy, I'm in, I want some payback." Michael was hurting he considered Emma and Carol as much his own family.

"This isn't about payback. Louise is right if we

confront him head on, we are as good as dead and so are my mum and sister. If he see's anyone other than me he will kill them."

"So, what is your plan?" Robin asked.

"I'm going to distract Devaldros try and lead him away. I need someone to get my mum and sister into the circle and then someone else to activate it. That should bring everyone back to Camelot." It was a terrible plan, and he knew it.

"What about you?" Robins' eyes narrowed.

"I don't matter. I will try and get back in time. If I do or I don't you go, it's not open for debate. No one is to risk their necks." He could tell they wanted to argue but no one could think of a better plan. They were all terrified, Michael, Louise and Jack knew first-hand Devaldros' power. Jack did not want to ask this of his friends he knew the danger he might be putting them in, but he could see no other choice.

"I'll be back in an hour." Robin said, no one said a word they knew he was going to spend some time with Rachel, in case the worst happened.

Jack, Michael and Robin arrived at Stonehenge just before sunset, they needed to get in position before Devaldros arrived. It was important that Michael and Robin were well hidden, they had agreed it would be too risky to attempt to use magic to conceal them in case Devaldros could detect it. Michael had insisted Louise remained in Camelot, ready to operate Stonehenge. She would be the safe there they knew.

"come on, come on." Jack's body was shaking he never been so nervous in his life. Jack did not know exactly what time Devaldros was to arrive or even if he

The Dark Heart

would but all he could do know is wait.

It was nearing midnight Jack knew that Michael and Robin would be growing restless, he was himself, the faintest sound would cause him to jump in fright, if things went badly tonight, he didn't know what he would do. Sweat was pouring from his body several times he had wiped the palm of his wand hand on his jeans the moisture starting to stain. A strange shift in the air caught Jack's attention. Air bubbles felt as though they were building in his ear's, he had to blink several times as he could not understand what it was, he was seeing. In the middle of Stonehenge, the world seemed to be twisting and convulsing it looked as though the air itself was melting into a strange twisted black monstrosity. It took a fraction of a second for Jack to realise what was happening, but Kaiba had been right, Devaldros could transport himself to wherever he wanted. Jack had not counted on this and he had no time to change his plan without warning Devaldros of his friend's presence. The black mass began to separate, and Jack stared to see four clearly defined shapes. This was another blow he was only expecting three people who was the other person. Just before Jack could make out the person's face a blinding red flash swept out in a wave hitting Jack, dazzling him. Blinking furiously Jack struggled to see anything but the air pockets burst in his ears allowing him to hear again three separate muffled anguished cry's told Jack that Devaldros had arrived.

"Arthur, I'm so glad you came." the same cold gravelly voice echoed around the monument. Still blinking Jack stared up at Devaldros somehow, he seemed even more monstrous than before his hair had grown slightly longer and he now carried a gilded edged red handled sword with a dragon's head carved on the hilt. The blue flames which had previously covered his body had now disappeared.

"Let them go it's me you want." Jack said pointing to his mother and sister Jack's eyes still had not recovered and he could not see the third person who seemed to have been thrown behind Devaldros. Jack stared at Devaldros as he laughed.

"Why should I let them go? I have already told you they belong to me as much as you." Jack gritted his teeth. A small flash caught his attention. It was Michael sneaking up to a better position behind, the flash the signal for Louise to prepare Stonehenge.

"Why do you want me to join you? They are far Stronger than me and you haven't asked them I take it?" Jack was desperately trying to draw Devaldros' attention away from Michael. The grin which Devaldros had worn slipped from his face.

"You have far more power within you then any of these. You are after all, Arthur King of this land, even if they don't realise it." Emma jerked her head upwards at Devaldros not believing what he had said. "What didn't you know, didn't your weakling of a husband ever tell you the secret of his family." he mocked looking at Emma.

"Shut your mouth." Jack roared. Devaldros' face tautened.

"If you want your family to live then I suggest that you learn some respect." Devaldros slashed his hand through the air an invisible force slashed across Jack's cheek, his blood splashed onto the ground. Jack refused to clutch his face letting the blood fall, whilst Emma and Carol screamed at the sight. "That will do for the first lesson, shall I continue to the next?" Devaldros was toying with Jack showing him just how defenceless he was. He spotted Michael again creeping closer Robin was following, Jack was going to have to make his move soon or risk his friends being caught. Jack raised his head to eye level with Devaldros.

"If you're going to kill me, then fine but I'm not going to become your lapdog." Jack spat at his feet.

"Defiant till the end, eh?" He mocked. "Your father was the same and you know what happened to him." Devaldros was in his element laughing at Jack. "You know of course, your husband was murdered. Would you like to know who killed him?" The relish in his voice was unmistakable. Emma shook her head refusing to believe him, tears streaming freely down her face. "Would you like to know who killed your father?" Devaldros leaned over Carol, he had not noticed Jack slip his wand into his hand. "Well, if you're not going to answer me then I'll tell you anyway." Jack gritted his teeth he needed to get him away from his family. "It was Arthur there he killed him. He killed your husband, your father." Devaldros long bone like finger pointed to Jack. "See, he doesn't deny it." Emma and Carol stared at Jack longing for him to say something, anything, but he couldn't. Devaldros pulled the person laying on the floor behind him to his feet. Jack was shocked by what he saw a beaten and bloody Grey was being held in the air by one hand barley alive. "I would have preferred your brother, but this thing hid him rather well, I must say I was almost impressed." Devaldros dropped Grey at his feet.

"I swear I'm going to kill you." Jack seethed. Devaldros flicked his hand again but this time Jack was ready, he dived to his left producing a hex of his own. Devaldros' spell hit with Jack's in mid-air exploding in all directions. Devaldros roared, furious, his face contorted in rage.

"I offer you the world and this is how you repay me?" Devaldros' attention was fixed firmly upon Jack.

"if you want me, come and get me." Jack shouted running outside the circle using the stones for cover, Jack cast a multiply spell on himself his body seemed to split into multiple versions. "If you can't tell which one Is me, you'll have to take us all out." Jack shouted.

Devaldros seemed disorientated by what was happening he hadn't expected Jack to put up a fight. He pulled a dagger from his waist hurling it screaming as he ran, it found its target impaling one of the fake Jack's, the duplicate faded into mist. Devaldros screamed in rage chasing after the duplicate's sending spells randomly at the Jack's.

'now Michael.' Jack thought. There must have been only a few more seconds until Stonehenge was ready to take them all back. All he had to do was keep Devaldros distracted a little longer, he could see him chasing after a duplicate dragging him further away.

Michael and Robin had dragged his mother, sister and Grey into the circle.

'yes.' Jack shouted in his head all he had to do now was to get into inside without Devaldros noticing. This was easier said than done, as only two of the duplicates remained. He had to run for it, Jack sprinted as hard as he could for the circle, he heard the last duplicate scream and vanish. A few yards remained. A scream echoed out

The Dark Heart

of nowhere Jack raised his head to see Robin shouting he grabbed Jack by the back of the neck and threw him into the circle, Jack hit the floor, turning he saw Devaldros' last spell coming directly at him, something moved in the way just in front of him. Robin didn't scream but looked at his friend's, shock on his face. A dark red stain soaked through his top where the spell had hit him. Everything seemed to be in slow motion, Robin's body began to fall as Stonehenge fired taking them into Camelot and safety. They appeared seconds later just a little away from the confines of the castle wall. A thud broke the silence, as Robins body hit the floor, dead.

Chapter 22

A Friends Love

Jack felt nauseas was it like when he had first travelled by Stonehenge, or was it what he had just seen, a silence total and pure filled the air, everyone stared at Robins fallen body. It took seconds for Jack to understand what it was he was seeing, in a flash of a memory the horror hit him.

"Robin." he muttered hoping against hope that he would somehow answer him back. Michael crawled over to Robin, tears filling his eyes

"Jack, help me." Michael shouted, he placed his wand over Robins wound he tried every healing spell he could think of, but it was too late.

"Michael stop, he's gone." Jack said softly almost emotionless.

"he can't be gone, he's our friend." Michael was in denial refusing to believe that his friend had passed on. Jack got to his feet, his head felt strangely light and empty. He walked over to his mother and sister freeing them from their bonds. He looked at their faces and they somehow looked different. The joy he had expected at their reunion was there, but Jack could not feel it. His mother cried, hugging Carol. Emma jumped to her feet grabbing Jack in an embrace.

"thank you, Jack my gods, how are you?" She checked

over him brushing the dirt from his clothes.
"I'm fine mum." he said absently. Carol looked at Jack with fear.
"this is all your fault Jack." she hissed.
"shut your mouth Carol." Emma shouted before diving back down and hugging her again. Clearly torn between her joy at there being safe and her unhappiness with what she had just heard. Jack did not care though; he knew it was true.
"you're right, it is." he turned and walked over to Grey who was still severely injured. Jack stood over him with hand in hand. Seven times in all he performed the helixius spell before Grey was well enough for Jack to sit him upright. "where's Joe, is he safe?" Jack asked again without a hint of sincerity. Grey nodded, gasping at the pain. Jack did not have the magical ability to fully heal his wounds. He was barely skilled enough to keep Grey from dying. It was clear he had been tortured and that would require help he couldn't provide.
Instead, he walked over to the body of his fallen friend, Michael sat by Robin his head in his hands. Jack picked up Robin's wand and passed it to his mother.
"can you help Grey please, we need to get going I don't know if he can get into Camelot or not." Emma Ran over to Grey using the Helixius spell with each new casting Grey became Stronger, until he could stand.
"we should be safe in Camelot, Devaldros can only enter once every hundred years, and thanks to you he's already been here so whilst in Camelot he can't touch us." Grey whispered. Jack thought he was in pain, probably from broken ribs.
"Do you feel well enough to tell me where Joe is now?" Emma and Carol could not believe how cold and

callous Jack was being.

"he's here in Camelot, safe." Grey muttered. Jack rolled his eyes.

"I should have known." looking around they were only a few hundred yards from the castle. 'worked better than I thought.' Jack felt numb, a nasty feeling kept trying to creep into the back of his mind, it filled him like water being tipped in a vase and soon it would overflow. Jack reached down gently as he could he heaved up Robin's body. He slung it over his shoulder. "we need to get to the castle his parents should be informed." Michael looked up at Jack,

"stop it." he gritted.

"stop what? we have to tell his parent's, it's the right thing to do isn't it?" Jack said as if describing the weather.

"stop acting like this isn't a big thing, don't you get what's just happened?" Michael looked as though he might be sick. Everyone was still in shock at the night's event's and had no will to stop Michael. "we have just pissed off the most powerful being in the world, our friend was just murdered in front of us and you're acting like some fucking zombie." Michael rose shoving Jack, he almost dropped Robin's body; Jack clutched hard to Robin he was not going to allow him to fall again.

"Michael, I know it's been a difficult day, *but don't ever shove me again.*" he screamed in Michael's face. An explosion of emotion hit Jack, all his fear, anger and loathing that Jack had been bottling up boiled over. "*Don't you think I know what's happened. One of my best friends just died saving my life, He was an idiot, worth a hundred of me.*" Jack's blood was boiling he felt sick with himself. "I don't care what you think, I'm taking his

The Dark Heart

body to the castle, I need to tell his parent's that their son was the best man I have ever known." Emma and Carol got to their feet following Jack up towards the Castle. Jack turned to Michael. "would you like to tell them what happened as well?" Jack walked off, Michael helping Grey back.

A scream echoed around the entrance hall, a girl that Jack did not recognise had seen Robin's body. He had been hoping they could make it to Merlin's office without being noticed. Everyone within ear shot came running.
"what is it? what's happening?" Levell came running around the hall, stopping dead in her tracks when she saw Jack's group. Silence filled the hallway everyone stared at them as though they were a carnival sideshow.
"Miss Levell, will you please kindly inform the headmaster that we need to speak with him." Grey had stepped forward lending Michael's arm for support. "now, if you don't mind." He whispered holding his ribs.
"of course." she stuttered running away to get Merlin.

Merlin had arrived promptly thrusting his way through the group.
"come this way." he grabbed Grey helping him, "we need to take you to the infirmary. And as for the rest of you, to your dormitories, you shouldn't be out at this time anyway." the assemble group dispersed. "and as for you, we need to talk. Miss Levell will you please escort the two ladies to the infirmary." Merlin was calm almost business like.
"what about my friend." Jack asked he did not like the

way Merlin had avoided talking about Robin.

"I will see to him, please place him on the floor." Jack lowered his body laying him gently on the floor.

"please be careful." Jack implored. Merlin looked at Jack.

"I will be far more careful than you obviously were." Merlin flashed angrily.

"you can expel me or send me to the council for punishment later just make sure that my family is safe and they don't leave Camelot, you may want to contact the council as well." Merlin waved his wand Robin's body vanishing.

"to my office, I will meet you there once I have escorted Professor Grey to the infirmary. I believe you two have a lot of explaining to do and believe me you will be severely punished." Jack and Michael started their slow walk to Merlin's office.

"I guess this is when we get the death penalty then." Michael said.

Jack and Michael were interrogated by Merlin for hours. He scoured over every detail of Devaldros, his appearance, his power even the tone of his voice. The only reprieve they had was when Merlin had been called away to discuss with the high council. The only thing Jack had not told Merlin was about Grey and the other Elders, the two of them had also deliberately left out Louise's involvement. They did not want her to be punished either.

"I don't believe the council will be holding the death penalty over you, I want you to understand that isn't my choice, if this had happened within the school, I would have seen you hung." There was as much venom in

Merlin's voice as Jack had ever heard. "You won't be getting off the hook easily. Because of you risking your friends lives a young man is dead." Merlin's eyes bore into Jack.

"He wasn't just a man, Robin was a hero." Michael said exhausted. Merlin looked at Michael he seemed to soften.

"Until the council come to a decision. I'm confining you to the safety of the infirmary you can see your family there, but I suggest that you get some sleep and allow us to worry about Devaldros. I have nothing but contempt for you, Jack London. Leave my sight" they did as told, leaving the office. Once outside Michael turned to say something, he caught Jack's eye, mouth ajar. They stood for a moment as though suspended in time. The full weight of the night's events had crushed their voices, slowly Michael turned away from him and they continued to the infirmary. Jack knew that there was nothing he could say to make Michael feel better. He was going to suffer because of Jack again, because of him, someone else was going to pay for his actions.

Jack laid in his bed the familiar blue and white stripped curtains fluttered around his bedside giving him the impression he was outside in a gentle breeze. The curtains had once brought him a sense of safety that nothing could harm him in the world, but he had lost that illusion along with his friend. His mother and sister laying in the beds next to his and his friends body lying on some unknown slab had seen to that. Tears stained his already swollen cheek he could hear professor Grey wheezing through his broken ribs.

Memories of Robin haunted him, it scared Jack to think of just how easily his life was lost, a mere boy whose life was vanquished in the faintest heartbeat. It hurt Jack worse than any cut.

'it should have been me.' Jack thought, he still expected Devaldros voice to answer back. Sickness raised to the back of his throat. He had felt comforted by the voice when he was in the tower, a friendly presence that had helped him stay sane. How was he to know the horror that Devaldros would bring. Jack felt the world was as bad as it could possibly be but deep down, he knew it was going to become a lot worse.

Jack was awoken in the dead of night, his mother's hand stroking his forehead. He jumped startled by her presence.

"I'm sorry dear, I didn't mean to wake you." she said between sobs. Jack's eye's puffy and sore looked fine compared to hers.

"are you ok mum?" he asked his guilt weighing like a led weight on his chest. It was all his fault his family knew, his friends knew, and by now the whole world would as well.

"I'm ok, just concerned about how you're coping." Emma was different, something in her tone she seemed formal as though caring for a high official instead of a son.

"I'm fine." he lied. "just wish that things didn't happen the way they had, if I had been quicker or had a better plan then Robin would still be here. I was stupid to risk my friends lives I should have done it alone." Emma looked sullen.

"you did an amazing thing today, you rescued three

people who should never have been captured in the first place. We failed you and your friend gave his life to protect you. There is no greater honour he can bestow upon you; he was willing to die for you." Emma's speech would have seemed rousing if she had not sounded like she disbelieved what she was saying. He could tell she had been rehearsing this speech. He had seen her to many times at home practicing a difficult speech in front of the mirror not to recognise the signs.
"I just wish it had been me, Robin was a worth a thousand of me. It should have been me. Maybe Devaldros would have let you all go if he had just killed me." Jack grieved.
"my Lord, you can't feel that way." Emma's hand had drifted onto his own she squeezed tightly trying to let him know he was not alone. Jack's heart rose a little but something she had said was wrong.
"what did you say?"
"I said you shouldn't feel that way." She answered her eyes drawn to his.
"not that, why did you call me Lord?" anger welled within his chest the same familiar feeling of an animal clawing its way through him. It was like before Devaldros had ever spoken to him. Emma stuttered clearly not sure what she was going to say.
"I said it because of who you are. Your blood is that of." Jack stopped her in her track's.
"My blood is the same as yours mum. I don't care what anyone says I'm not the descendant of Arthur, I'm your son." Jack implored her he did not like the feeling of being set aside from other people.
"but you are. There was always a rumour that had been passed down through each member of the council

about a possible heir to the Throne, and it is you." She gazed at him, but she appeared almost spellbound by his sight.

"I'm not Arthur." he shouted waking the others in the room. Emma was on the verge of tears again. "please I just want to get some sleep." Jack rolled over pulling the blanket over his head. Fresh tears rolled down his cheeks as he heard his mother edge out through the curtain.

Michael held his manacled hands to his eyes. Walking out of their tower room the light seemed unnaturally bright. Two elven knights stood guard behind them. It felt unnecessary it wasn't like they were going to attempt to escape. Both Jack and Michael felt dead inside, it was only a week ago their friend had been murdered. Robin's funeral was being held today. Jack and Michael had been worried they would not be able to attend. They were awaiting trial over the release of Devaldros and their involvement in Robin's death. Jack almost hoped to be punished, he wished it would somehow balance the cosmic scales. He knew it wouldn't, Robin was dead, nothing would change that. Jack couldn't allow Michael to be found guilty though. He had committed no crime; he couldn't let him down as he had Robin.

Everyone stared at them as they made their way through the castle. Their fellow student's faces showed revulsion and hatred, some shouted abuse others whispered behind their hands as they passed. The castle's normal decorations had been replaced by black hangings. As was tradition even for a knight in training a garrison of knights lined the hall, their scabbards tied by black silk. Today was a day for mourning not fighting. Jack passed by them, his head bowed, he stood waiting to enter the hall, a rock struck him in the back of the head. The Elven knights sprang forward to check he was ok. Jack held them back turning to look at the hate filled faces.

"Not today." he snapped. Jack didn't care if they tore him to pieces. He knew he deserved it. Today was about Robin though. They would not tarnish this day, not for him.

The hall like the rest of Camelot was covered in long flowing black flags hung from every corner bearing the Arthurian crest. Jack and Michael pulled the hood of their cowls over their heads, they had discussed it, saying it would be better if Robin's parents did not see them. They had almost backed out of coming, until they realised that if Robin were so willing to help them at any cost, then the very least, they could do would be to attend his funeral. The black hood's twitched and moved all over the hall it looked like a sea on a rough night, breaking over the shore. Jack watched as the trail of his friends passed up the walkway each placing a dragon's tear on Robin's coffin, they could help grant the person his last dying wish and were given in more hope than expectation, no one could remember the last time it had occurred. Jack longed to join them his one last chance to say goodbye to his friend, he knew Michael felt the same his head bowed deep. In his pocket the tear felt red hot against his leg, he pulled the tear it surprised him because it was cold and wet, dragon tears were usually diamonds engraved, very few actual dragons' tears existed, after all when had anyone seen a dragon cry and lived to tell the tale? The tears shone on Robin's coffin. The light seemed to dance around the room flicking across the sullen faces. Jack watched as Kim walked side by side with Rachel, they leaned on each other tears pouring freely without shame or embarrassment. Kim had tried to see Michael, but the conditions of their trial meant they could have no visitors until it was over. She had not attempted to contact Jack. Each of her footsteps falling like a hammer, heavy and full of pain. The entire school was distressed hurting, Robin had touched so many lives everyone was reminiscing about how he had helped them in some way or another, guilt descended upon Jack, guilt for letting his friend down and for not being a better person. How could Robin sacrifice himself to save the piece of dirt he was? Jack hated Robin for throwing away his life the way he did. He did not understand why Robin would think that his life was worth more than his own. Jack held his head in his hands and wept.

Jack's tears soon dried with Merlin standing on the stage dressed in his formal attire staring down upon the school he looked gaunt. His eyes too often would rest upon Jack and Michael, boring a hole into them.
"I wish he would look away or at least blink every now and then." Michael whispered to Jack.
"let him look, there's nothing he can do to you." Jack whispered back.
"I know, but I still want to know why he won't let us alone; you know he was trying to get us the death penalty don't you?" Jack was not surprised he had already told them as much the night Robin died.

"so, why haven't we already been sentenced then? I mean if Merlin asks it's normally done before he can finish his sentence." someone tapped Jack on the shoulder he felt their hand clasp him softly telling him it was a friend turning around Jack expected to see Levell, but it was someone who surprised him.

"oh, hello." Jack said not daring to look into the woman's eyes.

"Hello Jack, how are you doing dear?" The woman answered in docile tones sitting next to him. Quickly he faced forward he could not bear to see her fresh tears.

"I'm alive, which is all thanks to your son, he was a real hero." Robin's mother clasped his hand squeezing it tightly thanking him.

"he was a good boy, far too good for this world." Jack nodded in agreement. Not daring to hope she might not revile him like the rest. Jack looked up at the stage, Merlin's face was like thunder.

"Rob was one of the greatest friends I ever could have hoped for and far better than I deserved, I just wish I hadn't failed him." Merlin stood down from the stage and walked towards him.

"Jack, please don't think like that you didn't fail him, Robin chose his friends well you risked your life to save your family and Robin risked his life to save yours. Robin's father and I both know this, he wanted to talk to you, but he decided to talk with Michael instead." Jack looked around Michael was missing, Jack suddenly felt very alone in a room with people. Merlin was stood before Jack and Robin's mother.

"what do you think you are doing talking to her? you have no right!" Merlin was furious.

"but sir I…." Jack put his head down. 'let them shout

at you' Jack thought the shouting was better than the soft calm it was easier to hate himself then not.

"if you ever speak to her again, I will personally see to it you will never again see the light of day." Robin's mother stood up to look Merlin in the eye, Robin's dad came rushing over as well.

"don't you dare ever speak to him like that again. *Bruce.* He was my son's friend, and I was his mother don't you dare think that you can tell who can honour our son's memory, I heard you tried to stop these boy's attending." She shouted Jack was grateful to her but still felt that he did not deserve it.

"I am acting in your family's interest and you must call me Merlin." Robin's father jumped in he looked like he might strike Merlin.

"You have never acted in anyone's interest but your own. You forget we are council members. We know the dirty secrets, so don't you ever speak to my wife like that again. *Bruce.* These boys, you are trying to persecute are guilty of nothing more than trying to save their loved ones. You could have helped you the all-powerful Merlin could have helped them. And then maybe my son wouldn't be dead." The final word came as a wail, it was as though the word wounded Robin's father.

"I did not know what was happening." the whole hall was now looking at this verbal battle. Jack just wanted it to stop he didn't want to be the cause of this at Robin's funeral.

"oh, don't give us that bull." Robin's father shouted exasperated. "the council all know you were spying on Jack here, after what happened when he collapsed. You knew exactly what was going on. And if anyone is responsible for my son's death it would be that monster

The Dark Heart

Devaldros, followed quickly by you." the hall was silent no-one knew what to say the entire council and from what Jack could see the Elders as well, were sitting awestruck at the head table.

"if you feel that way, perhaps it would be better if I left." Merlin stormed from the room spite left in his trail. He still did not dare to glance at the family he had helped to destroy. He sat there hoping they would turn on him, shout, scream and hit him, anything to dull the pain Robins death had left in him.

"Jack, I'm sorry you had to see that." Robin's father said kneeling down so he could see his face.

"Sir, I don't know where you and you wife get this strength from and I can't believe that you would ever talk to me after what happened. But you need to know Michael had nothing to do with this it was all my fault." more tears swelled in his eyes. 'my god how can I cry again? there's nothing left.' Jack thought his emotions so close to the surface now.

"we get our strength from the memories of our son and as for you and Michael it wasn't your fault, Robin died saving you it was his final act of goodness, I could never have been prouder of him." Robin's father clasped his knee. Standing, he was about to leave, when Jack called out.

"sir, if I can ask just one thing." he nodded. "can you please place this next to Robin?" Jack held out the tear in his shackled hands. The father took the tear.

"I will place it next to his heart. Along with mine." He took both Jack's and Michael's and quietly walked their way up to the coffin, Robin's mother clung to her husband she could barely walk the tears were streaming down her face. No matter what they had said Jack could not help but blame himself, all he wished for was for Devaldros to come and end his misery. They laid the tears on Robin's heart trying the best they can to be Strong. Robin's mother unable to cope with the strain fell to her knees over the coffin weeping as hard as Jack had ever seen anyone cry. Jack hung his head not wanting to intrude on their grief, he wished more than he could say that the tear would work so they could see their son just one more time. But he knew it was hopeless the tears were a tradition, a myth, he was sure. Jack sat there in his chair watching as the funeral went by all he wanted to do was to get out of there as fast as he possibly could. People Jack had never seen before talked about the type of man that Robin had been,

'they're wrong.' he thought they did not understand how he could laugh sing and love. He felt a new level of guilt with each person that passed to say their piece thinking they knew the man Robin was, but Jack knew the hero he was, it hurt him to think of the price it cost to learn that though. Slowly the funeral began to come to its climax, men and women held together in their love for Robin cried together as his body was lowered into a new sarcophagus where he was to be buried under Camelot the place he loved. And where Jack hoped he would find peace.

Chapter 23

The Trials End

The trial was fast approaching, Jack spent the time since the funeral laying on his bed. He was barely eating; a consistent fear had taken hold of him. Devaldros was out in the world even now plotting. Jack could not bring himself to think of the forth coming trial, he had attempted to think of how he could explain his actions. It all seemed so stupid now he thought of what he had done. He could only say his piece when given the opportunity. He just hoped it would be enough to help Michael. In contract to Jack other than the day of the funeral Michael had been busy studying the most complex law books. Michael of course had no issues in not only understanding the finer points of the law but was able to remember the texts almost word for word. He had found multiple precedents of cases being excused when someone had been under the influence of mind control. Jack had sarcastically asked if there was a precedence for someone releasing an unstoppable evil on the world who was responsible for mass murder? it was an uncomfortable moment, when Michael had reminded him Arthur had done just that. They had been appointed a legal specialist in Nefarious, elves unlike wizards did not separate their warriors from other roles. Nefarious was apparently a legal genius. Being over seven hundred years old he knew most of the law's known to Wizard and Elf kind. He had been deeply impressed with Michael's intelligence, how quickly he was able to understand complex legal procedures. Nefarious had stated he would be wasted as a council member. It was during their laughter Jack reminded them if found guilty not only would they not be on the council, but they would likely spend the rest of their lives in jail.

The morning of the trial Jack and Michael were chained by their elven guards and escorted to the courts. They walked through the castle in silence. Their classmates lined the halls as they went, no-one said a word, staring at the two as they descended the stairs into the hall. Jack spotted Kim as they passed, she reached out and held Michael's hand for a moment. Jack saw her smile at Michael, she never even glanced at him.

"We must move on." Said one of the guards gently prodding Michael forward. Out into the courtyard and through the city they walked. The citizens of Camelot now lined the roads. He had never heard Camelot so quiet. The only noise the clattering of the steel boots on the cobbled stone. Their trial was to take place in the ancient courts in the centre of the city. They entered an immaculately kept garden area, small iron railings kept the public from walking on the perfectly green mown grass. The garden smelled unnaturally sweet as though the scent from the nearby flowers was being magnified. The court sat at the centre of the gardens. Like most of the official building was built from thick grey stone. Marble pillars held up the heavy stone roof. A glass dome sat on the centre of the roof. Two large oak doors opened as they approached. A mosaic floor depicted a large scale, on one side the council represented by the round table the other the knights shown as an armoured helmet. Doors led off to administrative areas, smaller courts and waiting areas. Dozens of pictures of ancient, aged wizards were mounted on the walls. These were old and existing judges. The oldest looked terrifying, they reminded Jack of the inquisitors from before Arthur's time. They had been barely more than torturers under the employ of the king. Jack was prodded inside as they approached the main court one of the guards stopped them.

"Wands." He held out a box. Nefarious reached into his pocket and placed his wand inside. "You'll get it back at the end of the day. Go in." Rows of benches ran the rear of the room these were for the general public and family members to watch the trial unfold. It had no window's being at the centre of the room. The only natural light from the large dome above them. A wooden platform sat at one end where the judge would sit high above them. Jack and Michael would sit nearby in a separate box. It was shielded by a protective glass in case anyone decided to take matters into their own hands.

Once seated in the box the knights removed their manacles. The court slowly began to fill. Jack watched as his family entered taking their seat's. Emma and Joe gave him a nervous smile. Carol wouldn't look at him. He knew she still blamed him. Louise had sat with them. Levell came in, spotting Emma she ran over and embraced her. Jack should have known they were old friends. After all, Levell was best friends with his father.

Emma and Ben had met at school of course they were friends. Rachel appeared next; she was being escorted by Robin's parents. They all looked at Jack and Michael a small nod of support. Jack's heart fell at their selflessness. When Michael's mother and father arrived, Jack felt him tense. Michael's mother attempted to approach their box, but two knights blocked her path, Michael's father gently pulled them away. She would not be allowed near them at this stage. It was with a sickening feeling Jack spotted Melfice in the upper gallery, he had brought popcorn, as though this was a sideshow. Not that he had expected it but there was no sign of Kim. Nefarious took a seat at a bench in front of them. Michael gave Jack a prod with his foot nodding to the prosecutor's position.

"Jack that's Merlin." He whispered; Michael was right. It seemed the headmaster would be their prosecutor.

The judged entered the court. All within rose waiting for him to address them. The judge an elderly man slowly walked to his seat, he wore the traditional red and black gown, powdered wig and a small ruff. He pulled a pair of steel spring nose spectacles from his pocket wiping them with the handkerchief in his top pocket. He waved, smiling at both Merlin and Nefarious.

"You may all be seated." Everyone sat at once. "Good morning all, I am His Honour Judge Thwaites. You will address me as My Lord." He looked at Merlin aware of his unusual appearance at court. "Now, I would like to hear the charges against the accused." He put out his empty hand waiting for the charge sheet to be delivered to him. One of his aides ran over and whispered in his ear. The room began to whisper at this unusual turn of events. "Prosecutor, I have just been informed that we are still awaiting an official charge for the accused is this correct?" Judge Thwaites seemed to chew on his words.

"I'm afraid the charges could not be formalised until this morning this being such an unusual case." Merlin pulled a scroll from his robes and handed it to one of the aides. They snatched it away, running over to the judge handing it to him. After several minutes of reading, he looked back over at Merlin.

"The crown is charging the accused with releasing Devaldros and assisting in a murder? As far as I am aware there is no law regarding Devaldros? He was believed a myth until the unfortunate recent events." The crowd continued to mutter whilst Merlin sat nonplussed by Judge Thwaites' question. Once the crowd had quietened, he handed another scroll to an aide.

"My Lord, a law was passed under an emergency act last night, by the high councillor. Due to the fact both defendants have parents on the council it was felt it could not be placed to a vote as per our regular decree. The law is also retrospective in this case relating to the time Devaldros was released from his captivity." The crowd erupted, it was apparent the high councillor was abusing his emergency powers in order to punish Jack and Michael. Never before, had a law been created after an event especially without the consent of the entire council. Nefarious was shouting about abuse of power and how it was a disgrace to wizard kind. Banging his gabble to be heard over the noise Judge Thwaites eventually regained control of the court.

"Anymore outbursts from the gallery or the court and you will all be removed." Nefarious apologised retaking his seat. The audience fell to a whisper. Jack could see the fury on the faces of the council members in the audience. "Whilst I do not appreciate the outburst from the court, I personally agree with the sentiment behind it. This is a court of law, not some plaything for the high councillor. This law." He waved the scroll in the air. "This law will be judged fairly; it must be evidenced beyond doubt the accused are guilty. As the prosecution appear to know more than myself on this new law please inform me of the punishment if found guilty?" He slammed the parchment to his desk. Merlin smiled sweetly.

"Death, my lord." Emma screamed standing in horror reaching for Jack a moment later she passed out Joe barely managed to catch her. Two aides rushed over helping Joe to place her back in her seat checking she was ok. The court rushed around holding back some of the audience who screamed at Merlin. He paid them no attention his eyes fixed on Jack.

"Recess, for thirty minutes." Called Thwaites he looked as shaken as Emma.

The court resumed once everyone had time to absorb the bombshell Merlin had dropped.

"I will now hear the opening arguments, Defence if you would please." Nefarious rose at Judge Thwaites invitation.

"My lord today has already been an extraordinary day. As the defence we have had no time to prepare a case for the charges brought forth only once the trial had begun. A law that was not passed until after the alleged

The Dark Heart

crime. The council have accepted the manner in which Devaldros returned as true. They knew of this as soon as Jack London was able to report it. In this instance the defendant Michael Smith was unable to have assisted in the release of Devaldros, as Jack London was in isolation in a tower. There is no way he could have assisted in the release. This truth was already accepted by the council. I can only ask my learned colleague how he can explain away their sudden change in feeling on the matter?" He turned to Merlin, he held up his hand to pause Nefarious. Something not normally allowed during the opening arguments.

"My Lord, I apologise for the intrusion, but I feel I must say this now to stop the court from wasting it's time." Angered at Merlin's lack of respect for court proceedings Judge Thwaites glowered from the docks.

"You have one minute, but I warn you any further interruptions and I will throw this case out. Do you understand prosecution?" he snapped.

"Thank you, my lord in regard to the defences point concerning the involvement of Michael Smith in the crimes they are accused, the crown has decided to withdraw the charges against him. The crown after studying the evidence no longer believe him to be guilty but rather dupped into the events." No one could believe what they had heard. Michael was free, the relief swept through Jack he hugged Michael as hard as he could. He seemed to be in shock.

"Very well, Michael Smith you are free to go." Ordered Judge Thwaites, he sounded relieved. As the guards opened the door to take Michael away Jack's attention was caught by the sight of Melfice throwing his popcorn to the floor and storming from the court.

Michael wished Jack luck, they knew he would no longer be able to talk to or see Jack. He was alone now.

The next two weeks were spent with Merlin and Nefarious arguing their respective cases. Merlin had called Carol, Emma and Grey as witness for the prosecution. It was a clever move Nefarious had told him as he wouldn't be allowed to call them in his defence. Merlin had worded his questions so no matter the answer given it wouldn't help Jack's case. Nefarious under cross examination was only allowed to question them on the answers they had given. So far it seemed they were losing badly. Merlin had finally called Jack to the stand once he was sure the case was firmly in his control. He had made Jack repeat over and over what had happened between himself and Devaldros, each time Merlin making suggestions on how things might have really happened, twisting Jack's words against him. It had been with relish he forced Jack to tell the court how Devaldros had taken over his body as a child and killed his father. The court had gasped when they heard this. Merlin had begrudgingly revealed Jack to be the descendant of Arthur, he could not have hidden it. He had been forced to hand over the documentation the council had only apparently discovered that day on Devaldros. It had been written by the first Merlin explaining how Devaldros would pass through the bloodline of Arthur's children. The whole world now knew about his lineage.

Nefarious' arguments had revolved around the accountability of Jack's actions. He quoted law's stating Jack could not be held accountable for the actions of another being. Merlin had scoffed at this saying that in Jack's own words he had released Devaldros from captivity. If Jack hadn't of taken the series of actions he had, then Robin would be alive and Devaldros would be contained still. He sat there for the rest of the day listening to one legal argument after the other never hearing anything that resembled what had happened that night. At the end of the day Jack had been excused to his room he had been told that tomorrow he would be able to tell his side and deliberations would be made afterwards.

His throat was dry, sweat dripped from his harrowed brow; the dock suddenly seemed like a cell. His fear intensified how was he going to make them understand all what had happened. Jack knew that his life depended upon what he said today and yet his mind was blank, he began to panic what if he couldn't think of anything? he would be done for; he would never be able to see Kim again he couldn't tell her how sorry he was about what had happened to her. He would never be able to tell her he loved her more than anything.

Judge Thwaites sat perfectly still his steel spring nose glasses clamped to his face. He seemed deep in thought. Jack felt sorry for the judge, he seemed to be aware of how the high councillor had twisted the laws turning this trial into a kangaroo court, but the law was the law, and he had a duty to uphold it. Jack knew in his heart of hearts Merlin's case was watertight, he was guilty he had said as much himself when questioned. Jack sat watching as courtroom filled, Nefarious below did not turn to look at him, he too knew it was a lost cause. Jack wished he had been allowed to see him last night he had hoped Nefarious could have told him what to say instead of it being left to him. He guessed it was because they wanted it all to be in his own words with no outside influence. A dark cloud seemed to have descended upon the court as the judge raised his head.

"Court is now in session, anyone who will object to what is said today must leave I will not stand for any more interruptions." Judge Thwaites was referring to several events of abuse being hurled at Jack during the trial. Merlin seemed to have rather enjoyed it. Jack had a suspicion that he may have arranged it. No-one moved from their seats. "Good, now we can begin. Jack London you have heard the case the prosecution has presented you have also heard your own defence, now you can speak your own piece. But I feel I must warn you that anything you say could have serious implications either way, so you must choose what you say carefully." Jack understood, not that it helped his nerves any. He had half decided on what it was he would say, this was his last opportunity to set the world straight on that night, he wasn't going to miss this opportunity.

Jack rose from his seat looking around at the crowd. Sitting in the back of the court was Robin's mother and father, they sat with his own family. Michael, Grey, Kaiba, Levell, Rachel, Barry, and Ben Mclambeth had all come. He wished they hadn't. The one face he longed for still was nowhere to be seen. He was grateful, Jack didn't know if he could have done this if Kim was there. He turned back to face the judge.

"My Lord, I don't have much to say, but I need to say this." Judge Thwaites nodded for him to continue. "It has been argued that there is no precedence for this case, as my friend reminded me shortly before we began the trial, that's not true. Devaldros was released onto the world once before by my ancestor, Arthur. I'm not as strong as he was and even he, wasn't strong enough to stop it. I never knew of Devaldros' existence, I don't know how I could have fought against him. A couple of weeks ago I was laughing with my friend. My family was safe, and no one had heard of Devaldros other than from a nursery rhyme. The voice in my head talking to me I believed to be Draxon, my Avatar." He explained to the puzzled faces looking up at him. "I have seen my friends attacked; I have been forced to reveal details about my father's death that had nothing to do with their attack under the Serene potion. I myself, almost died. I was in isolation as I attacked a student and a teacher when I was tricked into thinking they had done something terrible to a person I love. Devaldros convinced me in my isolation to release him, he told me he would save the person I love. None of that matters though, I have been accused of releasing Devaldros, this is true. I have said it with my own words. I am responsible for my friend's death, if I hadn't of asked for his help he wouldn't have been there. Devaldros may have killed him, but it was my fault. I'm guilty, I trusted in my own ability. I believed my friends would do as I asked, that they would have left me to die. I should have known Robin wouldn't have left me. I thought I could protect the people I love; I can't protect them. I don't know if anyone can, the council are here in Camelot hiding from Devaldros, I am here on trial because the world needs someone to be punished for Devaldros returning, that can only be me. If you are going to sentence me to death, I need to say this Robin was a great man he would one day have been a great leader. But he was far more then that he was a hero if it wasn't for him, my family would be dead. Please honour him, honour his memory, revere him as you do Arthur, the truth is he was a better man than either me or Arthur." Jack sat down, he had said what he needed, he had honoured his friend's memory and now no matter the result he could rest.

   Nefarious had escorted Jack back to his cell the judge had called a halt to the proceedings for the night so he could sum up all the evidence. The night came and went to quickly in just a few minutes a man whose face Jack had never seen would decide if he would need to return here if only for a few days until the execution was set a date. Or even if he was to be moved into the old dungeons. They had changed since the days of Arthur, Jack had recurring nightmares about the dungeons and if they did indeed look anything like they did in his dreams, then he was glad they been changed. although he was sure that Merlin would have changed the cell back for him, after all he had gone out of his way so far to make his life difficult. Nefarious came at eleven, he rapped gently on the door, allowing Jack time to prepare himself.
   "I'll only be a minute." Jack's numb voice whispered from within. Jack pulled his dragons leather coat onto his shoulders. "ok, I'm ready." the door on Jack's cell opened allowing him a false sense of freedom. Standing beside Nefarious were the two knights holding his manacles.
   "After today, you won't have to wear these again."

Nefarious meant it to be comforting. He was right though. If innocent Jack would be free of them, if guilty well he would still be free of them.

The knights opened the glass box, releasing the manacles from Jack's wrists. Judge Thwaites re-entered the courtroom, the chamber was silent, the gather crowd awaiting the answer they had been hoping for since the trial began.

"Good morning all, please be seated. I realise you have attended today for my verdict in this most high profiled of cases. I have deliberated overnight, for the entirety of the trial in truth. The defence has made an impassioned argument, they have been able to argue using historical precedence and laws. The prosecutions arguments however align perfectly to the new law. I have found this case to be very trying on my conscience. Many nights I have lost sleep since these past few weeks. It wasn't until yesterday, when I heard the defendant's own statement that I finally was able to put the entirety of this case into context in my mind." he allowed this to sink into the crowd before continuing. "I do agree that through his desire to save his family the defendant endangered the life of his friend. His action resulted in the tragic loss of life of the accused friend. Does this constitute as the defendant aiding in the murder of the boy? I cannot say that it does, the responsibility of the murder in the opinion of this court rests solely on the shoulders of Devaldros." Merlin shifted uncomfortably in his seat; Jack knew this was the flimsy part of their argument. Releasing Devaldros on the other hand there was no way around. "As for his helping Devaldros to return, we have heard in the defendant's own words he considers himself to be guilty." Merlin's smile broadened. Any moment now Jack would be sentenced to death. "I trust that the defendant genuinely believes this. Throughout this case he has shown tremendous remorse for his actions. I am not as convinced of his guilt in this manner. At no point has anyone proven that the defendant intended to release Devaldros from his prison. Indeed, we have all heard testimony from the accused and the prosecution informing us he believed it to be his Avatar." Merlin jumped to his feet.

"My lord, I object. What you are saying is irrelevant. It does not matter he didn't know it was Devaldros, he still released him." Merlin screamed, fury in his voice.

"The prosecution will remember that under law an individual who is to be sentenced to death must only be done so under the case of premeditated crime. An accident may not result in someone being sentenced to death." Judge Thwaites stared down at Merlin, who had thrown his own wig onto the desk.

"No, he will not get away with this. He must die, Arthur must die. He will not take our place." Merlin stormed.

"What do you mean take your place? That's what this whole trial has been about. Your worried about him replacing the council? Only those with the blood of Arthur can remove you. You knew all along who he was. That was why you were asking him questions about his father under the serene test to see if he knew." Nefarious was disgusted, the whole court had heard Merlin.

"Of course, we knew." Merlin shouted positively deranged now. "The council has existed since the time of Arthur, how could we not know?" Merlin stormed

The Dark Heart

around his desk; the audience was in shock.

"So, the council knew. You knew and did nothing to aid the boy. It is you, you and the high councillor that helped to release Devaldros by your inaction, not the boy!" Judge Thwaites was incensed, the Council's lies had been laid bare in public now. Their fear of losing power had shown the corruption at its core. Merlin stopped his pacing, realising his mistake. "Jack London, I find you innocent of all charges. You have had a grave injustice brought on your name. Knights arrest the former headmaster Merlin, and someone issue a warrant for the arrest of the high councillor."

Jack sat opened mouthed, he had been freed, found innocent he could not believe it. He watched as Merlin shouted at the judge, never hearing a word he said. Merlin grabbed a wand from inside his pocket pointing it at Jack.

"He will die!" Jack did not understand what was happening he was innocent; the court had said so. A knight rushed at Merlin trying to disarm him he did not even have time to reach for his sword before Merlin cut him down. A woman screamed in the back of the court several people dove to the floor. The knight lay injured his blood sliding down the courtroom floor, like a snake across hot sand. "I don't want to hurt anyone else I just want him dead." he shouted firing a spell at Jack's box smashing the protective barrier that had surrounded him. Shards of glass showered Jack cutting his face and arms. Merlin whipped his wand round his head, Jack felt a force grab him around the waist pinning his arms to the side. An invisible lasso held him fast. Merlin ripped his arm back pulling Jack from the box onto the concrete floor below. Jack felt sickened as his face hit the floor, blood sprayed from the top of his eye. "you will die, you will die at my hands!" Merlin pulled his wand high above his head. Jack still tied, unable to move, waited for the blow to fall. "Evortorus." The dome above Jack's head split glass rained down, splinters showered him cutting his body like ribbons. "You will not survive this time." everyone was running for cover as the ceiling began to crack. The steel dome barely clinging to its supports. Jack knew it would give way any moment and come crashing down on him. Without his wand he stood no chance. Merlin had placed a barrier between them and everyone else. Jack could hear his brother hammering on the barrier. Knights furiously attempted counter curses to remove it. Somewhere in the distance he could hear Grey screaming for his wand. Merlin blasted one of the supports a chunk of the ceiling dropped towards Jack. With the last of his strength, he rolled to one side. The stone ceiling smashed to the ground cracking the floor where he had been moments before. "WHY WON'T YOU DIE!" Merlin was beyond insane, "Evortorus." he screamed; Jack couldn't even close his eyes, his body had given up on him, it had prepared itself to die. Everything seemed to move in slow motion he could see the last support give way. The steel dome began to fall toppling towards him,

'MOVE' his head screamed. 'can't' his body replied, this was it. "I love you Kim." he shouted without the words escaping his lips. The dome crashed on top of him, the sound of steel snapping filled the court. People screamed as Merlin laughed. Grey appeared wand in hand easily dismissing the barrier before blasting Merlin across the court with ease.

"Jack." Joe screamed, those that had not run rushed over to where Jack laid, buried beneath the dome. Desperately they cleared the beams and glass until Jack was uncovered. Grey pressed his head to Jack's chest.

"He's breathing, but barely. We need to get to the infirmary now." Joe heaved him up in his arms. Jack wheezed as he tried to breathe through his crushed ribs. He tried to tell Joe something, but he couldn't get the words out before he fell into the inky black of sleep.

Chapter 24

The King

"Merlin why do I have to continue to come to these banquets? I have a kingdom to defend, I shouldn't be running around here I should be at Camelot there are still enemies within Briton." the young Arthur said to Merlin.

"my Lord there will always be enemies of this beloved country and if you don't learn to relax then you will die far before your time. Even I have my vacations, I remember my last time in the lands of Spain. Ah the girls." Arthur grinned at Merlin.

"I never knew you had it in you, you sly old dog." Merlin chortled.

"I haven't always been an old man you know, the story's I could tell you, but a king shouldn't hear such things." Arthur hung his head,

"As a King I should live my life as way of an example. That's what you have told me since the beginning." Merlin nodded. "is that why we keep coming to these banquets?"

"I don't know what you mean." Merlin protested his innocence.

"don't be coy with me. My spy's have already told me that this Guinevere you keep trying to introduce me to is here tonight. If I didn't knows better, I would think that

The Dark Heart

you're trying to marry me off." a knock on the door prevented Merlin from answering.

"come in." Merlin shouted. Arthur laughed. Or rather Jack laughed. He had only just realised it, but he was dreaming again. Or was he dead? The door opened and to Jack's amazement Michael stepped in.

"what the hell?" Jack shouted. But Arthur did not say a word he was trapped.

"Lancelot what is it my dear friend?" Arthur jumped up hugging his friend. "good news, I hope. A deadly battle that needs my urgent attention?" Arthur asked hopefully.

"I'm afraid not sire, I called Sir Lancelot here." Lancelot looked over at Arthur.

"I'm sorry but Merlin ordered me here. Do you know the reason why?" Lancelot eyed Merlin cautiously.

"I think we have been set up by the original matchmaker." Merlin held up his hands in protest. "

sir this is a disgrace, a mockery of my name I have never been so insulted in all my life." Merlin looked sincere.

"My dear Merlin, I'm sorry, we will stop in our obvious discrepancies against your character. Please tell us what it is you would like us to do." Arthur held out his hand as way of an apology.

"thank you Sire." Merlin bowed even deeper.

"what I ask is that your talk with the lady Guinevere and you Lancelot meet this lovely lady I have handpicked for you." Merlin grinned.

"why you fickle old…." Arthur held out his hand to stop Lancelot laughing so hard Jack felt his knees buckle. Jack enjoyed seeing this Arthur and his friends laughing about the same things his own friends did.

Were these memories, could this really have happened? it seemed far too real to be a dream, did that mean he was alive. "Merlin I couldn't believe that you would use our feelings like that." Arthur said still laughing.

"my lord I only do what is necessary for the betterment of this kingdom. And if that means I must haggle you to into marriage then so be it." Arthur did stop laughing now.

"now look Merlin, I can understand that you do what is best for this country but if I don't want to marry then I won't." Jack could feel a small amount of resentment from within Arthur towards Guinevere. Arthur had not ever meet Guinevere and yet here he was being pressurised into meeting this woman with the prospect of marriage. It made Jack think maybe Arthur's entire marriage to Guinevere was a sham.

"I understand my Lord all I ask is that you meet with these lady's just for a possible allegiance in case of another invasion, if nothing else. The gods know our troops are spread thin trying to hold back the Orc and troll invasion army's and if the people found out just how thin the forces are stretched there would be panic in the streets, as I told you before Arthur sometimes it's just about keeping up appearances. If the public think we are winning, then there will be calm. So please just meet with the ladies and for once Lancelot, try to be charming, you may be one of the greatest warriors who ever lived but you're also the most exceedingly arrogant." 'my god it is Michael to a t.' thought Jack. Lancelot smiled

"Merlin my arrogance is maybe a downside, but have you ever seen someone so good at it." Merlin shook his head.

The Dark Heart

"I give up please be ready and, in the clothes, picked for you in an hour." Merlin walked from the room leaving Arthur and Lancelot alone.

"does Merlin know anything yet?" Arthur whispered to Lancelot.

"not that I know, but he does always seem to know everything. So, I can't be sure." Jack did not understand what they were talking about, but they seemed to be plotting something. "are you sure he can't hear us my Lord?" Lancelot asked. Arthur smiled,

"Morgan gave me this." He held up a dragon's claw engrained around a stone wand. "it protects me from him hearing whatever I don't want him to. But in saying that Merlin did teach Morgan everything that she knows so there may be ways that he can still hear." Jack did not like what he was hearing, it was far from the Arthur he had ever heard about.

"we had better get ready, but don't look to happy or he will become suspicious." Lancelot nodded.

"we'll get him this time he'll never realise this whole banquet has been set up to celebrate his birthday. Is Boars back from the north yet? he would hate to miss this." Lancelot was as giddy as a schoolgirl. Jack could not believe it. Arthur was trying to play games with the greatest Druid ever. But it somehow humanised him. He had always been a god like figure, but Jack now realised he was a man just like him. An hour passed, Jack listened to Arthur and Lancelot, it amazed him at just how similar it was to himself and Michael. It was strange to him how natural it seemed he did not feel like he was intruding upon another person it felt like a distant memory. Arthur and Lancelot were prepared in their finest clothing and armour. Merlin met them in the hallway. Jack had no-idea what castle they were in, but it was not as grand as Camelot. But when Arthur approached the hall, he dropped back allowing Merlin to overtake him and enter first. A tremendous cheer rang around the hall at the sight of Merlin. He stopped in his tracks almost stunned.

"my dear Lord if we live past tonight remind me to kill you in the morning." he laughed at Arthur.

"consider it done my friend, but come tonight is for you, it took a lot of work to keep this from you and I have no intent on letting that energy go to waste." Arthur watched as Merlin was dragged around the hall like a prized hound. Jack was amazed, faces he had never seen before kept on coming over to Arthur talking as far as Jack was concerned, they were only talking to him to marry their daughters off to him. He found it disgusting the way they were almost selling them to secure a better future for themselves. Apparently, Arthur felt the same way he decided to pretend that he had to rush to see Lancelot over some urgent business. Over in the distance something court Jack's attention. But Arthur continued to walk, the more Jack looked the more people he thought he recognised. At one point a man had run over and bowed to Arthur Jack did not see his face fully. But when Arthur called him by his name his face was slightly visible. It was Boars but it shook Jack.

'Robin.' his friend alive, could it be? "Robin." he screamed but it was useless the man standing before him was not Robin, Jack himself was not even there he was a prisoner in a memory. Jack hated the fact that Arthur left quickly he wanted to spend more time with Boars even if he was not Robin, it comforted him. But

The Dark Heart

Arthur seemed more intent upon staying on the move so he could not be pinned down by anyone. But his plan did not work after twenty minutes or so Merlin called out to him. Arthur walked over; Jack could tell he would rather not be with Merlin it reeked of a trap.

"My Lord, I have been hoping to corner you for the night if you would observe." Merlin pointed into the corner Lancelot seemed to have been abducted by a group of sniggering girls.

"very amusing." Arthur sniggered clearly glad his knights were enjoying a night of relaxation.

"yes, my lord and now it is your turn."

"what, no?" But before Arthur could stop him Merlin seemed to pluck a girl out from thin air.

"My Lady Guinevere, may I present the King of England Arthur Pendragon." Arthur had not even looked at the woman's face, he bowed and gently kissed her hand.

"my lady I am honoured by your presence, Merlin has been trying to bring together our persons for quite some time no……." Arthur looked for the first time at the lady. He was stunned, and so was Jack Guinevere was Kim.

"my Lord, what is the matter?" Guinevere asked concerned.

"I'm sorry, Merlin has often told me of your beauty, but I'm afraid he has been dishonest with me." Guinevere took a step back.

"I'm sorry my lord, if I do not please your sight." Guinevere curtsied and went to leave.

"please my lady, I did not mean offence." Arthur shouted at her. "I merely meant that he hadn't told me of your full beauty, he had informed me you were a chased woman but not that you were capable of stealing a man's heart with just a glance." Guinevere blushed furiously

"my Lord, I don't know what to say. You honour me."

"I'm sorry if I have offended you by my comments. And I must say that it is you whom honour me with your presence, but I would like you to know I meant no harm, indeed I would wish death upon myself a thousand times before I ever would allow anything to hurt you." Jack laughed as he watched Arthur stumbling through his words. A man who could defeat any enemy but present him with a beautiful woman and his words became his greatest enemy. Maybe they were not so unalike after all. Jack was just enjoying the scene before him nothing complicated was happening here, you could tell the bad guys from the good. Jack only wished he could warn Arthur of Lancelot's eventual betrayal. A thought hit Jack, what did Michael's resemblance to Lancelot mean?

'Michael wouldn't betray me.' Jack thought then again it was possible he was already dead. For all he knew there was no way he could escape from this memory or whatever it was. He might not ever be able to see his own Guinevere again, even if she did not want to see him again.

Jack watched as the party wound down. Arthur had spent the rest of the banquet with Guinevere he had even tried to dance a couple of times. But again, his similarities to Jack were exposed. He could not keep in time with dances several times he had trod on Guinevere's feet. Jack could not stop laughing at Arthur he was seeing all his own insecurities through someone

The Dark Heart

else's eyes and it amazed him just how stupid he was being.

A light occasionally dazzled Jack from nowhere it would appear and disappear just as quickly. Arthur did not seem to have noticed. So, Jack just shrugged it off thinking it must be something to do with the banquet, but occasionally it would break into Jack's eyes directly.

"what the hell is that?" Jack held his non-existent hands to his eyes, but the light still shone through.

"it's your way home." Jack shook his head he was hearing things.

"who said that?" the light vanished, and Merlin's face replaced it.

"young Jack, I have come to show you the way back to your world, this isn't the time for you to see this." Jack did not understand how this was possible.

"is it really you, the first Merlin?" Jack asked in awe.

"I'm more than the first Merlin, I'm the only Merlin, anyone else who held my name would have a weight of expectancy that would surely break any man." the real Merlin talking to him it was too much to believe.

"but Mr Merlin sir." Jack started.

"Jack you should not use such words with me, rather it is I whom should be calling you Lord, you are after all King in your own time." Jack blushed.

"I'm no king, in fact I was just stabbed by the future headmaster and Merlin of the school Camelot." Merlin nodded,

"so that's what brought you here then, I had never expected this magic needed using. But how aren't you King I don't understand?" Merlin was puzzled.

"I have only just found out and am beginning to

believe that I am descended from Arthur. And that only happened because I released Devaldros." Merlin was still puzzled.

"I don't understand, who is Devaldros?" Merlin Jack came to realise did not know all. He could just see Arthur's bloodline.

"Devaldros is the foulest being in all the worlds." Merlin stopped him again.

"my king I must stop you, I cannot know anything about the future, it might affect your past destroying everything you know. You must leave but please know that one day when ready these memories will be available to you; I can sense what they mean to you. But for now, my king goodbye and good luck and remember if you need my help, search for me." the light began to descend upon Jack.

"what do you mean?" Jack shouted his voice trailing into the light.

"we always return." Merlin's voice echoed through. He could feel the light pulling at his insides pulling him into his true world.

"Merlin, I don't want to go back I want to stay." Jack shouted into the light, but it continued to drag him further back he could not move away, every time he tried it pulled harder against him. At the end of the light, he could see the world coming into sharp focus. The disgusting infirmary drapes were again there. He knew his body was there in the real world. His body was slunk he could see the nurse working tirelessly trying to save him. Jack began to slip into his own body, he could feel the pain returning. He gripped his teeth determined not to cry out. Finally, he rested into his body and blackness came over him.

The Dark Heart

Chapter 25

Friendship

Jack woke sputtering as though drowning, a pain in his chest matched only by that of piece of jagged steel protruding from his side. He retched, why hadn't they pulled it out? Was it possible he was still dreaming? He tried to move again but a terrible pain ripped through him. He was awake.

"Jack, we need you to stay still." The nurse panted working hard against the steel.

"Pull it out!" Jack hissed.

"We're trying to. Bite down on this." She shoved a piece of leather in his mouth. The taste nauseated him but that was as nothing to what happened next. The nurse had climbed onto the bed "ok Jack, bite down now. Professors, please hold him." Grey and Kaiba ashen faced walked into the cubicle, Grey nodded to Jack holding him down. Jack did not much like the idea of having a vampire around him with half his blood laying on the bed sheets, but he was not about to complain. "Ready, Go." She twisted and pulled on the steel trying to free it from within Jack. He screamed out praying to any god that would listen that it would soon pull free. Kaiba turned his head away as blood flicked up onto his clothes. The nurse stopped; Jack welcomed the numbness that was beginning to fill his body. "Kaiba

The Dark Heart

there's no chance that I can move this, you're the strongest one here you're going to have to do it." Kaiba began to shake his head. He did not seem to want to get any closer to the blood than possible. "Kaiba now, or he'll die." Kaiba placed his shaking hands on the metal, the drying blood warm against his skin.

"Kaiba, if you don't pull this out of me, I swear I will stake you myself." Jack shouted his words muffled by the leather rag in between his teeth. Kaiba gritted his own and pulled hard, it began to come inch by inch Kaiba straining, the steel was tearing at Jack's skin the jagged edges ripped along his bones. He screamed and screamed; the gods were ignoring his plea's. He could almost hear them shouting down upon him, calling him a heretic. Delighting at the torment ripping through his body.

"Kaiba, I need that out now; he's losing far too much blood." The nurse was pouring potions into Jack trying to replace his blood faster than he was losing it, but it was proving difficult. Kaiba climbed upon the bed and pulled with all his strength his feet sinking into the bed lifting Jack's body into the air. His teeth began to tear into the leather. The nurse and Grey pounced on Jack smashing his body back into the bed, but it worked the steel pulled free, sending Kaiba crashing to the floor. Jack spat the leather to the floor, he felt like his bottom rib had come out with it. The nurse rushed over and placed a fizzing gauze on his wound, a feeling of calm spread over his body allowing him to relax whilst the nurse began to bind his wounds.

"have I ever told you how pretty you are?" Jack asked the overworked nurse, whom with her hair flapping wildly and muttering incarnations like a crazy woman looked anything but beautiful. But will all the potions and spells circulating his body, he had become a little disorientated, almost inebriated.

"thank you, Jack, but lie down you can tell me how beautiful I am later when you're comfortable in bed." she grabbed his arm to stop him peeling at his bandage.

"ok, if you say so nurse but I don't think you should get in bed with me whilst he's here, it might look unprofessional." Jack slurred his words becoming more incomprehensible. Grey grinned but the nurse seemed shocked she almost shouted at him but thought better of it.

"your right Jack, some other time." Jack winked trying to be subtle and failing miserably.

Jack's hand fumbled feebly over the cabinet next to his bed his throat felt as dry as a dragon's tail. He held a jug of water in his shaking hand the ice rattled within. He poured himself a glass but could not bear to sip it his lips felt shrivelled and chapped.

"how are you feeling today?" the nurse had appeared around the corner. Jack hung his head. "that well then. Let us have a look at you, see if have lost any of your charm from last night." she grinned.

"what do you mean?" Jack's memory was a little fuzzy as though he had dreamed the events of last night, and the harder he tried to find them, the further away they became.

"oh nothing." She laughed. Jack stared at her he did not know if she was being serious but decided not to question her.

"oh, I'm sorry I think I was a bit out of it." Jack grovelled.

The Dark Heart

"If you need anything you should know how to contact me by now." the nurse smiled and walked out of the cubicle.

'one day I'm going to have to find out her name.' Jack thought embarrassed.

Michael came to see Jack later in the day, it felt slightly strange to Jack that he no longer needed someone's permission to see his friends or as Jack now feared friend. They had wasted the best part of the day discussing the trial and Merlin's betrayal. He had been captured and was to be transferred to the new prison called Mordredstien it had been created to hold the most powerful of fugitives and Merlin fitted the bill. The high councillor was on the run. He had managed to avoid capture when the knights had come for him. After dark had fallen Michael got on to the subject Jack had been keen to avoid.

"the entire school has been asking about you." Michael told him rather sullenly.

"oh goody, how many of them said it's a shame they didn't lynch me?" Jack was scared about what the school's reaction to him would be.

"no-one has said anything like that." Jack scoffed.

"not really, since they heard about Merlin attacking you and about your lineage."

"what?" Jack interjected. "what about my lineage?" Jack asked even more afraid,

"the court issued their report only hours after the case finished and it mentioned about you are being descended from Arthur." Michael was trying his best to reassure Jack, but it was just making him feel worse.

"as if they did not have enough reason to hate me,

first they think I'm in cahoots with a murderer and now they think that I'm going to be just like Mordred." Jack sat in silence Michael tried to break the silence a couple of times, but Jack could not even think properly. Michael seemed distracted "What else has happened then." Jack asked Michael was even more sullen with the question.

"it's nothing really." Michael tried to wave Jack's question away.

"it matters Michael, what is it?" Jack asked sincerely.

"Well, it's just that Kim found a note from Louise, she's gone. Apparently, she said she couldn't be here any longer not after everything that had happened." Jack tried to comfort Michael, but it was no use, he pretended that everything was ok even though Jack knew he was dying inside. The nurse came a little while later telling Michael Jack needed his rest, Michael seemed a little relieved to leave. Jack was relieved, he just wanted to sleep and forget that the name Arthur or Devaldros ever existed.

"oh, good news Jack." the nurse said just as he was settling down. Jack looked up at her hoping she was going to tell him he had some terminal illness with no cure. "you can go back into the school tomorrow." She said cheerfully.

"oh, thanks that's great news." Jack lied dread filling every nerve there was no way he could sleep now.

The morning came too quickly the sun had barely risen when the nurse woke him.

"come on sleepy head I'm sure your just desperate to get back to your friends and to Jousting." she smiled at him delicately.

"Miss, do you really think that I should be allowed

out so soon? you normally keep me here for at least a couple of days." Jack was trying desperately to stay in the infirmary where the other students could not gawp at him.

"yes, but then there were concerns about your mental health, this time it was wounds, and the body can be healed much faster than the mind. I mean look at your stab wound, you see you don't even have a scar." Jack could tell she was showing off a little, but he did not want to upset her. She had after all saved his life and was only trying to be friendly and Jack guessed he was going to need all the friends he could get now. He gave a cheery grin thanking her for all she had done before setting out into the school.

Outside the infirmary Jack found Joe waiting for him. Without a word they walked to each other and embraced.

"You have got to stop nearly dying, it's aging me." Joe broke their hug pointing to a singular grey hair.

"Sorry about that, I'll do my best to remain alive for the next month." Joe slapped him on the back.

"Come with me. I want to talk somewhere I know we can't be heard." Joe led Jack through the castle. They entered an area he had never been in before. "This section of the castle used to be housing for the knights. It hasn't really been used in the last century since the council decided to remove us and allow the school to use it. I think they just didn't want us close to them. Camelot has never had enough pupils to use the whole castle." Unlike the rest of the castle the enchantments that kept the school running didn't appear to work here anymore, Dust covered the floor and windowsills; the torches did not burn as they passed. The corridors were cold and unwelcoming. The house banners which hung here were tattered and moth eaten. The carpet that remained had faded from the sunlight. Suits of armour long neglected rusted to the point holes had worn through the steel. Joe pulled a torch from its holder. "Would you do the honours?" Jack pointed his wand to the torch.

"Ignescotus" flames burst to life, the torch shone brightly.

"Still got it I see, come on we still have a way to go." Joe walked on. Jack felt awful seeing the castle like this. It was just like the ship Excalibur; it was all show from the outside but rotten inside.

'Just like the council' he thought. Finally, they reached the base of a tower.

"Up here." Pushing against the wooden door it collapsed from its hinges. The crash echoed around the empty halls. Steadily they climbed the crumbling stairway until eventually they reached the top, Jack puffed out of breath.

"Where the hell are we?" he asked Joe his hands on his knees bent over double trying to fill his lungs.

"The central beacon." The tower they stood in was open on all sides. A large brazier sat in the middle of the tower. "This is the largest of the warning beacons in Camelot. There were over a hundred recorded as being operational. The towers used to always be manned in case of attack. Now like most of this country they are abandoned." Joe looked mournfully out over the horizon. In the distance Jack could make out some of the other beacons. They seemed to be crumbling and in disrepair also. As Jack scanned the city below, he saw

The Dark Heart

the remains of the court. The building's roof was gone. What struck Jack other than this was how from above the city seemed different, it somehow shined less. Camelot looked wounded from here. "I'm told this was once the best place in the city to see how beautiful Camelot was, now it just shows us the truth of what the high councillor and his type have done." Joe was sullen, Jack had never seen his brother like this. He knew he had misgivings about the council, but this seemed beyond his usual reticence.

"What's going on Joe? Why are we here?" Jack was worried, with Devaldros out in the world they all needed to pull together not fall apart.

"We can't be heard here, and I need to ask you something. Things are about to change for you. The council are going to do one of three things. They are either going to try and recruit you make you their poster boy to keep things the way they want. They might try and discredit you to the public now everyone knows your descended from Arthur or they may bury their head in the sand. Without Excalibur it would be impossible for you to claim the throne." It was an uncomfortable thought, all Jack wanted was to be left alone. Jack considered another option that Joe hadn't. The council may offer him to Devaldros if he agreed to leave them alone. He shuddered at the thought. He knew some like his mother wouldn't allow this to happen but as he knew the council had layers and those that would protect him probably weren't able to.

"Ok, thanks for that." Jack still didn't get where Joe was going. "What are you actually trying to ask me?" Joe turned to face him leaning against a rotten pillar.

"I want to ask you to do one of two things. If the

council do ask you to support them and you accept, don't be a puppet. Try and make a difference here. They will try and convince you this is fine." Joe pointed to the broken beacons and rotting city below. "This is what I really want to ask you though. I want you to run. Take Kim and get the hell out of here. Run and hide leave Devaldros to me and the other knights." Jack was overwhelmed he had not expected Joe to say that. "You know he's coming for you; from what you have said he's coming for Kim as well. Get her and go live your life you don't need to sacrifice yourself for this." It sounded so simple when said aloud.

"Joe, I love you but you're an idiot. Do you really think I would let the council use me? As for running and hiding. Like you say Devaldros is coming, there is nowhere in the world that I could hide. He has already used mum and Carol against me. How long do you think it would be until he killed you all! Nothing will stop him." There was no escape from his future, he knew. Under any other circumstances the thought of running away with Kim sounded heavenly. He didn't even know if she would ever talk to him again now though. "Maybe you can convince Kim to hide though Joe. Take her family far away and see that she is safe." Joe shook his head.

"She wouldn't leave you, same as you won't her." Jack wished that were true. He missed her more than he could stand.

"Things have changed, I'm sure you noticed she wasn't at the trial. She rightly blames me for everything, I've lost her. I'll never get to tell her…." It hurt too much to say. A set of swans took flight from the lake Jack watched them as they flew above the city and out towards the harbour before disappearing from his sight.

"Jack, Kim cares about you, she was there I saw her, every day she was in the gallery watching. She was one of the first to your side when the ceiling collapsed on you. She waited outside the infirmary the entire time you were there. That isn't someone who doesn't care. Maybe she needed time to take everything in. It's a lot to find out, I'm not sure I can take it in myself." Jack suddenly felt selfish, he hadn't considered how the revelation of his bloodline would affect Joe and Carol. They too were descended from Arthur, though they didn't have his memories or the weight of carrying Devaldros within.

"I don't know what to say to her. I can't think of anything that will make it better." He admitted.

"Well, you had best think fast." Joe said pointing down the spiral stairs. Jack could make out the faint glow of a torch ascending the stairs. "She will be here any moment." Joe tapped his brother on the shoulder and started his own climb down. Jack felt his heart in his throat, this seemed to be the reason he had called him here. There was nowhere to run nothing to distract them. They would have to thrash this out one way or another. Jack sat himself on an old wooden crate he could hear Kim climbing the steps her breathing heavy as her pace slowed the closer, she came to the top. Finally, the blonde hair emerged from the gloom of the staircase. Kim's beautiful features seemed to glow brighter than the torch she held in her hand.

"Hey." She said as soon as she clasped her eyes on him.

"Hi." Was all he could manage. He had no idea how this conversation would go, he prayed for once his mouth would allow him to say the right thing.

"You seem better." Kim pointed to where the steel had pierced him.

"Yeah, you know the nurse a miracle worker that one." Kim nodded whilst looking out across the city.

"Did you ask Joe to bring me here or was it his idea?" Jack said just to break the uncomfortable silence.

"Mine, I didn't want us to be disturbed. Although I didn't realise we would be quite so isolated." Kim continued to scan the world below her. Jack wondered if she was seeking the strength to say what she had come to. Jack decided to stay silent allow Kim the time she needed to gather her thoughts. After some time, she turned and face him.

"Do you know why I haven't spoken to you?" Kim sounded tired almost resigned.

"You blame me for everything that's happened." Kim struck him across the face.

"Don't you dare say that." She shouted so loudly birds took flight across the rooftops. Jack reeled from her strike. His face suddenly red stinging. Kim made to reach for him before pulling away shocked by what she had done. "I'm sorry I didn't mean to…." Kim held her mouth ashamed.

"If you don't blame me for what's happened, I don't know why you shut me out." He threw a pebble over the side and watched as it bounced from rooftop to rooftop.

"How do you feel about me?" It was the one question he dreaded. Jack steeled his resolve forcing himself to look her in the eye.

"I love you. I've told you before, you are my queen." It was the pure naked truth of the matter. He didn't look away as she blushed.

"That day down by the lake before all this, I thought I knew the truth at last. Now I don't know what to believe. I don't know if you really feel that way. Is it some lingering feeling from Devaldros." Jack went to speak but she held her hand to his mouth. "I can't believe you love me. Not until you know for yourself, really know that's how you feel. When I can believe you, we can talk about it." It was a reasonable request, but Jack couldn't help feeling disheartened. She didn't believe he felt that way. Jack knew his love for Kim was true. Neither Devaldros nor his memories from Arthur could stop that. It would take time for her to believe him until then he would have to wait. "Can we be our old selves at least for now?" she implored him; he could see her eyes holding back a tear.

"Whatever you want." He promised brushing the hair from her face. Kim took his arm and lead him down the stairs. Just her touch, being close to him made Jack feel like a new man, free from Devaldros and the weight of his future, in this moment he was Jack and the woman he loved was at his side. Tomorrow might bring more pain and horror but this feeling in this moment could never be taken from him.

Chapter 26

The Dark Round Table

Jack had barely finished putting his clothes back into the unfamiliar bedroom when Michael rattled on his door, spotting Kim sitting on Jack's bed, he walked in. He checked around the room searching for something.

"What are you doing?" Jack asked.

"Just making sure that there's no sharp objects in sight." Kim tutted.

"Michael, shut up." Kim was hiding a grin under her stern grimace. Jack smiled to himself he did not think a few hours ago that he would ever be in the same room again despite laughing and joking together like nothing had happened. It made him happier than he could say, and he did not want to try to explain it. If Kim wanted to be his friend, then he was not about to ruin that by telling her his true feelings, no matter how deeply he wanted to run to her screaming his love all the way.

"So, what's up then?" Jack asked Michael

"I've been sent to get you and Kim. There's an emergency meeting of the council and the school council has been called to assist." Jack eyed Michael he knew what this meant.

"it's bad isn't it?" Kim whispered she too understood.

"I don't know what going on, it could be they want our suggestions on the new Merlin." Michael said unconvincingly.

Silence filled the common room when Jack entered. People stopped and stared shamefully at Jack as though he was a prize animal being paraded for their enjoyment.
"Yes, he's back so there isn't any reason stare." Kim scolded the room. Most of the room walked away but one boy stayed behind, he had been a close friend of Robin, but he and Jack had never really been awfully close.
"What's bothering you then Steve?" Michael asked him, Steven stood still anger etched across his face,
"I think it's disgusting that a murdering son of a bitch can show his face here." Steven threw his bag down onto the floor.
"What the hell do you know?" Michael shouted. Jack grabbed Michael
"It's not worth it, let's just go." Jack did not want to cause any more trouble. He could happily have gone through the rest of his life without anyone looking at him again.
"No Jack I'm not letting this pass; these guys are going to have to learn that your innocent." Michael steamed shoving Steven into the couch. What surprised Jack the most was the fact that Kim was letting Michael get away with it.
"Michael, I said leave it we have far more important things to deal with." Jack pulled Michael out of the way. Steven took his chance though jumping to his feet and punching Jack in the face. Taken by surprise Jack stumbled onto the floor. Michael pushed Steven over the couch, but again Jack stopped him.

"Michael, leave it, I told you I don't want any trouble." Jack wiped the blood from his lip standing he walked over to see his attacker.

"You can take this as your one free hit." Jack pointed to his lip.

"Guess what, you ever touch me again and I swear I will rip your arm off and beat you with the wet end." with his threat firmly seated in Steven's mind Jack left the room, Kim smirking behind him.

The council sat gathered around the infamous round table which had been brought with them, Emma was sat opposite the door Jack guessed she had wanted him to see her to show him he had a friend there. Kim's mother and Michael's father were sat either side of Emma whilst Robins mother and father sat on there right showing a solidarity for the three. Jack thought it was nice of them but the seventeen other faces staring back at them seemed less friendly.

"Jack, Kim, Michael, please sit." Grey sat in the high councillor's chair. He had been appointed to Merlin's position until a full promotion could be issued. This made him second in command to the High councillor only.

"May I ask why we're here?" Jack asked sitting between Michael and Kim.

"All will be explained in a minute." one of the councillors said shortly. Jack took an instant dislike to him; he was a short man almost dwarf height a deep scar ripped across his lip which appeared to have been torn away. Kim nudged Jack's arm.

"What's wrong?" he whispered to her.

"All the seats are full." Jack looked around she was

The Dark Heart

right.

"Yeah, so what's your point?" Jack asked unsure what she was pointing out to him.

"We are the only members of the school council here where is everyone else?" it had not occurred to Jack that they were the only ones, but she was right.

"Why do you think they only wanted us here?" Jack mouthed at Michael. He shrugged clearly as bemused as Jack was. Emma rapped her fingers on the table, Jack knew that she was nervous he had seen her do this when waiting for both Carol and Joes exam results. Once or twice, she smiled over at Jack mouthing at him if he was ok.

Grey tapped his goblet to bring the circle to silence, everyone turned to look at him, their utmost attention directed at him.

"Good morning everyone, I know that the hour is still early and that we have some guests within our chambers this morning." Grey pointed out Jack, Michael and Kim. "Now that the trial of two of the individuals is now over, I must tell you all about some terrible news." Grey shifted uncomfortably in his seat. Some of the council members looked at Jack not understanding his presence there, they didn't seem to appreciate it either. Grey took a deep breath preparing himself for what he was about to say. "I see that not everyone is happy with my young friends being here. If you wait, I will reveal to you why they have been summoned here." the council tapped on the table consenting to Grey's request. "As you are all aware the headquarters for the council's training was destroyed earlier in the year, and some of the next generation of council members were killed I'm sad to say." Jack hung his head the people sitting next to him had lost their children in the explosion caused by Devaldros.

'No wonder they are staring at me.' he thought 'as far as they're concerned, I helped to kill their children.' Jack felt cheap and used no matter how he rationalised it he knew that it was his fault. Once Michael had said that maybe it was his destiny that the gods had decided it was time for Devaldros' return. Jack would have liked to believe Michael's story, but he did not believe in the gods, and if he did, they must have forsaken him.

"This was the last we had heard of Devaldros until the incident at Stonehenge. Where I, Ms London and her daughter owe are lives to these two gentlemen and their friend who lost his life." Grey again pointed to Michael and Jack. "Last night I'm sorry to say we have two separate reports of incidents, the first Merlin whilst being transported to Mordredstien escaped with the help of an unknown entity, on top of that a group of knights searching for Devaldros were killed whilst on patrol." Gasps rang around the room.

"How many?" Kim's mother shouted aghast.

"Six in total, it appears that they were caught in a surprise attack. It appears we have a new player on the board. They appear dedicated to helping Devaldros obtain power. They may be the same group that helped Merlin escape. I have set up a new organization intent on nothing more than stopping Devaldros. They are to be called the Avartarians the most powerful of wizards." A growl of disapproval met his words.

"I don't believe it; a wizard would never do such a thing. It must have been vampires or trolls something else. And as for your avatar wielding group it's the most pathetic thing I've ever heard." the dwarf like wizard shouted. Grey shook his head at the wizard.

"There is no doubt that it was wizards, and I also don't like your thoughts about our allies we cannot discriminate because they are different to us. I also believe the Avartarians are one of our safest chances of helping to fight against this other group of wizards, they are already searching the area." Grey was attempting to keep his voice calm; it was clear though he thought little of the man in front of him. Jack felt ashamed of the wizard, vampires and trolls were no more inclined to evil than wizards. He could see that the man was a small-minded bigot. He knew that if this were Arthur's council then the wizard would never be allowed near the table apart from to pour them wine.

"Frank." Emma scalded him. "Grey is correct, with Devaldros returning and Merlin's betrayal were open to attack, we must show a united Front." A mutter of agreement echoed across the table at Emma's words. Frank shuffled his hands but did not say anything.

"As I was saying, we are facing a war not seen since the times of Arthur, this is why are young friends are here." the group turned to face the trio.

"You're not honestly expecting us to believe the rumours that have been said about this boy." Frank shouted.

"That boy is my son." Emma seethed.

"It doesn't matter who he is. You can't honestly expect us to believe that he is the descendant of Arthur?" He scoffed. Jack felt as though he was watching a ping pong match, the arguments passing back and forth.

"You forget Frank, the high councillor Is gone, Merlin is gone. The truth has been exposed. Those at the height of the council know the truth. There is no longer any denying the truth." The gathered council members stared at Jack, he hated sitting there being judged by them. Sick of being treated this way Jack decided it was time to say something.

"Who the hell do you think you are." Jack said calmly. "I don't care who you think that I am this is my life, I won't have it dictated by all of you. I've lost my friend my family was nearly killed my father was murdered and his murder was covered up by the very people in this room. If you think I'm going to be used by you all your all mistaken. Camelot is the best representation of this council, shining on the outside, rotten from within." Jack was not angry he was tired of the games. He had a sudden flashback to when he had started at the school. He had scored low for his diplomacy.

"Jack you are mistaken." Grey tried to reassure him.

"No, I'm not. The council sit here and decide on how they can best retain power whilst doing the minimum to keep the people of this country safe. You have done nothing in centuries of real note to protect this land, you have systematically restricted the lands and rights of other species. You have destroyed our relationships with our allies and allowed our cities to rot. Since the real Arthur's council died their seats at this table have been passed down through their family's line. Arthur didn't intend that; he wanted the country to be run by a fair government. He wanted to see the people cared for. Most of you here aren't decent enough to run a village shop." Jack rose to his feet his pulse beginning to race. "I don't know why you called me here or my friends but let me tell you that I don't care what you think. If Devaldros, Merlin or anyone else comes looking for me,

I will fight. No-one will threaten my family, my friends or anyone I love again. I do not care if I am Arthur and if Michael is meant to be Lancelot. In my dreams Robin was Boars but he's dead MY knights are dying just the same as yours but I'm not going to stand for it." Jack turned to leave but Kim stopped him.

"Jack, we should hear them out they wouldn't have called us here if we weren't needed. I mean we all want the same thing don't we." Her eyes glistened gently Jack just wanted to leave but for Kim's sake he sat down.

"Fine, but I'm not staying for them."

"Why are we here then?" Michael asked he had lost his illusions about the council long ago.

"Jack is right when he called you Lancelot you know Michael." Grey said the council looked at him Frank the wizard scoffed again.

"How would you know this then?" Grey slipped his hand between each other.

"I know because I was his servant. I remember them all from Arthur to Lancelot to Guinevere." He pointed to Kim. Kim 's draw dropped slightly her hand gripping Jack tighter but said nothing.

"Kim, I'm sorry if you don't know about this but it must be said." frank slammed his goblet on the table.

"I don't believe this we destroyed the immortal magical creatures everyone knows that." Jack's blood was boiling, a pot exploded just behind Frank. Grey looked at Jack his eyes imploring him to remain calm.

"I'm not a magical creature I'm an elder." he boomed over Frank. no-one seemed to understand what Grey was talking about, "There are only a handful of us handpicked by Merlin and taught by him to aid the future decedents of the council. But as Jack pointed out to me, we haven't done a particularly good job, the people sitting before you are our only hope of defeating Devaldros and I need your help Jack, your blood ties to Devaldros it might be the key to destroying him. Guinevere's love for you made you strong enough to defeat him the last, and we have need again of Lancelot's sword. The council sat open mouthed not daring to believe a word he was saying.

"This is madness, there is no way he could know about any of that." Frank screamed a few of the councillors seemed to agree with him.

"You have no idea of what has transpired over the last few hundred years this council has abused its position as has been demonstrated by the recent betrayal of the headmaster Merlin. He cared more for his own beliefs then he did the people's. And now we have no ideas as to his intentions." Grey said as though this was an open subject, but no-one seemed to want to answer him. A black smoke began to arise from the table.

"what's happening." frank shouted falling backwards off his chair in his hurry to get away from the table. Flames shot upward sending the remaining councillors sprawling. Jack grabbed Kim, holding her behind him.

"Get everyone out of here." He ordered. A group of knights burst into the room pulling the councillors away. Nefarious appeared grabbing Michael and Kim, Jack managed to pull himself away, he watched as the flames burned higher and higher the black smoke crawled along the wall forming words. The elves formed a shield around the council only Jack was outside the shield.

The smoke cleared and the council stood aghast. *Fear the Black Council.* These words were etched across the wall as the blackened surface of the Round Table told them there was a new enemy one that had no fear of the darkest arts.

"They reached us in here, they have managed to attack the council in our very own chambers." Michael's father said disbelievingly.

"How can we stop them?" Emma looked at Jack scared. He looked back at her with no fear. Devaldros he had faced, Merlin he had faced and if he would have to face this Black Council as well then so be it.

"So, you think that Devaldros has formed his own army?" Michael asked once they were in the safety of his room.

"Why not, it would make sense even someone as powerful as he would need help to control the country, imagine if he has ideas about the entire world?" Kim shuddered at her own words.

"He doesn't care about the world, it's Camelot he wants. And Arthur or the closest thing he can get to Arthur dead." Jack shrugged like it did not matter.

"Why do you think he wants you dead Jack?" Michael asked Jack thought it was another rather stupid question, but Michael seemed earnest.

"Well how about the fact that he kidnapped my family and fired spells that killed a person standing where I was only a second before." he could not believe Michael would not think of that.

"But he wanted you to join him, and he only used those spells as a last resort. I think he wants you with him. No offence, but he had plenty of time to kill you when we were at Stonehenge." Michael's memory was much better than Jack's he had forgotten that he was asked to join Devaldros.

"Yeah, well let's face it he won't exactly be handing me out an application form to join now." Kim laughed loudly leaving Michael and Jack to stare.

"What's so funny?" Jack asked bemused.

"I'm sorry, I'm sorry." Kim gasped wiping some tears from her eyes. "it's just that I can see Devaldros handing out application forms asking people what they think of how well he would rule the country." Kim laughed even harder, falling off the bed and laughing on the floor.

"Ladies and gentlemen allow me to present Guinevere." Michael sniggered.

Jack did not sleep that night he could not get comfortable in the soft bed he found It stupid that he was missing the cold hard lumpy bed of the tower but miss it, he did. As he lay there his thoughts kept drifting to Kim. A tap on his door gave Jack a distraction from his self-torture.

"Who is it?" He called out.

"Michael can I come in?" he whispered through the door. It was half four in the morning Jack guessed he could not sleep either.

"Yeah, you had better not be naked though because I'll know this is a nightmare then." Jack shouted back. Michael walked in fully clothed a small grin on his face. "What's up I guess this isn't a social call at this time of the morning." Jack was a bit blunter than he had meant to be.

"Sorry, I can come back later, its nothing really." Michael was already stepping back out the door.

"No, it's alright I was awake anyway I couldn't sleep after everything today. I must admit I'm glad we didn't bump into Melfice today, I did not need my patience tested. What's up?" Michael sat on the end of Jack's bed.

"It's just that what Grey said earlier about me being descended from Lancelot." Unlike Kim Michael was obviously in turmoil over this revelation.

"What's the issue with it?" Jack knew how much of a shock it had been for himself to find out the truth. If it hadn't of been for Devaldros he still wouldn't have believed it himself.

"He betrayed Arthur." This story had been passed down through history. Jack wasn't concerned but clearly Michael was taking this to heart.

"Why is that bothering you?" Jack was trying to be sympathetic, but he couldn't understand why Michael would be affected by this. It was ancient history.

"What if I do the same thing to you? What if the is the Lancelot legacy to betray his best friend?" Michael sat smoothing the creases on the letter Louise had given Kim, he had taken to carrying it with him everywhere.

"I don't think legacy has anything to do with our futures. We have their memories, their blood, it doesn't mean we will repeat their mistakes. I trust you Michael, completely." This seemed to improve Michael's frame of mind.

"Maybe we do know better." He agreed.

"Do you know how Kim is taking the news? she barely blinked when she found out." Jack was trying to ask casually but Michael may have picked up on the desperation in his voice.

"Not to me, I think it's been another shock after everything that's happened." Jack couldn't blame her he remembered the conversation at the top of the warning beacon. He was yet to show her his true feelings.

"She doesn't know how I feel about her, she thinks my

feelings were being influenced by Devaldros. Probably thinks Arthur's memories are me think I love her as well now." Michael looked at him shaking his head laughing.

"You are without doubt the biggest idiot I've ever known. I've been friends with you both for as long as I can remember. Do you think I don't know how you both feel about each other?" he sat grinning stupidly. "You two love each other you always have. What you have never done is shown each other. Its driven me mad for years. Show her once and for all for the love of Merlin." Michael slapped him hard on the back. He was right, Jack needed to show Kim how he felt. Not because anyone else made him feel that way, but because she was the one for him. He realised he had a way to show her, something from before Arthur or Devaldros something that was just them.

"Michael, I need your help in a little plan of romance." Michael shook his hand,

"Anything you need. Just don't tell anyone I still have a reputation as a cold-hearted bastard I want to keep it. It stops everyone from asking for help."

Chapter 27

Timeless Love

"What's going on, Michael will you answer me?" Jack could hear Kim through the door he was trying to compose himself, no matter what happened this was the time. Carefully Jack slipped the small vial of golden potion Louise had given him months before under the cushion next to him. He no longer needed it for the original purpose and hoped this would be a better use for it.

"I told you I want to show you something, you'll have to wait and see." It wasn't hard to imagine Michael with a huge grin on his face, there was a delight in the voice he hadn't heard from his friend since Louise had left. The door handle twisted and slowly the door opened, Michael pushed Kim into the common room and closed the door behind her.

"Not that I'm upset with you, but what's going on?" she asked suspicious seeing Jack all alone.

"Would you like to sit down?" Jack patted the seat next to him.

"come on Jack, tell me what's going on?" she was apprehensive,

"Kim, you know me, I'm not going to bite you." she seemed to agree he was telling the truth and sat in the seat next to him. The vial cracked underneath the pillow and a gold thread began to envelop the two of them.

"Jack what is it what's going on." Kim had started to panic; he hadn't thought she would react like this.

"Kim do you trust me?" Jack shouted over the sound of air rushing past their ears.

"What?" she screamed back holding Jack as though scared the thread might break them apart.

"If you trust me, just wait a few more seconds and it will all be over." Kim clung even harder to Jack. He felt her warmth against him a hole that had existed in him for so long began to fill.

The thread ravelled around their head so they could no longer see. Jack clutched Kim's hand to let her know she was safe. she squeezed back Jack could tell she was unhappy, but she was doing it for him. Finally, the thread began to loosen allowing them some movement, but Kim clung even closer. The thread fell from their heads, but Kim kept her eyes closed.

"It's ok Kim, open your eyes, go on." Jack pushed her. She slowly opened her eyes and was astonished by what she saw.

"Jack where are we?" Kim gawped looking around the common Room had been replaced by the same ball room Jack had dreamed about after being stabbed by Merlin.

"it's a memory of a time long ago." Jack did not want to spoil the surprise of what was yet to come. Blurry shapes began to appear out of the air.

"what's happening now?" Kim brushed her hand against the blur.

"I can touch it." she said surprised.

"it's a person, as I said it's a memory that we can interact with, Louise made this for me, I was going to use it on the orb of my father's murder. But I wanted you to see something, it is especially important to me so please play along. Oh, and look down." Jack explained.

"what do you mean look…" Kim stared open mouthed her clothing had changed from her school clothes to an elegant ball gown.

"will you join me?" Kim Looked up at Jack his shirt and trousers had been replaced by a blood red cape over a white dragon hide tunic with a black dragon emblazed across the Front a uniform fit for a king.

"oh my." Kim was stunned.

"why have you done all this Jack? I don't understand." Jack smiled.

"just enjoy it." an elegant music began to play along with several dozen people talking. Jack grasped Kim's hand and led her to the dance floor.

"Jack please, you're not the greatest dancer I've seen that." Kim laughed looking around the room she was still in awe of what she could see. The ball room was splendid all her dreams were coming true in this room. Jack pulled her close to him. "Jack even though I appreciate all this, what is it were actually doing here?" Kim held Jack close swaying to the music.

"look over here." Jack span her around so her back was to his front.

"ok, what is it I'm meant to be seeing?" her head twisted towards his. Jack could almost taste her lips. Her eyes fixed upon his with his arms wrapped around her, but he dared not look back into her own.

"the man in the red armour." Jack stuttered. Not wanting her to ever look away from him again. But she did twist away.

"Michael?" Kim asked unsure of what she was seeing

sounding a little disappointed. She pulled away from Jack before he even thought. "Michael what are you doing here?" Kim was almost cross.

"I'm sorry my Lady, were you talking to me?" the man was confused. Jack came running over.

"I'm sorry, she mistook you for someone else, how are you my Lord Lancelot?" Jack tried to sound calm, but he had not really wanted to spend time with Lancelot.

"I'm fine thank you, may I ask, have you seen your King? I have urgent business with him." Jack shook his head he knew that about now Arthur would be meeting Guinevere for the first time and even if this was just a remake of a memory, he did not want to spoil that first time. Lancelot kissed Kim's hand and left to search for Arthur.

"that was Lancelot, but he looked so much like Michael?" Kim was astounded.

"well yeah, Grey told you, Michael was Lancelot." Jack took a deep breath. "And you were Guinevere. Would you like to dance again?" Jack said quickly hoping to bypass what he had just said. Kim had other ideas though.

"is that why we're here? so you can show me this and make me try to remember." Kim was being very protective.

"no that's not it at all, I wanted to show you something. I wanted to show you this." Jack pointed into the far back of the room. Kim clutched at Jack seeing Arthur and Guinevere for the first time shocked her. Jack was a little thrown himself he had not ever seen Arthur before. But it was the double of him.

"why do you want me to see this?" Kim asked hesitantly. Jack watched as Arthur dressed the same tried to speak with Guinevere but finding it hard to speak.

"You're Guinevere. Do you understand that now, you are her and she you, I think that Merlin brought us together here for the first time? And I wanted you to see our first meeting." Jack led Kim over towards Arthur. Whom seemed thankful so he could stop making an idiot of himself. "my Lord," Jack bowed, before tapping Kim reminding her to curtsy.

"Please Jack, it is not necessary, and I see you have brought another with you. Whom may I ask you are?" Kim clasped her arm around Jack's.

"My name is Kim my Lord." Arthur looked from her to Guinevere.

"Oh, I understand. She will be the other." Kim guessed that Arthur knew she was meant to be Guinevere and wanted an explanation.

"How does he know, I thought this was a memory?" Jack nodded.

"Well yes, it is but as it's mine, well ours," Jack pointed to Arthur.

"He knows everything that I know as well." Arthur grabbed Kim by the hand.

"I know that we are the worst dancers in the world in fact, normally I would prefer to fight a hundred mountain sized dragons than dance but when surrounded by such beauty I feel like I'm dancing already." Arthur smiled.

"I'm sorry." Kim paused.

"He wants to dance with you." Jack explained. Arthur led Kim away to the dance floor. He was as ungraceful as Jack, but he no longer found it funny. He had come here to try and show Kim that they had loved each other before they were even born and yet she now seemed to be enjoying herself more with Arthur.

'It's stupid, I'm jealous of myself.' Jack thought. But decided to intervene anyway with a quick whisper in Guinevere's ear they entered the floor Jack headed straight for Kim and Guinevere Arthur.

"May I interject." Jack asked politely.

"My dear self, it would be an honour." Arthur held out his hands for Jack to take.

"That's not funny in any time." Jack placed his hand on Kim's Shoulder and the other on her waist turning from Arthur.

"Jack that wasn't very nice." Kim scorned him a pulse red vein throbbed in Jack's head.

"I'm sorry but I have something else to show you before we finish." They stopped dancing; Jack closed his eyes concentrating as hard as he could. The world around the began to twist changing to a memory that was purely his own.

"Wait I know this place." Jack saw himself a child sitting on the bridge across the lake near the henge. He was eleven years old; this moment was one of his special memories. In the distance he could hear his family laughing and joking holding a picnic.

"Come on Jack, everyone is waiting for you." His mother called.

"Why are we here Jack?" Kim was watching the child version of him as he dangled his legs over the water.

"Do you remember this day?" Jack asked her, at that moment a child Kim came walking over the bridge and sat down next to the child Jack.

"Yes, it was a picnic with your family. It was a lovely day; I think it's the first time you ever acted like a

gentleman to me." Kim laughed looking at the two young versions of themselves.
"It holds a special meaning to me. Watch." Kim watched as the children laughed tickling each other. Eventually calming they saw Jacks fingers crawl like a spider across the timber until he was holding Kim's hand. The memory stopped in that moment. The sun setting over the lake and the smile of the young boy's face.
"What is the special meaning?" Kim struggled to ask her voice a little broken.
"It was this moment I realised something. I should have said there and then but something held me back. It has up until now in truth." He knelt by the small boy and ruffled his hair.
"What did you realise?" Jack dangled his legs over like his younger self. Kim sat beside him. He mimicked his earlier action, this time Kim aware of his hand inching across the wood until he held her own.
"I realised, in this moment, that I loved you." Kim stood still not saying a word the colour had drained from her face. Thirty heart pounding seconds passed before she opened her mouth, but she shut it quickly not saying anything. Jack's pulse was racing he had never been so scared waiting for someone to say something.
"Jack how can you be sure, how do you know this is what you feel? You had Devaldros and Arthur in here." She stroked his face and Jack's heart sunk.
"I love you with my soul, not because of Arthur, not because of Devaldros. Because of this moment right here. I wanted to show you Arthur and Guinevere. They loved each other." Jack stressed this it was important she understood this. "I don't love Guinevere. It was this

moment before Arthur's memories before Devaldros whispered to me. An eleven-year-old boy realised the young girl sat there was the only person he would ever love." Jack looked into Kim's beautiful eyes. She seemed shocked by what he was revealing.

"Say it." She whispered she needed to hear the words.

"I Jack London, love you Kimberley Illsley. You are my Queen from that moment, to forever more." It was as plain as he could make it. Whatever happened now he had been honest at last. He waited as Kim looked at to the water, the young versions of themselves sat frozen in time, their hands clasped.

"You can't love me Jack." She muttered almost to herself. He walked over and placed his hand on top of hers.

"I never thought that you would really love me, not even in my dreams, I thought you would laugh at me if I told you how I felt." Kim's hand gripped his own she was grinning. "I love you too. I have for as long as I can remember." She clasped the back of Jack's head and kissed him. Her lips as soft as clouds on his own. Warmth, love, affection, happiness, pleasure, lust, hate, despair, everything was lost in that moment. Jack had never felt less, but it was overwhelming he felt intoxicated, unable to take in the moment. Jack fell into the embrace, it was as though his soul was floating away, this was surely heaven.

They sat together on the sofa Kim huddled against him, he sat there Kim's head resting on his chest the smell of her hair invigorated Jack.

"can you pinch me please." Jack asked Kim.

"what, again?" Kim laughed.

The Dark Heart

"I just need to make sure I'm not dreaming, because if I am, I don't ever want to wake up." he wrapped his arms around her even tighter.

"you know that I'm not letting you go don't you."

"if you do ill grab you, I haven't waited this long to let you slip now. Can you tell me again." she whispered?

"ok, but I'm going to set you an allowance you can only ask me to say it a hundred times in one day ok?" Jack grinned.

"ok, but you will have to keep count. Now tell me." She wriggled against him teasing him.

"ok, I love you." Kim squealed with delight turning she kissed him again and again. "do you know I don't think I will ever get tired of this." Jack knew he would not.

"shall we test that then my dear girlfriend Kim?" Jack wanted to emphasis this.

"I think we should my lovely boyfriend Jack." And again, they kissed their lips pressed together and angels fell from the sky because this was perfect a perfect love that the world would cherish.

"do you think Michael is still out there warning people not to come in?" Jack laughed.

"I hope so if they did, they would find us in an awfully compromising position." Kim said stroking Jack's cheek. Jack thought for a second,

"what's that meant to mean then, I thought that you would want people to see us together. Or are you ashamed of me?" Jack wanted everyone to see them together.

"no, I'm not ashamed of you. And yes, I do want people to see us together just not when I'm doing this." Kim grabbed Jack and started to kiss and nibble his neck.

"ok, maybe not now then." Jack played along sliding down the sofa wrestling with Kim kissing and writhing with pleasure.

"JACK," a voice shouted from behind the sofa.

"oh, shit it all." Jack swore loudly pulling his t-shirt down. He jumped from the sofa and to his horror saw Louise standing there clutching the table for support. She looked exhausted and ragged her clothes were torn and blood was flowing from wounds in her arms and face. Jack ran over and helped her sit into a chair.

"what the hell." Kim looked on astonished, no-one had seen Louise for weeks since she had left during the trial. And for her to suddenly turn up in this condition did not mean anything good,

"what happened to you?" Jack asked binding her wound with his wand.

"Jack, I need to warn you and Michael the dark council their planning something it's going to happen soon." Louise collapsed before she could say anything more.

"get Michael and clear the corridor." Jack told Kim.

Chapter 28

A Dark Plan

Louise had been placed in Michael's bed; she was unconscious. Whatever had happened to her she seemed to have used the last of her strength to get to them to try and warn them of some impending danger. Jack had bound her wound's as best he could, but he was not particularly skilled at it, Louise herself was their best healer.

"what did she say again?" Michael asked holding Louise's hand, he was if possible, whiter than Louise. All the blood seemed drained from them both.

"she said the dark council was planning something. But I don't understand how she would know." Kim fretted rebinding Louise's wounds for the third time.

"I don't know she is the dark priestess after all. Maybe she has a connection somehow." It made no sense that Louise would be connected to the dark council. She had detested being associated with dark magic.

"It doesn't matter right now. We need to get the nurse. I don't think we should risk moving her." Kim was watching Michael carefully, as he cleaned the blood from Louise's Hair with a cloth. He waved his wand over the bowl of water that had turned red for the third time. Jack wondered how many more bowls it would take to clean all the blood. There was no two ways about it. She had been tortured and for a long period of time judging from how some of her previous cuts had healed.

"Michael, do you have that note she left Kim still?" an idea struck him, but he prayed he was wrong. Michael pulled the note from his pocket and handed it to Jack. He took it studying each word as carefully as any ancient text.

"What are you expecting to find?" Kim asked after his fourth read through.

"I don't know exactly, nothing seems wrong, it's just a thought but what if Louise didn't write this or was forced to write it?" Michael snatched the letter back studying it again.

"Why do you think that?" she asked.

"It never made sense to me that she suddenly left. I thought she may have felt guilty about Robin but now with this maybe she was forced to leave someone threatened her, or us, or her family." It didn't feel like a stretch to imagine this.

"Maybe Merlin knew about her involvement after all. He wanted us dead, didn't he? Michael said still studying the letter, Jack saw him stop reading, he stood walking over to his bedside drawer he opened it and pulled one letter from a stack. It was clear Michael and Louise had been writing to each other for a long time. And from the fact he had kept them all next to him, showed Jack how much they meant. "Do you see this?" Michael handed Jack the two letters pointing to her signature on the bottom of both sheets.

"What am I looking at?" Michael rolled his eyes and handed them to Kim. She too seemed to struggle for a moment suddenly, she clapped her hand to her mouth in horror. "Is someone going to explain?" he asked.

"The signatures don't match." Kim whispered.

"Maybe she just wrote it differently, it doesn't mean I'm right." He reasoned.

"if you copy someone writing using magic the signature will never match, It's a hex on your own to stop anyone forging it. That's why when you sign a document you use your wand. How do you not know this?" She asked him, exasperated.

"So, she couldn't have written this if the signature is different is what you're saying?" Kim nodded. Michael collapsed in his seat next to her mortified.

"How didn't I notice?" He asked rhetorically.

"Michael, you can't blame yourself. None of us did." Kim knelt beside him taking his hand in hers.

"I should have seen it, I tried to find her after I was released. I sent letters everywhere I could I asked my parents to speak with hers, but no one had seen them at the council meetings. And now she turns up here having been tortured. I wasn't there when she needed me." Michael was trying desperately to hold in his tears, he was physically shaking. Jack understood how he felt. It had been the feeling of helplessness that had allowed Devaldros to use him.

"I'm going to get Grey rather than the nurse, I think its best if we keep Louise's appearance a secret for now, it will probably be safer. He will be able to heal her just as well." Jack put his hand on Michael's shoulder. "We will make whoever did this pay, I promise you."

"Jack searched the entire of the castle from the council chambers, the headmaster's office, through the dungeons, his old office, he even knocked on the

knight's chambers where he had been told to search by the river Pendragon. It had taken him almost an hour, but he found him eventually by a large oak tree that had been felled the year before by a large storm.
"it's amazing don't you think that even the mightiest things can come crushing down with the smallest efforts." Grey had not even looked around, but he knew he was standing there.
"Sir." Jack puzzled looking at the oak tree. "I think it took more than a little effort to bring that to the ground." Grey chuckled to himself.
"I'm sorry Jack, I was trying to say something else. I meant it takes so little to destroy a man of all his morals and sense of justice they just disappear when thing is do not go his way. Humanity is in a poor way." he added grimly. Jack watched as a carp blipped to the surface of the water and swam away, he pretended to be interested in the fish but all he could think about was how right Grey was. Jack after all had only just thrown away his morals about not involving himself with Kim for her protection. A fact he did not share with the professor.
"sir, I need you to come with me. I can't really explain here but it is particularly important, the only thing is no-one can see." Jack whispered barely audible over the river. Grey smiled.
"I understand I shall be very discrete, where am I to meet you?" Jack could have sworn that Grey had said nothing at all. He told him all he dared and rushed away to tell Michael he was coming.

Grey escorted Jack and Kim from Michael's room leaving him alone with her. He looked very grim. He took them to his personal chamber where he was sure they would not be overheard.

"Jack, I'm going to ask you to carry your sword with you at all times. I will change the charm so it will be its normal size whenever you deem necessary." Jack nodded his understanding.

"Sir, I want Kim and Michael to have Knight's training and the three of us additional lessons in practical defensive magic. When Louise recovers for her to join us." Jack thought this was sensible. If Devaldros was coming for them, any training they could get was now possibly the difference between life and death. It was no longer about being in school and learning new spells but about winning a war.

Grey had agreed readily to Jack's request for additional training for him and the others. Whether it was because he agreed with Jack, or because he didn't think he could deny him now he knew his lineage Jack didn't know. At this moment he didn't care either as long as it happened.

"Do you think we should get Michael some dinner?" Kim asked, they knew it was unlikely he would leave Louise's bedside at this point until she made any signs of recovery.

"Yeah, I'll go to the dining hall and get us all something." Kim kissed him and headed off towards the common room. He felt slightly dazed still every time she kissed him.

People hissed and whispered behind their hands as he passed, the students all now knew of his lineage since his trial. They knew too that he was responsible for releasing Devaldros and Robin's death. Most students were giving him a wide berth happy to leave him alone. Others were more hostile, whenever they saw him hurling abuse or jinxes at him. He mostly used the secret passages to get around as so few students knew about them but unfortunately none nearby lead to the dining hall. As he passed beneath a balcony overlooking the main hall water poured all over him soaking him. He stood there for a second spitting the water dripping down his face and shaking his hair dry. It was then he saw Rachel coming over to him along with Barry.

"Are you ok?" Rachel asked her voice hollow. This was the first time he had seen her since the night Robin had died. She was different, he almost didn't recognise her. Rachel had always been immaculate, perfect makeup, hair, clothing standing before him now though her hair looked slightly wild, she wore no makeup and looked as though she had been wearing the same clothes for several days.

"Yeah, I needed a shower anyway." He said looking up at a pair of Lancelot's who were high fiving at his appearance. "I'm sorry I haven't spoken to you since…" He couldn't bring himself to say it. He knew how much Robin and Rachel meant to each other.

"It's ok, I haven't really been out of my room much, I didn't really want to face the world. I heard what you said during your trial about Robin being a hero." She took Jack's hand in her own. "Thank you." She had tears in her eyes.

"It was true, every word. Robin was a hero; he was my friend. I'm so sorry I couldn't bring him back to you." Tears filled his eyes now. He was letting his friends down. Robin dead, Louise lay unconscious.

The Dark Heart

Michael and Rachel broken, his family still recovering from their own nightmare. He suddenly felt a sense of hopelessness wash over him. The ray of light that had been the kiss with Kim only moments ago, disappearing in his mind like a cloud had moved in front. Rachel squeezed his hand lightly.

"Are you getting food, Barry convinced me I needed to eat." Barry was looking exhausted.

"Ive been keeping an eye on Rachel, a favour for her older brother." He explained unnecessarily. Jack knew he was trying to explain he wasn't hitting on Rachel. He was grateful, Robin wouldn't have appreciated how he hadn't taken time to comfort her. He knew he was going to have to do better.

"I'm taking stuff away to the room but let's get some together." A voice sneered behind them

"I'm surprised your talking to him again, after he got your boyfriend killed." It was Melfice, his face twisted into a sneer. It was clear he had been waiting for something like this. Barry made for Melfice but Jack stopped him.

"I clearly didn't hit you hard enough." Jack taunted.

"Yes, well greatness does require sacrifices sometimes." It was clear the memory of Jack's attack rocked him a little. Jack did not have a clue what Melfice was talking about,

"Melfice your just full of crap, so say whatever it is that you have to say then do everyone a favour and get lost." Jack was getting angry no-one could get to him like Melfice even Joe was an amateur by comparison.

"How's Louise?" Rachel and Barry looked confused they of course didn't know she was back; the shock must have slipped on Jack's face.

"How would I know?" Jack lied.

"She's here in the castle, I know. I'm presuming in the other idiots room." Something important was happening Jack knew he was trying to grasp the hidden meanings behind Melfice's words.

"and how would you know where Louise is or isn't?" Jack asked.

"You still haven't worked it all out yet have you. What does Devaldros see in you?" a stone slid down to his stomach at the look on Melfice's face.

"What did you do?" he felt sick to his stomach.

"You're finally starting to understand aren't you. How it's all connected, from the moment you got here right up to this second." Melfice had been waiting on this his grand reveal. "It was me; I was working with Devaldros all along. My family knew all about him. You think only Arthur had people in place ready for his return?" He was lying he had to be. There was no way that he could have known. If he was lying though why was he saying this here in front of the entire hall. Even pretending he was involved would get him in trouble. And the other students wouldn't take kindly to it. "Connect the dots Jack, I have been tormenting you at every stage, pushing you to your edge. Who do you think was assisting Devaldros when he took over your body when you were asleep? I helped him to find the high chancellors son. I took him to Michael and Louise, I wanted him to kill them, but he had other ideas. I made you attack me getting you locked away in the tower, to give Devaldros time to convince you to release him. Then when you were ready, I popped in and a little push made you tip over and free him. My mother and father got him the access to the council in Dublin. Louise had started to suspect I was involved so whilst you were on trial, we convinced Merlin to cause a little distraction. All so I could get her out of the city without anyone noticing. Devaldros wanted her for some reason you see. She thought she got away, but we already had what we needed from her." Rachel clutched her mouth as though she were about to be sick. Barry stood shocked. It made a twisted sense, Devaldros would never have been able to do these things alone.

"I'm going to ask you one more time, what have you done?" Jack was attempting to keep his breathing steady, he wanted nothing more than to draw his sword and stab It through Melfice's heart. The crowd around them was beginning to grow restless.

"I did what I needed to, I distracted you." Melfice burst out laughing. Unafraid as the students began to gather around him their anger close to boiling over. "I would be asking why I needed Louise by the way. Rather why I needed an Arthurian specifically. Or don't you know how we access the common rooms, its old blood magic. How's Kim?" The crowd was now within touching distance of Melfice.

"Grab him and get a teacher." Jack shouted before running for the common room. Blood magic they had used Louise's blood in order to gain access to the common room. Melfice's quip about Kim couldn't be a coincidence either. Had the dark council come for Kim.

He pushed the door open to see her normally immaculate room in tatters a heavily hooded wizard stood in the far corner of the room with Kim's head being held by her hair, her body lying unconscious at his feet.

"what the hell?" Jack raised his wand but too late the wizard was lightning quick and struck his arm it shook uncontrollably making Jack drop his wand.

"I'm leaving here and I'm taking her with me. As for you, stay here for now at least." the wizard wheezed. Jack could not see his face, but he could just make out something sparked a familiar feeling.

"what have you done to her." Jack was appalled Kim looked as bad as Louise the same type wounds almost ritualistic.

"I have prepared her for what is to come." The man boasted as though Jack proved no more of a threat then a fly.

"and what is to come?" Jack's voice jogging from his arm.

"don't worry you'll find out at some point, but I'll be having my fun with this one first." The wizard reached down for Kim.

"if you touch her again, I will kill you." Jack screamed at him. The wizard laughed at Jack.

"you are as nothing your strength could not even stop this feeble body." again he laughed at Jack almost maniacally. He had not noticed his charm wearing off on Jack his arm returning to normal. Jack had been waiting for this he screwed his fist into a ball.

'screw it.' he thought faking a dive for his wand the wizard fired upon his wand hitting stone, but he was no longer there. Jack jumped across Kim's bed tackling the wizard around the waist forcing him to drop his wand and Kim.

"I will kill you fuckers, each and every one of you." Jack punched and punched the wizard he did not stop until a cough behind him brought him to his senses.

Kim's body was wracked in pain thrashing about like a fish gasping for the water. "MICHAEL, ANYONE HELP!" Jack screamed as loud as he could, he held Kim in his arms praying to any god to save her. Jack wiped Kim's blood-soaked hair from her face the wizard had cut into her flesh leaving symbols behind. "Kim please talk to me, Kim it's Jack please I need you." her eyes opened for the smallest of seconds and smiled at him.
  "I love you." she mouthed before falling unconscious again. Jack cried out desperation in his voice.
  "what the hell is going on here?" Levell had been passing and heard Jack's cry for help.
  "Miss, please help her. I can't do anything help her." Levell came rushing over holding her wand aloft. She stood still not doing a thing. "What's wrong why aren't you helping her?" Jack shouted.
  "I don't know how; I never could do this part of magic." Levell was almost hysterical. Jack grabbed the wand from her hand and started to bind her wounds.
  "Run and get Michael and then get Grey," He shouted to her as she ran from the room. Within thirty seconds Michael rushed in.
  "Who did this?" he jumped across to the wizard laying beaten unconscious on the floor. He pulled the cowl down to reveal Frank, the councillor. "Him." Michael exclaimed looking at the bloody mess that was once a man.
  "I don't care who he is." Jack was fretting over Kim, he longed to finish off Frank. "Just help Kim." Jack pleaded holding her as tightly but delicately as he could. Levell reappeared at the door along with Grey.
  "Jack, Stay back." he commanded placing chains around frank. Who had just started to regain

consciousness, Kim was still in a bad way though.

"Let's get her onto the bed." Michael said. They laid her carefully against her thrashing it was difficult.

"You think this will make any difference the Master will have her. It is his will, and it shall be done." Frank laughed seemingly lost to madness. Jack rammed the chained Frank to the floor. He pulled his father's sword from his side.

"Jack, no." screamed Levell.

"I'll do it." Hissed Michael, they wanted blood for what had happened here.

"Jack, we need him alive. He may have information we need." Grey was right but his desire for revenge was nearly overwhelming.

"One reason and I mean a good one, not to kill him now." Behind him Kim started thrashing on the bed again. Jack released Frank and ran to her bedside trying to calm Kim.

"Get him out of here." He whispered pooling all his strength to remain calm.

Since Louise being at the school was no longer a secret both she and Kim had been moved to the infirmary. Michael and Jack had gone with them. Kim and Louise's parents had been informed but were unable to attend. The council had been put into lockdown due to the betrayal of Melfice's parents and Frank. They were deliberating over what to do with them. The Trelane's residence had been raided but found empty, the former owners no-where to be found. Jack knew they would have all left when Melfice had been revealing his master plan to Jack. His only hope being they may have left some clue for them to follow. At eleven the nurse had told them they had to leave but both had refused. She instead had allowed them to sleep in the empty beds. Under the condition that they would not try to wake either of them. Jack had explained to Michael everything that had happened, how Melfice had confessed to everything. Michael had attempted to force his way into the dungeon when told. Jack knew full well if Michael had managed to get to him, he would have Killed Melfice in a horrific manner. It had taken Grey to stop him, he had reasoned with him once under restraints Louise needed him more than he needed revenge.

Now that Michael had calmed or at least wasn't about to try and kill Melfice in the immediate future he and Jack had slowly started discussing the events of the day.
"What worries me is why Devaldros used Frank? He was a council member, along with Melfice's parents." Michael said quietly.
"Because he just threw away three perfectly positioned spies along with Melfice." Michael nodded. "I guess this explains why he freed Merlin. He would have been able to tell him how to get into the common rooms. Either that or he was always a member of the dark council, like Melfice's family. It feels strange though he's throwing away people in the best positions to advance his plans with no regard." It was difficult to think straight, their fear overwhelming their desire to understand. In the darkness Kim coughed sending Jack running to her side. He grabbed a damp flannel cooling her head. He felt infuriated at his uselessness. "you know, I really hate this room." the weather outside reflected Jack's mood. A storm had battered the castle from all sides ever since Kim had been moved. The

lightning had struck the tower several times making tiles crash to the ground far below. The thunder was so loud that the nurse had placed a silencing charm on the walls so that it would not awaken Kim or Louise, but you could still occasionally hear the ferociousness inside. "how is she doing?" Jack asked Michael who so far still had not left Louise's bedside.

"the nurse said with a little rest she should be better in no time." he sat still her hand in his as though he was pouring his strength into her.

"can I ask you something?" Jack quizzed; Michael shrugged not paying any real attention. "Do you love Louise?" He slowly turned to look at Jack.

"She loves me, and I love her." Michael looked as broken as he felt.

"Good." Jack said calmly. "you should love her. You should stay be her side and never let go. We're at war again and they're coming for the people we love. Me and you were meant to be generals in this war, and we need to stay focused." Jack stroked Kim's hair was it only this morning they were sharing their first kiss. Jack smiled down at her willing her to awaken and everything to be ok.

"It's why I dreamed of her; I think. I know she's connected to Lancelot in the past. Old souls seeking out love across time." Michael held Louise's hand. It was strange to see him like this, vulnerable. "I forgot to ask you how things went between you?" Michael asked not looking away from Louise's unconscious body.

"We were finally honest." Jack did not want to say anything more right now, he didn't think it right. Michael shouldn't hear that Jack had been enjoying the best moments of his life whilst his own love was

The Dark Heart

desperately clawing her way to them, trying to find safety. Kim's last words seemed to scream in his mind. She loved him. Did she think them to be truly her last words?

"will you get some sleep? or they will be awake before you! I'm all for heart-warming moments but not at three in the bloody morning." the nurse shouted from her room. Michael half grinned at Jack.

"come on, she's right let's get some sleep." Jack kissed Kim on the forehead. "Please wake up, I can't be without you." He whispered to her not wanting Michael to hear.

Jack had a restless night's sleep, he had dreams of Kim, Louise and Robin sinking into a sea of sand screaming for him to help them, but every time he tried to grab them, they had sunk further away from him. He awoke, sweat pouring from his body.

'a nightmare.' He panted hoping never to hear the screams again. 'how did Arthur ever live with the responsibility of protecting a kingdom, When I couldn't even protect my friends?' He walked to the end of the infirmary were a bowl of water glistened in the early morning sun. The blue surface shimmered and seemed to break as Jack approached even though the floor was still. He dove his hands into the water throwing it against his face, the coolness refreshed his weary eye's but did little to alleviate the weight in his heart. Michael stirred early he too appeared to have been having nightmares.

"You ok?" Jack asked. Michael waved his hand at Jack.

"give me a second I just need to make out my bearings ok." Michael panted hard placing his head between his knees. "sorry just a bad dream." he looked intently at the floor Jack thought he looked like he was going to throw up.

"yeah, I know the feeling." Jack said running his hand through his untamed hair.

"what was yours about?" Jack asked casually. Michael kept staring at the floor.

"Arthur killing Lancelot." all the air seemed to have been sucked out of the room. Neither of them could speak for a few seconds.

"oh," Jack said finally. "so not your best night's sleep I guess?" it seemed a rather lame thing to say but what else could he do the idea of someone seeing your ancestor killing them was a rather strange one.

"no, not my best night's sleep. "How are they?" Michael asked quickly changing the subject.

"Louise stirred a few minutes ago, but that's about it I haven't seen the nurse yet to ask her." a strange awkwardness fell between the pair. The idea of Michael seeing Lancelot's death at the hands of Arthur unnerved them, although neither would say so. Jack walked over to Kim's bedside and held her hand. "Michael where do you think that Excalibur was hidden?" Jack asked as casually as possible.

"I don't know, then again, who could apart from the person who hid it? I mean, pretty much every inch of England has been searched since the time it was hidden. You would have thought someone would have found it by now." he sat on his bed watching Louise like a hawk searching for any sign of life.

"yeah, maybe unless they needed something they didn't have." Jack was thinking more out loud then really asking Michael.

"what, you think that we would have a better time finding it then some of the most powerful wizards who have ever lived?" Jack smiled at Michael.

"we have been two of the most powerful knights who ever lived, so why not? maybe there is something about us that will help us find it, what is the harm in looking? Don't you think that we would have a better chance against Devaldros with Excalibur than without it?" the door to the infirmary came crashing open interrupting them, Grey walked in a storm in his eyes.

"Sir, what is it? what's the matter?" Grey slammed the door but quickly checked on Louise and Kim.

"They killed him." Grey seethed.

"what, who?" Jack asked.

"the council killed Frank. Executed him for crimes against them in the dungeon only minutes ago, his body will remain there until they can work out what to do with it. I pleaded with them, I told them he might prove useful. But they had to kill him to prove they were doing something to the public. And after what happened yesterday, I can almost blame them." Grey slumped into a chair defeat in his eyes.

"What happened last night sir?" Michael said looking concerned.

"Mr Trelane escaped, it appears Bravo helped him." Jack and Michael roared their fury. "It appears even more people are already on his side than I originally thought. It's not the worst of it." How could it be worse, their two best sources of information had either been killed or escaped. "A hospital was destroyed last night. Over three hundred patients and staff were inside at the time. Every Knight and the newly formed Avartarians were there within minutes, but they couldn't help." Jack and Michael bowed their heads at the horror they had just heard. "Michael, I know how you feel about Miss Harrison here, but we must wake her by magical means. We need to know what it is she knows before anything like this happens again." Michael looked horrified at the prospect.

"could it hurt her?" he asked.

"nothing serious, but she may have a headache for a while. I will not do this unless you say it is ok Michael, and Jack I need to ask the same of you with Kim. We need to know what the dark council wanted with her also. Their parents have already consented." Michael and Jack exchanged glances. They knew that it wouldn't cause any lasting pain, and they knew that after the horror of the night before they couldn't say no, but still they weren't sure if they wanted the girls to awake in such a way.

"it needs to be done." Jack whispered. Michael seemed to be thinking the same nodding his agreement.

"let's face it, we can't do anything else, can we?" Michael walked over to Louise and looked at her, just looked. Jack thought he was almost saying goodbye. "when you do this, I want to be here ok?" Grey agreed walking off to prepare the necessary potions.

The death of over three hundred people rocked Jack, whenever news of Devaldros reached the school he had always prayed it wasn't something like this, no matter if someone did manage to defeat Devaldros it could never bring back those three hundred people whose lives had been lost. But Jack was also shocked at just how unlike Devaldros this attack was. What did he stand to gain from this senseless killing, there simply was not any logic to it? Jack and Michael sat in silence waiting for Grey to return with the potion, each thinking about the loss they could so soon be facing. Out of nowhere Michael slammed his fist into the beside cabinet.

"Why do this now Jack, why must that thing always commit some atrocity when were just beginning to become happy again?" Jack knew Michael was talking about having Louise back in his life. But he did not answer, how could he, the truth was there was no answer. "I'm asking you Jack why he does this?" Michael was almost pleading with him. Jack knew Michael was just taking his frustrations out on him he understood it, but he was getting tired of it.

"MICHAEL, HOW THE HELL DO I KNOW WHAT HE'S THINKING?" Jack was shouting without even realising it. "I mean, the monster just had three hundred people killed for no reason as far as I can tell. Why do that? I ask you, why change his style after all this time? he's always used subterfuge before now." Jack was trying to sound calm he did not really want an argument in the middle of the infirmary. Michael had a strange expression on his face, his mouth hung half open like he was about to sing. Jack blew a great breath of frustration. "Michael I'm sorry, I didn't mean to…"

"Ssh." Michael hushed him,

"what?" Jack asked confused.

"what you said your right, he doesn't do the whole blow everything up just for laughs. He would only do it if there was something in it for him. Think about it, Grey said it himself, every knight and every member of the Avartarians were there within minutes. It was a distraction he wanted them there." Jack started to understand what he was talking about, "what do you reckon that the explosion happened at the same time as that scum attacked Kim?" Jack asked.

"I don't know, I mean what would they accomplish by sacrificing Frank to us? I mean let us face it he was in a prime position to pass on information from within the council itself. He is now dead, Devaldros still cannot enter Camelot and the black council are not any closer to getting to us. But what bugs me the most is what Frank wanted with Kim?" Michael rubbed his temple.

"god I'm getting a headache, I just can't work this out." Jack was thinking hard about what Michael had just said something seemed wrong. "why did you say that Frank wanted Kim." Jack asked.

"that's what you said, he told you he wanted her." Michael said bemused.

"no, I didn't say that I said he wanted her. But Frank meant Deval……" Jack jumped from his seat. The truth hit him like a hammer to the chest. "stay here and don't let anyone in." Jack cried out to Michael crashing through the door. Michael called out behind him, but Jack was already halfway down the hall. He ran as fast as he could not stopping when people called out to him or swore at him. Even when a boy almost pushed Jack down the stairs. He managed to tiptoe quickly down most of them, but his momentum made him trip down the last couple. In one motion though he managed to make the fall into a roll and was on his feet in seconds. Darting forward as hard as he could, the hallways were almost a blur. Further and further down the castle he ran until finally he reached the dungeons, panting hard Jack reached for his sword, the dungeon hall was dark and dank water seemed to be dripping from the walls soaking the torches that lit the way. Jack kicked open the first door, but the room was empty. He blew a great breath of relief, his stomach tied in knots again as he reached the second again, he kicked through and again there was nothing except a few rats scurrying on the floor. Again, he breathed a sigh of relief. As he approached the third a sensation pulled at his insides drawing him to the furthest door sealed from the outside, but this was it he knew it.

'it's always the last.' Jack told himself staring at the oak door in Front of him. 'just think of Kim.' he thought an immediate feeling of strength arose within him. Quickly he unsealed the door and entered, sure enough lying in the middle of the floor was Frank, dead. Jack walked around the body observing it carefully. Once he had circled, he closed the door.

"Get up." He said to the body. "I said get up." Jack kicked out at Franks corpse. The leg flayed out coming to a rest and stayed still. 'maybe I was wrong.' Jack thought to himself. A great relief swept over him as he turned his back to leave, but the sound of metal dragging over the stone floor chilled his blood. Jack turned back to see the body of Frank sitting up from the floor raising from the dead. "Hello Devaldros." Jack said calmly. Frank's face twisted into an ugly warped smile.

"Hello Arthur, it has been too long. I missed you." this time there was no mistaking the cold gravelled voice it sent more chills down Jack's spine.

"I suppose I should be surprised that you're here, but I guess I always knew you would be back, in fact the only thing that bothers me is that you used that body you're in to get back into the castle." Jack was trying to mock Devaldros but was making a poor job of it.

"there were other reasons, I do want your queen."

Jack's blood was heating up.

"you don't scare me anymore, so why don't you tell me why you have come you can't hurt me in that body and I'm guessing it's taking a lot of strength to keep that dead weight upright." Jack was right Franks body was beginning to sweat heavily. Devaldros ran his hands over Frank showing nothing but contempt for it.

"This wizard wasn't as powerful as I wanted but this body got what I wanted done." Jack looked over at Devaldros

'He does have his limits.' He thought. "Why do you want her?" Jack was clutching his wand under his coat.

"She is as much mine as yours." he sneered. Jack bit his tongue he needed to find out as much as possible, Franks body was drooping what was left of his life edging away.

"Kim isn't anyone's, we love each other, That isn't ownership. There isn't any way you could convince her to love someone like you." Franks failing body was sickening, the skin seemed to be slipping from his bones. The muscles tearing away. Jack could smell the body putrefying far quicker than it should.

"You think that I would want a pure Guinevere no." Devaldros shook his head vigorously it made Jack feel sick as an eye slipped from its socket and flopped around his cheek. "Your queen will be my dark reflection. Even now I am awakening her dark heart. She soon will no longer love you." Jack watched thinking about what Devaldros was saying.

"Is that why you wanted Louise you were attempting to corrupt her?" Jack understood the plan. Devaldros rushed forward at Jack but the body had degraded too much. The legs of Frank snapped barely more than dust, collapsing to the floor.

"She provided me an opportunity to explore her mind. But her own affinity with dark magic would have protected her from my efforts. Your queen though as pure as snow it will be all too easy." He paused allowing the sinister tones to fill the room. "I'm going to take your queen as my own, I will kill your family and destroy your Knights as I did all those years ago." Jack looked at him fury in his eyes. The skin of Frank's body now opaque as it liquefied in front of his eyes. Bubbling and popping releasing a sickening smell Jack would never forget. Devaldros pulled himself up on his crumbling stumps. Jack stared him down though as disgusting as Franks body now was a white fire had lightened within him.

"you will never touch any of my friends, you won't get near my family and as for my queen. If you ever manage to find a way near her again, I will find a way to destroy you just as you killed my friend. This is for him." Jack grabbed his sword and thrust it into the abdomen ripping his sword up splitting Frank from head to toe. Devaldros screamed but only for a second as the body fell to the floor in two pieces. Jack smiled as the sound of Devaldros screaming still filled the room. "You do feel pain." something sparkled at his feet Jack picked it up he was surprised to see it was an amulet. "This must be how Devaldros was able to possess him." Jack realised but he had no time to dwell he needed to see Grey.

Chapter 29

Awakened

Jack crept into the infirmary, seeing Grey and Michael were seated waiting for him. Grey jumped to his feet at the sight of Jack.

"Jack, my goodness, what has happened." Grey was in a state of shock. Jack pulled an amulet from his coat pocket and threw it to Grey.

"that was around Frank's neck." Grey held the amulet up to the light.

"what is it?" Michael asked.

"it's what allowed Devaldros to possess frank." Jack explained all about Devaldros' plan. Grey had been concerned about Devaldros being able to enter Camelot.

"I told them, they shouldn't have killed him, the council overruled the acting Merlin in Camelot, it has never happened before." Jack could see his thinking.

"You believe more of the council are on his side? They needed him dead, not to be able to reveal who they are." Grey said nothing but they all knew it was true. Jack suddenly imagined they were at the centre of an ever-shrinking iceberg with sharks waiting around to devour them.

"We need to start taking control of this Jack, we need allies." Michael said. He was right they could no longer act like children, if they were to ensure the people they loved were protected, he was going to have to step up.

"What did he mean about awakening Kim's dark heart though? We need to wake her and see if there was any psychological harm." Grey stared at the two women laying in their infirmary beds. The three of them stood looking at them, terrified about what they may soon find out.

Jack cleaned himself up quickly and stepped out from behind a curtain.

"I'm sorry, I suppose we had better get on with this then." he watched as Grey placed two clear vials onto a nearby table.

"what's in the potion then?" Michael asked eyeing them curiously.

"I think it would be better if you didn't know, forgive me but it would take a tremendous amount of time to explain it all correctly and we just don't have the time." Michael was not happy, but he did not object to continuing. Jack sat watching, all he wanted was for Kim to wake now, he needed to see what Devaldros was trying to do. He had promised himself that he would never allow anyone to hurt her again. And he had failed. Grey pierced the bottom of the vial and ran a tube from the vial into the girl's arms.

"the knights have started to experiment with this form of introducing potions to a person. So far it seems a far more effective way of introducing the potion then tipping it down someone's throat. I believe they call it a drip." Grey explained.

"what do you mean by experiment, this is safe isn't it?" Jack did not like the look of the drip. Grey smiled understandingly.

"it's far safer, people ran the risk of drowning before. The potion is administered directly into the body. It allows the potion to take effect far quicker, they should wake within the hour." The nurse had done a fantastic job on healing the girls there was no discernible injuries to their body's all that was unknown was the damage to their brains and they did not know about that until they were awake.

Jack and Michael sat patiently by the girl's bedsides waiting for any sign of them awakening.
"what's taking so long?" Michael shouted looking at the clock the hour was almost up and so far, neither girl had so much as twitched.
"patience Michael, it will be soon. We can't rush this." Grey had no more finished saying this when Louise's arm flicked out almost hitting Michael.
"Louise." he said unsure. She suddenly lurched forward throwing up violently. Michael jumped up out of the way of the sick and started to rub her back. When she had finished being sick, he helped her to lay back down.
"it's alright, she's ok," Michael shouted looking around at Jack. But he was sat motionless waiting for Kim to awake nothing was happening.
"sir, why isn't she waking up?" Jack asked desperately.
"I'm sure she just needs a little more time that's all, her injuries occurred after Louise's that's all let's just give her a few more minutes before we worry ok." He smiled down at Jack. The nurse was fluttering about Louise checking that everything was ok. Three minutes passed Jack with one eye on the clock the other intently

on Kim.

"sir, it's been an hour and ten minutes since you administered the potion, why isn't this working?" Jack was beginning to panic; Grey called the nurse asking her to check on Kim's vitals. Jack was biting his nails, the nurse straightened giving away nothing from her posture.

"There's no need to keep us all in suspense we've had enough of that today." Jack said rather quickly his nerves getting the better of him.

"she's the same as before, if your potion was working professor, we should have seen some improvement by now." Jack jumped to his feet. "That's not good is it?" Grey shook his head at Jack.

"that potion should have woken her unless,"

"unless what?" Jack pushed. Grey did not want to answer.

"UNLESS WHAT?" Jack shoved Grey. "what is it you have done to her?" he snarled; the room almost shook with his anger.

"I think she is catatonic. In other words, in a coma."

"no, she can't be." Jack argued. "Louise's awake and she had the same potion why wouldn't she be in a coma as well then?" Jack looked on despairingly. But no-one answered him. Looking around Michael bowed his head. Louise was still out of it and not able to tell him anything. "fine if you can't wake her, then I will." Jack grabbed hold of Kim but as soon as he made contact an electric charge sent him flying across the room smashing his head into the stone wall behind him.

"Jack." Michael called running over to him.

"I'm just going to sleep here for a while." Jack whimpered grabbing the back of his head. Blood trickled down his neck.

"Are you ok?" Grey asked checking his pupils for concussion.

"I'm fine just what the hell did you do to her?" electricity buzzed around Kim blindingly bright.

"I didn't do this, there's something else happening here." Grey was astounded not knowing what to make of what was happening before his eyes.

"Devaldros." a soft voice muttered from the corner.

"Louise. You're ok take it easy." Michael said to keep her calm. "he isn't here he can't hurt you ok." he grabbed the sponge and mopped her forehead,

"Not me, Kim he's changing Kim, changing her mind her memories" she blacked out having used all her strength.

"he's doing what?" Jack ran over desperately hoping she would answer him. Michael grabbed hold of him.

"Jack stop it, she's told us all she can." Michael pleaded. Jack felt he was on the edge of insanity. He wanted nothing more than to rip the room apart. He turned upon Grey.

"You're this great and powerful Elder, so tell me how do we wake her if Devaldros has planned this then it's obviously not going to get better on its own?" the fire inside of Jack blazed white hot.

"I'm sorry Jack but there is nothing that I can do this is magic beyond even me, until we know what is happening if I tried anything else it could do more harm than good." Grey was so apologetic it only succeeded in making Jack angrier.

"Don't say that, there has to be more that we can do. A potion, a spell, a charm, something?" Jack stormed Grey did not answer though infuriating him further. He grabbed the nearest chair and threw it across the room smashing it against the wall.

"TELL ME." he exploded but Grey shook his head.

"there is nothing that can be done, I don't think we could get close enough to her to try another potion anyway her body is being protected by that shield." Grey was almost scared of Jack backing away from him.

"Devaldros did this to her right. Then if he's dead the spell will end." Jack seemed to have completely lost his mind.

"Jack you can't be serious, it's suicide." Michael shouted at him.

"I couldn't be more serious; I don't care what happens to me your supposed to be her friend and you're just going to stand there and let this happen to her?" Jack was seething. "you would rather not even try to help her, thinking it was too dangerous well stay here and enjoy what's going to be the rest of your life." Jack pushed his way past Grey and towards the door.

"Jack you won't be able to leave the castle it's been sealed, I'm not willing to let you throw your life away for a vendetta." Grey attempted to explained.

"This isn't a vendetta; this is a war. Devaldros is going to win, you think hiding here is going to stop that?" He felt sick with worry, what else could he do.

"Jack, give me some time, I might be able to think of something or find something in the dark magic section. I spent forever in there with Louise I know it well now." Michael implored him. Jack looked at the nurse.

"Is Kim in danger?" He asked, she looked around at them all.

"I don't know. She could remain like this forever or recover in a week. I've never seen this before." Jack stood thinking trying to calm himself think rationally.

"One week. If we haven't come up with anything by then I will hunt down Devaldros, and no seal will stop me." They all nodded.

"Professor Grey I need all reference books brought to me here unsealed. If we have any hope of knowing what this is, I'll need access to the darkest magics." Michael commanded.

The following week was the longest of Jack's life. He and Michael had spent every waking moment pouring through books, Louise was still weak but helped where she could. Michael had made some advances in an idea he was working on, but without the details on the amulet he had said it wouldn't work. Jack had left him attempting to discover the secrets of the amulet whilst he had gone to pack his things. He was collecting an arsenal of weaponry and potions. Emma and Grey had attempted to talk Jack out of his plan, but he had refused to listen. Joe had offered to go with him to hunt down Devaldros and attempt to finish him off. So far neither the Dark Council nor Devaldros had made any further moves. Kim's condition hadn't changed, she was still unconscious, but without any signs of physical harm. Devaldros wanted her, what was his master plan? Jack finished collecting his items, staring around his room. It was likely this would be the last he saw of it. He pulled his bag onto his shoulder and started to make his way towards the infirmary. He needed to see Kim one last time before he set out.

As he neared Jack could hear raised voices. It seemed Michael and Grey were arguing again. They had spent hours arguing over different theories on how they could help Kim. As old and experienced as Grey was it felt to Jack he didn't have the passion or natural inquisitive nature of Michael. It felt as though he was stuck in what he knew. It reminded Jack of his first lesson with him, he had warned of the dangers of exploring magic. He of course was right but as Michael had pointed out the advancement of magic had taken risks.

"What's going on?" Jack asked entering the room. He was surprised to see Michael looking exhausted but happy. Grey on the other hand seemed defeated.

"I think I have it." Michael shoved his scribbled notes to Jack. Louise nodded encouraging Jack to read it.

"What are you talking about." Jack started flicking through the notes. It made no sense to him at all. It was written in some language Jack had never seen. "Um, what is this?" Michael ripped it back out of his hands.

"Sorry, forgot you don't know runes. Thought it was best not to make it easy to understand, we don't want it falling into the wrong hands. I think we have a way to wake Kim up." Michael was almost hyperactive.

"Are you serious?" Jack asked suddenly excited.

"It's a workable theory." Grey begrudgingly agreed.

"That's more than we've had so far. Tell me?" Jack pulled a chair over as Michael began.

"Kim's mind is trapped, and her body is being shielded. But Devaldros gave us a way to get inside her mind." Michael picked up the Amulet holding it high for them to see.

"Tell me how?" He asked wanting to get started straight away.

"Jack, I'm working on a theory here, it's possible it won't work." Michael looked unsure if he should tell

Jack or not, but he knew Kim's life could be at stake,

"Michael would you do this even if there was only the smallest chance it might work, no matter the risk to you?" Michael looked over at Louise and nodded.

"Professor, what do you think are the chances of this working?" Grey bit on his lip.

"I can't say, I'm still not sure I understand how Devaldros was able to inhabit the body of Frank using the amulet. Miss Harrison is the expert here. I want to bring in Lord Kaiba, he is far more proficient in dark magic than myself. But you need to know this. Even if we are able to replicate this spell you would only be able to take over her body not her mind." He was right but Michael seemed to have an answer ready for this.

"We managed to identify the amulet in a horrific section of magical artifacts. It's a necromancer's amulet." Jack was now confused; Necromancy was used on the dead. When Frank had attacked Kim, he had been very much alive.

"I know what you're thinking, it's been modified. See the writing on the amulet. It's the ancient language like that on the Diasis. Grey was able to decipher it, as he was alive when it was spoken. Kaiba will be helpful but we will also need Levell. If one of us can inhabit Kim's body, we would then be interacting with her subconscious and that's her specialty." Michael suddenly hesitated. It seemed they had come to the problem part of the plan. "You need to know, only one of us can do this." Michael explained fretful. Grey tried to offer his services, but Jack interjected.

"I'm doing it, this is on me. You keep saying I'm descended from Arthur, well its time I act like it. That is an order from the King." He looked at Grey who stood defeated. "Professor, can you please get Lord Kaiba and explain the situation. I'll get Levell. Michael you start preparing the room." Jack was trusting Michael with the most important thing in his world Kim.

"We are also going to need blessed salt, dusted fairy wings and Adder venom. There's a few more things but I'll get them." Jack raced out of the door not wasting anytime. "Hey Jack." Michael called from the doorway. "ask Levell to bring one of her charms." Jack waved letting Michael know he heard and carried on towards Levell's Room.

Jack knocked hard on her door tired and out of breath, he panted hard people smiled at him as they passed.
'probably hoping I'm choking.' he thought.
"who is it?" Came Levell's voice from within the room.
"it's Jack London Miss, I need a word with you urgently." He shouted back through the door. Jack waited a second hearing whispering within the room.
"One moment please." Levell appeared shortly. "What is it Jack, is everyone ok? Has something else happened to Kim?" Levell was tear streaked and shaking she was clearly hiding something.
"Miss, I need you to come with me and to bring some of your charms. It's a matter of life and death. I cant explain anymore right now." She took a moment to compose herself.
"Very well, give me a couple of minutes and I shall be with you." He waited patiently outside, all the time trying to ignore the two voices whispering inside the room. As hard as he tried, he could overhear the conversation going on inside. It seemed Levell and Mrs

Bravo were fretting over what they were to do now that Bravo had run away with Melfice. Mrs Bravo clearly felt in danger, along with their daughter, Kestra. Jack felt terrible for pulling her away at this time. He didn't want to be the cause of pain to anyone and if something happened to Kestra because of this, it was something else to weigh on his soul. "Very well, lets get going." Levell said shortly after.

"I'm sorry miss, I didn't want to pull you away but like I say, its life and death. I hope this won't take too long and you can get back to your friend." Levell stopped suddenly. Looking all around before whispering.

"What did you hear?" she seemed frightened.

"Nothing really, just you and Mrs Bravo talking. She seems worried that something will happen because her husband has gone over to Devaldros' side." She grasped Jack's shoulder.

"Jack you can't tell anyone about this please. Louise and I, if people found out." Of course, how hadn't he seen it before.

"Miss, I won't say a word to anyone, but please we must hurry. We still need to stop by the store cupboard." Jack hadn't seen it before, but it was obvious now. Levell and Michelle Bravo had been having an affair. Bravo clearly knew hence their fear, he no longer felt bound by the council's law's. Once tonight was over he would ensure that they had additional protection from the knights, he wouldn't have to explain why exactly just it was required until Bravo was captured.

"we're back, how are things going?" Jack shouted walking into the infirmary.

"almost ready, we just need your ingredients." Michael said looking at the items in Jack's arms. "I take it Jack explained everything to you Miss?" Michael asked eagerly. Jack walked over as close as he could to Kim's bed.

"No, just it was a matter of life and death, what is going on here?" She asked looking around at them all.

"Kim has been injured and we need some unorthodox medicine to help her otherwise, she will probably remain in a coma for the rest of her life." Michael explained quickly. Watching Kim being so still and lifeless hurt him, tears threatened to pour forth. He hated how he felt he hated loving Kim because of it, but then he hated himself for hating how he felt.

"Jack you are an idiot, if you had only said I would have gladly helped." she said seeing the passion he felt for Kim.

"I'm sorry, but I couldn't risk anyone overhearing us. Michael, get started with whatever it is that you're going to do." Jack just wanted to help Kim.

"Grey has got Kaiba up to date." He put the amulet around Jack's neck.

"We think we have it figured out. The theory is Avatars are made of mystical energy right, but when summoned they take physical form." Miss Levell shook her head.

"that's not right, they're not mystical energy they're made from the dreams and wishes the inspiration from the person that they come from." Levell announced whimsically.

"That's a very romanticised view isn't it. They're still energy and that's energy projected from the person's subconscious turned into a physical apparition. Now if we can turn energy into a solid why can't we turn a physical form into energy, that will enable us to get past that barrier. The problem then comes with how to get you inside of Kim's subconscious." Jack felt the amulet around his neck. "Exactly, the amulet. We know it can be used to take over a person's body and transfer that into someone's body, if Miss Levell can help to guide you into Kims mind, like she would in your own, then you should be in her subconscious." Michael's explanation seemed logical to Jack, but he still was not sure if it could be done.

"ok, let's say we can do this absolutely crazy idea of yours how will it help?" Grey asked, Jack guessed it was because he knew he could not stop him.

"psychologists believe that when a person is in a coma their consciousness it stored within their subconscious. That is why if we can access her subconscious, we might be able to find her hidden there, it may also explain what Devaldros was trying and hopefully we might be able to wake her up." Michael was making it sound extremely easy, something Levell was quick to call him on.

"Michael, this isn't like opening a doorway and stepping through. A person's subconscious is a world of chaos, it is where your thoughts are processed your deepest desires and your darkest wonders are buried, it could easily drive anyone mad. You have not even explained how you propose to turn someone from a physical form into energy. I'm sorry but I just can't see this working." Jack was not listening anymore he just wanted to get this over with.

"listen it's really simple, how do you summon an avatar? you have to feel the avatar within you, the reason it's difficult is because people are far too self-absorbed to be centred enough to feel their Avatar. We don't have this problem we can see Jack we know he exists, so all we need is for you Miss, to summon Jack whilst with the aid of some other little charms myself, Lord Kaiba and Professor Grey perform a reversal spell so instead of turning him into a physical form it will turn him into energy. And then you need to direct his energy towards Kim, the rest is up to him from then, but he would have to leave her mind before she awakens, or you might disappear or die. I don't know." Grey looked at Michael astounded.

"this could actually work." Grey congratulated him.

"I'm just really smart, what can I say?" Jack laughed.

'There's the Michael we know and love.' he thought only the nurse seemed concerned, even Levell now seemed convinced.

"I know I may not be an expert at these ritual's, but this all seems very high risk and with the condition that this poor girl's mind is in, this could very well destroy what's left of it." the nurse warned.

"that is why if there looks to be even a hint of trouble, we have the Adder venom, if we inject it with that drip Jack's mind will react as though he has been injured and should bring you out of her mind. That's only if you can stop what is ever causing that shield though." Michael seemed confident in the plan.

"Jack are you sure you want to go through with this It could be very dangerous, we don't know what her mindscape will be like." Grey wanted Jack to be sure that he knew what he was doing.

"I know what I'm doing, don't worry about me, I'm going to get this done no matter what. And I don't care if it does look like I'm in trouble, you're not going to bring me out until Kim is ok, do you understand me?" He scanned the others for their reactions there was no way he was going to allow any more harm to come to Kim whilst he was still alive. "Fine, I only have one more question Michael, what's with the blessed salt?" Jack knew the others were lying, they would use the drip if necessary, without them seeing he slowly pointed his wand at the now empty drip at the base where it couldn't be seen he cast a blocking jinx, no venom would be able to pass through.

"it acts as an amplifier, because this is such an unusual spell, we will need all the power we can get. You need this by the way" Michael handed Jack two bracelets. "This is how you get out; they both contain a small amount of venom, not enough to hurt but enough to cause you both to wake. Just press it on and it will inject you." Jack nodded he had all the information he needed and yet he was still nervous.

'I can't let her down.' he groaned, Kim was his world, and he was not going to let whatever was happening to her happen without trying to stop it.

Michael ran a ring of salt around Jack and Kim,

"so how exactly will my energy be transferred into Kim?" Jack had just thought of this tiny point.

"well, you see if you had ever paid attention in class then you would know that energy can be contained by a circle of blessed salt, it not only works as an amplifier, it's also a barrier to stop your energy from escaping. I'm hoping that between Miss Levell and yourself, you will guide into Kim naturally." Jack looked in disbelief at Michael.

"we all know that your incredibly smart Michael, but for the love of god, stop showing off and get on with it!" Jack was waiting as patiently as possible, but he did not have time to stroke Michael's ego.

"ok but Jack, I need to ask once again are you sure about this? I don't want to lose two of my friends. And we don't even know what it's going to be like in there." Jack did not care. He knew Michael was just trying to let Jack know what the dangers were.

"I'm sure, we will be back before you know it." Michael understood he gathered with the others around Jack.

"now, everyone knows what they need to do." Grey, Kaiba and Levell gave Michael a nervous smile. "ok then Jack, get ready this is where the fun begins."

"ok here we go." Jack gritted his teeth. The room seemed small with everyone crowded around him.

"ok Miss, you can start." Levell began to chant fixing her eyes upon Jack. Michael, Kaiba and Grey began to make complicated and confusing patterns with their wands whispering under their breath. Jack's body began to feel light.

"Uh guy's, is this meant to be happening?" he asked. His body began to glow a variety of colours he felt as though he was floating away. He was finding it hard to concentrate as though his mind was losing its cohesion, his vision and voice were both rapidly disappearing. "it's working keep it going." he tried to shout but his voice was gone. Electricity crackled within the air Levell looked stunned at what was happening before her.

"Jack are you ok?" He heard someone shout. But the rushing of wind past what used to be ears made it impossible to tell who had shouted it. Sickness passed through him like a smoke, it was extraordinary he could no longer see with his eyes, but he could see everything all at the same time. No, he was not just seeing everywhere, he was everywhere. He was energy Michael's plan had worked but he was still nowhere near helping Kim. He could not understand how to enter her mind. Levell seemed to be directing him he could feel himself being pulled towards something. Michael grabbed the adder's venom and threw a few drops into the energy field that Jack had become. Pain shot through him like a bullet. Hurting every part of him, not just where it struck. He screamed but again, no sound escaped, he fell back towards Kim. Michael was forcing him into Kim three more times the pain struck, blinding white, but Jack could now feel himself being pulled into Kim's mind. Distorted images flashed into his vision he was both outside and in Kim's mind at the same time. Jack was disorientated, not knowing what was happening, he did the only thing he could think of closing his mind. Everything went calm relaxing him. He reopened his mind but the sight before him was chaos, a realm of horror and intrigue, but at least here in this realm he was whole again, a physical form so to speak. He was successfully inside of Kim's mind.

'what in Avalon's name.' he gasped opening his new eyes. Kim's subconscious seemed a twisted landscape, a perverse version of Camelot stood before him. The beautiful castle had been transformed into a nightmarish monstrosity; the pillars of knight had been twisted into hideous versions of themselves. Instead of Excalibur Arthur carried the head of an Orc, Guinevere was dressed in a black high collared dress making her seem vampiric in nature. The city wall lay crumbled in places, huge rocks crashed down on the burnt structures below. Jack could make out through the broken wall where the moat was in the real Camelot. Its water had been replaced by spikes. It took a moment to realise on top the spikes were the heads of victims. In the distance Jack could see the harbour on fire as waves of flame crashed against the ships. Eyes peeked at him from the windows of the destroyed town as he passed through. The only sounds in the city were cackles of maniacal laughter, the wails of what seemed like people, but not quite. Jack thought it was rather more like the Camelot Devaldros would wish existed.

'ok Kim, let us set you free from here.' he thought looking at this world of despair. He started towards the dark Camelot hoping that he would see the real one again. Finally, entering the school itself, he saw Michael talking with Louise "How did you get…." They turned and looked at him. Louise was dressed in a little black slip whilst Michael in an expensive three-piece suit. They looked away returning to a deep embrace. It took Jack a moment to realise they were a representation of thoughts and memories that Kim had never processed.

Jack was worried, why was Kim's subconscious so dark? it seemed her mind was full of fear and hate, but why was it like this? She was an angel to Jack not this neurotic, almost psychotic person this landscape represented.

"Kim, where are you?" Jack began to dash around the bizarre Camelot, every room he entered seemed filled with pain. When he had entered the dining hall, he saw Rachel screaming over the top of Kim telling her she was hideous a monstrosity whilst a version of himself embraced Kestra. He was laughing at her tear soaked. He ran forward to pull Kim away as he reached to grab her, his hands passed through. It wasn't the real Kim another vision of her inner torment.

Jack was beginning to understand why the subconscious was such an important part of human psychology, its ability to suppress pain was a good one, he didn't believe that anyone could survive carrying their darkest thoughts with them all the time. He left the hall but instead of entering the main entrance hall like he expected it had been replaced by the outside courtyard.

Melfice was pinning Kim to the wall, again he went to step forward to try and stop this, but another version of Jack came to her rescue. Both he and Melfice appeared as monsters fighting over her like a piece of meat. The fake Kim cowered below as they beat their chests at each other, was this the way she honestly thought of him? Jack thought that he knew where Kim would be, but he was frightened of what he would see the further he travelled.

It was rare to see but every now and then he would see something differently. A memory of them together, like the snowball fight, it was in pure light as though shielded from the outside darkness unable to be twisted as so much else had.

Jack crept slowly through the common room, a hundred different memories seemed to fill the room, including the memory of Kim and Jack having their first kiss, but instead of Jack being depicted as a monster like he had seen so many times, he was bathed in a glorious

white light so bright and intense the real Jack had to shield his eyes. Jack watched their first kiss, Kim's hands clasped hard around Jack's neck holding the kiss for far longer than he remembered. It seemed that Kim had waited upon that kiss for even longer than Jack,
'she always did love me.' Jack thought sullenly. Why had he wasted so much time in telling Kim how he truly felt about her. It did not matter now he was going to free her and then spend the rest of his life with her, not letting her go for one second.

Jack pressed his ear against Kim's bedroom door, the silence was almost as deafening as the screams from the Joust, which seemed to be located next door.
'ok here we go.' he took a deep breath and opened the door. Kim was sitting in the middle of the room tears flooding her carpet. "Kim it's me, Jack." he called out to her.
"Go away, you're not real your just another vision, a fake.!" She screamed throwing a book at him Jack caught it inches before it hit him on the nose. "You caught it?" Kim was stunned, "Then you really are. Oh Jack." Kim ran and jumped onto him kissing him. All feeling left Jack's body all sense of reality, this is what he lived for, to be in Kim's arms, but he had to get her out of here,
"Kim do you know why or even how you're here?" Jack asked breaking their embrace.
"Someone attacked me in my room, I didn't even see their face, but where are we why do these horrible manifestations keep coming to me?" Jack closed his eyes praying he knew the words to say this right.
"It was Devaldros, he was possessing the councillor Frank, they were working together. It looks like some of

the council have gone over to the other side." Kim broke away from Jack.

"it was Devaldros!" Fear flushed across her face.

"Frank was executed by the council, probably to hide who else has changed sides. Melfice and his parents were involved as well. There is something you should know, this world we're in, well, it's your mind. These figments you're seeing, I think they are either memories or your deepest subconscious thoughts." The screaming from next door died down. Jack guessed the joust must have finished. He didn't know if it would start again soon or be replaced by another twisted version of a memory. The world whilst chaotic in its layout, didn't feel right. Kim clung to Jack he noticed the tighter she held him he began to emit a small glow from his skin. It was like the light that had shone over the memory of the snowball fight or their first kiss. He suddenly felt stronger, more confident. He shook away the feeling trying to balance his mind. "I don't think your mind is normally like this. The way Michael explained it, your mind should be a world of pure chaos, this feels organised somehow. Has it been this way since you got here?" She shook her head.

"It's changed, they keep changing." Kim pointed out the window. Jack walked over and could see a dozen or more memories outside. It seemed like a black fog was descending over the city. Corrupting anything it touched. Only the memories shielded in brilliant light seemed able to withstand the corruption. "What's happening to me?" She cried reaching out for Jack. "I can't think straight." Jack held her tighter, this was what Devaldros had meant.

"I think your memories are changing. Devaldros is

The Dark Heart

trying to change how you think. He wants you as his Queen. I don't know how he's doing this though. We need to stop it." A cold merciless laugh echoed from behind them.

"I just love memory lane don't you Arthur?" Jack and Kim looked up in horror. "Are you surprised to see me here in the mind of our sweet? I think your starting to understand what is happening now." Devaldros laughed at Kim's look of fear, his black veined face delighted at the scene in front of him. Jack pulled Kim around behind him.

"How are you here?" Jack was terrified he couldn't understand how this was possible.

"Do you really believe that I would allow myself to be caught? or I would have told Melfice to reveal himself unless I had an ultimate plan? I didn't need that amulet to control that little fat wizard. I needed you to find it to bring you here. Arthur, I'm disappointed in you, once upon a time you would never have fallen for this." Devaldros tossed his head back laughing. Everything now fell into place Jack could see the plan laid out in front of him. He had been so stupid; he had acted exactly as Devaldros had known he would. His desire to play the white knight and come riding to Kim's rescue.

"You wanted me in Kim's mind all along. Why? so you could torture me in seeing you twist her mind? Or are you going to try and kill me?" Devaldros mocked Jack waving his finger at him.

"if you ask me no questions, I'll tell you no lies, I told you I want her as my Queen and that is true. But here in this place you have no friends to help you, and I am not limited by the protection of Camelot. I can unleash my full strength at you." Jack made sure that Kim was safely hidden behind him. Devaldros laughed again

"You're the reason this world is so dark, you're trying to pervert her mind. Make Kim something she's not." Jack gritted his teeth trying to buy time he knew he was going to have to battle Devaldros, but he was being reminded of something that Michael had said.

"This was my primary aim I admit, like yourself Arthur I love Guinevere. You're stripping me from ourselves did not remove that love. Shortly she will begin to see the world through my eyes. Not the lies your kind have tried to fill her mind with. It would have happened sooner but some of her memories are strong." Jack had never considered that Devaldros truly believed himself to love Kim.

"You're never going to corrupt me." Kim shouted stepping out from behind Jack. Her eyes filled with fire. "This is my mind. You're going to have to kill me, I will never be with you." She advanced on Devaldros her anger making the room shake. Devaldros made no move against her as she shoved hard into his chest. "You will never change how I feel about my friends. I love them I love Jack; never will it be you." She slapped Devaldros as hard as she could across the face. Jack had to pull her away, sure Devaldros would strike back. Devaldros did not move though.

"You're already changing." He smiled; Kim's anger was proof of this. "Your thoughts are darker. You begin to see him as the monster and me in a softer light. Your clothing's not the cottons and light colours you're used to. Even your makeup darkens. It is only a matter of time now." Jack hadn't noticed before but Devaldros was right, Kim's mannerisms weren't quite her own. She was suddenly dressed in a long flowing black dress. Jack was sure she hadn't appeared like this moments ago. "This is going to be so much fun." Devaldros eyed Kim greedily.

"So, you want fun, do you? I mean let's face it this isn't exactly a challenge is it?" Jack started stringing words together just hoping that they made sense.

"oh, a challenge what do you propose?" Devaldros asked, not taking his eyes from Kim, she shied away from the intense gaze.

"A one-minute head start. I mean if you're as powerful as you say you are it should be no problem for you to track me down, should it?" Devaldros laughed.

"Why would I let you go? There are so many ways in which I can torture you. Also, you will have a way to escape, otherwise your friends would have never let you enter." Devaldros wasn't going to be fooled so easily.

"You want my way out? here it is." Jack placed his hand in his pocket and carefully removed a bracelet he threw it to Devaldros. "You have my way out. A minute's head start and then we can see who really is more powerful, you or me, unless you're scared that is?" Jack tried taunting him, hoping that would get the reaction he needed.

"Very well, I will be even more generous you have two minutes. Go." Jack Grabbed Kim and pulled her from the room. He burst through door after door trying to find a room which would give him space. The screams and laughs deafened him as he passed by dozens of memories. Finally, they made it outside of the front doors and into the courtyard. This would have to be where he made his stand. Kim was breathing hard she ripped at her clothes, horrified by her own appearance. "Kim you need to listen to me, take this."

Jack handed her the other bracelet. "This will free you from here, all you need to do is press it on." Kim blinked at Jack.

"What about you? you gave yours to Devaldros." Jack calmed himself, he knew what was about to happen.

"It was a fake." He lied. "I don't think I'll be able to stop him. If we wake up now Michael thinks it will destroy anything that shouldn't be in here. Devaldros will be gone. We need to do this now, before he gets here." Kim took the bracelet in her fumbling hands. She placed her arms around Jack's neck. "I love you; we will be together I promise." Tears were in his eyes. Jack blinked them away. His body glowing brighter than before. The darkened makeup wiping away from Kims face. Her clothes brightened a shade, before they could say another word Devaldros burst through the doorway.

"Hide and seek is over." He screamed. Jack rushed forward firing as many spells as he could, Devaldros blocked most but one hit him in the shoulder causing him to scream aloud as the black steel started to melt over his skin. Jack dived behind the cloister wall as a spell from Devaldros missed by centimetres blasting apart a statue. Jack could see Kim pinned down behind another wall. Devaldros like him was doing all he could to avoid her. A tearing noise above Jack alerted him to the gargoyle Devaldros had pulled free from the castle wall, it fell towards Jack. He dived blasting it with his wand but Devaldros had been waiting for this. He grabbed Jack lifting him from the floor and rammed him through a pillar. Jack collapsed to the ground. He was still breathing somehow; in fact, he was barely in pain. He realised the glow was shielding him somehow. This was the opportunity he needed.

"Kim do it now." Jack pleaded.

"But Jack." She called unable to help with the battle raging on.

"Kim, I love you, if you love me you will do It now!" Devaldros turned to face her.

"NO." He screamed; distracted Jack tackled him from the side, they launched into the side of the fountain. Bits of stone flew everywhere with the impact. Jack threw punch after punch at Devaldros who screamed in agony. The sound of bone crunching under the blows, black blood sprayed across the floor. Devaldros' arm shot up from the water grabbing at Jacks throat. Barely able to breath he shouted.

"Kim do it now. It's the only way to stop him." Kim placed her hand over the bracelet and pressed down onto her arm. "I love you Kim, I will always love you." he called wrestling to hold Devaldros down. They suddenly recoiled in pain as the venom soaked into Kim's body. The twisted memories created by Devaldros began to explode all around.

"Jack what is happening?" She called, shielding herself from the light beaming from her old memories. It was no good though, Jack could not answer her. She was slipping out of her unconscious mind. Kim could see the world beyond now. She reached out, her fingers stretching for Jack. Her final vision of his hand reaching for hers. A smile on his face.

Kim woke calling for Jack, Michael rushed over to her, the barrier which had protected her now gone. A tube at her side was filled with venom. Grey was shouting something about it being stuck. Michael looked at her.

"Kim, my god, where is he? where's Jack?" He asked

desperately.

"I don't know, he was fighting Devaldros he told me to go, it was the only way to save us both, where is he?" tears flooded down her cheeks. She sought any sign of him around the room.

"He gave me a bracelet, told me to use it, he told me he had given Devaldros a fake, where is he?" she pleaded It took Michael several seconds to answer, collapsing to the floor.

"Kim… he's gone!"

Chapter 30

The Death of a King

Joe sat at the round table his head held in his hands, Grey had just told him of his brother's death.

"You're lying he can't be dead." Joe said finally.

"I wish I was. He died saving Miss Illsley, he loved her very much." Joe threw his sword onto the scorched table.

"You're not listening to me. Jack is not dead, he can't be dead, he's my brother!" Joe was furious throwing his chair splintering it against the wall. Grey almost laughed. "What's so god dammed funny?" he ordered.

"I never realised how alike you were. When he heard about Miss Illsley, he did the same thing." Joe looked at him in disbelief.

"I'm going to kill you, you're laughing. My brother is dead and you're laughing." Joe was raging but Grey seemed perfectly indifferent to his anger.

"Joseph, please believe me no-one is as devastated at the death of your brother more than myself. He was our one hope against Devaldros. Now I fear the world is doomed." Joe realised Grey wasn't calm he was defeated. "I tried to watch over him, when I disappeared, I was attempting to discover who had killed your father. I had become suspicious. I had seen the likeness in the three of them. It seemed that the time for Devaldros' rise was at hand. I wanted to protect them. I wish I could have done more." Grey slumped down in his chair. "My champion is defeated." Grey saluted the air as though honouring an invisible enemy.

"That's all he was to you wasn't it the descendant of Arthur, the person who would defeat Devaldros for you. Are you too scared to fight him after he kicked your arse last time? My brother saved my family, he saved his friends, he was falsely put on trial by a corrupt government and almost murdered by his headmaster. Please tell me how you tried to look out for him?" Joe was disgusted. "He carried the weight of Devaldros for seventeen years, he had to be coerced and tricked into releasing him. He was better than Arthur, so don't you sit there feeling sorry for yourself. You are going to get the Avartarians and the Council. I'm going to get the knights and we are all going to go and slaughter that son of a bitch for what he did to my brother!" Anger was all that was keeping the despair away from Joe.

"We will lose. Devaldros is too powerful now, we will be sending men to their deaths with no chance of victory. We will fight and we will lose." Grey sipped from his glass, Joe wasn't willing to hear this, how dare Grey give up so easily. They had already lost Jack and Robin, hundreds of innocent lives across the country. The lives of the knights on patrol. This act of self-pity was not acceptable.

"Your meant to be some powerful ancient wizard, a great man, Merlin's protégé and yet here you are cowering in your castle. Jack defeated Devaldros, even if it did cost him his life, he wasn't willing to let other people get hurt because his enemy was stronger."

"Three times." Grey interrupted. "Firstly, at

Stonehenge when he rescued myself and your family, it cost him his friend. Secondly, Frank the councillor after we had executed him Devaldros had possessed his body. It was Jack who realised what was happening and he who stopped whatever he was planning.

"What was the third time, what else happened that you're not telling me about?" Joe warned, his voice cold.

"When Jack was in Miss Illsley's mind, he sacrificed himself so she could live, Devaldros had somehow implanted himself in her mind. Probably something he did when he was in control of Frank, it seems he was trying to turn her over to his side. Jack convinced her to free herself breaking the spell held over her. It killed Jack and the piece of Devaldros in her mind. Jack lied to her you see, he told her he would be ok to convince her to leave him to fight off Devaldros. In sacrificing himself he defeated him for a third time. There was never a more caring boy and yet I still think he should have let Devaldros have her, for the good of the world I should have killed her." Joe struck Grey as hard as he could sending him crashing to the floor.

"He was willing to give his life to save the person he considered to be his queen. If you ever go near her!" Joe grasped his sword from the table and slammed its point into the floor besides Grey's head.

"I will do that to you. Now if you will excuse me headmaster, I have a queen to see." Joe stormed out of the room determined to see what Kim had to say.

The infirmary seemed more like a morgue Michael sat between Louise and Kim, all three tear-streaked, the nurse fluttered between them trying to console them but breaking into tears herself, wailing like a banshee. Fear

met Joes eyes when he entered. Michael stood wanting to take the blame almost standing guard over the girls. But Joe had no anger left, he placed his hand on Michael's shoulder and nodded no words were exchanged but they all felt the same. The loss of Jack weighed heavily on all their hearts. Joe hugged Kim hard as her tears fell on his shoulder, he whispered
"You're the luckiest girl alive. He loved you more than anything else in the entire world." All five of them sat there in silence filled with the memories of their brother, friend, champion and patient. Joe had never realised just how much people cared for him, he had heard the abuse shouted about Jack after the trial, it had even been shouted about the knight's chamber. Joe had been suspended for a week after hitting a fellow knight, their accusations had stopped after that, at least whilst he was in the room. But to see this the unparalleled remorse and grief he knew that even if only the five people in this room had cared for Jack, he would have been considered a greatly loved man.

Jacks' funeral had been arranged for two days after his death. With no body, an empty coffin was to be buried. Grey had attempted to insist on Jack being buried in the royal crypt. Emma had refused and Jack's final resting place would be underneath the same tree as his father. His family all agreed it would have been what Jack had wanted. Two battalions of knights had been ordered to attend the funeral. Emma had revealed that multiple council members, who had never met Jack, would be attending. They knew the council had seen it as an opportunity for some key members to attend and try to repair their image in the public eye. Joe found it sickening that a game of politics was being played at the funeral. He knew it would be safer for those in attendance if there was a guard of Knights. Joe had secretly agreed with his superiors to hand pick those attending.

"Do you think that dad would have been proud of Jack?" Carol asked Joe on the morning of the funeral.
"Dying protect the person he loved. It's how he would have wanted to go." Joe said shovelling a sausage into his mouth.
"That's not what I meant." Carol sounded affronted. Joe placed his fork down and thought carefully about what he was about to say.
"I know all dad wanted was for us to be true to ourselves. He was a man of honour. Jack proved he would do anything for those he loved. He was also smarter than I gave him credit for. Has Kim told you he knew how to make an invisibility potion?" Joe laughed considering what he would have probably done with a potion like that during his time at school. "All those times I called him an idiot and he could perform magic like that." He hung his head.
"Yeah, I know I miss him too." Carol gripped Joe's hand, "Joe I have something to ask you, will you help me today? I think it would be what he would have wanted." she asked tear's welling up in her eyes.
"I would be honoured; I just hope that you don't expect me to have a fancy speech prepared, Jack will get the sending off he deserves and if any of those politicians want to try to make this into a media circus then things will get ugly." Joe warned not wanting his brother's memory to be ruined by the council.

"you just say what you need to, but please remember this isn't about revenge, this is about saying goodbye to our little brother." that was it, Carol burst into more tears, Joe handing her a tissue trying not to cry himself. "I blamed him." she suddenly cried. Joe sat back horrified.

"You blamed who for what?" he asked unsure if he wanted to know the answer.

"Jack, I blamed him for mum and me being abducted, for his friend being killed, the last thing I said to him was it was all your fault." she cried harder still. Joe slipped around the table and leant his sisters head on his shoulder.

"Jack would have known you didn't mean it. No one could have known what was about to happen. Jack knew you loved him. He loved us all. We need to be strong and keep that love in our hearts." he could feel the tears coming but pushed them down he wasn't going to cry, he had to be strong for his family.

Joe hated the sight of this tree, he was always reminded of death, or more precisely the death of those he loved. The fact that his family gathered around this tree so soon after his father felt like a personal torture. He watched as people he never knew gathered, all wanting to pay their respects for Jack.

"Jack was well liked." He laughed to Carol she smiled weakly.

"I don't think they were all his friends. Most of them probably believed the story of him being Arthur and wanted to see him." she said coldly. "At least Kim and Michael are here." Carol pointed over to a small group in the corner. "She blames herself you know." Carol told him.

"What why?" Joe was astonished, there were a few to blame for Jack's death in his mind, but it certainly wasn't Kim.

"They had begun to date the day she was attacked, so when she was comatose Jack sacrificed himself to save her. She told me that if they hadn't started dating, she thinks that Jack would not have let himself die to save her. You don't think she's right, do you?" Carol was examining the look on Joe's face.

"I thought they were smart the new generation. You knew how Jack felt about her. He had been in love with her forever. It was always just a matter of time until he told her that he loved her, there would have been no stopping him. And he would have done it even if they were just friends, he would have done it for anyone." Joe was serious it was why he had asked Jack to leave with Kim, he knew this was likely the outcome. Michael appeared walking towards them, Louise on one arm and Kim holding his other.

"I'm sorry were late, Kim wanted to look presentable she didn't want to disappoint your family or Jack." Michael told them; they had spent a great deal of time together over the past few days. Their grief over losing their friend and brother strengthening their bonds.

"If it were Jack standing here you could be wearing nothing at all, and he would have been pleased. Incredibly pleased in fact." Joe tried to joke.

"Yeah, he would have done." Michael agreed. The pair grinned, but only succeeded in making Kim sniffle, she smoothed down her dress.

"How are you Kim? Holding up?" Joe asked more delicately. Kim nodded, almost as though the shock of

Jack's death had stolen her voice. Louise wrapped her arm through Kims. "We're not due to start for a while, why don't you guy's and Carol get a drink? I just want a quick word with Michael." Joe pointed to a small outcrop near the road. They walked over in silence Michael looked nervous unsure of what Joe was about to say. "How many of them do you think are going to survive this war?" Joe asked seriously looking back towards the gathered crowd. Michael was taken aback at the question.

"I don't know." he answered truthfully. "I do know that Jack would never have given up. I won't either, not whilst there's breath left in me." he vowed. Joe chuckled

"Somehow, I knew you would say that. I want to ask you something I once asked Jack. Leave take Louise and Kim and leave. You're Lancelot after all. Devaldros will want you. Melfice seems to want Louise, get out of here and protect yourselves." Joe knew the answer before Michael opened his mouth.

"No!" Michael has no interest in running. "I'm guessing that was the answer Jack gave as well." Joe nodded, he found himself surrounded by heroes.

"If you won't run, then work with me. Jack tried to do this on his own and it cost him his life. It almost cost you, Louise and Kim their lives. If you hold Lancelot's memories like Jack held Arthurs, then you can help the knights to fight this war." Michael agreed they knew it was going to take all of them to have the smallest chance of winning. Carol re-emerged from the crowd and waved for them to come over. "it's about to start." Joe whispered.

The sun beamed down on the tree a strong wind blew

The Dark Heart

through the crowd making them shiver. Joe pulled his coat tight about him, an attempt to shield himself from the wind. The coffin had been brought to the resting spot and everyone had finally gathered. "Welcome everyone," someone shouted from beside Carol. Joe turned is head to see who it was.

"Bastards." He whispered. It was a leading council member clearly trying to make this a state funeral.

"I'm glad to see so many faces here today, under these terrible circumstances that we find ourselves in. Today is a harsh reminder of the price of freedom. Jack London was a proud boy who never let anything get him down, he was greatly athletic and academically sound, a real loss to the community of Camelot." Joe was gritting his teeth this wizard was trying to make Jack out as some martyr.

'I'll sort this.' He thought. Joe was not great with a wand having none of Jack's skill he flicked the point of his wand from the inside of his coats sleeve setting fire to the hem of the wizard's robe. The wizard scrambled trying to stamp out the fire. "the reason we are here today." Joe shouted over the yelping of the wizard. "is to say goodbye to a brother, a son, and a friend. My sister and I have elected to speak for Jack today, seeing as he never had any religious beliefs. Carol has prepared a speech so if you would please be quiet and listen." Joe looked daggers at the wizard who was still yelping in the background. Carol nodded towards Joe and stepped forward.

"Jack London was more than people thought, I don't mean the rumours about him, I mean as a person. He was an uncommonly kind individual brave, smart and unyielding in what he thought right. He was a King, a boy who faced a monster and won, he saved this family and it cost him a friend. He was betrayed by those meant to protect him, yet he continued to care for us all. He died saving the person he loved, a king doesn't describe him there isn't a person alive today that can fill his place so let us please keep him alive in our hearts." Carol finished. Emma and Kim allowed silent tears to slide down their cheeks.

"thank you, Carol." Emma whispered. Joe stepped forward to the podium now hugging his sister.

"Carol has a way with words that defeats me. A lot of people have said what a brave, innocent boy Jack was, they have all told me how proud they are of him and how smart he was." The crowd smiled at Joes kind words. "The truth is Jack was a kind, caring boy. He loved his wolf Galahad; he had a passion for history. He would have done anything for you. Carol was right, Jack was better than most of us. He was willing to die for what he believed in. What he believed in was us, everyone gathered here today. Jack loved his family, he loved his friends. He lost his life to protect the love of his life. I know I speak for those who truly knew him, we couldn't have been prouder of the man he became." Joe climbed down and hugged Carol again.

He walked over to the empty coffin and opened the lid inside was a picture of Jack with a goofy smile on his face. Joe pulled his dragon tear from his coat and placed it inside the coffin.

"Come back." Joe whispered walking away as more and more people laid their tears inside the coffin he could not bear to watch as Kim and Emma broke down in each other's arms. "She really did love you." Joe said looking towards the sky, hoping his brother was somewhere up there smiling down on him.

Del Smith

Printed in Great Britain
by Amazon